RUNAWAY DREAM

Obeying her parents' orders, petite Rachel Robinson has traveled far from her home in the Kentucky hills to a remote Army outpost in the Dakotas—to join the stranger she married by proxy. But when Major Shelby Bruckenridge turns out to be an abusive cad, the self-sufficient mountain miss knocks him cold on their "wedding night"—and runs off to seek refuge among the Cheyenne.

DREAM CATCHER

A proud, magnetic leader, Strong Elk is irresistibly drawn to the tiny, tempestuous beauty who has stumbled into his camp. Though Strong Elk mistrusts whites, Rachel's radiant spirit warms the handsome warrior like the sun—and her sensuous form fills him with a perilous desire. For their love courts the vengeance of a spurned husband and his soldiers—and commands Strong Elk to choose between the needs of his people . . . and his heart.

First in the *Dream Seekers* Series

KATHLEEN HARRINGTON

DREAM CATCHER

An Avon Romantic Treasure

AVON BOOKS ◆ NEW YORK

DREAM CATCHER is an original publication of Avon Books. This work has never before appeared in book form. This work is a novel. Any similarity to actual persons or events is purely coincidental.

AVON BOOKS
A division of
The Hearst Corporation
1350 Avenue of the Americas
New York, New York 10019

First Avon Books Printing: May 1996

AVON TRADEMARK REG. U.S. PAT. OFF. AND IN OTHER COUNTRIES, MARCA REGISTRADA, HECHO EN U.S.A.

Printed in the U.S.A.

RA   10   9   8   7   6   5   4   3   2   1

*With love and thanks to my dear friend and
colleague of twenty-five years,
Bernice Chin Woo,
who encouraged me to write a story
about a spunky little tomboy,
and who's always willing to demonstrate a new
and exciting strategy for hand-to-hand combat*

*If Rachel Rose lived today, she'd have
a master's degree in Kung Fu San Soo,
just like you, Bernie!*

I would like to thank Kathleen Whitaker, Ph.D., Chief Curator, Southwest Museum, Los Angeles, for generously sharing her knowledge of the Dream Catcher myth, its probable origin, and of the dreamcatchers themselves, which have become such a beloved part of our present-day Native American crafts.

Down in the valley, valley so low;
Hang your head over, hear the wind blow.
Hear the wind blow, love, hear the wind blow;
Hang your head over, hear the wind blow.

Roses love sunshine, violets love dew;
Angels in Heaven know I love you.
Know I love you, dear, know I love you;
Angels in Heaven know I love you.

If you don't love me, love whom you please;
Throw your arms 'round me, give my heart ease.
Give my heart ease, love, give my heart ease;
Throw your arms 'round me, give my heart ease.

"Down in the Valley"
Folk song

Prologue

Clear Creek, Powder River Basin
Cheyenne-Sioux Hunting Grounds
Autumn 1866

*I*t was the rutting season. The bull elk stepped out of the tall, sheltering timber and stood on the crest of a knoll. He was an imperial stag in his prime, each antler on his enormous rack branching out to eight deadly points. A black mane on his neck and throat accented his sleek coat of coppery brown. Nearly a thousand pounds of solid muscle, the solitary male was ready to fight anyone foolish enough to cross his path.

On a limb overhead, two black-billed magpies ceased their chattering at his approach and deserted the scene with a swish of their long tails. The bull swiveled his pointed ears and listened to the sudden, ominous silence. He looked across the high gramma grass toward the tumbling river, sniffing the autumn breeze. The wind was in his face, and the heavy scent of a mountain lion filled his nostrils. He stood perfectly still and studied the open meadow between him and the frothing, gurgling water.

A sudden movement caught the bull elk's attention.

The lazy flick of a long, tawny tail stirred a plume of beargrass. The big cat was crouched in stealth, its powerful hind feet gathered beneath its body, its strong muscles bunched and tautened for the kill. Almost completely hidden in the golden grass, the feline watched and waited for its prey to come closer.

But it wasn't the elk the lion stalked.

From the thick rushes along the river's edge bounded a white-tailed fawn. The graceful youngster stopped for a moment, lifted her velvety nose, and sniffed the air in curiosity. She wagged her short tail, quivering all over with excitement as a bright orange-and-black butterfly fluttered past. Her smooth coat, spotted with white, glistened like a flame in the setting sun. For a moment, she seemed to teeter precariously on her trembling legs, but made no quick leap for safety. Her predator was downwind. Completely unaware of the marauder's presence, the red fawn gamboled in childish glee, seeming to frolic for the sheer enjoyment of being alive. There was no sign of a doe, whose mature experience would have ended the carefree dance with a motherly snort of rebuke.

In a sudden explosion of grace, the mountain lion leaped out of hiding. The tiny deer scampered frantically, dodging back and forth in her doomed race for survival. In ground-devouring leaps, the bull elk charged across the meadow. The lion, forced to swerve off the intended course, dodged the sharp hooves aimed at its head, knowing instinctively that one well-directed blow would easily crush its skull. In a long, sinuous motion, the cat twisted and slashed out with one deadly forepaw, the splayed claws coming within inches of the bull's thickly muscled shoulder. It snarled and hissed, baring long canine teeth in undeterred ferocity. The cat's yellow eyes glittered with deadly intent.

Head lowered, the elk lunged to his right. He caught the great cat with the full force of his charge, lifted his

*ancient enemy on his massive antlers, and tossed it sky-
ward. Gored in the hindquarter, the lion screamed in
pain, but somehow managed to land on its feet. Within
seconds, it had raced into the thick cover of buckbrush
nearby.*

*The bull whirled to see the white rump of the little
deer disappear into the undergrowth as well. Stranded
from her mother, she would inevitably perish without
protection. Moments later, the shrill, agonized wail of the
outraged cat carried through the deepening dusk like the
cry of a demented woman. The elk knew the wounded
lion would circle back in a great arc to intercept the
helpless fawn.*

*The majestic stag lifted his head and bugled his chal-
lenge in clear trumpet tones. The defiant notes echoed
for miles down to the flatlands below. Then he charged
into the brush after the little deer . . .*

Strong Elk Heart awoke, the heated blood in his veins
throbbing like a war drum. His dream had returned, the
dream that had so frequently invaded his sleep for the
last three moons. Instantly alert, he looked up through
the smoke hole to find the stars still glittering in the night
sky. Taking a deep, calming breath, he glanced to the
back of the lodge, where his grandfather Flying Hawk,
the Old Man Chief, snored peacefully. On the far side of
the tipi, the Old Man Chief's two gray-haired wives
snuggled comfortably beneath a warm buffalo robe. The
Elk rose and moved without a sound to the entrance,
where he lifted the closed flaps and stepped out into the
night.

The entire village slept as serenely as the three inside.
Only the usual sounds were carried on the cool fall air—
the muffled stamp of hooves, the soft nicker of horses,
the hoot of an owl. Far off in the distance, a coyote complained to the moon.

As his pulse returned to normal, Strong Elk shook his head in a futile attempt to dispel his worried thoughts. He knew he'd experienced more than just a dream. It was a foretelling of things to come. But what did the haunting images mean? Surely a man renowned for his ability to interpret the visions of others could understand his own. He was the elk, of course. That was clear enough.

The corners of his mouth curved up in wry amusement. Every time he woke from that particular dream, his sex stood out beneath his breechclout, as swollen and heavy as a bull elk's in rutting season. Perhaps his hard male arousal had nothing to do with the vision itself. He'd been living with his grandfather's band for two winters now. It wasn't always easy following the customs of his own people after so many years of riding with the horse soldiers, who were notoriously lax in their morals. Around the forts, there were always females available who'd willingly sell their bodies. He'd paid for his share of their time with the money he'd earned as a cavalry scout.

Here, it was different. Cheyenne women were known throughout the Plains tribes for their chastity. A warrior didn't court an innocent maiden without the sincere intention of marriage. There were always lonely widows, whose gentle solace helped ease the emptiness inside, if only for an evening. But they, too, deserved to be wooed by someone seeking a second wife. So until his heart was captured by a pair of lovely eyes and beguiling lips, he would spend most of his nights alone.

Strong Elk's bachelor way of life sometimes made him want to tip his head back and bugle, long and loud, in sexual frustration—just like a great bull elk. That part of the dream was easily understood. The rest of the events remained a mystery, though he'd tried before to decipher the prophetic symbols. For an elk to purposely save a white-tailed deer was contrary to the ways of nature. A bull would instinctively protect his own harem of cows and calves from a mountain lion, but never an animal of a different species, not even a helpless youngster.

Nearly lost in contemplation, Strong Elk felt the presence of his grandfather behind him and glanced over his shoulder. The Old Man Chief had wrapped a buffalo robe around himself to ward off the night chill. In the moonlight, his long gray braids shone silver against the robe's shaggy fur. His weathered face betrayed his concern.

"Did something disturb your sleep, *nixa,* my grandchild?" Flying Hawk spoke softly so as not to wake the women inside. His dark eyes scanned the circle of tipis illuminated by the full moon, alert to any possible danger. Since the butchery at Sand Creek two autumns ago, no Cheyenne warrior ever slept deeply.

"No, *namsem,* only a dream."

"Ah, then you had the vision again. Was it the same as before?" At the Elk's affirmative nod, Flying Hawk clasped his grandson's shoulder. "And this time, did you understand its meaning?"

Strong Elk scowled in deliberation. "I think, perhaps, the little fawn could be our own small band of people. The Maker of Life may be warning me that we are in danger of becoming devoured by the white man's civilization."

"Such a thing may be inevitable," Flying Hawk said, his farseeing eyes dulled in resignation. "They are many, and we are so few. And as helpless as the tiny deer in the jaws of the lion."

"No!" Strong Elk disclaimed. "We are not helpless. If we remain true to the ways of our ancestors, if we listen to the words of our wise ones and tell our children the tales of Cheyenne courage around the lodge fire, we will survive. But the white man's road can only lead to our destruction."

"You are so certain, *nixa*? You, who are familiar with their language and their strange customs?"

"I am certain," the Elk replied. "They are a vile breed, made up of liars, cheats, and thieves. We must remain apart from them, or we will become as contemptible and greedy as they."

There was a long moment of silence as each man gazed out across the camp circle. Then Flying Hawk rubbed his chin pensively. His quiet, speculative words rumbled like far-off thunder. "I have wondered, sometimes, if the little fawn could be a symbol of a white woman."

"Never!" Strong Elk denied. Behind them in the lodge, one of the elderly sleepers stirred on her soft pallet of fur. He stepped closer to his grandfather and continued in a low voice. "That could never be the meaning of the prophecy, *namsem*. Their women are selfish and argumentative. They speak in strident, high-pitched voices that grate on a man's ear. And when they are startled or frightened, they emit the eerie scream of a wounded lion. No, it is the mountain cat who represents the entire race of white people. I'm certain of it."

Flying Hawk shrugged, unmoved by his grandson's vehemence. "You are the one with the gift to interpret prophecies, *nixa,* not I. When Maheo wants you to understand completely, he will send a messenger spirit to guide you." The older man stretched and yawned contentedly. "At the moment, I am interested only in returning to my mattress."

Alone with his troubled thoughts once more, Strong Elk frowned up at the stars. His grandfather's suggestion had occurred to him several times before, although he didn't want to admit it, not even to himself. He disliked the white eyes and everything about them. To even contemplate the possibility that a woman of that despicable breed could turn him into a rutting bull, trotting back and forth in frantic, sexually charged aggression, bugling his possessive ownership to all other males within sound of his call, filled him with disgust.

That couldn't be the meaning of his vision.

What the prophecy did portend, however, he had yet to discover.

Chapter 1

Ashwood Hall
Lexington, Kentucky
April 1867

"**D**ang it, I ain't a-goin'. And nobody here can make me, neither." With those rash words, Rachel plopped down on the settee across from where Papa sat in his favorite chair, folded her arms across her chest, and scowled in open rebellion.

"Now, Rachel Rose," her father began in his quiet, measured way, only to be interrupted by his wife's shrill voice.

"You'll go, little missy, and we won't hear another word to the contrary. Your father and I are only trying to do what's best for you." Eliza stalked across the library's handsome Aubusson rug to stand directly in front of her stepdaughter. She leaned over and shook her plump finger in Rachel's face. "This is your one chance to snare a husband, and you'd better take advantage of it. You'll never get another, Rachel Robinson."

Rachel lifted her brows in honest befuddlement. "Who said I wanted to catch a husband, for God's sake? A body

8

doesn't have to jump over the broom with a feller to have a happy life, particularly not with some stranger she doesn't even know.''

At such outrageous talk, Eliza straightened up so fast, her corset creaked alarmingly. The thirty-eight-year-old matron prided herself on her hourglass figure. She insisted her laces be tightened every morning until she could barely breathe and then spent the afternoon complaining of a headache. Rachel thought it ridiculous the way some females went around encased in corded boning on top and steel birdcages on the bottom. It was scarcely a wonder, considering all those store-bought contrivances cutting off the blood supply, that her stepmother's face flushed a brilliant rhododendron-pink whenever she got excited. Which was plainly happening now.

Turning to her spouse, Eliza flung out her hands in desperation. ''See what I've been trying to tell you, Garrett? She uses the Almighty's name in vain like some unchurched heathen. Her grammar is an abysmal disgrace, as are the scandalous clothes she insists upon wearing. Why, she's nothing but an ignorant savage.''

''I ain't no savage!'' Rachel cried as she jumped to her feet. ''Jest 'cause I can't read and write, don't give you no call to flout me. Leastwise, I never asked to come here in the first place.'' She slipped past her stepmother and hurried to where her father sat. Dropping to her knees, she grasped his hands and looked up into his worried eyes. ''Please, Papa, let me go back home to Sugar Holler. I can live with Aunt Delinthie or Saphronia and Lemuel, if you won't let me stay in Gramps's cabin by myself. There's nothin' a-goin' to harm me in Sugar Holler, and you know it. Why, there's not a body there who ain't my kin.''

''That's exactly the point!'' Eliza snapped. At the scowl of annoyance on her husband's face, she clenched her hands and reined in her shrewish temper. With an immediate change of tactics, she offered her stepdaughter a smile as sweet as sorghum on a johnnycake. "That's my very point, Rachel," she cooed. "If you return to your mountains, you'll never meet an eligible beau. You don't want to end up a forgotten old maid, do you?"

Rachel rested her cheek on her father's knee and made no attempt to hide her grin. "Seein' as how I'm only seventeen, I don't think I need to be a-worryin' 'bout bein' on the shelf jest yet. All that frettin' is liable to make me crotchety afore my time."

Garrett Robinson rested his hand on Rachel's mop of unruly curls. She could feel the love in his touch, but also the uneasiness he tried to hide. Eliza hadn't given either one of them a moment's peace since the day, four months ago, when he'd returned from the Cumberland Mountains with Rachel in tow. Papa had hurried to McDougall's Mill on Sugar Creek as soon as word of Gramps's death had reached him. It was time for his eldest daughter to live with her family at Ashwood Hall, Judge Robinson had announced in his most authoritative manner. But Rachel wasn't ready to leave the only home she'd ever known. Gram and Gramps had been her family since her mother had died birthing her. This time, however, Rachel's father hadn't given in to her pleas to let her stay in her beloved hollow.

"Rachel," her father said now, "I'm not worried about your becoming a spinster." He cupped her chin in his hand and lifted her face to meet his gaze. "But I am interested in making the best possible match for you that I can. Major Bruckenridge is a gentleman of means with a fine career ahead of him. He's a graduate of West Point and distinguished himself quite brilliantly during the war."

"Humph." Rachel sniffed. "I wouldn't call it brilliant. He fought on the Union side."

"How dare you look down your nose at my cousin?"

Eliza demanded. She propped her hands on her hips and glared at her stepdaughter. "Shelby comes from a long line of military heroes. Our great-grandfather fought the Redcoats at King's Mountain. I imagine that's more than the McDougalls can claim. Why, the Louisville Bruckenridges have mingled with the cream of Kentucky society since before the Revolution."

"Could be," Rachel said, meeting her father's twinkling eyes in a moment of shared amusement. If there was one thing Eliza Bruckenridge Robinson was proud of, it was her own illustrious family tree. "But I know for a fact that Gramps's pappy come over the Cumberland Gap with Daniel Boone. And when he was barely fifteen, Gramps took his squirrel rifle down the Mississip to New Orlins with Andy Jackson. So I guess my pedigree is jest as fine as Major Bruckenridge's. And no McDougall I ever heered of fought for the Federalists."

Eliza's face drained to the pale shade of a frog's belly. Rachel suspected the woman was secretly mortified that her first cousin had donned a blue uniform. What Eliza didn't realize was that her stepdaughter didn't give two hoots and a holler which side the major had fought on. Gramps had believed staunchly in the Union cause, while Papa had served with the Lexington Rifles in the Confederate army. The entire populace of Kentucky had been sorely divided in those terrible, agonizing years. During the war, Rachel hadn't prayed for either side to be victorious, only that the fighting would end soon and her father would come home safe and sound. So Shelby Bruckenridge's political sentiments didn't count one way or the other in toting up his assets as a future bridegroom. The truth of it was, Rachel simply had no intention of marrying some fellow she'd never even met.

Eliza dropped down on the gold satin couch that Rachel had abandoned as though her knees were about to give way. With a tragic moan, she pulled an embroidered handkerchief from her pocket and dabbed at the corners of her eyes in a display of melancholy fit for the stage. Lord a'mercy, she was bringing out the heavy artillery now. Papa never could withstand a female's tears. If they both started bawling, he'd likely head for the stables and hide out in one of his hunters' stalls for the rest of the day.

"Mr. Lincoln's war caused enough heartbreak on both sides," Eliza said in a strangled voice. "It's time to set aside past animosities and work for the common good. Which is why it's so important for your father to win the coming election to the Senate. If you have no feelings of compassion for your family, Rachel, you must at least be moved by a spirit of patriotism. This country needs levelheaded men like your father at the helm."

"Now, Liza," Garrett cautioned, "whether Rachel marries Shelby or not has nothing to do with my winning the campaign for senator."

"Oh, but it does!" Eliza exclaimed. She turned the full force of her china-blue eyes on her husband in open astonishment. "Just wait till some horrible newspaper reporter espousing the Radical party discovers she's your daughter!"

"Rachel is my legitimate child," he said sternly. "Her mother and I were married, even though it was only for a brief ten months. There is absolutely nothing any journalist can write of a defamatory nature about my little girl. And should one try, I'll take the lying bastard to court—after taking a horsewhip to his backside first."

"Defamatory! Hah! What about holding her up for public ridicule, and you along with her?" Eliza's words rose to a hysterical pitch as she pointed an accusing finger at her stepchild. "Look at her, Garrett! She's unlearned, ill-mannered, and dresses like a boy half the time. Unless I force her to put on shoes, she runs around barefoot, indoors and out. And she continues to speak in that atrocious mountain dialect, though heaven knows, I've tried and tried to correct her. If a *Gazette* reporter starts to sharpen his talons on your daughter, you'll be the laughingstock of the entire state. And I'll never be able to show my face outside our door again.''

''You ever try goin' possum huntin' in a dress, ma'am?'' Rachel countered, scrambling to her feet. She glanced down at the loose flannel shirt and baggy britches she wore, then wriggled her bare toes in the soft carpet. ''Didn't I jest bring in the fixin's for a nice possum pie? Why don't you never praise me 'stead of faultin' me all the time?''

''Young ladies do *not* go possum hunting,'' Eliza stated coldly. ''And I would praise you if there was anything worth praising you about!''

In a quick, defensive motion, Rachel tossed her head and lifted her chin. ''Well, then, I guess I ain't no lady, am I?''

Despite her audacious reply, tears burned Rachel's eyes at her stepmother's mean-spirited remarks. She bit her lower lip, trying to stifle the sobs that clogged her throat. The sadness she'd glimpsed in her father's gaze whenever she caught him watching her unawares brought an ache that couldn't be eased. No one knew better than Rachel how wanting she was in every way.

First of all, she was far too short. The Robinsons and McDougalls were tall, elegant people, but she'd taken after Gram's family. No matter how determinedly she'd thrown back her shoulders and stretched her spine, she'd never passed the five-foot mark on her grandmother's pantry door. And like Gramps when he was young, she had a head of thick red hair and a sprinkling of freckles across her nose. Her voice, unlike anyone on either the spear or spindle side, was a deep contralto, several octaves lower than any other female she'd ever met. And in a society that admired full bosoms and well-rounded hips, she was far from amply endowed.

Worst of all, she'd never had a lick of schooling. She was as ignorant of the world outside Sugar Hollow as Papa was learned and wise in the ways of the law. She suspected that her own father thought she had no chance of attracting a husband, suitable or otherwise, which was perfectly understandable. She had her doubts on that score, too. But if Garrett Robinson believed he might lose his race for the Senate because of her many inadequacies, it would truly break her heart.

Rachel folded her hands and looked at her father with pleading eyes. "It ain't that I'm a-wantin' to contrary you, Papa," she announced in a desperate attempt to thwart her destiny. "But I can't go out to Wyomin' Territory to marry Major Bruckenridge. Somethin' terrible will happen to me, if'n I do."

Both parents peered at her in disbelief.

"Why, Rosie, child?" her father queried patiently.

"Why, indeed?" Eliza demanded.

"'Cause if'n I go out to the prairies, I'll most likely be killed or somethin'." Meeting their dumbfounded stares, she wrinkled her nose and solemnly explained. "Gram had a knowin'. She saw it all clear as day. She made me promise I would never, ever cross the Mississip."

Her father sighed as he ran his fingers through his graying brown hair. When he spoke, his tone was only mildly curious. "What exactly did your grandmother see?"

Rachel took a deep breath and went on in a rush. "Gram saw me a-runnin' from someone. I was a-runnin' and a-runnin' through the tall buffalo grass, and every oncet awhile, I'd look back to see if whoever it was was still a-comin'. Then I'd take off again, like the devil himself was on my heels."

"That was it?" her father asked. The corners of his mouth twitched up, though he tried his best to hide his amusement. It was as plain as the moon in the harvest sky, he didn't place any credence in "knowings."

"No, there was more," she said breathlessly, as if she really had been running. "In the distance behind me, a fort was a-burnin'. The log stockade was a-goin' up in flames more'n ten feet high. The sky overhead was darkened with smoke and ash, though it was still daylight out."

"And that's why you don't want to marry my cousin?" Eliza scoffed with a brittle laugh. "Because your grandmother had some foolish dream?"

"Oh, 'twasn't no dream, ma'am," Rachel said earnestly. "Gram had the second sight. She inherited it from her mama."

"What unadulterated nonsense!" Arching an eyebrow, Eliza looked over at her husband. A disdainful smirk twisted her Cupid's bow mouth. "That's what you get, dear, for letting your eldest daughter be raised by Scotch Presbyterians. They filled her head with imbecile superstitions brought over from the Highlands."

"That's enough, Eliza," Garrett warned. He rose and walked over to take Rachel's hands. "You can't make important decisions based on dreams, child," he told her gently. "Major Bruckenridge has assured us that you will be perfectly safe with him. Fort Laramie is one of the oldest military outposts west of the Missouri River. The soldiers quartered there have their wives and children with them. There'll be teas and balls and quilting bees, just like here in Lexington. You'll be surrounded with all the gaiety and social life we could offer you at Ashwood Hall. And as an officer's wife, you'll find yourself part of a close-knit group of women friends, who'll help make your adjustment to married life easier."

"You should tell her there'll be turkey shoots and

horse-swapping and knife-throwing contests, Garrett,''
Eliza said scornfully. "That's the only thing that would
tempt Rachel to go.''

"Ain't no need to tell me nothin','' Rachel stated
baldly. She hurried to the door, grasped the polished
brass knob, and turned to meet their incredulous faces.
"I ain't a-goin', Papa, and that's my final word.''

"I hear you're getting married,'' Ben called as he
scrambled up the giant bull bay tree. He climbed out on
the limb and perched beside Rachel, hidden from the
house by the dense foliage.

She glanced at her younger brother, then stared down
at her bare feet, swinging them back and forth despon-
dently. " 'Pears so,'' she admitted. "Guess I'm a-headin'
out to Wyomin' Territory whether I like it or not.''
Despite her bold words less than an hour before, she
knew she would never purposely jeopardize her father's
chances of being elected to the Senate. If, as Eliza
claimed, a newspaper reporter could hold Judge Garrett
Robinson up for ridicule because of his eldest daughter's
shortcomings, it would be better if Rachel was as far
away from Kentucky as possible come voting time.

"Do you think you'll see any Indians out there?'' Ben
asked.

Rachel braced her hands on the thick branch and stared
up at the canopy of green leaves soaring eighty feet
above them. "Reckon I will,'' she said glumly. "Reckon
they'll see me, too. Reckon they'll jest lift my hair right
off'n my head.''

"Whoa!'' Ben exclaimed, his hazel eyes bright with
excitement. "You're not going to let them scalp you, are
ya? If they get too close, you can shoot 'em with that
long-barreled squirrel gun of yours. I've never seen you
miss a shot with it yet!''

Rachel laughed in spite of herself. Although her fifteen-year-old half-sister, Lucinda, was the spitting image of her mother, Ben favored their father, right down to his dry sense of humor. "What's meant to be is goin' to be," she told him with unqualified fatalism, "whether I take my rifle along or not."

"They probably won't want to scalp you anyway," the twelve-year-old added. "Not with your short hair and all."

Rachel reached up to touch her tousled curls. She couldn't be bothered with all the fussing and fretting most females suffered over their elaborate hairstyles, so she kept her own locks cropped to chin length. "I don't know 'bout that," she said doubtfully. "Injuns scalp men with hair shorter'n mine, don't they?"

"Well, maybe they won't want it 'cause it's red."

She grinned and punched his upper arm. "Yeah. Maybe they'll jest fill me full of arrows and leave me, at that. Thanks for raisin' my spirits."

Her little brother returned her grin and then spat impressively. They sat side by side in companionable silence, peeking through the magnolia leaves at the colonial brick mansion with its tall white columns and fanlighted entryway. The home had been built by their illustrious grandfather, who'd been one of Kentucky's greatest criminal lawyers and, later in life, a successful breeder of Thoroughbred horses.

"You ever met your cousin Shelby?" she asked, breaking off a broad leaf and twirling the stem between her fingers. She glanced at Ben from the corner of her eye, not wanting to give away her anxious thoughts.

Ben shook his head. "Nope. But I heard Mother say once that all the Bruckenridges are tall and fair and good-looking, and Shelby's the best-looking of all. She said it was a downright shame I took after my father."

Rachel bristled. "Jumpin' Jehoshaphat, she said that to you?"

Ben laughed at her irate expression. "No, she was talking to Lucinda. I just happened to overhear."

"Shucks, I think our papa's 'bout the handsomest man in the whole dang world," she said, glowering at the leaf she held in her hand. "And you're goin' to grow up to look jest like him."

"Don't pay any attention to what Mother says," Ben advised. "She's always complaining about something. I think it's those headaches that make her so cross."

"She's plumb tetchy, all right," Rachel agreed. She tore the glistening leaf into shreds and watched the pieces float to the lawn below. "I'll miss you, Ben," she said softly.

"I'll miss you, too, Rachel Rose. As soon as I'm old enough, I'll come out to Wyoming Territory and join you," he promised. "I've always wanted to see the Wild West."

Rachel reached out and patted his hand. She smiled bravely, while inside her heart was breaking. There wasn't a chance in a month of Sundays she'd still be alive by the time her brother was old enough to make that journey west. When Gram had a knowing, it always came true. Sooner or later, events unfolded just as Mattie McDougall envisioned them. Rachel knew, without a doubt, that once she left Kentucky, she'd never see any of her family again.

"C'mon," she said. "Let's go saddle up two of Papa's best hunters. I'll race you to the stable. Winner gets first choice."

"Come away from the window, dear, and turn off the lamp," Eliza complained. "It's getting late. You know I can't sleep with the light shining in my face."

Garrett stared out at the great magnolia tree on the front lawn and sipped his bourbon. Earlier in the day, he'd seen Rachel and Ben climb down from its sheltering branches and race around the house toward the stables, laughing uproariously over some joke between them. He braced one hand on the window jamb and fought the overwhelming guilt that assailed him. If he had it to do all over again, he'd never have allowed Rachel to stay in Sugar Hollow, rather than being raised here at Ashwood where she belonged. But at the time, it had seemed the right thing to do.

Heartbroken when Jenny died, he'd left his tiny baby girl with her maternal grandparents. Two years later, upon his marriage to Eliza, it still seemed the best solution, for his second wife had been reluctant to take over the care of her stepdaughter, and Nehemiah and Mattie McDougall loved the child to distraction. The elderly couple had pleaded with Garrett to let them keep her. Seeing how happy Rachel was in the mountain cabin, and the scowl on Eliza's face whenever she looked at the laughing, carefree child, he'd given in to everyone's wishes. Through his irresponsibility as a father, Rachel had grown up an untutored waif with little chance of making a favorable alliance. Yet Garrett Robinson loved his oldest daughter even more than his other two children. Her heart-shaped face and petite vivacity reminded him forcibly of her mother, whom he'd adored beyond reason. He'd married Jennifer Juliette McDougall in the face of his parents' adamant objections. Through the years, he'd never regretted that decision for an instant.

He prayed he wasn't making a mistake this time. He'd only met Shelby Bruckenridge once, in Louisville, before the outbreak of hostilities had divided the nation. The attractive young man had been scrupulously well-mannered. And his career in the army seemed exceptionally promising. The match itself had been Eliza's idea. Garrett had cautioned her to be perfectly honest about Rachel's mountain upbringing and lack of education. Promising to be forthright to a painful degree, Eliza had penned a letter to her cousin at Fort Laramie, and to Garrett's surprise, the major had written back, proposing a marriage to Rachel by proxy. Apparently, it was damn lonely out there on the frontier without a supply of marriageable young women.

Garrett emptied his glass, turned out the lamp, and climbed into bed. "Good night," he told his wife quietly.

"Good night, dear," she replied.

He folded his hands beneath his head and stared up at the ceiling. He hadn't touched his wife intimately in over twelve years. Not since their son was born. Eliza wasn't to blame for the fact that he'd never loved her. He'd married her at his father's urging and with the intent of producing a male heir. Through the years, Garrett had learned to accept her megrims and countless other ailments, knowing that they were the only way she could get his attention.

For the past four months, however, their estrangement had grown deeper, the chasm between them wider. Rachel's presence at Ashwood had brought images of Jenny, like a beloved ghost, flitting through the rooms. His heart ached unbearably for what might have been. Dear God in heaven, had she only lived . . . had his sweet, adorable Jenny only lived . . .

Eliza turned on her side and smiled to herself in satisfaction. Eighteen years ago, Jenny McDougall had stolen Garrett right out from under her nose. She hated the little girl who'd grown up to look exactly like her conniving mother. Determined to be rid of her bumpkin stepdaughter once and for all, Eliza had come up with a brilliant plan.

She covered her mouth to keep from chortling out loud. She hadn't written Shelby that his new bride was as skinny as a fence rail and no bigger than a minute. Or that she was illiterate, red-haired, and freckle-faced to boot. He'd never have agreed to the marriage, if he'd known. Eliza had implied, instead, that Rachel looked a lot like her father, tall, slender, dignified. The impatiently waiting bridegroom would probably fly into one of his horrible rages the moment he laid eyes on the flat-chested tomboy. With any luck, he might even beat her insensible.

For what Eliza had failed to tell her husband was that Shelby had a twisted side to his nature. When he was a boy, her cousin had been shockingly cruel to helpless creatures and seemed to get a perverse pleasure from inflicting pain. But that wasn't her fault, Eliza rationalized as she plumped up her pillow. All the Bruckenridges had a mean streak flowing through their blue-blooded veins, and that had never kept any of them from getting married.

Chapter 2

Fort Philip Kearny
Dakota Territory
June 1867

"**G**'yup! Hyar!" The driver cracked his whip and gave an ear-splitting whistle. As they reached the summit of the hill, the wagon's six-mule team seemed to sense that their destination was in view and bawled in jubilation.

"Up ahead, ma'am!" Captain Feehan called to Rachel over the raucous braying of the animals. He edged his bay gelding closer to the side of the canvas-topped army wagon. "Look over there," he said, pointing into the distance. "There's Phil Kearny on that plateau to your left."

Rachel clutched the wagon seat with one hand and shaded her eyes with the other. On the grassy tableland, a log stockade rose up against the blue sky like an impregnable fortress. "Yup, I see it," she told the cavalryman with an answering smile. Her heart thrummed with excitement. "Lord A'mighty, I can't believe I'm here at last!"

22

Rachel gazed around her with a mountain girl's appreciation of the rugged scenery. On the slopes of the Big Horns not more than five miles away grew dense forests of evergreens. A breeze from their towering, snow-covered summits cooled her cheeks despite the warm summer sun. Tall pines stood like sentinels along the crests of the rolling foothills, while in the bottoms of the ravines that crisscrossed the open plains, lush grasses grew so high a horse couldn't pass through them any faster than a walk.

"Those shinin' mountains over yonder ain't my blessed Cumberlands," she said, with a sense of burgeoning exhilaration. "But, jumpin' Jehoshaphat, they sure are plumb beautiful. The hollers are bound to be full of game, and the creeks jest burstin' with trout. I can't hardly wait to unpack my rifle and go huntin'."

"Major Bruckenridge is going to be mighty happy to see you, ma'am," Captain Feehan said with a boyish grin.

His confident words brought her plummeting back to reality. "Leastwise, I hope so," she replied solemnly. " 'Cause afore that sun goes down, I'm a-goin' to meet the man I've been married to for over six weeks."

Terence Feehan understood her nervousness. She'd explained to the astonished captain back at Fort Laramie that she was a proxy bride, who'd never even met her husband. "Don't worry, ma'am," he assured her. "Everything will work out fine."

"Well, the major knows what I look like, anyhow," Rachel said. "Afore I left Ashwood Hall, my stepmother told me that Shelby Bruckenridge knows all about me. Eliza penned him a complete likeness, includin' my red hair and puny size. She claimed Shelby wrote back that he'd already fallen half in love with me jest from my description alone."

Captain Feehan smiled encouragingly. "I'm sure he did."

"Shoot, that part don't exactly ring true," Rachel contradicted skeptically. "I took a closer look at myself in the mirror and figured Eliza must have stretched the truth a mite tryin' to sell her cousin on the idea of gettin' hitched. 'Twasn't nothin' in the lookin' glass that'd make a man swoon at the mere sight of me."

"You'll be as welcome as the flowers in May, Mrs. Bruckenridge," replied Captain Feehan. "No doubt about it."

She grinned at him, unable to withstand his unfailing good humor. "Yep," she agreed, "I'll be jest like the dogwood at bloomin' time. A regular spring bouquet."

Feehan chuckled at her show of bravado. The bluff, stocky Ohioan had served in the late war. He'd admitted to Rachel on their way to Fort Reno, however, that he was a raw recruit when it came to fighting Indians. Like herself, he'd never been west of the Missouri until four weeks ago.

The blue Studebaker wagon and the ambulance behind it carrying medical supplies were escorted by a platoon of twenty-five men, all of them, except for their civilian guide, as new to the frontier as their leader. They'd accompanied the mail from Fort Laramie, a journey of thirteen days, stopping at Fort Reno, where Rachel had expected to catch up with her husband. But then, she'd expected to find him at Fort Laramie in Wyoming Territory before that.

There'd been a letter waiting for her at Laramie, instructing her to continue on to Fort Reno, where Shelby had been ordered to lead a company of men. Upon arriving at that small military outpost, she'd been greeted by its flustered commander with the information that her bridegroom had been reassigned to Fort Phil Kearny the previous week. So the next morning, she climbed back atop the high-spring wagon seat and continued northward up the Bozeman Road with the mail.

"You must be weary of all this traveling," Feehan said, his hazel eyes warm with concern. "The fort will be a welcome relief."

"Seems like I've done nothin' but chase after Major Bruckenridge's coattails for nearly a month," she admitted. "But this last leg of the trip has been the best part. Everyone has been doin' his utmost to make it as easy for me as possible."

"The men are tickled to have a lady along, especially the Southerners, who'd go twenty miles out of their way just to talk to a young woman from Kentucky."

Rachel lowered her lashes, suddenly shy. "If'n Major Bruckenridge is anything like these kindhearted soldiers, Captain Feehan, wedded life might prove to be a mighty pleasant experience."

The thought that she was actually a married woman filled her with dread. The feeling of noble self-sacrifice that had motivated her back in Lexington had dissipated by the time she'd reached St. Louis. Since then, she'd had plenty of opportunity to repent her hasty decision, but the vows had been said and her X marked on the paper. She wasn't going to let Papa down through sheer cowardice, when he'd seemed so pleased with her. Not when she'd finally done something to make him proud of his eldest daughter.

Rachel leaned around the canvas side to check on the stallion tied to the back of the wagon. McDougall's Pride was one of her father's prize Thoroughbreds, descended from the finest hunter in the Ashwood stables. "Mac's taken the trip from Lexington in stride," she said happily. "Even that swayin' railroad car didn't put him off his feed none. But he's goin' to be as pleased as we are to reach Phil Kearny."

"We'll be there before you know it, Mrs. Bruckenridge,'' Captain Feehan promised. ''We'll stop for a nooning on the trail, and you'll be eating supper with your husband this evening.''

Rachel hoped the alarm didn't show in her eyes. ''Reckon that sounds jest wonderful,'' she lied. The captain must have believed her, for he touched his wide-brimmed hat in salute, gave his horse the go-ahead, and galloped to the front of the line.

Once inside Fort Phil Kearny's main gate, the wagon pulled to a stop in front of the general headquarters building. Rachel scrambled down from the high seat before anyone could assist her. Momentarily forgetting about the full skirt of her traveling dress, she caught her heel and nearly tumbled on her head. She regained her balance, tried unsuccessfully to smooth out the travel-worn garment, gave up, and looked around.

Hesitant to leave the haven of safety the vehicle had provided for nearly two weeks, she hovered close to the tall wagon wheel, while all around her, uniformed men were milling about good-naturedly. Bags of mail and brown paper parcels were being tossed to waiting arms, while boxes of medical supplies were quickly unloaded from the ambulance. It seemed as though everyone in the fort had come running to greet them with a shout of welcome. That wasn't surprising, of course, considering the arrival of mail anywhere always got people excited. Nor were the soldiers' curious stares. After all, the appearance of an officer's new bride was bound to attract attention.

''Tell Major Bruckenridge we brought his wife,'' Captain Feehan called to a private lounging on the porch that ran the length of the building. The captain dismounted and came to stand beside Rachel, while the soldier disappeared inside. Moments later, three men hurried out—two officers and a portly civilian.

Rachel knew immediately which one was her husband.

Tall, slender, and blond, with wavy hair and an enormous mustache, Shelby Bruckenridge looked exactly like the daguerreotype his cousin had shown her. The hopeful smile on his attractive face quickly faded. He stopped mid-stride and stared at her in shocked silence. Mortified, Rachel glanced down at her wrinkled cotton dress and then reached up to push the windblown curls off her damp forehead. When she tried to step away from the wagon, the pointed toe of her half-boot snagged in her hem. She would have pitched forward on her nose if Captain Feehan hadn't reached out and caught her elbow.

"Drat it," she muttered. "I keep forgettin' 'bout this confounded skirt." With Feehan's assistance, she made it safely up the wooden steps.

Giving a snappy salute, her escort introduced himself to the senior officer, then added, "Sir, this is Mrs. Bruckenridge, come all the way from Lexington to meet her new bridegroom." Feehan turned and smiled encouragingly at Rachel. "Ma'am, may I present Lieutenant Colonel Henry Wessells, commander of the post."

The dark-haired gentleman gaped at her in astonishment. He seemed to recall his manners with a start. "How do you do, Mrs. Bruckenridge," he said politely. He gestured to the civilian at his side. "This is our doctor, Surgeon Hines." With a fatherly smile, the middle-aged Wessells turned and clapped Shelby on the shoulder. "And I gather you've never met Major Bruckenridge?"

"Howdy," she croaked, looking from one man to another. "My name's Rachel Rose. Papa calls me Rosie." In her nervousness, her voice was even deeper than usual.

Shelby winced at the sound of it. Stepping forward, he took her hand. "Welcome to Fort Phil Kearny," he said with only the faintest hint of a Louisville drawl. His years in the Union army had put their stamp on him. "I trust you had a safe trip," he added as he looked her up and down. Tarnation, she could have sworn his thin nostrils actually quivered in disdain. His chilly eyes were the pale hue of apple cider, almost golden. A cat's eyes.

"Safe enough," she told him, her heart lurching painfully. "I'm a far piece from Sugar Holler, and that's for dang sure." She included the other men in her gaze, wanting to avoid the spleen in the major's strange-colored eyes. It was plainer than blue blazes, he was vastly disappointed.

"No doubt you'll want to refresh yourself after the rigors of your journey," he said curtly. "I'll show you to my quarters and then have an orderly bring you some hot water."

Rachel felt the heat of a flush suffuse her cheeks at his obvious attempt to hurry her out of sight. She knew she must look like a bedraggled mudlark. But by the eternal, who wouldn't, after nearly two weeks of traipsing through the wilderness? "If'n you'll excuse me, Colonel Wessells," she said, her mouth suddenly dry as a ball of cotton in a sun-baked field. She swallowed convulsively and continued. "I allow as how I'll jest take Major Bruckenridge's advice and wash up a mite."

Wessells stepped forward and extended his hand. "Your arrival is cause for a celebration, ma'am," he said kindly. His dark brown eyes offered a silent apology for her husband's unenthusiastic welcome. "We'll have a full-dress affair this evening in your honor. So get some rest and be prepared to join in the dancing."

"I'm lookin' forward to it, sir," she said as she pumped his hand. She glanced at her husband, whose jaw was clenched in ill-concealed aggravation. Maybe a little coddling would sweeten him up eventually, but at the moment he looked like he'd been eating a green persimmon. "Papa sent you a weddin' present, Major Bruckenridge." She pointed to the chestnut stallion tied to the back of the mail wagon.

His fair brows lifted in disparagement, Shelby followed the direction she indicated. This time, however, his golden eyes lit up with sincere regard. Without a word to his spouse, he stepped off the porch and approached the magnificent animal. "He's marvelous," he said in a whisper.

McDougall's Pride tossed his head and neighed his displeasure as Shelby came near. In a flash, Rachel was beside the skittish Thoroughbred. Untying the lead rope, she patted his velvety nose and crooned to him lovingly. "It's all right, Mac. It's all right. Major Bruckenridge is your new owner now." The other men followed the couple to stand beside the stallion.

"What a beauty," Surgeon Hines said with a low, appreciative whistle.

Rachel reached up and proudly stroked the stallion's long, graceful neck. "His grandpappy was Liberty Bell, one of the finest racers in all Kentucky. Ain't no horse can pass McDougall on the track nor outjump him in the field, neither."

At such high praise, the beautiful creature nickered softly and nuzzled Rachel's hand, hoping for an apple. But when Shelby reached out to touch him, the horse shied away. "He'll get used to you," Rachel said in a consoling tone.

"Damn right, he'll get used to me," her husband snarled as he grabbed the rope from her hand. McDougall snorted and shook his mane in warning. Shelby jerked down hard, and the confused horse reared up. Clearly startled, the major let go with a vicious oath. The four men stepped back in awe as the stallion's front hooves pawed the air dangerously close to their heads.

"Easy, boy," Rachel soothed in a motherly fashion. "Easy, now." The sound of her voice calmed the excited animal, who immediately settled down and started to nuzzle her once more. "He was gentled as a foal by kindness,'' she chided the ham-handed man beside her. ''Ain't nothin' will spoil a high-spirited horse faster'n rough treatment.''

''Don't tell me how to handle a horse,'' Shelby gritted through clenched teeth. ''I've been riding since I was six. I'll teach him who's in charge quick enough.''

''The little lady's only trying to help,'' Henry Wessells admonished. He motioned to a soldier nearby. ''Take this horse to the stable, Private Hoppner, and see that he's given the best of care. And be gentle with him.'' Turning back to Shelby, the colonel added, ''Perhaps you should escort your new bride to your quarters, Major, where she can refresh herself after the long journey.''

Shelby belatedly gathered his manners about him. ''Follow me, please,'' he said with a brief nod.

This time, Rachel remembered to lift the hem of her skirt clear of her toes. Awarding the other three men a grateful smile of farewell, she trailed after her husband across the parade ground, finding it impossible to keep up with his long, angry strides.

The moment the couple was out of earshot, Lieutenant Colonel Henry Wessells turned on Feehan with a thunderous scowl. ''Were you aware, Captain,'' he growled, ''that the women and children of this fort were evacuated over four months ago?''

Terence Feehan stared at the officer in shock. ''No, sir!'' He looked at the retreating pair and then back to Wessells. ''If . . . if that's the case, sir,'' he stuttered, ''why did the commander at Fort Reno allow me to escort Mrs. Bruckenridge here?''

Surgeon Hines sent a spew of tobacco into the dirt. ''Major Van Voast probably didn't want the responsibility of sheltering a female until the mail wagon returned on its way back to Laramie. He knew damn well when Mrs. Bruckenridge got to Phil Kearny, she'd have to turn right around and go back where she came from. She should never have been allowed to leave Fort Laramie in the first place. Sometimes I can't believe the naiveté of the United States army.''

"Is that true, sir?" Terence asked the colonel in dismay.

"I'm afraid so, Captain. Tomorrow, Rachel Bruckenridge will start back with you and the mail escort.''

"Then shouldn't we tell her now, so she won't begin unpacking needlessly?"

Wessells shook his head. "No, let's allow the bridal couple to enjoy their wedding night. There'll be time enough in the morning to spoil their happiness.''

Terence hooked his thumbs in his sword belt and frowned. He hadn't liked the petulant look that had crossed the major's haughty features at the sight of his diminutive wife. "Major Bruckenridge didn't seem all that happy with his new bride."

"Nonsense," Colonel Wessells replied. "He's merely a jittery bridegroom on the eve of his honeymoon. Why shouldn't he be happy with her? She's chopped her pretty hair off shorter than some men, but otherwise she seems like a sweet young thing.''

"She's a peach," Terence stated emphatically. "Every man-jack of us took an enormous liking to her on the trail. No complaining. Not a bit of whining. Just a cheery hello for all, and an eye to what she could do to help. Not many women would have suffered such a rough journey without complaining once.''

"Sounds like you've fallen a little bit in love with her yourself, Captain," the white-haired doctor jested. He smoothed his pudgy hands over his belly and winked conspiratorially.

"A man could do a whole lot worse," Feehan answered with an exasperated shake of his head. He looked across the parade ground to see the two disappear into the major's cabin. "If that preening popinjay doesn't appreciate what he has, he's a damn fool."

"Well, if nothing else, she's a brave little soul," the colonel said in admiration. He absently plucked at his dark goatee. "Not many women would willingly come to the site of the Fetterman Massacre."

"I don't think she even knows about the massacre, sir," Terence stated. "She never mentioned it once."

"Impossible!" The surgeon snorted. "Everyone knows about the butchery that took place on Peno Creek."

Henry Wessells pursed his lips in calm deliberation. "The news was printed with banner headlines on the front page of every paper in the country. Mrs. Bruckenridge has to be aware of the fact that eighty-one men rode out of this stockade last December to be brutally killed and mutilated by two thousand Sioux and Cheyenne."

"Not if she can't read," Terence pointed out. "And unless I miss my guess, Rachel is totally illiterate, though she'd probably be humiliated to have to admit it to anyone."

"Surely someone must have told her about it at the time," Wessells countered.

The captain shrugged. "Until four months ago, Rachel Bruckenridge lived in a hollow in the Cumberland Mountains with her grandfather, who probably didn't know how to read or write, either. Luckily, we didn't sight a single red man the entire way here. When I realized the extent of her ignorance about the savages, I warned the men not to discuss the danger of Indian attacks while we were on the trail. Or to say anything at all about massacres or mutilations. I didn't want her frightened unnecessarily."

"I'll be damned," Hines said softly. "She really is a babe in the woods."

"Then we'll say nothing of this at the festivities to-night, either," Wessells cautioned the two men. "There's no point in her learning now that she's landed herself right in the middle of an Indian war. She's got to go back through two hundred miles of hostile territory to reach the safety of Fort Laramie. I don't want her frightened out of her wits before she starts the journey."

"Amen to that," the doctor prayed fervently. "Or we'll never get Mrs. Bruckenridge on board the mail wagon in the morning."

"You don't have to worry about her," Terence said with an unabashed grin. "That's one little gal with true grit."

Rachel glanced at her reflection in the cracked mirror over the bureau. She'd washed her hair during her bath in the hip tub, and the damp curls clustered about her face. Before dressing for the evening, she'd rested awhile on the large double bed, though she hadn't been able to fall asleep. She kept expecting Shelby to come back any minute. He hadn't said more than two words—"Good-bye"—before leaving her in his quarters. To her immense relief, he hadn't made any attempt to kiss her or put his arm around her. She sure as heck didn't want any of that mushy stuff—especially from a man who was a whole sight prettier than she was.

She looked around at the rustic abode. The three-room cabin was made of pine, and the familiar, woodsy scent filled the air. Pieces of old sheeting curtained the win-dows. The dirt floor was covered with gunny sacks sewn together. Her new home wasn't fancy, but there was lots she could do to make it more livable. Plenty to keep her busy, anyway. When her husband realized just how handy she was to have around, he'd likely change his mind about her. If they took their time getting acquainted, it might all work out yet. Rachel tried to ignore the uneasy feeling inside that this marriage would never work out, no matter how much time they gave it.

With a sigh, she looked down in disgust at her fanciest gown. Eliza had insisted upon supervising the bride's trousseau, as she'd called it. The choice of patterns and fabrics wasn't all that Eliza had insisted upon. Every dress in the new wardrobe had been fashioned to fit over a pink rubber device that was meant to compensate for Rachel's small bosom.

"It was designed," Eliza explained with a condescending sniff, "to augment the inadequate female figure. You needn't worry that anyone will suspect you're wearing it. The artificial bust will follow the movements of your respiration with perfect precision."

"Lord A'mighty," Rachel had muttered rebelliously, "I'll be so top-heavy, I'll fall flat on my face and bounce back up like an India rubber ball."

As if that wasn't enough, Eliza had insisted that the gowns be designed to go over a horsehair bustle. Rachel had promptly tossed away both contraptions, bust and bustle, on the second morning of her journey. But the dresses, which had been molded around them, sagged on top and bottom, making Rachel look like she was wearing her older sister's garments. If anything, she now appeared shorter and slighter than she really was. Worst of all, Rachel had to remember to lift her skirts well off the ground when she moved, or she'd catch her toe in the hastily stitched hems she'd sewn on the trip west.

A polite tap on the door interrupted her musings. Rachel froze before the mirror. Drawing a deep breath, she met her own frightened eyes. Would Shelby understand her desire to move slowly when it came to this business of being married? The thought of lying down with him in that big pine bed, wearing only her cotton nightgown, seemed downright indecent. He was, after all, a total stranger. If he wouldn't agree to wait a spell before demanding his conjugal rights—whatever the heck that included—she was at a loss as to what to do. One thing for dang sure, a bride was expected to sleep with her groom. She couldn't appeal to Colonel Wessells or the kind Captain Feehan. A man wouldn't understand a female's instinctive shyness. But any married woman would sympathize with Rachel's predicament. If necessary, she'd confide in Mrs. Wessells or one of the other officers' wives. Papa had assured her that the ladies she'd meet on the frontier would want to be her friends. Perhaps one would offer Rachel the shelter of her home until she was ready to sleep under the same roof with her spouse.

She opened the door a crack and peeked out, to find the young soldier she'd seen earlier.

"Beggin' your pardon, ma'am," he said, touching two fingers to the leather visor of his forage cap. "I'm Private Hoppner. The major asked me to escort you to Colonel Wessells's quarters."

Rachel pinned on a bright smile, determined to hide the fact that her husband's failure to come for her bothered her even more than his hasty departure. The two of them were going to have to have a serious talk before bedtime. She grabbed the gaily colored shawl she'd set out and tossed it over her shoulders. "Jest lead the way, Private," she said. "I'll stay on your trail like a hound chasin' a possum."

Hoppner's broad, freckled face creased into a delighted grin. "Yes, ma'am," he drawled. "I sure do like the way you talk."

"Where you from, soldier?"

"West Virginie, ma'am."

"Tarnation, if that don't explain it," she said, laughter bubbling up inside her. "Only a West Virginian would have the gall to be born with hair redder'n me and more freckles to boot." Her deep chuckles must have been infectious, because he tipped his head back and boomed with mirth.

The setting sun had painted the sky in glorious streaks of red and purple. As they walked across the parade, Rachel took stock of her surroundings. She'd been in such a daze when they first arrived, she'd hardly glanced around. The fort's single-story buildings were made of logs, their bark to the outside, and roofed with shingles. A continuous banquette ran the length of the stockade walls, which had loopholes for firing rifles. Two massive blockhouses with portholes for cannon stood at diagonal corners of the stockade. Huge gates, at least twelve feet wide, had small wickets just large enough for a single man to pass through in a stooping position.

"Have you been here long, Private Hoppner?"

"Since it was built, ma'am." He pointed proudly to the score of buildings that stood along the edge of the parade. "That there's company quarters, of course. Over there's the sutler's store, the laundry, and the hospital. Behind us is officers' row."

"I'm plumb amazed at such an almighty bastion a-sittin' smack dab in the middle of nowhere," Rachel said in awe. "Why, I doubt there's a livin' soul within a hundred miles of this fort. Seems like they kinda overgreased the skillet, don't it?"

Hoppner looked at her, his blue eyes wide. He opened his mouth, hesitated, then scratched his head beneath his cap. "Well, shucks, you know the army, Mrs. Bruckenridge. Nothin' they do ever makes much sense."

"Guess I don't know the army, a'tall," she confessed. "Ain't been married to a soldier more'n six weeks." She paused and looked across the parade ground. "Before we go to the colonel's house, I'd like to see how McDougall's gettin' along. Would you take me to see him?"

"You bet," Hoppner replied. He gallantly offered his elbow and led her across the dirt roadway to the stables.

* * *

The levee was a full-dress affair held in Colonel Wessells's spacious private quarters. Shelby met Rachel at the door and guided her to a small group that included the post commander. The men had traded their short cavalry jackets for frock coats that almost reached the knees of their blue trousers. Looking about, she was disappointed to find not a single woman among the roomful of officers.

"Is your wife feelin' poorly this evenin'?" she asked the colonel, barely able to hide her chagrin.

"Mrs. Wessells is visiting her parents in Baltimore," he explained. His brow puckered in an apologetic frown. "She'll be sorry to learn she wasn't here to welcome you."

"I'm plumb sorry, too," she said sincerely.

As Rachel was introduced to each officer, she discovered that, for one reason or another, all of the women and children were back East on extended visits with their families. She tried to hide her disheartenment at the news, for it meant that any confiding in a sympathetic female ear would clearly be out of the question.

The bridal couple was placed at the center of the head table, with Colonel Wessells at the groom's side and Captain Feehan and Surgeon Hines on the bride's. Along with thick elk steaks and canned lobster, the guests were treated to a fruit punch liberally laced with the colonel's finest Irish whisky. The newlyweds were the target of warm congratulations and frequent toasts. Despite the friendly raillery, as the evening progressed and the drinking continued, the handsome blond officer seated next to Rachel grew more and more surly.

"I don't know why we have to be so damn cautious," Bruckenridge muttered to a young lieutenant across from him, his words edged with ill-concealed belligerence. He shot his commanding officer, who was conversing with another man at the moment, a glance of pure contempt. "We're all tired of hiding behind these stockade walls like a bunch of cowards."

"The colonel specifically expressed his wish that we refrain from any talk about Indians," Terence Feehan remonstrated. He threw his napkin on the table in apparent disgust and met Shelby's amber eyes. To Rachel's amazement, the two men seemed to be trying to stare each other down.

"I don't know about you, Captain," Shelby sneered, "but I, for one, am not afraid of filthy savages." He tipped his chair back, lounging insolently. "Hell, a single company of U.S. cavalry could ride right through the entire Sioux nation."

Rachel cocked her head and looked at her husband in surprise. "Ridin' through a passel of natives don't sound like much of an accomplishment to me," she blurted out. "A body'd have to be downright chicken-livered to be afraid of 'em." At his stunned expression, she hurried to explain. "I saw them camped in their tents near Fort Laramie. The soldiers called them Laramie Loafers. They were a plumb sorrowful lot, if'n you ask me. One poor old woman come up to our wagon, beggin' for coffee. I didn't have any, but I offered her some apples I'd brought along for Mac. She gave me a string of beads in return."

"I trust you threw it away," Shelby said with a curl of his lip. He brushed the tip of one finger across his mustache in a finicky gesture.

"It's a right pretty necklace," she protested. "Whyever would I do a fritter-minded thing like that?"

"Because all redskins are vermin," he replied in a tone of undiluted loathing, "and anything they touch is covered with vermin, too."

Now that she looked at him closer, Rachel decided, her husband definitely had a weak mouth beneath that overgrown yellow bush.

"Let's steer the topic into calmer waters, shall we?" Colonel Wessells suggested, once more attending to their conversation.

"By all means," Feehan agreed. "In fact, I think I hear the regimental band tuning their instruments in the front parlor. I'm hoping for at least one dance with Mrs. Bruckenridge before the evening's over. Once the music begins, every man here will be lining up for a waltz with the new bride."

"Seein' as how I'm the only female in the room, Captain," Rachel said, chuckling, "I'm bound to be a powerful disappointment. I'm warnin' you here and now, I'm a whole lot better with my squirrel rifle than I am on the dance floor. But I'm willin' to give it a try, if'n you are."

"I believe the first dance belongs to the bridegroom," Colonel Wessells pointed out. He shot the major a piercing look.

Shelby waved his glass with scornful indifference. "Go on and dance," he said to Rachel, slurring his words slightly. "I prefer not to get my boots stepped on, if I can help it. My orderly just spent an hour spit-shining them."

"In that case, Mrs. Bruckenridge," the colonel said as he pushed back his chair and rose, "would you allow me the honor?"

"Reckon I allow how it's my honor, too," she replied with a grin. She laid her hand on the commanding officer's sleeve, not even deigning to glance at her spouse. If Shelby Bruckenridge thought he was going to weasel up to her later, after behaving like a foul-smelling varmint in front of her new friends, he had another think coming. With every minute she passed in his company, he reminded her more and more of his briggoty cousin Eliza. And Rachel never could stomach her pompous airs for more than a quarter-hour at a stretch.

Chapter 3

During the dancing that followed the meal, Shelby tried to rectify his shameful behavior. He stopped guzzling the colonel's whisky like some decrepit old moonshiner and switched to drinking hot coffee instead. By the time the band struck up the last waltz, he was sober enough to ask Rachel politely for a dance. She hesitated, well aware that everyone in the room was watching them in hopeful expectation. Ignoring the small voice inside that told her Major Bruckenridge was a low-down polecat, she nodded her acceptance. They twirled around the floor together to the spontaneous applause of his fellow officers.

Rachel could barely keep from gloating. Despite her earlier warning, she didn't once trod on the toes of Shelby's shiny black boots. Waltzing was the only thing Eliza had managed to teach her willful stepdaughter. Under the woman's critical eye, Rachel and Ben had galloped around the Ashwood drawing room to the rousing cadence of Lucinda's piano playing, till their feet were numb and their hearts were pumping.

The celebration ended at midnight in proper military fashion. Captain Feehan approached Rachel just as the newlyweds were about to leave the colonel's quarters. He took her fingers in his broad hand and gave them a compassionate squeeze. "Are you all right, ma'am?" he asked hesitantly.

"I'm jest dandy, Captain," she told her friend, forcing a smile for his benefit. "A body'd have to be plumb techeous not to be pleasured by all this attention." She wagged an admonishing finger under his nose. "Now don't you dare go hightailin' it out of here in the mornin' without tellin' me good-bye."

Rachel had seen the cantankerous looks exchanged by her husband and the barrel-chested Ohioan. The last thing she wanted was to cause a ruckus that would end in disciplinary action for either of them. Terence Feehan had been far too kind to be served in such a shabby manner. And although she knew he was deeply concerned about her well-being, she couldn't bring herself to discuss her grievous disappointment in her bridegroom with any other man. Somehow, it seemed downright traitorous to her father, who'd agreed to the match. Papa had met Shelby once, before the war. What the learned judge had seen in the cocky young braggart to earn his admiration, she couldn't begin to guess.

"Good night, then," Terence said, his worried eyes searching hers. "I'll talk to you in the morning."

Outside, the grassy parade ground was lit by the faint glow of a crescent moon. A sprinkling of stars peeked through heavy drifts of clouds. Along the banquette, one sentry after another called out a comforting "Twelve o'clock and all's well."

Rachel walked stiffly beside Major Bruckenridge toward officers' row. In her smoldering anger, she found it impossible to make even simple conversation. Peering up at her tall, silent husband from the corner of her eye, she read his baleful expression and wondered if she'd done the right thing in turning down Terence Feehan's unspoken offer of help. When the captain had told her earlier that he was leaving in the morning to escort the mail wagon back to Fort Laramie, she'd fought against a rising tide of homesickness. With Feehan's departure, she'd be losing the only person in the fort who truly cared about her welfare.

But it was best to get this matter of conjugal relations settled with her husband tonight. Granted, he'd behaved like a skunk, but he still deserved to be told personally the conclusion she'd reached during supper. For she had no intention of sharing a bed with Shelby Bruckenridge any time in the near future. Fact was, she couldn't envision *ever* sharing a bed with him. The man was a swaggering, puffed-up fool.

Thankfully, at the moment, he was also stone sober. His commanding officer's reproachful glare had apparently brought Shelby to his senses—leastways, as far as decent manners were concerned. Once inside their own quarters and safe from curious ears, she would explain to her chastened groom that they needed to get to know each other first, before there could be any intimacy between them. If he wasn't gentleman enough to sleep on the floor, she would. She'd made her decision, and it was unshakable. He'd have no choice but to abide by it.

Rachel never had a chance to explain her newly formed resolution. The moment they stepped into the darkened cabin, Shelby slammed the door behind them, grabbed her by the upper arm, and yanked her into the bedroom. With a wordless snarl, he shoved her rudely toward the big pine bed. He lit the coal-oil lamp on the scarred bureau and turned to stare at her, disdain marring his handsome features. In the flickering lantern glow, his golden eyes were as hard as agates.

"Take your clothes off," he ordered. "I want to see just how badly I've been tricked."

"No one tricked you," she denied, suddenly short of

breath. His uncalled-for roughness left her more irate than frightened. There was no reason for him to kick out like an ornery mule. She was every bit as disappointed as he was. "You went into this marriage willingly," she reminded him, "which is more than I can say for myself."

"Willingly?" he bit out. "What man would willingly marry an illiterate red-haired midget, who croaks like a goddamn bullfrog?"

At the needlessly cruel words, tears stung Rachel's eyes. "Eliza wrote you what I looked like," she said in a suffocated whisper. "I don't rightly see how you have any room for complaint now."

"Oh, don't I?" Shelby stepped toward her menacingly and stood with hands clenched and feet braced wide apart. His amber cat-eyes were filled with loathing.

Something about his aggressive stance rang an awakening chord of fear inside her. "I'm gettin' out of here," she gulped as she tried to scoot around him toward the door. "We can jaw about this in the mornin'."

He caught her forearm and twisted it painfully, forcing her down to her knees in front of him. "You're not going anywhere, you little bitch," he growled. "Do you actually think I'll let you run to Wessells and make me the laughingstock of the entire fort? Not when I've got the only petticoat in Phil Kearny right here in my bedroom." Shelby's chuckle was as low and evil as the devil's himself. "You're not going to refuse your wifely duty, Mrs. Bruckenridge. Not tonight. You're going to give me everything I want. You're going to pay for your contemptible deceit, and you're going to keep on paying every day for the rest of your life."

Holding her arm so tightly she was afraid he'd snap the bone, Shelby slowly unbuckled his sword belt. With a twisted leer, he threw the belt and saber, sheathed in its scabbard, onto the gray army blanket that covered the mattress. His fringed silk sash followed.

"Come on, you freckled-face whore," he taunted. "You wanted a husband so badly you were willing to lie and cheat for one. Hell, you came all the way from Lexington to entrap me. Don't pretend to be a shrinking virgin now. I'll bet you've spread your legs for at least one strapping mountain lad. What decent, God-fearing woman would cut her hair nearly as short as a man's?"

Rachel looked up into his pale, glittering eyes and knew no pleas for compassion would move him. His face was contorted with hate and a driving need for revenge. Eliza had lied to them both, but he'd never believe it. "Wait," she implored. "Jest give me a chance to explain what happened."

Shelby snatched a handful of her hair and jerked her head back brutally. "First, you undress me, Mrs. Bruckenridge, starting with my boots. Then maybe, just maybe, I'll listen to your lying explanations." He released her and sank down on the edge of the grass-filled mattress. "Go on," he commanded, extending his black leather boot out in front of him. "Take it off."

Rachel slowly regained her feet. Certain she could never make it to the front door before he caught her, she cupped the low heel of his cavalry boot in one shaking hand, its square toe with her other, and pulled it off. He stuck out the other foot, an insolent grin on his thin, bloodless lips. "That's better," he said as she removed the second boot. He rose and stood in front of her. "Now for the coat."

She unfastened the double row of brass buttons, her fingers trembling visibly. With her help, Shelby eased out of the dark frock coat and tossed it aside, then removed his shirt. He shucked off his sky-blue trousers and stood before her in nothing but his drawers and gray woolen stockings.

Rachel had been raised in the mountains. She'd seen horses, cows, and goats mate. She had an instinctive and rudimentary understanding of how human beings coupled. When she saw the bulge in Shelby's underwear, she knew what he intended to do.

"And now for the dress," he said in a low, sinister tone.

She stepped back, her heart smacking against her breastbone. "No," she begged. "Please. I . . . I can't. Not like this."

"Then we'll try it like this," he snarled. He doubled his fist and punched her viciously in the stomach. Rachel crumpled forward, holding herself in agony. She fought the roiling blackness that threatened to swamp her. Raising one hand, palm outward, in a silent plea for mercy, she gagged repeatedly with shock and anguish. Tears scalded her eyelids and blurred her vision. Worse than the violent, stabbing ache in her belly was the searing mortification. No one had ever purposely inflicted pain on Rachel in her entire life.

She clamped her lips together, unable to stifle the moan that welled up inside her. Through the excruciating fog, she heard Gramps's voice: *If'n any low-down skunk ever tries to harm you, Rosie child, you jest get in close-like and smack him right in the jingle-berries with yer knee jest as hard as you can. Then while he's a-staggerin' round, conk him on the head with anythin' you can lay your little hands on.*

Shelby's chilling command cut through the red haze of misery that clouded her brain. "I said take off that damn dress."

"I think I like you better drunk," she gasped. She undid the tiny pearl buttons that ran down the front of her ill-fitting ball gown, her fingers shaking so hard she could barely manage them. That task completed, she paused and looked at him warily.

"Go on." The two words were edged with feverish anticipation. In that instant, Rachel realized that Shelby enjoyed inflicting pain. Her suffering and humiliation excited him. Any begging or pleading on her part would only whip him into a frenzy, and what further depths of low-minded savagery he might sink to, she couldn't imagine.

Stubbornly, she clenched her jaw and glared at the bully, guessing intuitively that the least show of fear on her part would add to his sexual arousal. Without a hint of emotion, she pulled the green satin dress down over her shoulders and let it fall to the floor, along with her snowy white petticoats. She lifted her chin and stood before him, clad only in her delicate chemise and embroidered cotton drawers. Her cheeks burned with anger and shame. Rachel could hear his swift intake of breath as he raked her with his covetous gaze.

Without a hint of warning, Shelby grabbed the front of her lawn chemise with both hands and ripped the fragile bodice down its center seam, exposing her high, firm bosom to his view. "Well, I'll be damned," he chortled. "This is turning out to be quite an evening for surprises."

He clenched a hank of her hair and dragged her to him. His cruel fingers squeezed her breast, digging into the tender flesh. Rachel recoiled in pain and disgust. He bent his blond head, and she turned her face away, refusing even to look at him. She felt the brush of his thick mustache against her collarbone as he lowered his mouth, still holding her hair in an agonizing grip.

With his hands and mind occupied, she took advantage of the only opportunity she was likely to get. She grabbed hold of the waistband of his drawers with both hands, brought her knee up with all the force she could muster, and nailed him square in the crotch.

Shelby bent forward, clutching his groin and swearing

a blistering oath. As his head came down, Rachel butted the bridge of his nose with her hard forehead and heard the satisfying pop of cartilage severing from bone. He staggered and groaned, unable to see through his watering eyes. His comely features were screwed up in shock and pain. She didn't give him a chance to recover his senses. She grabbed the sheathed cavalry saber and, swinging it high over her head, struck him with the heavy hilt. It cracked against his skull with a sickening thud, and he fell to the floor, unconscious.

Rachel struggled for breath, her chest heaving, tears of fright and revulsion streaming down her cheeks. Waves of nausea rolled over her. She looked around wildly, searching for something to bind him with. Her frantic gaze lighted on his hat, and she quickly tore the double-looped hatcord off its wide brim. She lashed his hands together behind his back, then fastened his stockinged feet with his silk sash and brought them up, hogtying him securely. Rachel stood up and stared at him in horror. She'd probably tied his hands too tightly in her panic, but she couldn't take the chance of loosening the gold cord now.

Her whole body shaking uncontrollably, Rachel dragged her carpetbag out from under the bed where she'd stashed it that afternoon. She removed her torn chemise and pulled on another. Then she scrambled into Shelby's trousers and gray flannel shirt and slipped on his short cavalry jacket. Plopping down on the edge of the mattress, she drew on her worn riding boots and stuffed the long pant legs inside. She piled some underclothes and toiletry articles into the bag, along with a few apples and a tin of biscuits. Hastily, she threw in the britches and shirts she'd hidden from Eliza's prying eyes when she'd packed back in Lexington. She snatched up her Great-granddaddy McDougall's plaid, which she'd draped across the foot of the bed, and rolled the purple-

and-pink wool around her Bowie knife. Last, she stuffed in her powder horn and shot pouch, closed the bag, tossed the bedroll over her shoulder, and picked up her long-barreled flintlock rifle.

Her heart stopped when she heard Shelby groan. Whirling around, Rachel stared at him in blank confusion. He moved his head slowly back and forth, blinking repeatedly as he struggled to regain consciousness. Lord A'mighty, she couldn't let him wake up and holler for help.

Before he could summon enough strength to yell bloody murder, she dropped the rifle and plaid, snatched up the china pitcher from the bureau, and smashed it over his head. Water sprayed over them both, soaking his wavy blond hair and the blue pants she wore. In the morning, he'd thank her for sparing him the gun butt. Course, she wouldn't be there to listen to his words of heartfelt gratitude.

Deep in the shadows, Rachel waited beside the water gate, holding Mac's reins in one hand. "Shh," she warned him when he started to nicker. She patted his quivering nostrils comfortingly. "Steady, feller. Don't give us away."

She'd learned earlier at the levee that a mounted picket would be sent out at exactly two in the morning to relieve the lookout guard on the hill north of the fort. It would be her only chance to get away before sunrise. Clouds drifted across the moon, blanketing the yard in darkness, just as two sleepy-eyed soldiers lifted the heavy beam down and swung the gate open.

Four men rode into the quartermaster's yard. Five men rode out. The last one, a small fellow, kept his head down and the wide brim of his cordless hat pulled over his eyes. He rode his showy chestnut a little behind the others. As the detail crossed Big Piney Creek and headed toward Pilot Hill, the last cavalryman dropped farther and farther behind, until he veered off into a deep coulee that followed a streambed.

The heavy bank of clouds rolled past, allowing a sliver of moon to shed its faint light on the landscape below. Just enough light to see by. Rachel looked up at the stars twinkling in the black canopy overhead and let out a sigh of relief. She hadn't dared to tell Colonel Wessells or even Captain Feehan what had happened between her and her bridegroom. The men might listen to her with sympathy, or they just might side with their fellow officer. She couldn't take that chance. Lots of folks thought a husband had the right to discipline an uppity wife. But Papa would understand, once she told him what kind of fiend Eliza's cousin really was. Papa would annul the marriage, and she'd never have to go near Shelby Bruckenridge again.

She urged the restive stallion into the swift-moving stream, where the clear water came up to his knees. "Come on, Mac," Rachel whispered. "We're goin' home to Kentucky."

Rachel kept to the rocky creek bottom as much as possible, following it northeast the rest of that night and all the next day, certain her pursuers could never track her. The soldiers, led by Major Bruckenridge, would gallop southward with the idea that any frightened female would surely try to reach Fort Laramie by going down the Bozeman Road the same way she came up.

There was never a doubt in her mind that Shelby would come after her, if for no other reason than to recover his horse. Besides, he'd shrink from having to admit to Garrett Robinson that the judge's daughter had run away on her wedding night. Not a pleasant thing for a body to have to write to his brand-new father-in-law. Added to that, the gleam of pure hatred in the major's eyes just before she'd hit him with that pitcher made it dead certain he wouldn't give up easily.

Two days later, Rachel discovered she'd been wrong about deceiving them. From the top of a tableland, she spotted a group of horsemen in the distance coming at a gallop. One of the civilian guides was out in front, leading the company of cavalry after her like he was Uncle Ephraim's prize coon hound. Criminently, how could the fellow have tracked her over the rocks?

It must have taken them a full day, at least, to discover she hadn't hightailed it south. They were sure making up for lost time now. Rachel hadn't been in any particular hurry, seeing as how she was heading in the wrong direction in the first place and would have to double back as soon as she felt it was safe. She'd shot a couple of rabbits and cooked them under the shelter of a jutting ravine in the evenings. Directions hadn't given her a lick of trouble. She'd just kept those shining mountains on her left.

"Well, Mac," she said sorrowfully, "looks like this is where you and I part company." She hugged his neck, laying her cheek on the smooth chestnut coat. "Lord A'mighty, I hate to send you back to that mule-eared scoundrel. But as soon as I reach Kentucky, I'll have Papa send for you. You'll be back in the Ashwood stables afore the frost sets in."

With the sheathed Bowie fastened to her belt, she took the woolen plaid and rolled her clothing and necessaries into it. She slung the bundle over her shoulder, along with her powder horn and bullet pouch. With any luck, they wouldn't have realized she carried a rifle and ammunition. She hoped the men would think she'd fallen off her mount and been attacked, maybe even killed, by a wild animal.

She slapped Mac's rump. "Go on, now!" she shouted.

"Git!" Startled, the stallion took off, racing toward the oncoming horsemen.

Rachel picked up her musket and scrambled down the opposite side of the plateau's steep bank, careful to trample as little grass as possible. She knew she had to leave the creek behind, though she hated giving up the surety of fresh water each evening. The guide would assume that even a woman going in the wrong direction would have enough brains to follow a streambed.

For three more days, Rachel wandered eastward, hoping she wasn't overshooting her mark. Her trick had worked. The soldiers must have dismounted and scoured the countryside inch by inch, trying to find her—or what was left of her. She tried to judge just how far east she could travel before she had to turn south or risk missing Fort Laramie altogether. She'd never seen such a confounded, confusing country. From a distance, the plains looked as flat as a flannel-cake. But traipsing up and down the coulees and draws had sapped her energy and made the going far harder than she'd first supposed. At last she had to admit to herself that, considering her slow progress, it'd take her over a month to reach Laramie.

What was far worse, the loneliness was starting to prey on her spirits. She missed Mac's company far more than she would have imagined. During the night, coyotes howled incessantly. Owls hooted at irregular intervals, while small creatures rustled in the surrounding brush. Dreams of running across the open grasslands, chased by some evil, unseen being, just as Gram had warned her about, brought Rachel awake and trembling with fright. Her long, sleepless nights began to rival the endless emptiness of her days for pure, point-blank misery.

On the sixth morning of her trek, Rachel discovered she was no longer alone. She found a high, swift-flowing creek and followed it south. As she rounded a sharp bend, she spied a village of natives. The cone-shaped tents, spread out in a great half-circle along the creek bank, looked similar to the ones she'd seen near Fort Laramie. She remembered the poor creatures who'd hovered around the stockade, pleading for coffee and tobacco. Still, beggars or no, they were fellow human beings, and she smiled to herself in elation at the welcome sight.

Cutting through a thick stand of willows, she entered the village from the creek side. As she walked through the open area, covered with trampled grass, the people stopped what they were doing and stared at her as though she were some ghostly apparition dropped from the sky. She couldn't blame them. Coming from the water's edge as she'd done, she must have taken them completely by surprise.

The silence that descended on the camp brought Strong Elk Heart to his feet. He'd been working on a small bow for Sleeping Bull's oldest son, when the unexplained quiet in the middle of a busy summer afternoon captured his immediate attention. Searching the camp circle, he spotted the intruder. It was a white boy. The youth, wearing a horse soldier's hat pulled down on his head, strode across the buffalo grass, waving a confident greeting to the people who watched him in utter amazement.

"What is it, my grandson?" Flying Hawk asked from the entrance to his lodge. The unusual silence had attracted the Old Man Chief's attention, and he'd stepped out of the tipi to investigate. Nearby, his two gray-haired wives stopped their work on a deerskin staked out on the grass. Good Robe Woman and Standing in Water laid down their scrapers and rose to their feet.

"It's a white boy," Strong Elk replied. "About eleven or twelve winters and carrying a long-barreled rifle slung on his back."

Together, the four hurried to join the gathering of men,

women, and children who'd surrounded the youth and now stood staring at him in solemn contemplation. No one said a word. Strong Elk was the only person in their band who spoke the language of the white eyes. The people waited patiently for his approach.

"Hello," he called to the child, the moment he was close enough to be heard.

The boy answered with an engaging smile. "Howdy!" He tugged off his wide-brimmed blue hat, and a murmur of appreciative *ahs* ran through the fascinated crowd. The youngster had a head of thick coppery curls, their flaming highlights dancing in the sunshine. The Cheyenne were especially fond of red hair.

"Why have you come here?" Strong Elk demanded with a scowl. He stopped directly in front of the lad, whose appearance meant that other whites were somewhere close by. "Aren't you aware that you're trespassing?"

"Hey, I didn't see no fences," the youth answered with an injured mien. "But I didn't bother nothin', neither. I was jest sorta . . ." The boy paused and sliced through the air with his small hand, indicating a southeasterly direction. ". . . passin' through."

Astonished, Strong Elk realized that his first assumption had been far wide of the mark. The youngster was dressed in the baggy trousers and shirt of a white boy, all right, but the delicate features and long, curving lashes were those of a girl. She spoke in a deep voice for a female. The soft, husky tones were wonderfully charming. They seemed to strike a responsive chord somewhere inside him, for he smiled without conscious thought.

"Are you lost?" he asked kindly, deciding she must have wandered away from a wagon train going up the Bozeman Trail. Or perhaps it had been attacked by Red Cloud's band of Bad Faces, and she was the only survivor. Yet aside from being dusty and rumpled, she showed no signs of ill treatment.

"No, sir, I'm not lost," she replied with a gurgle of laughter, as though the question were patently ridiculous. She ran her slender fingers through her matted curls, fluffing them up off her damp forehead. "But I'm plumb weary of travelin' alone, I can tell you that for a fact."

"What does she say?" Flying Hawk asked.

"She says she is not lost," he told his grandfather in their own language. "Just lonely." Suppressing a grin, Strong Elk met the older man's astute gaze. Clearly, the girl was lying. She had to be lost. She also had to be extremely frightened, but she was certainly putting up a brave front. He was impressed with her courage. Most white girls would have been running around in circles, screaming at the tops of their lungs in horrible, ear-splitting wails.

All about the circle of bystanders, people started to murmur in speculation, repeating what he'd just told their chief.

Strong Elk turned back to the girl and felt his heart pause for the space of a beat. She was watching him with enormous eyes the color of rich spring grass. Fringed by incredibly long russet lashes, they were the most guileless eyes he'd ever seen, without a hint of the contempt or fear he would have expected from one of her race. Unaccountably, he felt a rush of heat through his body and was instantly ashamed of his lustful reaction. She must have barely crossed the divide between childhood and maidenhood. Certainly, she was no older than fourteen. Far too young and innocent for a hardened warrior of twenty-eight, who'd slept with more women than he cared to remember. And she was white.

"If you're not lost," he said in a gentle tone, "where are you going?"

"Home." She looked around at the interested faces,

seemingly at ease in their midst. Noticing the chubby, round-cheeked Prickly Pear hanging on to his mother's fringed skirt, she wiggled her fingers at the two-year-old in a playful gesture. Then she turned her head to meet Porcupine Quills's curious eyes and smiled as though the white-haired woman was a long, lost friend.

She kept glancing away from Strong Elk, as though embarrassed to meet his gaze. The strange feeling that she'd somehow read his carnal thoughts brought to him an unaccustomed surge of guilt. "Where's your home?" he asked curtly, starting to lose patience.

Rachel lifted her eyebrows in surprise at the man's irritated tone, wondering what she'd said to displease him. She tilted her head, indicating the southeast. "Over yonder."

She glanced around at the natives once again, striving her utmost to keep from staring gooey-eyed at the tall man in front of her. Lord A'mighty, here was no pathetic beggar! He had to be, beyond a doubt, the most beautiful human being she'd ever laid eyes on. And there was enough of him exposed to view for her to make that hasty judgment. Fact was, she'd never seen so much bare male flesh in her life.

Except for his loincloth and beaded leather footwear—and the string of ferocious bear claws he wore around his neck—the man was stark, blinding naked. His straight, blue-black hair fell nearly to his waist, with two narrow side braids and a shorter braid on the crown of his head, all three decorated with fur and feather ornaments. Two large, barbaric gold hoops hung from his earlobes.

What was most amazing, however, was the tattoo of a buck elk, sporting a magnificent rack of antlers, on the man's left breast, just above his flat, brown nipple. As hard as she tried, she couldn't keep her gaze away from that one particular spot. The primitive, stylized elk was caught in mid-leap, with legs outstretched as though flying over a wide mountain hollow. She'd never seen anything so exotic. She longed to reach out and touch it.

His clipped words interrupted her wandering thoughts, and she forced herself to meet his eyes once again. "By treaty," he explained, "the Cheyenne and Sioux hunting grounds stretch for hundreds of miles in an easterly direction from where we now stand. You'd have to walk for weeks before reaching the first white settlement." He paused and glowered at her like an angry schoolmaster. "So where exactly is *over yonder*?"

"Kentucky."

He blinked, then slowly shook his head, relaxing his taut stance. He seemed to smile in spite of himself. "What's your name, child?"

She grinned, wanting to reward him for finally recalling his company manners. "Rachel Rose Robinson. My kinfolk call me Rosie."

"Where are your parents, Rachel?"

The man might be as gorgeous as a ridge full of piney roses, but he surely was thickheaded. "I jest told you," she responded with an audible sigh. "Kentucky. Sugar Holler, to be exact."

He folded his arms across his broad chest and gazed over the top of her head toward the creek bank, which wasn't hard for him to do, considering she didn't quite reach his shoulder. His dark, almond-shaped eyes glinted suspiciously. "Who were you with, before you became lost?"

"I already answered that one, too," she said emphatically. "I ain't lost."

"Then what are you doing out here in Dakota Territory, Miss Robinson?"

At the proper form of address, she surveyed him with heightened regard. He spoke English fluently, with just a trace of an accent. One she couldn't quite put her finger on, but it sounded kind of fancy-like. There wasn't a doubt that he'd spent lots of time with white folks. She wondered, unhappily, if he were acquainted with any cavalry officers in the area. All these questions were starting to give her the jitters.

"I was visitin' some folks out here," she explained. "You talk pretty fair English for an Injun. What's your name, anyhow?"

He ignored her inquiry. "Who were you visiting?"

At his insistent tone, she shrugged, jammed her hat back on her head, and hooked her thumbs in her belt. "Jest friends. Say, listen, I don't mean to be makin' a nuisance of myself or nothin'. So I allow as how I'll jest be moseyin' along." She started to step around him.

"You're not going anywhere, Rachel Robinson," he said as he moved to block her way. His words had the ring of authority. She guessed he must be the headman of the village. If that were true, and he persisted in trying to keep her there, she could be in a heap of trouble. Her grandma's warning never to go west of the Mississippi had been right on the button.

He turned to the old man beside him, and they spoke at length in their strange-sounding language. The elderly woman Rachel had smiled at earlier stepped forward and talked, quickly and earnestly, to the two frowning men. She was every bit as short as Rachel, with sparkling black eyes and a merry expression. A knowing smile skipped around the corners of her mouth, as though she kept some marvelous secret. Rachel was reminded of Gram.

Others in the group added their opinions, till pretty soon it seemed that everyone was talking at once. Rachel studied them in captivated silence. Their costumes of soft deerskin were lavishly adorned with colorful beads and feathers. Unlike the natives she'd seen at Fort Laramie, they were all beautifully groomed. Their shiny black hair fell around their shoulders like thick curtains of satin. And everyone appeared well fed and healthy. At last, they seemed to come to some sort of agreement. The elk man turned back to Rachel with a satisfied expression on his sharply honed features.

"Porcupine Quills has offered to share her lodge with you until your people come," he told her. "She's a child-less widow and lives alone. She'll be happy for the com-pany."

"Reckon that's mighty nice of her," Rachel said, "but I really can't stay, 'cause my homefolk ain't never comin' to find me. Like you mentioned afore, it's goin' to take me a powerful long time to get back to Sugar Holler. I thank you all right kindly for your offer of hos-pitality, but I'd best be gettin' on my way." She touched the brim of her hat in farewell, praying someone would have the decency to step aside, so she could pass through the tight circle of onlookers without bumping into any-one. Instead, they crowded even closer.

"Give me your rifle," the elk man ordered, thrusting out his hand.

Rachel took a quick step back. "Whoa, now," she said. She raised her hands in a peace-seeking gesture. "I ain't givin' up my gun, nohow. I'm willin' to swear on a stack of Bibles that I don't mean no harm to a soul here. But you're burnin' green wood for kindlin' if'n you think I'm goin' to hand over my granddaddy's rifle."

"Give me the gun, Rachel." He took a step closer, his strong jaw set like a lawman's at a hanging. "And I'll take that knife as well. We can't let you wander back out onto the open plains. There's a war going on. Only the guidance of the All-Knowing One led you safely to our camp. Had you run into Red Cloud and his warriors, you wouldn't still have that pretty mop of hair on your head."

She gulped at the image his words conveyed. "It ain't that I'm wantin' to contrary you none," she said. "Why, I'm plumb pleased that you're invitin' me to stick around for a spell." She looked at Porcupine Quills and offered a wide smile of gratitude. "It's jest that I've got to be goin'."

While the girl's gaze was momentarily diverted, Strong Elk calmly lifted the rifle off her shoulder with one hand and removed the Bowie from its sheath with the other. He gave the hunting knife to Flying Hawk and stood the gun, butt down, on the ground beside her, measuring its length against her short stature. The long, slender barrel extended a good six inches past the top of her head. "No one should have to carry a gun taller than she is," he teased. He made no attempt to hide his tickled sense of humor at the unusual sight.

Rachel glared at him, her narrowed eyes snapping with green fire. "A body could get himself in a whole lot of trouble stealin' another body's weapon. My gramps carried that rifle all the way to New Orlins and back. I don't aim to lose it out here in the middle of nowhere, and that's a fact, mister."

"My name is Strong Elk Heart," he told her. "My people call me the Elk." He was unable to keep from grinning. That a young white girl would dare to threaten a Cheyenne warrior who'd counted numerous coups in hand-to-hand combat was hilarious. She was like a tiny hummingbird getting ready to attack an eagle.

"I'm not stealing your rifle, Miss Robinson," he continued. "I'm merely holding it, till your father comes for you. Your entire family must be searching the countryside right now. If you're worried that we plan to harm them, I assure you, they are in no danger. My grandfather, Flying Hawk, signed a new treaty with your government two months ago. We are a peaceful band of Cheyenne on our way north along Powder River. We planned to break camp in the morning, but we'll wait here, until you're safely reunited with your loved ones. I'll return your weapons to you when you leave."

Propping her hands on her hips, Rachel shook her head

in disgust. "I don't aim to tell you but one more time, Mr. Elk. All my kinfolk are back in Sugar Holler. There ain't nobody a-goin' to come lookin' for me."

"Then I suppose you'll have to come with us," he replied, clearly unimpressed with her predicament. "We'll be hunting the buffalo all summer. Either way, you're not going back out on the plains alone. I forbid it. And I'll take that powder horn and bullet pouch while I'm at it."

"Shoot, if that don't beat all," she grumbled as she handed them over. "You're the second most contrarious man I've ever met. Fact is, I do believe by the time I get out of here, you jest might take the prize."

Chapter 4

~~~♦♦~~~

That evening, Strong Elk went to Porcupine Quills's lodge to question the *vehoka*. He had returned to camp late in the afternoon, his pack horse laden with deer meat, expecting to find that someone had come searching for her. Prepared, even, to learn that she'd already departed in the company of her grateful family. He'd grown more and more perplexed as the hours wore on and no white man appeared. Stranger yet, none of the warriors who rode into the campsite after a day of hunting had reported seeing any white eyes in the vicinity.

The Elk waited until the evening meal was over, not wanting to impose on the elderly widow's hospitality. Promptly at sunset, he walked across the open circle to Porcupine Quills's small tipi. Beautifully decorated with four large stars, it sat beside Clear Creek near a cluster of large willow trees.

Although it was June and the days were warm, the evenings remained cool. The lodge's buffalo-skin covering, which had been raised in the midday heat to allow the summer breeze to float through the interior, was now lowered. Strong Elk courteously waited outside until the

61

old woman called for him to enter, then he bent and stepped into the tipi.

Porcupine Quills and Rachel were seated beside the fire, their heads close together over a piece of tanned deerskin. The coffee-colored leather would soon become the upper part of a summer moccasin once the darker, buffalo-hide sole was sewn in place.

The white girl had pulled off her scuffed riding boots and stockings and piled them beside a backrest covered with a soft buffalo robe. Still wearing trousers, she sat cross-legged like a boy, intently watching the older woman's nimble fingers fly. Using an awl and a long strand of sinew, Porcupine Quills stitched the colorful dyed quills in an intricate pattern on the toe. The two looked up as he entered, and smiled their welcome.

"*Hamestoo-estse,*" Rachel called cheerfully.

Strong Elk stared at her in disbelief.

Grinning widely, she rose and slowly sank back down on the bearskin that covered the floor. Before he could say a word, up she popped again and repeated the movement, her arms floating out gracefully at her sides like a dancer's. "*Hamestoo-estse,*" she said with pride as she demonstrated the meaning of the command once again. Her green eyes sparkled in delight at his incredulous gaze.

Strong Elk sat down on the men's side of the lodge, momentarily speechless. He'd brought a haunch of deer meat to Porcupine Quills earlier that afternoon in appreciation of her willingness to shelter their uninvited guest and to provide for the extra mouth the older woman now had to fill. Once he was seated, Rachel pointed to the roasted venison, left over from their supper, in a small wooden bowl.

"*Ne-a-ese,*" she said with a spontaneous gurgle of laughter. The throaty, uninhibited sound lit a fire deep in his groin. "That's all I've learned so far," she explained in English, completely unaware of his reflexive reaction. "'Sit down' and 'thank you.'"

"The white girl is a quick learner," Porcupine Quills announced in Cheyenne. Her wrinkled face beamed in a smile of approval. "I am teaching her the correct way to adorn moccasins. Tomorrow, she can learn how to make a proper dress. She will need one. All she has in her little bundle is boy's clothing."

"She will not be here long enough to make a dress," Strong Elk declared more sharply than he'd intended. In respect for the widow's advanced years, he lowered his voice and continued in a subdued tone. "By tomorrow, her family will come for her."

Porcupine Quills tipped her snowy head, her long braids falling in front of her, and gazed at him. "You think that is so?" she asked. "Mm." She made a face that meant she doubted it. "Whether or not they come, she will need moccasins." She motioned to Rachel's feet and went back to her work.

"What's the matter with your feet?" he questioned the *vehoka* in her own language.

Without a moment's hesitation, Rachel stretched her legs out in front of her, presenting her bare toes for his inspection. They were blistered and raw. "All that walkin' in boots 'bout did me in," she confessed. She wrinkled her nose in dissatisfaction. "I'm used to runnin' around barefoot durin' the summer. Don't generally put on shoes till the first frost."

Strong Elk's gaze moved from her injured feet to her pert little nose, reddened from too much exposure to the sun. A sprinkle of coppery dust trailed across its narrow bridge. She shook her head in apparent disgust at her own frailty, and a shiny lock bounced down over one eyebrow. Moving shadows from the firelight played across the fragile bones of her face. Her features were small and delicate and utterly feminine. He felt the blood hit his heart in a rush and swore silently to himself in English. What in the hell was the matter with him?

She wasn't much more than a baby.

And she was white.

He cleared his throat, willing his overheated pulse to return to normal. "Porcupine Quills can prepare a poultice of herbs for you," he told the *vehoka* with all the solemnity of an Old Man Chief. "She's very skilled in the healing arts."

Rachel's smile lit up her heart-shaped face. "I know. *Niscem* poured a warm mixture over my blisters after I bathed in the creek this afternoon. Whew!" She shook her head, and the unruly curls danced around her face. "The stuff stank to high heaven, but my poor toes are startin' to feel better already."

Strong Elk turned to Porcupine Quills with a frown. "Teaching the white girl to call you Grandmother was unwise," he reproached her in Cheyenne. "She is not one of us."

"For as long as she is with our band, I will be her grandmother," Porcupine Quills said with a shrug, unmoved by his disapproval. "The young woman will need someone to explain our customs, to show her where to get fresh water each morning, and where to wash every afternoon. There are some of us who have not forgotten how to treat a guest, particularly one who is in mourning." With an admonitory sniff, the widow chose another quill from her little case made of buffalo pericardium and returned to her sewing.

"The child is not in mourning," he informed her. "White people do not cut their hair as a sign of grief."

The old woman's alert black eyes bespoke her doubt, but she was too polite to argue. "Still, I will teach her what she needs to know while she lives among us."

Strong Elk was aware that Rachel had gone with the other women to the secluded spot where they bathed each day. He'd seen her in their midst as they'd left the camp, the entire group of females chattering like a flock of magpies. When they returned, the *vehoka* had changed her soiled clothing for a clean shirt and pair of trousers. The loose garments looked as though they were made for someone twice her size. Her freshly washed hair was caught back on one side by an ornament crafted from an oriole's bright yellow and black feathers. He recognized the trinket as belonging to Choke Cherry Blossom and wondered if Rachel had given the young woman a gift in return. The white girl had certainly lost no time in making friends. She had a natural vivacity that was extremely appealing. The sooner her parents came to claim her, the better.

"Rachel," Strong Elk said, folding his arms across his chest in his most authoritative manner, "I want to ask you a few questions about how you wandered into our camp today. I had expected someone to come looking for you by now. How long were you alone before you found us?"

"Six days," she replied sweetly.

The obvious falsehood provoked his usually even temper. "Weren't you taught better than to lie to your elders?"

Her green eyes widened at the rebuke. She glanced quickly over at Porcupine Quills and then met his gaze once again, a glow of winsome humor lighting her face. A playful smile skipped about the corners of her soft, pink lips. "I ain't a-lyin', Mr. Elk, and that's a fact. I've been on my own for six days. And if by an elder, you're meanin' Porcupine Quills, I don't rightly think she can understand me. If'n you're talkin' 'bout yourself . . . well, in Kentucky, we usually wait till a body's got at least one gray hair on his head afore we call him Grandpa."

Strong Elk glared at her, scarcely able to believe her

audacity. "Watch your tongue," he warned softly. "I'll tolerate no insolence from an impudent little girl."

Her gaze entangled in his, and she sobered immediately.

"Now," he continued, mollified by her chastened expression, "I know you couldn't have been wandering about on your own for nearly a week. You'd have collapsed of starvation before you reached us, if you hadn't died of thirst. So think about it again, Miss Robinson, and count up the days more carefully."

She folded her hands neatly in her lap and stared at him with the serene, unblinking eyes of an owl.

"How long were you lost?" he prodded.

"Six nights."

He braced his hands on his knees and leaned toward her. "Rachel," he said in a near-whisper, "do you know what the Cheyenne do to little girls who don't tell the truth?"

She opened her mouth, no doubt to deny her bald-faced fabrication, and thought better of it. Pressing three slender fingers against her lips, she looked up at the smoke hole. For the space of two long, seemingly interminable minutes, the silence in the lodge was palpable. This time, however, he intended to outwait her. At last, she lowered her gaze and met his eyes. "Come to recollect," she said in a strangled voice, "it was more like a day and a half." She swallowed noisily. "What do they do to girls who tell lies?"

He had to bite his cheek to keep from smiling. Now he was starting to get at the truth. He ignored her question and asked another of his own. "Who were you with, before you became lost?"

"Well, like I told you," she said with a long, drawn-out sigh, "I was jest visitin' friends. They were goin' on up the Bozeman Trail to Montana to look for gold. I went along purely for the sport of it. But all that travelin' was plumb wearisome, so I decided to start back home without 'em.''

"What were these friends' names?"

She paused for a moment. Her smooth forehead creased in a thoughtful frown. "Tinsley. Elma and Shadrach Tinsley from up in Raccoon Holler. Actually, they're my fourth cousins on the spindle side."

He arched one eyebrow. He was fluent in seven languages, one of them being English. Apparently, people from Kentucky spoke a dialect all their own. "Spindle side?"

"Gram's side of the family."

His words were laced with skepticism. "And so, tired of your travels, you took off across the plains all by yourself?"

"Yep," Rachel said, wondering just how much bunkum she could feed the man before he realized she was merely telling him what he wanted to hear. "Figured I'd jest head on down to Fort Laramie and pick up a stagecoach goin' east."

His determined chin jerked up at that one, and she knew she was getting pretty close to the line. "What did you plan to live on?"

"Game. If'n you recall, I had a squirrel rifle with me when I arrived." She paused meaningfully. "You do remember as how it belongs to me, don't you?"

He had the decency to look proper flummoxed. "You'll get your gun back when it's time," he told her gruffly. "Were you planning to shoot and prepare your own food?"

"That's right."

Rachel watched the play of emotions on his strong face. Highlighted by the glow of the fire, his sharp features appeared to have been chiseled out of granite. High, wide cheekbones accented the prominent, slightly hooked nose. His sensual lips curved slowly upward as he continued to stare at her. The amusement in his ebony eyes told Rachel he put no store whatsoever in her ability to provide for herself.

"What exactly did you hope to bag?" he asked with a low chuckle.

"Well, I didn't plan on stalkin' no bear, that's for dang sure," she informed him testily. "A rabbit, maybe, or a prairie chicken."

"I see." He glanced over at Porcupine Quills, as though wanting to share the joke with her. Unable to understand a word of their conversation, the old woman paid him no heed. She stitched diligently on the tanned deerskin, seemingly unaware of the tension that swirled around her.

Rachel took advantage of the opportunity to study Strong Elk in the flickering light. Lord, he was a big man. Well over six feet, if she reckoned correctly. His body was corded with muscles, the bronze skin taut over sinew and bone. Scarce wonder he liked to go around half-naked!

He'd removed the necklace of bear claws he'd worn earlier that day, and she could distinguish a pattern of old scars across his massive chest. One welt ran over his rib cage all the way down to his right side. Her fascinated gaze swept down to a jagged scar on his left thigh, clearly visible below the beaded band that held up his loincloth. Somehow, Rachel just knew the wounds had been received in hand-to-hand combat. She gulped back a lump of fear and raised her lashes to discover him looking at her with searing intensity.

Her breath caught high in her chest at the smoldering glow in his eyes. Suddenly aware of how small and vulnerable she must appear to him, Rachel blurted out, "I'm a crack shot with that rifle, mister. I can drop a stag at two hundred yards. Or a man, for that matter. Not that I've ever shot anyone . . . yet."

Without warning, Strong Elk reached over and captured her hands in his. He turned them over as though inspecting her palms for more blisters. "Such small hands," he murmured, "to be so dangerous."

The spark of laughter in his eyes when he met her startled gaze sent a jolt of pure delight straight through her. She'd thought, at first, that their black depths were like frozen pools. She realized now that they were warm and beckoning. An unfamiliar ache spread deep inside her. Heat scalded her cheeks. She quickly lowered her lashes, afraid he might read her confusion in the telltale flush.

Lord A'mighty, her hands did look small compared to his. And very pale against his sun-bronzed skin. The backs of his hands were broad and ridged with veins, the fingers long, the palms callused. For the first time, she noticed the outline of a black hawk just above the inside of his right wrist. There was something so pagan, so primitive, and yet so breathtakingly beautiful about him, Rachel found herself enthralled.

She tugged on her fingers insistently, determined to break the spell. "I was hopin' one of your people would be willin' to guide me to Fort Laramie."

As though suddenly realizing that her hands were still entrapped in his, Strong Elk released her and sat back. "We're moving north up the Powder River Basin in search of buffalo. None of the warriors can afford to sacrifice the time it would take to lead you to the fort and then rejoin our band. Such a trip might mean the loss of an entire winter's provisions for the man's family."

"My father would reward anyone who helped me return to him safely," she promised. "He's a wealthy judge and can afford to be very generous."

Her words seem to ignite the Elk's precarious temper. "Your paper money is no use to us," he announced coldly. "It won't feed the hungry children when the snows come. Nor warm our winter lodges.''

''What about horses?'' she persisted. Unable to keep the desperation from her deep voice, she prayed she didn't remind him of a bullfrog. ''Papa has a stable full of Thoroughbreds, the like of which you ain't never seen afore. Racehorses so fast, they can't be passed.''

''I have all the ponies I need,'' he stated with finality.

''Then ask the others in the mornin','' she pleaded. ''Maybe they won't all feel the same way as you.''

In one swift, graceful movement, he rose to his feet and towered over her. ''I will ask the other warriors, Miss Robinson. But no man will lead you to Fort Laramie until after the summer hunt is over. In the fall, you might be able to convince someone to guide you there. That, however, is probably irrelevant. I'm certain your friends will come for you tomorrow or by the next day, at the latest.''

Rachel stood and braced her hands on her hips, meeting his ferocious scowl with one of her own. She wasn't afraid to be alone in the wilderness. Back home, she'd roamed the mountains, barefoot and carrying a rifle. She was a crack shot and could prepare and cook any game she killed. ''If'n nobody'll guide me,'' she said indignantly, ''then the least you can do is map out the way, so I can get to Fort Laramie on my own. All I need to know is the lay of the land, and whether there are any rivers or streams I can follow.''

He didn't bother to answer her. With a brief murmur of farewell to Porcupine Quills, he moved to the entrance of the tent.

''Strong Elk,'' Rachel called out before he could leave. ''What do the Cheyenne do to girls who don't tell the truth?''

He glanced back over his shoulder, a wicked light shining in his ebony eyes. ''Ask Porcupine Quills.'' He bent and started through the opening.

"But she don't speak nary a smidgen of English," Rachel shouted after him.

From the darkness outside, his muffled words rang with laughter. "Then learn Cheyenne."

The horse soldiers arrived late the next morning. A full company of U.S. cavalry, with a large white flag flying beneath their swallow-tailed guidon, came thundering over a ridge in the distance. Herds of horses grazing on the lush summer hillsides scattered before their approach. Warriors on spotted ponies rode out to meet the blue-coats, calling back their warnings to those in the camp. Some of the band's young men, their long black hair streaming out behind them, showed off their horse-manship by galloping back and forth along the flanks of the oncoming double column. A few daring braves even stood on their mounts' bare backs, as though thumbing their noses at the troopers' precise military formation.

Everyone in the camp was instantly alert and ready for danger. The piece of white cloth that snapped in the breeze meant little to the Cheyenne. Three years before, one of their most revered chiefs had been shot down at Sand Creek while waving a huge American flag in a sign of peace. All across the open camp circle, mothers snatched up their small children and cuddled them close. Cries of alarm were carried across the grassy bottomland on the clear morning air as men and women called to their elderly parents to seek cover. The entire village bristled with bows and arrows, tomahawks and war lances, while the few warriors fortunate enough to possess a rifle checked their ammunition.

Side by side, Strong Elk Heart and Flying Hawk rode out into the high grass to meet the soldiers. The approaching cavalrymen gradually brought their lathered horses to a walk some distance away from the circle of lodges. Although the troopers' new breech-loading Springfields remained in their saddle holsters, the Cheyenne took no chances. Every warrior carried several weapons, while the women and children remained close to the tipis, ready to flee in the opposite direction should shooting begin. The fierce Dog Soldiers, their painted war shields adorned with eagle feathers to give them swiftness and courage, formed a line of defense between the village and the approaching cavalry. They would be the last to retreat, should a battle erupt.

Strong Elk recognized the civilian scout who rode well out in front of the twin blue lines. The Elk held his powerful Henry repeater in one hand and returned Jim Bridger's salute with the other. The two men had ridden together across vast, uncharted territory as guides for several of the U.S. government's mapping expeditions. Strong Elk trusted Bridger, who was known as Old Gabe, to honor the white flag. The grizzled trapper had explored the Rocky Mountain area for over forty years and was well known by the plains tribes.

Bridger brought his big blue roan to a halt and slid down from his saddle. Holding his reins loosely in one hand, he strode through the tall buffalo grass to meet Flying Hawk and Strong Elk, who'd dismounted as well. All around them, warriors gathered, some on foot, some remaining on their painted horses.

"Strong Elk," Bridger said in Cheyenne, "it has been a long time."

"Yes," the Elk replied. "I no longer scout for the army." They shook hands in the custom of the whites, then he motioned toward the older man beside him. "This is Flying Hawk, my grandfather and Old Man Chief of our tribe. Only two moons ago, he signed a peace treaty with General Sully at Fort McPherson. We have no quarrel with the cavalry."

Bridger held up his hand in the traditional sign of

friendship, and the Hawk returned his greeting.

"We heard from the Sioux that you were with the soldiers at Fort Phil Kearny," Strong Elk told the trapper. "I am glad to see you still have your hair," he added with a smile.

Old Gabe grinned and scratched his graying red beard. "I may be getting old," he answered, continuing to speak in Cheyenne, "but I still have more sense than to follow a decoy over a ridge and into a valley swarming with Sioux and Cheyenne warriors." In his early sixties now, the scout knew more about the geography of the Big Horn and Powder River basins than any other white man alive.

From behind the raw-boned mountain man, an impatient voice barked an order. "Goddammit, Bridger, ask the stinking savage if he's seen her, and let's get the hell out of here. This place makes my skin crawl."

Strong Elk looked up to see a major in the U.S. cavalry on a magnificent chestnut stallion. The blond officer had a white bandage plastered across his nose. His spirited mount was giving him plenty of trouble, prancing and sidling and whinnying restively. The Thoroughbred was more horse than the man could handle, and Strong Elk made no effort to hide his look of amusement.

Beside the commanding officer, a stout young captain calmly sat a well-behaved bay gelding. The sandy-haired man shaded his eyes with one gauntleted hand and scanned the village behind them, a worried frown on his boyish features. He seemed to be searching for someone among the women and children.

Bridger made a nearly imperceptible motion for Strong Elk to follow him. They moved several steps away, so that neither the soldiers nor the warriors, who surrounded them, could overhear their conversation.

With his back to the two officers, Jim Bridger's weathered features broke into a wide grin. Beneath the brim of

his flat-crowned hat, his blue eyes twinkled merrily.
"Seems as how Major Bruckenridge, over there, has mis-
placed his wife," Old Gabe explained, switching to English. "The fellow's been mad as a hornet ever since."

"His wife?"

"Yeah, and on their weddin' night, too." Bridger
tipped his hat back on his head, and a low, furtive
chuckle rose up from deep in his chest. "We've been
trackin' her for the last week, but she sure as hell ain't
been anxious to get found. Led us on a wild goose chase.
She was travelin' north, while we were headin' south.
When we finally come about, she had the gumption to
abandon her horse and light out for the east. We spent
three days searchin' for her on foot, certain she'd been
killed by a grizzly—or worse."

Strong Elk looked over the mountain man's buckskin-
ned shoulder. Bruckenridge had managed to calm his excited mount and now sat glaring at the back of Bridger's
head. The major had a huge yellow mustache and pale,
amber eyes, the exact color of a mountain lion's. Looking
closer, Strong Elk realized that the man also sported two
purplish-blue shiners. The surly officer looked as if he'd
walked straight into a stockade wall.

The Elk had immediately recognized the major's
name. While the officer had been stationed at Fort Laramie, his reputation for cruelty had become widespread
among the Plains tribes. He'd severely injured several
young women in the satisfaction of his brutish sexual
appetites. One of their band's loveliest girls, Mysterious
Dancer, had been cruelly scarred on the face and breasts
when she'd tried to refuse his advances. No Indian
woman would willingly go near him.

"What does his wife look like?" Strong Elk asked,
sympathy for the poor female apparent in his voice.

"Little bitty thing," Old Gabe answered. "Cute as a
bug's ear, with curly red hair and big green eyes."

Strong Elk felt as though he'd just been smashed over the head with a war club. Dazed, he blinked at the scout, his mind unable to comprehend what his ears had just heard.

Bridger met the Elk's stunned gaze, misinterpreted his silence, and grinned once again. "Guess she must've got a peek at what was under the major's drawers and didn't like what she saw. We found him the next mornin' trussed up like a boar, ready for butcherin'. She'd managed to break his nose before she knocked him unconscious. Bruckenridge had a bump the size of a cannonball on his thick skull. The miserable bastard ain't stopped swearin' yet. Every time somebody mentions her name, his yeller eyes pop out, and he starts foamin' at the mouth like some ragin' maniac."

Strong Elk continued to stare at Bridger, dumbfounded.

"Don't suppose you've seen her?" the mountain man asked with a frown.

The Elk shook his head. "How old is she?" he asked hoarsely.

"Seventeen, but she'd pass for much younger. Wears dresses several sizes too big for her little frame. Makes her look kind of puny and helpless." Gabe winked broadly. "Guess the major learned better, didn't he?"

"What will happen to the woman when Major Bruckenridge finds her?"

Bridger glanced over at the two cavalry officers. "That's up to Lieutenant Colonel Wessells back at Phil Kearny. We'll make sure she returns safely to the fort, anyway. Captain Feehan don't aim to see her harmed none. He insisted on coming along for that very reason. The captain escorted her up from Fort Laramie and plans to take her back there again. Seein' as how she was a proxy bride, I have a hunch the colonel will let her go on back home to her family in Kentucky."

"But you're not sure?"

Bridger shrugged. "You know as well as I do that white folk don't hold to divorce the way Injuns do. Even if a little woman's beaten by a big lout of a husband, she doesn't have the right to just up and walk away from the marriage. Seems kind of uncivilized, don't it?"

It sounded absolutely barbaric to Strong Elk Heart. The thought of Rachel in the hands of that fiend chilled the blood in his veins. He fought the urge to pull the brutish Major Bruckenridge down off his horse and skin him alive. If he ever found out that the yellow-haired officer had actually hurt her, he'd track the slimy coward down and stake him out over an anthill.

"We're breaking camp in the morning," Strong Elk told the trapper. "But if we find a young, redheaded *ve-hoka* in a dress too big for her, we'll send word to the fort."

"Fair enough," Bridger said. "Let's go tell the rejected bridegroom I've come up empty-handed."

The two approached the waiting soldiers on horseback.

"Strong Elk ain't seen hide nor hair of your wife, Major," the frontiersman called.

"Filthy, thieving buck," Bruckenridge spat out. "He's probably lying through his damn teeth." He reached for the hilt of his saber, and fifty arrows were immediately pointed at his heart.

"Flying Hawk's band is peaceful," the scout answered, unruffled by the officer's venom. "They'd have no cause to harm a white woman. Now I suggest you let go of that sword, if you want to keep your scalp." The major wisely followed the mountain man's advice.

With his legs braced apart and the Henry rifle cradled in his arms, Strong Elk met Bruckenridge's glare of hatred. They stared at each other long and hard, each man taking the other's measure and neither liking what he saw.

"Did you ask the Indian to keep an eye out for Rachel?" Captain Feehan inquired. He pulled off his hat and smacked it against his dusty trousers. His eyes were red with fatigue and worry. Mopping his damp forehead with his blue sleeve, he silently appealed to Strong Elk with a look approaching despair.

Jim Bridger nodded sympathetically. "Strong Elk promised to send word if they find her."

Feehan met the Cheyenne's gaze and released a harsh, pent-up breath. "Thank you."

Bruckenridge glanced over at his subordinate with a grimace of disgust. "Shit, you're wasting your time, Captain. That idiot buck can't understand a frigging word you're saying." Turning his mount around, he jabbed his spurs viciously into the stallion's flanks, and the chestnut took off at a gallop. At Feehan's signal, the bluecoats followed their commanding officer.

Bridger ambled over to his horse and climbed into the saddle with a weary groan. He wiped the back of his big hand over his bearded mouth. "Think it's about time I quit workin' for the army, too," he said. "Usually those paper-collared soldiers they send out here from the East are just green and dumb, but that foulmouthed major makes the devil himself look like a mighty nice fellow." He stared pointedly at Strong Elk. "If that little red-haired gal does show up, it might be a kindness to keep it a secret."

"Major Bruckenridge's marital problems are none of our concern," Strong Elk said. "Should we happen to find his missing bride, we'll let her decide whether to return to Fort Kearny."

"Can't ask for a better promise than that," Old Gabe replied. He touched two fingers to the brim of his hat and rode off at a slow trot.

Strong Elk walked over to his grandfather. Together, they remounted and watched the twin columns disappear over the rolling hills. Beneath a cloudless blue sky, warriors on horseback followed the troopers out of sight, whooping joyously. In the village, people gradually returned to their daily chores.

"What did the soldiers want, *nixa*?" Flying Hawk asked as they rode back toward the camp.

"Rachel," his grandson replied.

The Old Man Chief's craggy face registered no surprise. "You did not tell them she was here." It was a statement, not a question.

"The officer on the chestnut stallion was Major Yellow Eyes. Rachel is his wife. She ran away from him a week ago, and they have been looking for her ever since."

"If she wanted to return to her husband," Flying Hawk pointed out judiciously, "she would have made herself known."

They continued in silence until they reached the circle of lodges, where they dismounted again. "What will you do with her?" the Hawk asked.

A muscle twitched in Strong Elk's clenched jaw as he tried to control his seething anger. "What I would like to do is cut a willow branch and give her a sound whipping for lying to us."

"Cheyenne do not beat their children," his grandfather reminded him.

"Rachel is no child," Strong Elk growled. "Nor is she Cheyenne."

Chapter 5

Strong Elk Heart looked across the camp circle at the small tipi flanked by the swift-flowing creek, searching for any sign of a dainty head of bouncing red curls. Before he could start toward the lodge, his cousin's young son raced up and skidded to a halt in front of him.

"May I take Thunder Cloud out to graze?" Little Man asked hopefully. His deep brown eyes were wide with excitement.

Giving a quick nod of assent, the Elk boosted the sturdy six-year-old onto the gray stallion's back. "Take Grandfather's horse as well," he told the child, handing him the reins. "Find a friend to go with you, *nis'is*, and be watchful. Stay within sight of our camp. If you see any soldiers, I want you to bring both horses back as quickly as you can and tell me immediately of the blue-coats' presence."

"I will," the youngster promised as he grabbed a handful of silky mane. Pride at having been given such an important duty shone on his happy face. Holding the other horse's reins in one hand, he kicked his heels against Thunder Cloud's flanks and rode off to find another lucky boy to go with him.

Strong Elk turned to his grandfather. "I am going to speak to the *vehoka* now. After which I will decide what is to be done with her. Perhaps we should have returned Rachel to her husband, after all."

His dark eyes saddened with the events he had witnessed in the last twenty winters, Flying Hawk bestowed a look of austere reproach upon his grandson. "Major Yellow Eyes is an evil man, *nixa*. No female should be forced to endure his mindless savagery, especially not a girl of such tender years. I do not understand how the whites can condone this kind of vicious behavior. If one of our braves disfigured a young maiden in such a bestial manner, he would be driven from our camp and shunned by every member of our band for the rest of his life. Yet this hairy-nosed soldier chief is allowed the honor of leading others into battle. How can their young warriors respect and follow him?"

Strong Elk knew his grandfather referred to Mysterious Dancer. The once lovely woman was the niece of Flying Hawk's two wives. The Elk also knew that if Major Bruckenridge had scarred a white woman horribly, he would have been severely punished. But Indian women were considered lowly squaws in the eyes of the whites, not worthy of the same treatment as females of fairer skin, no matter how honorable and unblemished their characters might be.

"The ways of their people are incomprehensible," Strong Elk explained. "I do not know whether the white man chief who commands Fort Phil Kearny will allow Rachel to go back to her family in the East, unmolested by her husband. If Colonel Wessells listens to the yellow-haired major's lies, it will be just as likely that she will be placed, once again, in the hands of her vengeful bridegroom. That is why I gave my word to Jim Bridger that I would let the *vehoka* decide if she will return to Major Yellow Eyes. And though I may one day regret it, I will keep my promise.'' Once again, the Elk's gaze searched out the small lodge decorated with four brightly colored stars. When he continued, his words were sharp with disapproval of the aggravating little redhead. "For her own good, the foolish young woman must stay with our band, until we can see her safely on her journey to her loved ones.''

"That would be for the best," Flying Hawk agreed as he grasped his grandson's shoulder in a warm gesture of affirmation and esteem.

With a brief farewell to the elderly man, Strong Elk strode across the open circle to the cluster of river willows, growing angrier with every step. The cunning *vehoka* had known that he believed her much younger than her years. She'd allowed him to continue in the foolish misconception, knowing his sympathy for her was based on that fallacy alone. She'd smiled coyly when he'd cautioned her not to lie to her elders. *Eaaa!* Why shouldn't she enjoy the jest? He'd been treating her like an innocent babe, believing her barely a year or so removed from childhood. And all the while, the runaway bride had cleverly kept her true age—and the fact that she was another man's wife—a secret. She'd played on his compassion for a lost little girl as skillfully as any infatuated young brave plays on his love flute.

But it wasn't her wicked deceit that had Strong Elk Heart stalking through the trampled buffalo grass, hands clenched and taut with fury. The thought that she belonged to another man—and that man the infamous Major Yellow Eyes—burned in the Elk's brain like a flaming arrow launched from an enemy's bow.

Only a self-serving snake would have brought his child-bride out to a fort surrounded by overwhelming hostile forces. Every inhabitant of the high plains, red or white, knew that the women and children had been evacuated from Phil Kearny that previous winter. With no thought of the risk to his wife's personal safety, the cold-hearted bastard had allowed Rachel to be escorted through unfriendly Indian territory to the very site where eighty-one men had been annihilated just six months before.

What was far worse, Major Bruckenridge had the legal right, under the white man's law, to keep her with him, willing or not. The knowledge that the corrupt officer held that kind of power over Rachel made the blood rage through Strong Elk's veins. Why had the little idiot agreed to marry that despicable carrion? The urge to pick the child-woman up and shake her till those beautiful eyes rattled around in her empty head was almost overpowering. One thing was certain. He would never allow the corrupt major to take her by force. Not while there was a breath of life inside him.

By the time Strong Elk reached Porcupine Quills's lodge, he was ready to tear it apart with his bare hands. He entered abruptly, not waiting for the welcoming invitation. Inside, the widow sat working on a fringed doeskin dress. She looked up at the Elk with an expression of mild astonishment, as though unable to believe him capable of such a breach of good behavior, but resigned to it, nevertheless.

"Where is she?" he snapped.

Porcupine Quills lifted her snowy brows, her eyes sparkling with humor. "Your manners are atrocious, Strong Elk Heart," she admonished cheerfully. "It is clear that you lived with the white men too long."

His gaze swept the tipi. A large bump protruded from beneath the bearskin that covered the floor. Rachel had burrowed under a pile of furs like a mole and wrapped her small frame into a tight ball. Her little *mazeton* stuck up, begging to be smacked. It was almost more tempting than a sane man could withstand. And at the moment, the Elk was feeling far from sane.

"Get out from under there, Mrs. Bruckenridge," he commanded furiously.

She remained perfectly still. Not so much as a breath betrayed her presence beneath the fur robes. He stomped across the lodge and shoved unceremoniously at the mound with the toe of his moccasin. "Get up, Rachel," he bellowed. "Now!"

She peeked out from under the pelts, her apprehensive green eyes round with fear. "Holy Moses!" she hissed. "Can't you talk any quieter than that? You're makin' more noise than a mule in a tin barn."

"There's no need to whisper, Mrs. Bruckenridge," he informed her coldly. "Your husband's gone."

Her voice squeaked with relief. "Then it's safe to come out?" She smiled up at him, the sweetest, most beguiling smile he'd ever seen. Strong Elk steeled himself against her false allurements. The winsome little redhead had fooled him as no other female had ever fooled him before. And he wasn't about to forget it. When she realized that no one else had accompanied him inside the lodge, she pushed the stack of furs aside and slowly rose to her knees. "Thank the Lord," she said fervently.

"Don't start your prayers too soon," he warned her. "I didn't say it was safe to come out, but it won't do you any good to try hiding from me, either." He reached down, grasped the deceitful wretch by her upper arms, and pulled her to her bare feet in front of him. After releasing her with a low growl, he folded his arms across his chest and looked down at the exasperating female from his far greater height. "Well, well, Mrs. Bruckenridge," he said acidly, "in all that talk about friends and family, kinfolk and homefolk, Sugar Holler and back yonder in Kentucky, you forgot to mention just one small thing. You forgot to mention you had a husband."

Rachel wasn't about to let the large man intimidate her. Mountain girls had more gumption than that. She crossed her arms in direct imitation of his arrogant stance and returned his glare, measure for measure. "Will you stop callin' me Mrs. Bruckenridge?" she demanded. "My name is Rachel Rose Robinson. And the major is *not* my husband. Why, I wouldn't be married to that ornery jackass if his head was wound with gold."

Strong Elk leaned toward her menacingly. In the tipi's dim interior, his eyes were blacker than a kettle in hell. "Oh, no?" he said caustically. "That's not what Major Bruckenridge says. He claims he's looking for his lost little red-haired bride. The one who ran away from him *six days ago.*"

Rachel peeped up from under her lashes, a smile curving the corners of her mouth. It served the cocksure warrior right to be proven so all-out wrong. She'd tried to tell him how long she'd been traipsing across the plains alone, and he'd refused, point-blank, to believe her. "Six days ago?" she queried in a commiserating tone. "My, my, seems like a mighty long time for a poor, helpless female to be—"

"Don't say it," he cautioned, his spine suddenly gun-barrel straight. "Not if you value your pretty hide." The ice in his deep voice sent a chill through her veins, and she gulped nervously, realizing with alarm that he was madder than a coon in a poke.

"Now, there ain't no call to be gettin' so upset," she placated. "Major Bruckenridge and I ain't *really* married." At the incredulous expression on Strong Elk's ax-sharp features, she tipped her chin up. "We're not," she repeated defensively. "Not really."

"There was an entire company of soldiers out there to back up his claim, not to mention Jim Bridger's word on it. I've known the mountain man for twenty years, and I've yet to catch him in a lie. I can't say the same about you, can I, Rachel?"

"Law, is that the scout who was trackin' me?" she

asked with genuine admiration. "He was doin' a better job of stayin on my trail than a pair of Cousin Lemuel's bawlin' hounds—and they took top honors on county court day." An unhappy thought struck her. Clasping her hands behind her back, she looked down in abashment and ran the toes of one foot back and forth across the silky, fur-covered floor. "Was there a kind-lookin' captain with them?"

"If you mean Captain Feehan, yes."

She shook her head. "I'm plumb sorry 'bout foolin' the nice captain. He's been a good friend. But I couldn't take the chance on them draggin' me back to Fort Kearny, nohow. I ain't sure Colonel Wessells will believe me when I tell him I ain't legally married to Major Bruckenridge, after all—and don't never intend to be."

His arms fell to his sides, and his voice softened imperceptibly. "Would you care to explain?"

Mortified, Rachel looked over at Porcupine Quills for help. The old woman smiled her encouragement, almost as if she knew what they were saying. "In order for a marriage to be legal," Rachel began in a near-whisper, "it has to be . . ." Her words trailed off in embarrassment.

Strong Elk watched the rosy flush spread over her cheeks, and his heart began to pound out an erratic rhythm. "Go on," he rasped.

"What I mean to say is, it takes more'n jest a weddin' ceremony." Wringing her hands, she looked frantically around the lodge as though searching for a second opening not blocked by his large frame. When she didn't find one, she met his eyes again, her lovely face aflame, and continued in a shaky voice. "The marriage has to be . . ."

He waited with glacial politeness, not daring to acknowledge the hope that spiraled upward inside him.

". . . completed," she finished in a reed-thin whisper.

Strong Elk's spirit leaped for joy. It was all he could

do not to lift her up and twirl her round and round the tipi. "Would you care to expound a little further?" he urged, somehow managing to keep the question cool and unemotional.

Rachel hesitated. "Well," she began reluctantly, "according to the laws of white folks, two people ain't really married until . . ." She halted and lowered her lids, the long russet lashes throwing her flaming cheeks into shadow. "*Hamestoo-este!*" she blurted out with a quavery smile. She gestured toward the bearskin at her feet. "Sit down."

"I'd rather stand," he said. "Please continue. You were saying that a marriage has to be . . . what?"

Looking up, she searched his eyes as though unable to believe he didn't comprehend what she'd alluded to so shyly. She ran her graceful fingers through her tangled locks. "When Shelby—that's Major Bruckenridge's first name—when he tried to . . . uh . . . legalize the marriage, so to speak, I . . . uh . . ." She pressed her lips together, unable to go on.

Strong Elk waited in silence for her to continue.

From the intense look on the warrior's hawkish face, Rachel knew he'd wait till hell froze over before he'd let her stop now. "I kneed him," she confessed. At his blink of astonishment, she continued in a rush. "Then I butted my head against his nose and broke it, and while he was staggerin' round, blinded and swearin' like the devil at a prayer meetin', I smashed his skull with the hilt of his sword."

"I see," Strong Elk said softly.

Unable to meet the man's shocked gaze, she kept her own eyes riveted on the buck elk leaping across his broad chest. "That's not all of it," she admitted on a mournful note. "When the major started to come round, I broke a pitcher over his head and hogtied him. Dang it, I had to," she explained. "I knew if'n he ever got ahold of me again, he'd kill me. Then I ran away, and that's how I ended up findin' your village. And that's why I've got to get someone to guide me to Fort Laramie afore the major finds me.'' She folded her hands in front of her and peered up at him from beneath her lashes, searching for some hint of compassion or, at least, understanding. "Will you help me now?"

"We'll talk more about this later, Rachel," Strong Elk said in a choked voice. Aside from the muscle that twitched in his cheek, his expression remained impassive. "For the rest of the day, I want you to stay inside this lodge. Tomorrow morning, we'll be breaking camp and moving north. You'll be going with us." Before she could contradict him, Strong Elk spoke briefly to Porcupine Quills in Cheyenne and left the tipi.

The moment he'd disappeared from sight, whoops of deep, masculine laughter rang out. Rachel could hear Strong Elk roaring with mirth as he walked back across the camp circle. Stunned, she turned to Porcupine Quills, who merely shrugged in bemusement. When Rachel made a circle around her ear with one finger, indicating the man must be plumb crazy, the old woman started to chuckle way down inside her. The merriment shook her thin body until, finally, she tipped her head back and cackled out loud in glee, like a hen who'd just laid a prize egg.

Rachel's wobbly knees gave way beneath her, and she slumped to the floor. Lord a'mercy, if those two were any example, the Cheyenne people were as fritter-minded and unpredictable as the city folks back home.

As soon as the sun came up the next day, Porcupine Quills showed Rachel how to pack their belongings for the journey. They gathered the wooden bowls, horn spoons, and clay pots used the night before and placed them in beautifully decorated leather pouches. All the widow's tools, including bone knives and scrapers, wooden sticks sharpened with antler points, stone hammers, pestles, and awls, were carefully packed in parfleches made of buffalo hides. Then they rolled the backrests and mattresses of willow matting and the thick bed robes into neat bundles and stacked them on the grass beside the dwelling.

Porcupine Quills talked constantly as she worked, pointing to each object and naming it clearly and distinctly. Then she'd look expectantly at Rachel, waiting for her to attempt the word.

"*Histai wittsts,*" the widow said, holding up a bladder skin filled with water.

When Rachel attempted to repeat the word, the medicine woman beamed her encouragement, in spite of the way her pupil garbled the strange sounds. "You remind me of Gram," Rachel told her with a grin. "Always talkin' while she worked, and always learnin' me somethin'." To which Porcupine Quills just smiled serenely and continued her instructions.

After all the household goods had been packed, they began dismantling the buff-colored tent. Its inner lining, made of skin and adorned with colorful scenes of warriors on galloping horses chasing endless herds of buffalo, was taken down first. Then the heavier outer skin, consisting of hides sewn together and embellished with painted stars, intricate quillwork, and red dewclaw ornaments, was lifted off the sixteen poles that formed the home's conical framework.

Porcupine Quills demonstrated the proper method every step of the way, from removing the stakes that held the outer covering taut, to releasing the strings that tied the entrance and smoke flaps. Next the lodge poles were divided and fastened behind each of the widow's two sturdy ponies to form a travois. The first animal was laden with the household items and the lodge skins. On the second, the elderly woman placed a saddle, ornately trapped out with brass tacks, beadwork, and long leather fringes. It was a ponderous wooden affair, with high curved pommel and cantle. Rachel grimaced in revulsion as she helped lift up the awkward seat, happy she wasn't the one who had to ride on it. With her comfortable new footwear, she was just as content to walk.

Earlier that morning, Porcupine Quills had presented her with the moccasins she'd been working on since Rachel had arrived. The tanned doeskin felt butter-soft on her sore, blistered feet. Rachel had gladly placed her riding boots in her small bundle of clothing, preferring to wear the comfortable moccasins. She had a hunch the Cheyenne would be covering quite a few miles that day.

All around them, the women were preparing to leave with the help of the adolescent girls and small children. Most of the men and older boys had left camp with the first ray of sunlight, and Rachel assumed they were in the hills nearby, hunting for game. In the midst of the hustle and bustle, she hadn't caught so much as a glimpse of Strong Elk, which was just as well, since she wasn't certain she could look him in the eye. After her painful confession the day before, and his outlandish reaction to her intimate secrets, she'd hunkered down out of sight in the tipi, drowning in humiliation. A girl from the Cumberlands never mentioned *anything* having to do with sex to a man, unless they'd been married for at least twenty years.

Just as she and Porcupine Quills completed the last of the packing, Strong Elk appeared. He was riding a big gray stallion and leading a black-and-white spotted mare.

"Ne-haeana-he!" she called in repetition of her earlier lesson with Porcupine Quills. It was the first thing the woman had said to her upon arising, and Rachel assumed it was a greeting to begin the day.

"Good morning," he replied, without the least trace

of embarrassment. "I see you're almost ready to go." His gaze swept over her, taking in her new footgear and moving upward to the yellow-and-black ornament in her tangled curls.

The prairie breeze whipped his long black hair about his shoulders and ruffled the four eagle feathers that adorned the short braid at the crown of his head. His gold earrings caught the bright sunshine, dazzling her eyes. Mercy, he was a sight to make a single gal weep for joy.

Avoiding his keen eyes, Rachel stepped closer and stroked the stallion's strong, muscled neck. Barbaric painted symbols decorated its gray coat, while a cluster of red-tipped feathers was fastened to each side of the halter. "Oh, what a beauty you are," she crooned to the magnificent animal. The Appaloosa nodded his head and nickered a polite acknowledgment of her well-deserved praise. She looked up to find the warrior watching her intently, his usually aloof features softened by the hint of a smile. "What's his name?" she asked.

"Thunder Cloud."

"Thunder Cloud," she repeated in admiration. "I like that. It fits him." She patted the soft muzzle absently as she glanced around the busy campsite, hesitant to broach the subject after yesterday's conversation, but unable to keep silent, nonetheless. "Did you ask if anyone was willin' to guide me to Fort Laramie this mornin'?"

Strong Elk's smile faded abruptly. "No. When the soldiers fail to find you in the area around Clear Creek, they're certain to head south toward Laramie. If you travel in that direction, you'll run right into them."

Rachel chewed her lower lip and debated her choices. She kept her gaze carefully averted from his bare, sinewy body, wondering if she'd ever get used to talking to a half-naked male. "Then maybe I could head straight east toward the Platte," she suggested, staring off in that direction.

Before Strong Elk could answer, the spotted mare he'd led up nudged Rachel's shoulder, as though to say she wanted some attention, too. Rachel turned with a laugh and patted the pony's velvety nose, noticing for the first time the colorful fringed and beaded saddlecloth on her back. "Yes, little girl, you're every bit as pretty as Thunder Cloud," she assured her, "even if your manners ain't nearly so fancy."

"You can teach her some proper manners while you ride her today," the Elk said. "I brought her in from the herd for you." He paused and studied Rachel thoughtfully. "We don't have a saddle you can use. Do you know how to ride without one?"

"I hope to shout I can," she declared. "What's her name?"

"Spotted Butterfly." Rachel lifted her brows in surprise at the fanciful title, and he added gruffly, "My cousin's young son named her for me."

"It's perfect," she assured him as she stroked the spirited mare's neck.

"You can ride her on one condition," Strong Elk announced in an uncompromising tone. He met Rachel's quick, upward glance with a look of implacable determination. "You must promise to stay with our band and not try to take off across the open country by yourself. Do I have your word on that, Rachel?"

"You mean I can either ride north with you or walk all the way to the Platte?" she clarified, not bothering to hide her disgruntlement.

"No, I mean you can ride Spotted Butterfly or you can ride up in front of me on Thunder Cloud. Either way, you're going north."

"You drive a downright nasty bargain, when you're holdin' all the aces," she said with a testy scowl. Raising her hand, she clicked her fingers impatiently. "All right, give me the reins."

He smiled benignly. "I'll have your word on it first, Mrs. Bruckenridge."

"Lord A'mighty," she exploded, "if'n you call me that one more time, I ain't a-goin' to be responsible for my actions!"

"I'm waiting for your answer," he replied with imperturbable calm. The blasted man was as cool as an icicle in January when it came to getting what he wanted. But little did he know who he was bumping up against. Rachel's kinfolk claimed she had the temperament of a firecracker on the Fourth of July.

She propped her hands on her hips and glared up at him. "There ain't goin' to be no answer," she avowed, "until you call me by my right name."

Quicker than hellfire could scorch a feather, he reached down and swung her up, sidesaddle, in front of him. Only there wasn't any saddle. Without so much as a by-your-leave, he slammed her up against his solid chest, imprisoning her within the confines of his muscular arms.

Rachel's temper soared. She squirmed and bucked against his far greater strength. But the more she fought him, the tighter he held her, and with seemingly effortless ease. The struggle was over in seconds. Panting for breath and nearly sobbing in frustration, she bent her head toward him, ready to take a good chomp out of his bare shoulder.

"Don't you dare," he warned in a low, terrible voice.

Something in his suddenly still form made her change her mind. She tipped her head back to meet his gaze. What she saw in those shimmering black eyes sent her heart into her throat. Her face was only inches from his, and his cool breath fanned out across her hot cheeks. The scent of mint leaves filled her nostrils. Mesmerized, she simply stared up at him, her lips parting ever so slightly as an unfamiliar thrill reverberated through the entire length of her body.

He wasn't angry. He might have been a moment ago, but he surely wasn't now. She pressed her hands against his massive chest, her nails grazing the hard bear-claw necklace, and he allowed her to move back ever so slightly. The feel of his sun-warmed skin sent lazy rivulets of pleasure coursing through her veins. As she shifted in his arms, she inadvertently brushed one flat nipple with her fingertips and heard him inhale a deep, harsh breath.

Strong Elk looked down into her enormous green eyes and grew heavy with desire. Beneath the oversized garments she wore, he could feel every soft, tantalizing curve. She was seated sideways in front of him, and her firm little butt rubbed along the inside of his bare thigh, her slender hip jutted enticingly against his aching crotch, which was covered only by the leather breechclout. The delicate curve of one high, round breast brushed impudently across his forearm. To his shocked surprise, hidden under the layers of loose clothing meant to be worn by a boy was an incredibly delectable female body—the waist tiny, the legs slender, the hips slim and seductive. Aware that they were surrounded by dozens of fascinated onlookers, he signaled Thunder Cloud, and they were off at a gallop.

"Hey! Where do you think you're goin'?" she cried. In the initial lunge forward, she wrapped her arms around him and hung on.

Strong Elk urged the stallion to even greater speed, relishing the feel of her clinging to him. Bending his head, he brushed his lips across the burnished curls on her temple and spoke in her ear. "We're going somewhere where we can speak privately."

He followed the creek bed around a wide turn for several miles, then pulled his mount to a halt in the shade of a stand of tall cottonwoods. At their unheralded arrival, a flock of meadowlarks rose from the open grassland nearby and circled overhead, the sound of their fluttering wings filling the air.

Rachel slowly unwound her arms from about the Elk's torso and sat up straight in front of him. "Jumpin' Jehoshaphat!" she scolded. "A body could use some warnin' 'fore she goes a-gallopin' lickety-split 'cross the countryside, barely hangin' on by the skin of her teeth. Next time, tell me afore you take off like a scalded dog." She paused to draw a long, steadying breath and continued in a calmer tone. "Now, what was it you wanted to talk to me about so private-like?"

Strong Elk bracketed her narrow waist with his hands, spanning it easily with his fingers. His voice was rough with tenderness. "I'll strike a bargain with you, *vehoka*."

"What does that word mean?" she demanded suspiciously.

"Little white woman."

"Mm," she said. "Three words in one. That's right handy." Her smooth forehead puckered in deliberation. "Is it meant in a nice way or a not so nice way?"

"In your case," he assured her, "it's meant in a very nice way." His thumbs traced lazy circles across her midsection, as the urge to slide his hands over her small breasts pounded through him like a war chant.

"Very well." She sniffed, apparently mollified. "What's the bargain?"

"I'll promise never to call you Mrs. Bruckenridge again if you'll promise never to leave our band without my permiss—" The look of rebellion on her face brought him up short. "Without my knowledge," he amended.

"You mean, if'n I decide to take off for Kentucky, I have to tell you first?"

"That's correct."

She tapped one fingertip thoughtfully against her upper lip. "Jest how long will this here bargain last?"

Strong Elk readjusted the cluster of feathers in her hair,

which had come loose during their ride, and the thick coppery curls wound around his fingers like satin ribbons. "For as long as you're with us."

"And I can ride Spotted Butterfly all I want?"

"Yes." He paused and added with deliberate emphasis, "But that means you have to tell me in person that you're planning on going. Not just leave me a note, after the fact."

Rachel flushed uncomfortably. "I won't write you no note."

At her guilty reaction, he arched an eyebrow in warning. "See that you don't, Rachel Rose Robinson."

"I said I wouldn't, and I won't, dang it!"

"Do you know what I'd do," he asked calmly, "if you broke your sworn word to me?"

She shook her head, her lower lip jutting out in a recalcitrant pout. "What?"

"I'd track you down so fast, you wouldn't get a full day's journey behind you. If you think Bridger was good at his job, wait till you have me on your trail." He traced the line of her stubborn jaw with the tip of one finger, his voice deceptively soft. "Then I'd make you walk all the way back, tied to my horse."

She jerked her chin away and glared at him through narrowed eyes. "When are you goin' to return my rifle like you promised?"

He grinned in delight at her spunk. She reminded him of a feisty little prairie dog, sitting bolt upright, muzzle to the sky, barking as loudly as it could in outraged defiance. "When I'm sure I can trust you not to try to put a bullet through me, I'll return your gun. Can you really shoot anything with that antiquated muzzle-loader?"

This time it was Rachel's turn to grin with smug self-assurance. "Jest try me."

"I don't think I'm ready to take that chance," he answered with an unworried shake of his head. His dark eyes grew strangely luminous as they brushed over her. "Then it's a bargain?"

"I guess so," she agreed with a reluctant shrug.

He grasped her shoulders and drew her slowly, inexorably, closer. "Good," he said, the timbre of his deep voice casting an invisible net about her. "Then let's seal it with a kiss."

"Why don't we jest shake on it instead?" Rachel suggested, her heart suddenly hammering against her ribs. "Seems more fittin' that way, seein's how we're all but perfect strangers."

"If you were a man, I'd shake hands with you," he agreed in a rational, compromising tone. "But since you're a woman, it seems more fitting for us to kiss. I've never shaken hands with a female before. Somehow it wouldn't seem right."

"Yeah? Well, I ain't never kissed no man-person before, so I guess we're even."

Strong Elk slid his fingers beneath her open shirt collar and stroked her collarbone with the pads of his thumbs. *"Vehoka,"* he coaxed huskily, "let's seal our bargain with a kiss." As he bent his head, his long side braids fell forward to bump gently against her breasts, sending a delicate shiver of excitement through her. He brushed his sensual lips across hers in a light, lingering movement, and every ounce of blood in Rachel's body rushed up to fog her brain.

Closing her eyes in a daze of wonderful sensations, she slid her arms around his neck and buried her fingers in his thick, straight hair. The ebony curtain felt like cool satin against her warm skin. Her audible sigh of pleasure seemed to encourage him. He crushed her to his wide chest, pressing his mouth firmly against hers.

When he stroked his tongue across the tight seam of her closed lips, Rachel's lids popped open in blank surprise. His black eyes were shuttered, and their smoldering fire poured over her, scorching every inch of tissue and bone in her body. She tried to pull back in a startled, reflexive action, but he held her fast as easily and harmlessly as a mama cat holds her baby kitten. Fighting against a riot of conflicting emotions, she yanked sharply on his long hair, but her unmistakable signal to stop only seemed to encourage him.

Rachel opened her mouth to demand that he halt this scandalous behavior, and he slipped his warm, moist tongue between her lips. The blood that had pooled in her brain cascaded downward to flood her private parts, and Rachel gasped and squirmed simultaneously as erotic sensations she'd never felt before—never even dreamed existed—pulsated deep within her.

Strong Elk felt her move against his hardened sex and knew he had to stop while he still retained an iota of common sense. It was all he could do to keep his hands from roving at will over her luscious body. The compelling, primal need to take her, then and there, threatened to overrule his deepest convictions. Only heartache and betrayal would result from such a mismatched union.

When she'd said they were perfect strangers, she'd been right about one thing. They were strangers in all the ways that counted: in their minds, in their hearts, and in their souls. He hadn't planned on this happening when he'd ridden away from the camp. He'd only meant to talk to her, to secure her promise not to leave on her own.

Gathering his iron resolve, he drew back. "Rachel . . ." he whispered hoarsely, and she slowly lifted her lids to meet his gaze. Her green eyes were dreamy and faraway, her heart-shaped face soft with sensual longing.

"I reckon that bargain's sealed till doomsday," she murmured in her deep, throaty way. The sweet resonance of her breathy voice seemed to wind around his heart, fettering him to her with silken bonds. Her dewy lips were swollen from his kiss. Without conscious thought, he bent his head and kissed her again, and once again, before finally regaining control of his senses.

With a muffled groan, he grasped her upper arms and held her from him. "We'd better return to camp," he said thickly, "before they leave without us."

As they rode back in silence, Rachel wondered what she'd done to offend him, for Strong Elk sat behind her as stiff and straight as the ramming rod on her Kentucky rifle. He jerked away from her every time she accidentally brushed against him.

It seemed to Rachel that everyone in the village looked up with a knowing smile when they returned. The moment he brought Thunder Cloud to a halt beside Porcupine Quills's two ponies, Rachel quickly slid down and ran to stand beside Spotted Butterfly. The painted mare had waited in the exact spot where Strong Elk had dropped the reins to ground-tie her. Rachel turned and looked up at him, searching for some hint of what she'd done wrong. To her surprise, she found him watching her with a look of profound tenderness.

"By the way," Strong Elk said, his thick-lashed eyes suddenly sparkling with laughter, "*ne-haeana-he* doesn't mean 'good morning,' if that was what you were trying to say when I first rode up."

Rachel gathered the reins in her hands and absently patted Butterfly's nose. "That's what Porcupine Quills greeted me with when I first woke up this morning. What does it mean?" she asked with a frown.

"Are you hungry?"

"Oh, no!" she wailed in disgust. "I was callin' it to everybody I saw. No wonder they jest grinned at me. They must have thought I was plumb crazy!"

"Don't worry," he consoled. "Your attempts to speak our tongue will be met with nothing but approval from every member of our band. Cheyenne is a very complicated language. Not many whites are courageous enough even to try it.''

"Do I mangle it pretty bad?'' she queried.

A wide grin flashed across his sharp features, lighting up his dark eyes with a spark of hellfire. ''No worse than you do English.'' Before she could think of a scathing retort, he wheeled the gray stallion around and galloped away.

Rachel stood watching in fascination. Strong Elk rode bareback, controlling the magnificent animal with just the pressure of his knees. There was perfect accord between him and the horse, as though they were a single, fluid unit. They looked like one of those magical creatures Gramps had told her about, part horse and part man. She put her fingers to her lips, recalling the feel of Strong Elk's warm mouth on hers and the incredible sensations that had rocketed through her at his slightest touch. Perhaps he was a magical creature at that.

Chapter 6

In minutes, the entire band of over two hundred Cheyenne were on the move. Men, women, and children rode their gaily caparisoned ponies, with brass bells jingling on harness and saddle, beads and bangles winking in the sunshine, and feathers and fringes blowing gently in the breeze. They took all their worldly goods with them, laden on pack horses or stacked on the lodge poles dragged behind. Toddlers, too young to ride and too big to be carried, sat atop the piles of furs on the travois, confined in small cages woven of supple willow branches so they wouldn't fall off. Babies were carried on their mothers' backs or rode strapped to cradleboards, which swung gently from the high pommels of the women's carved wooden saddles. Every boy from five years upward rode a spotted pony with an easy, natural grace that would have put a Kentucky racehorse jockey to shame, while dogs barked excitedly as they ran alongside. Little girls, with puppies in their arms, rode atop the packs in groups of twos and threes, on steady, dependable horses.

The seasoned warriors carried feathered war shields and lances, with strong bows and quivers of arrows on their backs. A party of high-spirited young men galloped

up and down the winding column, showing off their re-
markable horsemanship to lovely, sloe-eyed maidens who
pretended not to notice. Shouting war whoops, the enthusiastic braves hung by their heels from ropes looped
around their mounts' bellies, entirely hidden from view
on the far side of their horses. A few shot arrows from
under the ponies' necks to demonstrate their prowess,
then had to stop and retrieve the precious arrows before
riding off again.

The nomads followed Clear Creek in a northerly direction, with the magnificent Big Horn Mountains always
in sight. The sheer openness of the country was spectac-
ular. Vast, unbroken vistas of lush, green grassland
stretched as far as the eye could see. Wide valleys followed meandering streambeds lined with cottonwoods,
alders, aspens, and willows. The brilliant blue sky, dotted
with enormous puffs of clouds, seemed somehow larger
and nearer than Rachel could ever remember the sky before. Off to the west, a great herd of antelope moved
across the foothills toward the forests of pine and spruce
that covered the mountainsides.

Late in the afternoon, Rachel urged her black-and-
white mare to the top of a high knoll. She dismounted
and stood knee-deep in a drift of blossoming wild iris.
Barely noticing the beauty of the purple and yellow flowers, she gazed dispiritedly at the faraway eastern horizon.
Her traveling companions glanced at her questioningly as
they passed by, but no one interrupted her lonely sojourn.

A painful lump rose in Rachel's throat. Somewhere out
there, miles and miles beyond, was the wide, muddy Missouri River, and after that, the Mississippi and her own
beloved Kentucky. It came as no surprise to Rachel that
her grandmother's prophecy had proven true. Everyone
in Sugar Hollow would cheerfully swear on a stack of
Bibles that Mattie McDougall's knowings always came
to pass. In spite of all Rachel's efforts to avoid her fate,

she was now caught up in her grandmother's vision, and nothing she could do would change the course of events that Gram had seen with her inner eye.

Standing alone on the rise, Rachel was filled with a sense of utter desolation. She was terrified that she would never see Papa, or Ben, or any of her beloved mountain folk again in this world. Two fat tears rolled down her cheeks, and she swiped at them with the heel of her palm. Homesickness, as acute as any case of the tissick or winter fever she'd helped Gram tend, cramped her stomach and burned her throat. The longing to point Spotted Butterfly's nose toward the Cumberlands and ride off for the beckoning horizon was nearly more than Rachel could bear. But she knew she'd never survive such a long, hazardous journey without her rifle.

"You'd never make it, Rachel," Strong Elk said with quiet gravity. "Not even with your gun and your knife. You'd have to cross the sacred hunting grounds of the Sioux, and they happen to be feeling extremely hostile to all whites at the present time."

Rachel looked over her shoulder to find him seated on Thunder Cloud, only a short distance away. She'd been so engrossed in her solitary reflections, she'd hardly registered the fact that he'd ridden up. She blinked back the tears that pooled in her eyes, hating to be caught in such childish behavior by the strong, assertive warrior.

"Maybe so," she said mournfully, "but somethin' tells me we're headin' deeper and deeper into Injun territory with every mile we cover."

Strong Elk slid from the stallion's back and walked to her side. When he'd spotted the forlorn little figure standing on the crest of the ridge, he'd guessed what she was thinking. The sad droop of her slender shoulders was mirrored now in her tear-drenched eyes.

"Don't be frightened," he said gently. "The Cheyenne and the Sioux are old allies. No one will harm you while you're with us.''

''I ain't afraid of bein' killed,'' she declared with an irritated toss of her head. ''I'm bawlin' 'cause we're goin' in the wrong blasted direction!''

He grinned at her indignant expression. ''Where's your sense of adventure, Rachel?'' he exhorted. ''You're going to see sights that few white men have ever witnessed.''

She sniffed and wiped the corners of her eyes with her shirt sleeve. ''I'd rather see my papa,'' she answered in a tiny voice. ''And my cabin by the mill in Sugar Holler.''

At her woebegone snuffle, Strong Elk's heart went out to the young woman. She was only seventeen, alone in an alien world, and terrified that she'd never make it back home alive. ''Come on,'' he coaxed. ''Ride with me for a while and keep me company.''

He helped her remount, then vaulted up on Thunder Cloud's bare back. Side by side, they trotted their horses after the others. Eventually, the straggling pair caught up with the cavalcade that wended its way across the rolling grassland and let their horses slow to a walk.

They watched with amusement as a group of small boys on frisky colts took off after a startled jackrabbit, their bows and arrows at the ready. The youngsters waited until the frightened animal stopped its zigzagging flight and hid beneath a bush, then surrounded it on foot. A flurry of arrows followed, but the wily hare dodged through the undergrowth to safety, and the disappointed cries of the boys rang out in the warm, dry air.

''Looks like they're goin' to have to spend a little more time at target practice,'' Rachel said with a chuckle.

''And learn a lot more patience and caution when stalking their prey,'' Strong Elk added. ''But they'll grow up to be fine hunters one day, able to furnish food for their families' lodges.''

Although she'd promised herself she wasn't going to ask any more personal questions only to be rebuffed, Rachel's curiosity finally got the best of her. "How did you learn to speak English so well?"

This time he didn't ignore her query. "My father, Bellowing Bull, was a scout for the U.S. army," he answered, apparently unperturbed by her inquisitiveness. "My mother died when I was eight, and after that, I went with him on his travels. I accompanied him on a surveying expedition through the Sierras when I was only ten. At night, around the campfire, the officers took great delight in teaching the clever little Indian boy their language. I already spoke French, of a sort, from the Canadian trappers who crossed the high plains on their way to the Rockies. As the years went by, I learned other tongues.''

She studied the man beside her from the corner of her eye. He was dressed in the primitive loincloth of a benighted savage, yet conversed with the fluent ease of a traveling preacher man. "What other languages do you speak?''

"On my journeys with my father, I learned many native dialects, including Bannock, Shoshone, Crow, Blackfoot, Sioux, Pawnee, and Comanche. My father had a gift for languages, as well as a knack for recalling with amazing accuracy geographical features he'd only seen once. I was fortunate enough to inherit those talents. And I improved my French by talking with Father De Smet, who sometimes traveled part of the way with us on his missionary wanderings across the plains." Strong Elk shrugged as though his uncanny ability was no great matter. "Our work with the army took us all over the western territories. My father died when I was eighteen. After that, I continued to act as guide and interpreter for the

U.S. government's surveying expeditions until three years ago.''

Rachel wanted to ask what had made him decide to quit and return to his people, but she was reluctant to pry any further. "I ain't never been no farther away from Sugar Holler than Lexington till seven weeks ago," she admitted. "And everybody in the holler is kinfolk, on one side of the family or the other. So this is the first I've been among strangers for any length of time."

He gave her a searching look, his thick-lashed black eyes alight with sincere regard. "You didn't make the journey out to Fort Laramie alone, did you?"

"Oh, no! I traveled as far as St. Louie on a steamboat with Mr. Mason Yoder, an old gentleman friend of Papa's, who was goin' there on business. He turned me over to his nephew, Lieutenant Cuthburt McMeekin and his wife, Elodie, who were on their way to be stationed at Fort Kearney on the Platte in Nebraska. I was introduced to Annie Layman and her mother, Ophelia Banks, who were headin' for Fort Laramie. Annie's husband's a sergeant in the Second Cavalry there. Everyone was jest grand.'' She paused and added with a wry grin, "Leastways, till I got to Fort Phil Kearny."

"Had you known Major Bruckenridge long?" Strong Elk inquired gravely. He didn't seem to find anything amusing in her jaunty reference to the reception she'd been given by her bridegroom.

"Shoot, I never met that feller afore in my life," she said with revulsion. "If I'd a'known what a mean, lily-livered snake he was, I'd never have agreed to jump over no broom with him."

To Rachel's surprise, Strong Elk's features hardened perceptibly. His straight brows met in an angry frown. "Why in the devil did you agree to marry a complete stranger?"

"Papa wanted me to," she said simply, wondering

what had gotten the unpredictable man's hackles up, all of a sudden. "But it was Eliza's idea, sure as I live an' breathe. Shelby's her first cousin on her daddy's side. She's always rattlin' on about how wonderful the Bruckenridges are, till it makes you wanta . . . till it makes you sick to your stomach."

This time, Strong Elk's words were tinged with rueful amusement. "Who's Eliza?"

"My stepmama. Her people are from Louisville, and they're richer than bankers on Sunday. Papa's campaignin' for the Senate now, and the Bruckenridges are puttin' up a good share of the greenbacks."

"Were you forced to marry the major in exchange for their money?" he asked, clearly appalled.

Before Rachel could answer, Spotted Butterfly shook her head and snorted impatiently at their laggardly pace. The bells on her harness tinkled a pleasant melody, and Rachel patted her mare's neck in a soothing gesture. "Naw, that weren't the reason. Papa jest felt I'd be left hangin' on the vine, if'n I didn't grab my one and onliest chance. He'd met Shelby in Louisville afore the war and thought he was a fine, upstandin' officer and gentleman. Guess that mealymouthed skunk fooled Papa, all right."

Strong Elk's quiet reply was filled with contempt. "Some men behave with honor in public, but secretly vent their anger on their helpless families within the confines of their homes. It seems to be a practice all too common among the whites."

Rachel eyed him skeptically. "Not with your people?"

"My people live in small bands. There is little that takes place in a woman's lodge that is not known throughout the camp. For a man to mistreat his wife and children is greatly frowned upon by the Cheyenne."

"'Cept if'n they tell lies," she amended.

Baffled, Strong Elk searched her earnest face for some clue to her strange assumption.

"You warned me that they did somethin' awful to little girls who told whoppers," she reminded him, worry puckering her fine-boned features.

"Ah, that," he said with a sage nod. His mouth twitched with the hilarity of her wild supposition. It was all he could do not to burst out in guffaws. "It's always best to tell the truth, Rachel, especially to your elders," he instructed righteously. "Honesty is highly prized among my people. Almost as much as personal courage. Now tell me why you agreed to wed a man you'd never met."

Rachel wrinkled her nose in disgust. "I didn't, at first. I tried my dangdest to talk 'em out of the fool notion, 'cause I knew, if'n I crossed that ol' Mississip, I was as good as dead. But they wouldn't listen to me, nohow."

The powerfully built warrior reached over, grabbed Spotted Butterfly's tinkling halter, and brought the mare to a standstill. He was wearing an armlet over his massive bicep, and the burnished brass reflected a rosy glow in the setting sun. Rachel stared for a moment in fascination at the breathtaking beauty of his muscled form, then raised her eyes to his chiseled features. The tautness of his clenched jaw betrayed his intense concern. "Why would you be as good as dead?"

"My gram saw it all, way ahead of time," she explained blithely. "I told Papa and Eliza that she'd seen me a-runnin' for my very life out on the plains, but they paid no nevermind to me. They don't believe in knowin's."

"Your grandmother had a vision about your coming here?" He stared at her in shock, the tension in his deep voice unmistakable.

"Yep, Gram had the second sight right up till the day she died. She and Gramps were the most wonderfulest people I've ever known."

Strong Elk's dark eyes glinted with avid interest.

"Have you ever had one of these visions?"

Rachel shook her head, sorry to disappoint the tall warrior, when it seemed so almighty important to him. "Nope, never did. Oncet I threw an apple peelin' over my left shoulder to see if'n it'd spell out the first initial of the man I was goin' to marry, but Aunt Saphronia couldn't make head nor tail of what it said. They say the sight skips every other generation. But it didn't work that way this time, for it sure done skipped me."

"Did your grandmother have any other visions about you?" he asked gruffly.

"Not that she ever told me. Course she wasn't one to give away all her secrets. Gram was a healer, jest like Porcupine Quills. She taught me all about home remedies, and I often helped her tend to the sick and drindlin'. But there were other things she knew that she never shared with anyone, 'cept maybe Gramps." She looked at Strong Elk curiously. "Why? Do you believe in knowin's?"

"Yes, Rachel, I believe certain favored men and women receive visions from the spirit world." Strong Elk's eaglelike features were touched with something akin to awe, as though in his imagination he could see the same images that had frightened Mattie McDougall. A feeling of deep unease ran through Rachel, making her shudder involuntarily.

Just at that moment, a young boy with a small bow and a quiver full of arrows slung on his back rode up. He looked at Strong Elk with an expression of adoration on his radiant face. *"Haahe!"* he greeted the warrior.

"Haahe!" the Elk replied with a welcoming smile. He turned to Rachel. "This is Little Man," he told her. "He is my cousin Sleeping Bull's oldest son."

"Haahe!" she called cheerfully to the boy.

Little Man stared at her, his deep brown eyes as round and unblinking as a great horned owl's. Then, without any further provocation, he burst into a gale of laughter.

"Now what did I say wrong?" she asked the grinning warrior beside her.

"That greeting is used by men," he explained, fond amusement glowing in his eyes. "In Cheyenne, some words are used exclusively by males and others are spoken only by females. I warned you that it was an intricate language."

"Reckon it's goin' to be jest too darn difficult for me to learn," she acknowledged in defeat.

"No, don't give up," he said quickly. "Your willingness to try pleases everyone. Tell him, *'Pave-eseeva, Maceta.'* That means 'Good day, Little Man.' "

Rachel repeated the greeting as accurately as she could.

"Pave-eseeva, Maheszoocess," the boy replied with a shy smile.

To Rachel's surprise, Strong Elk frowned at the child.

"What did he call me?" Rachel asked gaily, trying not to sound hurt. From the warrior's thunderous expression, she assumed the child had mocked her with a bad word.

"Little Man addressed you as Red-haired Woman," Strong Elk lied, irked that the entire band had begun calling her Little Red Fawn. Flying Hawk had named the *vehoka* that the first day she'd walked into their camp, and the Elk knew it was because the Old Man Chief believed she was the trembling baby deer who had appeared in his grandson's recurring dream.

"Well, that's what I am," she said with an accepting lift of her shoulders. "Bein' a redhead's been a cross I've had to bear all my natural life. I'm plumb used to outsiders throwin' flaunts at me. So don't go scoldin' the child for only sayin' what's true."

Strong Elk stared at the young woman in amazement. She was completely unaware of her incredible beauty.

The Cheyenne prized the color red highly, for to them it symbolized life and joy. To the people of his band, it came as no surprise that the little white woman was always cheerful, friendly, and openhearted. Her very appearance among them denoted a renewal of their faith in life's bounty and goodness. Others besides Flying Hawk knew of the Elk's vision. And they were all determined to see her as a talisman of good fortune.

"How do you say your name in Cheyenne?" Rachel queried, interrupting his troubled thoughts.

"Mohehaszhesta," Strong Elk replied absently.

"Wope! That's a mouthful," she said on a gurgle of laughter. "How do you say my name?"

"Rachel Robinson," he answered with unnecessary curtness.

She couldn't hide her disappointment. "That's it?"

"It's impossible to translate the names of white people. They have no meaning," he said, knowing they were treading on dangerous ground. He wondered how long it would take before the clever *vehoka* understood enough of their language to know what people were already calling her and begin to question why they'd chosen that particular name.

"What about Rosie?" she suggested naively. "That's what all my kinfolk call me. Tell everyone to call me Rose in Cheyenne. It can be either the flower or the color. I don't care which."

"I'll suggest it," he agreed. "But they'll probably want to give you a name that holds more meaning for them. Perhaps something about your character or appearance that strikes them as being particularly relevant."

"Then it sounds like I'm stuck with Red-haired Woman," she said with a low, self-deprecating chuckle. "Sure as God made little green apples, that's the most strikin' thing about me." She turned and smiled at the youngster once again. "I guess Little Man knew what he was talkin' about all the time."

By the afternoon of the third day, the travelers were passing a series of red clay bluffs that overlooked Clear Creek. The swift, rushing water frothed and splashed over the boulders and rocks strewn along its gravelly bottom, filling the air with its babbling song. At their approach, squirrels raced up the trunks of the cottonwoods that grew along the grassy bank and spied on them from the branches overhead.

Strong Elk knew that Rachel had spent the morning riding beside Porcupine Quills. The old woman chattered continually to the bright-eyed *vehoka,* never seeming to run out of patience or words as she tried to teach their guest the Cheyenne language. Two of the band's loveliest young women, Sweet Feather and Choke Cherry Blossom, had joined the mismatched pair, and from their animated attempts to communicate in sign language, he knew it wouldn't be long before the white girl would be able to carry on a conversation with them, at least in a rudimentary fashion. When Rachel came galloping up on her black-and-white pony to join him, the Elk smiled a warm welcome.

"I was gettin' a little restless back there," she confessed with an impish grin. "All that concentratin' gets mighty wearin' on the gray matter. I thought I'd ride up here with you for a spell and talk plain English."

"That'll be a new experience," he teased. He waited for her expression of belated outrage as it dawned on her what he'd just implied.

Before Rachel could answer, a fusillade rang out from the bluff above them, and someone screamed in pain. As the wounded woman slumped forward, a friend riding alongside reached out to keep her from falling off her horse. People milled about in confusion, caught by complete surprise. The women and children were doing their best to keep their startled mounts under control when another burst of rifle fire raked their exposed position.

"Get behind the trees!" Strong Elk called out. He grabbed Spotted Butterfly's reins and charged into the stand of cottonwoods and willows that followed the stream, taking the skittish mare along with him. Everywhere, people quirted their horses and galloped madly for the safety of the trees.

Snatching his Henry rifle from its fringed leather holster, Strong Elk jumped down from Thunder Cloud. He pulled Rachel off her pony and dragged her behind a large tree trunk. Pushing her down into the grass at the base of the cottonwood, he shielded her body with his own.

Young Bear Running, one of the band's bravest warriors, crept to the Elk's side through the thicket of undergrowth, bullets zinging all around him. "Pony soldiers," he said softly. "Somehow they managed to evade our scouts and get in front of us."

Strong Elk met his friend's stunned gaze, finding the same bewilderment he felt himself. What were the soldiers doing so deep inside their hunting grounds? Such rash action on the part of a cavalry officer was hard to comprehend. Although Flying Hawk's band was peaceful, the entire area was rife with angry warriors, Sioux and Cheyenne alike, led by Red Cloud. The Bad Faces were waging war on all whites. Only an incompetent idiot would have led his troops so far east of the Bozeman Trail.

"What's happening?" Rachel demanded frantically in English, one cheek pressed to the ground. Strong Elk motioned for her to be silent, and she was instantly still.

Suddenly, a familiar voice shouted out in Shoshone from the cliff above them. "Strong Elk Heart! It is me, Striped Blanket! Major Yellow Eyes knows you are holding his wife captive. I have led him here. I have told him you speak English. He wants his woman back.''

The Elk glanced at Young Bear. "Striped Blanket is a scout for the army," he said with a grimace of repugnance. "I know him well. He will do anything for a keg of rum." Strong Elk tipped his head back and hollered up to the Shoshone, "Where is Jim Bridger? Let me talk to him.''

It was Major Bruckenridge who yelled back, his strident words echoing down from the bluff. "I sent Bridger and Captain Feehan back to the fort. All I want is Rachel, Strong Elk! I know she's down there. Striped Blanket saw her in your camp yesterday. Send my wife out, if you want to stay alive.''

At the sound of the major's voice, Rachel shook her head in resignation. "Lord A'mighty, he knows I'm here," she said. "There's no point in tryin' to pretend otherwise.''

Strong Elk put his hand on her shoulder, cautioning her to remain where she was. "The white woman is not a captive," he shouted back. "She is traveling with us of her own free will.''

"If you send her out," the officer promised shrilly, "I'll let your people go unharmed." There was a long pause as he waited for an answer. The silence that hung over the trapped Cheyenne grew heavy and taut with tension. "Can you hear me, Rachel?" Bruckenridge screamed, his piercing voice nearly hysterical with rage. "If you don't come out at once, I'll kill every last damn one of these savages, right down to the smallest child. Their blood will be on your hands!''

"Well, that tears it," Rachel muttered. Rising to her knees, she opened her mouth to call out her surrender. Strong Elk jerked her back tightly against his chest and clapped his hand over her lips.

"Don't be a fool," he admonished in her ear. "The

major is a lying bastard. He plans to kill us all whether you comply with his demands or not. Finding you in our midst is merely the excuse he needs to butcher a peaceful band of Indians.''

Rachel squirmed indignantly, but Strong Elk held her fast. He ignored her muffled exclamations and spoke rapidly in Cheyenne to Young Bear. ''Gather the seasoned warriors. We will need to storm the bluff. Have Sleeping Bull and the younger men see that the women and children stay well hidden behind the trees. They must not try to cross the river, where they will be exposed to any sharpshooters who might be hidden on the other side. My grandfather and the Dog Soldiers will guard them while we attack the bluecoats.''

The Bear signaled his agreement and left. The moment the warrior moved away through the thick grass, Strong Elk raised his voice and shouted across the space that separated them from the soldiers hidden on the cliff above. ''We must talk this over among ourselves,'' he cried. ''Give us a little time to decide what is best for our people.''

Then he bent his head and spoke softly to Rachel, his cheek pressed against her temple. ''If you promise to remain here quietly, I'll release you.'' He could feel her temper explode as she sputtered unintelligible epithets against his hand. She tried to pry his fingers away from her mouth. When that didn't work, she writhed and twisted and wriggled, trying to jab him in the ribs with her elbow. With all her efforts to break free, she merely succeeded in jouncing her compact little rump against his crotch, and in spite of the need for haste and cool, detached thinking, his manhood responded accordingly. ''Damm it,'' he swore under his breath, more irritated at himself than at her.

Rachel was well aware that the fierce warrior wouldn't remain there during the coming battle, just to hold on to her. And she wasn't about to let there be a battle, if she could help it. For if all it took to avoid bloodshed was her willingness to return to Shelby Bruckenridge, she would gladly agree to ride with him back to Fort Phil Kearny and take her chances explaining everything to Colonel Wessells.

"I'll gag and bind you if I have to, Rachel," Strong Elk warned in a low, threatening tone. He squeezed his sinewy forearm against her midsection till she gasped for breath. "Now, do I have your word?"

Rachel grew stiff with outrage, but she jerked her head in the affirmative. The minute he loosened his hold, she whipped around to face him. "Are you sure Shelby will murder everyone even if I give myself up?" she demanded.

"Yes," he answered with absolute certainty. "Now I want your promise you'll stay here with the other women, where it's safe."

He held her by her elbows, and she glared at him, uncertain what she should do. "I don't want nobody to die 'cause of me!"

"Good. Because if you say or do anything once I leave you to join the other warriors," he cautioned, "you risk endangering my life, as well as the lives of the entire band." He cupped her cheek with his hand and pressed the pad of his thumb against her lips to silence her protests. The corners of his mouth curved up enticingly. "Keep that curly head down, Maheszoocess. I want to look into those gorgeous green eyes and see you smile at me when this is over."

Before Rachel had a chance to decide whether to give herself up to Shelby, the Elk was gone.

Young Bear had gathered fifty of the band's most courageous warriors with their best war ponies in a draw that led from the streambed to a high, sloping incline on the far side of the bluff. The men had quickly stripped for battle, leaving on only their breechclouts and moccasins, so that any wound they might receive would be clean. Strong bows and quivers of arrows were slung on their backs. Several of the braves carried rifles, with cartridge belts strapped across their bare chests. They'd hurriedly painted their faces and bodies and checked the sacred medicine bundles that hung around their necks. Each man was prepared to die a hero's death that day, certain he would be honored in the memory of his loved ones for his sacrifice.

"Our scouts say there are nearly a hundred horse soldiers lying in the grass along the bluff's edge," the Bear told Strong Elk. "And twelve or more are hidden in the trees on the far side of the creek, waiting for us to try to ford the swollen waters." His dark eyes narrowed with amusement. "The yellow-haired soldier chief has foolishly left all their horses and pack mules in charge of ten men in a coulee behind the bluff."

While his friend was speaking, Strong Elk hurriedly painted his face for battle. In addition to the usual two black slashes straight across each cheekbone, he drew a vertical line from his forehead down the bridge of his nose to his chin in vermilion. Then he moved the four feathers in his scalp lock to an upright position.

A spate of rifle fire broke out as the Dog Soldiers took up their positions on the fringe of the trees, forming a line of defense to shield the women and children. The younger, less experienced braves would cover their rear against the sharpshooters on the opposite bank.

"Two men must stampede part of our herd into the coulee," Strong Elk directed. "The soldiers' horses are always poorly trained and will panic in the noise and confusion."

Crane Moving About and Moose Killer stepped forward, indicating their willingness to go. After the two volunteers left, the Elk addressed the rest of the warriors, many of whom belonged to the Red Shield soldier society. "We will move silently up the ravine and around the bluecoats' flank while they are busy holding our Dog Soldiers pinned down in the trees. No one is to make a sound or fire a shot until the signal is given. Then we will mount and charge the horse soldiers from behind."

"It is a good plan," Big Pipe Man said. His craggy features lit up with a broad smile. He had counted many coups and was known throughout the plains for his ferocity in battle. "We will kill them all."

"No," Strong Elk advised his uncle, who was headman of the Red Shields. "Whoever is not killed in the initial charge, we must allow to surrender. These soldiers are raw recruits. They will be terrified once they realize that we have caught them in a trap. We will let them walk all the way back to the fort. By the time they reach the stockade and gather reinforcements, we will be far away in buffalo country."

"But the soldiers attacked us!" Beaver Claws protested. The young brave gripped his war club in his large hand and brandished it angrily. "My mother lies wounded, and my little brother narrowly escaped being struck by a bullet. Should we throw away our chance for reprisal?"

"You will have your revenge and your scalps," the Elk told the infuriated man. "But we will not mutilate their bodies or kill anyone trying to run away."

"You would let their dead arrive in the spirit world with all their strength?" Big Pipe Man asked incredulously. "With their eyes and their hands and their feet, to enjoy the happy hunting grounds forever?"

"The white man's anger will be even greater should we wreak our vengeance on the corpses of their soldiers," Strong Elk told the listening warriors. "We must think first of our helpless women and children, not of our own need for retaliation. We do not want to rouse the entire American people against us, as the Bad Faces did at Peno Creek. But we will teach Major Yellow Eyes and the generals back in the East another stinging lesson.''

Some of the men nodded their agreement, while others merely turned and led their painted war horses up the draw in silence. In true Cheyenne fashion, each warrior would make up his own mind and follow the dictates of his heart.

Just as Strong Elk had directed, part of their herd was driven into the coulee, the two braves riding in their midst. The startled soldiers, unable to manage both their weapons and the horses, dropped the reins and scrambled for cover. Hidden in the confusion and dust, Moose Killer and Crane Moving About scattered the cavalry horses and pack mules, who jumped and bucked and screamed in fright as they raced out of the ravine and across the open countryside.

At the same time, Strong Elk led the rest of the warriors in a mounted attack against the soldiers. Whooping and yelling their war cries, they rode up the steep slope of the draw, their horses scrambling over rocky outcrops and leaping across ledges like pronghorns. Once on top of the knoll, the fighting Cheyenne charged at full gallop, shooting their weapons with deadly accuracy as they came. Their wild battle cries, together with the thunder of their horses' hooves, drowned out the shouted commands of the officers. The Elk held his gray stallion's reins in one hand and fired his repeating rifle with the other.

Major Shelby Bruckenridge rode his magnificent chestnut stallion back and forth in front of his men, calling out his frantic instructions. For a fleeting instant, the yellow-haired officer was in Strong Elk's sights. But before he could fire the Henry, another warrior galloped in front of him, blocking the Elk's view, and the chance was lost.

Some of the greenest troopers, unaccustomed to the turmoil and clamor of battle, immediately panicked and jumped off the edge of the bluff, straight into the withering rifle fire and deadly arrows of the Dog Soldiers below. Others were so terrified, they threw away their Springfields and raced along the grassy bank on foot.

The soldiers who survived the initial sweeping attack clustered together in small, disorganized groups, the officers vainly attempting to rally their squads. A haze of smoke swirled around the combatants, and the air was rank with the smell of blood and gunpowder. The hatless bugler tied his white handkerchief to his trumpet and waved it over his head in a frantic back-and-forth motion as the mounted Cheyenne began to regroup for another assault. The cavalrymen, fresh from the East and certain they were about to be captured and tortured to death, broke ranks in terror. They started to run along the edge of the bluff like fear-blinded sheep, abandoning their wounded without a backward glance. Realizing what was happening to his command, Major Bruckenridge spurred his Thoroughbred stallion and raced away.

The few Southern Cheyenne among them, whose blood still ran hot with hatred for the massacre at Sand Creek, cut several stragglers down with their war clubs and scalped them. The entire family of Walking Stone's brother had been slaughtered by Colonel Chivington and his Colorado volunteers. On the cliff overlooking Clear Creek that day, Walking Stone had his revenge at last.

But most of the warriors allowed the routed bluecoats to escape unharmed—even the yellow-haired major, whose bungling leadership had brought them there. The Cheyenne sat on their well-trained war ponies and laughed in mockery as they watched the rabble's ignominious retreat.

"We will never see those horse soldiers again," Young Bear predicted with a satisfied smile. "Major Yellow Eyes won't stop running until he is safe in his fort once again.''

Strong Elk drew his gaze from where Big Pipe Man was neatly and efficiently scalping Striped Blanket, the Shoshone scout, to meet his friend's amused eyes. ''I hope we have seen the last of Bruckenridge,'' he agreed. ''But if I ever meet the yellow-haired soldier chief again, I will have to kill him. For he will remember this day with shame for the rest of his life.''

The Elk turned Thunder Cloud about and rode to the edge of the cliff. The broken bodies of the soldiers who'd jumped off in their mindless panic lay on the rocks below. The corpses had already been stripped of their new Springfield carbines and ammunition, along with their scalps and any clothing or possessions worth keeping. Their naked white skin stood out in stark contrast against the red clay bank.

In twos and threes, the women and children came out of hiding, cautious at first, until they were certain it was safe. From her spot behind the large cottonwood, Rachel appeared, only to stagger and nearly fall. She leaned one hand against the rough gray bark for support as she gazed at the scene before her. Slowly, slowly, the *vehoka* raised her eyes, searching the crest of the bluff, until she found him.

Even from that distance, Strong Elk could recognize the revulsion that stiffened her small frame. Then she disappeared behind the tree once more, and he knew she was retching in horror at the grisly sight she'd just beheld.

''We killed sixteen pony soldiers,'' said Young Bear, who'd followed the Elk to the ledge. ''And there are four more wounded. One has been shot in the belly and lies near death. What shall we do with them?''

Strong Elk looked across the waving grass at the backs of the soldiers running in the distance, their mounted commander far in the lead, and debated the possibility that they would gather their courage and return for their fallen comrades. No Cheyenne would ever leave a hurt warrior on the battlefield. But the cowardice of Major Bruckenridge boded ill for the rescue of their wounded. And, in any case, there was no chance that a man who'd been shot could make it back to the fort on foot.

"Put the ones who can survive the ride on their captured horses," he said, "and send them after their retreating friends."

"And the soldier who is dying?"

"Put him out of his misery."

Chapter 7

❧⸺⟡⟡⸺❧

Powder River Basin
Dakota Territory
July 1867

"**H**urry, Little Red Fawn!" cried Thick Braided Hair. "It's your turn! Kick the ball!"

The sounds of the women's game being played on the far side of the circle of lodges carried across the distance in the warm summer afternoon. Seated cross-legged beside Young Bear Running on a robe spread in the shade of his grandfather's tipi, Strong Elk listened in dignified silence.

While Rachel lifted the round deerskin ball stuffed with antelope hair on her foot and balanced it on her instep, the rest of her team cheered excitedly.

"Noka, nixa, naha," they counted in unison.

With his eyes fastened on the flute in his hands, he continued to carve the figure of a bear into the juniper wood, all the while trying to ignore the voices of the high-spirited women, who chanted together.

"Four, five, six, seven!"

Strong Elk didn't need to see the players to know what was happening in the game of *ohaseovatoz,* which meant kicking the foot ball in Rachel's language. The young women had divided themselves into two equal parties of about ten each, and now the players of the two sets stood alternately in a large circle. With each number called, Rachel had to kick the ball up in the air and catch it again on her instep, never once letting the ball or her foot touch the ground. Usually the person doing the kicking counted out loud, while the opposite group listened to her count. But Rachel hadn't mastered the numbers in Cheyenne past ten, so the members on her side were counting for her.

"Nanota, soota, matota!" the women cried, their high female voices rising in excitement with each numeral. For every successful stroke on Rachel's part, their team would be awarded a counting stick. The side who succeeded in acquiring all the counters was the winner.

"The *vehoka* has learned the skills of the foot ball game very quickly," Young Bear commented.

Strong Elk's eyes darted to his friend's, searching for some hidden meaning in his words. Though the Bear's handsome features remained impassive, his brown eyes twinkled with deviltry. Returning his attention to his work, the Elk acceded in a tone of complete disinterest, "She is very clever."

"And swift," Young Bear goaded.

"Twenty-eight, twenty-nine, thirty," came the count.

The Elk raised his eyes from his task once more, his jaw jutting forward in a warning that only a foolhardy imbecile could mistake. He frowned at the reckless brave, daring him to say another word on the subject.

Young Bear could barely conceal the grin that threatened to spoil his pose of thickheaded dolt. "She is as swift as a little white-tailed deer outrunning a clumsy pursuer."

"Fifty-two, fifty-three, fifty-four," the women called encouragingly.

The Elk moved to his feet. "Your sense of humor is as flawed as your choice in horseflesh," he remarked with surly venom. "If your own attempts at courtship have been so successful with Choke Cherry Blossom, why is it you wish me to carve a flute with magical powers?"

Young Bear Running rose to stand beside him, his white teeth flashing in a jubilant grin, aware that he had succeeded, at last, in piercing the Elk's thick shield of indifference. "Do not try to insult me in order to change the direction of my thoughts, Dream Catcher. You are the one who can see into the future and explain the visions of other men. Where is your strong medicine now?"

The Elk snorted in disdain, refusing even to answer. He stared across the camp circle to the far line of tipis that hid the women at play from view.

"Perhaps you should spend more time carving a love flute of your own," the Bear persisted, "instead of glowering at every young warrior that the *vehoka*'s green eyes light upon. Little Red Fawn is scarcely more than a girl. She may never have been told about the sexual prowess of a mature bull elk."

"Ninety-five, ninety-six, ninety-seven."

Strong Elk Heart rammed the end of the half-finished flute into Young Bear's flat abdomen. "If any man in this camp tries to wrap his buffalo robe around the *vehoka*," he growled, "I will remove his prowess from the face of this earth."

Young Bear burst into loud guffaws, completely unintimidated by the carving knife Strong Elk flung into the dirt at his feet. With a snarl of disgust, the Elk shoved past his obnoxious companion and headed for the plateau on the other side of the lodges, where the women were playing in an open field of trampled grass.

By this time, the enthusiastic chanting had drawn many curious onlookers. People stood in groups of twos and threes near the circle of women and watched Little Red Fawn with growing admiration. She was dressed in her white boy's faded shirt and sturdy brown trousers, with the beautiful moccasins Porcupine Quills had fashioned on her nimble feet. The *vehoka* was extraordinarily agile. She was kicking a ball about eight inches in diameter on the instep of her right foot, her arms outspread for balance. When she reached the count of one hundred, she kicked the ball over and caught it on her left foot, then continued to kick the soft sphere, never missing a beat.

Sweet Feather, who was standing in the ring on Rachel's left, must have been certain that the *vehoka* would drop the ball, thus making Sweet Feather the next player. At the success of the dexterous feat, she covered her mouth with her hands. *"Noo! Noo! Ahh!"* she exclaimed, her pretty brown eyes glowing with wonderment that a young white woman could master the difficult Cheyenne game with such ease.

Now everyone took up the count. Rachel continued kicking, switching feet whenever she started to tire, until she reached three hundred, the exact number needed to take all of the counters that had been placed in the center of the circle. Flushed with exhilaration, she ran to Choke Cherry Blossom, who guarded the slender sticks, and accepted the trophies with a little hop-skip dance of victory. Laughing with the spontaneous joy of a winner, she presented the counters, in turn, to her exuberant teammates, who crowded around her, jostling and chattering with excitement.

Strong Elk braced his feet apart, folded his arms across his chest, and stoically watched her accept their exclamations of approval with good-natured modesty. Her fair features glowed with happiness, two bright stains of rose coloring her cheeks. In the two weeks since the surprise attack by the horse soldiers, Rachel had smiled at everyone in Flying Hawk's band. Everyone except Strong Elk.

They'd spoken to each other at length only once during that time. Immediately after the battle, she'd accused him of tricking her. She railed at him for not allowing her to give herself up to Shelby Bruckenridge, certain she could have prevented the deaths of the soldiers. What she refused to believe was that the bloodthirsty major would have doubtlessly massacred the entire band had the Cheyenne not struck first. And in typically white-woman fashion, she placed the blame entirely on Strong Elk's shoulders, as though he could have controlled the angry warriors whose loved ones had been callously murdered by the pony soldiers in the past. Rachel chose to ignore the fact that an entire company of U.S. cavalry had lain in wait on the bluff overhead and fired indiscriminately into a column of unsuspecting women and children.

Frustrated by her illogical accusations and convoluted female reasoning, he'd finally lost his temper. He'd told her in scalding terms just how childish her behavior was and suggested pithily that she grow up. After that, she'd barely wished him good day—in either language—whenever she chanced to encounter him.

"You do not look very happy, Strong Elk," Porcupine Quills said with a gleeful chortle, interrupting his morose thoughts. The medicine woman had come up quietly to stand beside him. She carried a large pile of necklaces, earrings, and bracelets in the lap of her skirt. "You should have bet on my granddaughter, as I did," she chided him smugly. "You would be collecting your winnings now, instead of sulking like a rejected suitor."

With his arms still crossed, the Elk glared down at the top of her snowy head. "For a lonely widow who depends on my generosity for her meals, you have a sharp tongue, old woman."

Porcupine Quills's alert black eyes danced in delight at his flagrant slip in good manners. No honorable warrior would ever begrudge the provision of food for a poor widow's lodge. "Your gifts of deer meat have been well enough," she informed him with a sly smile. "But there is one present you could bring to my tipi that would please even my finicky granddaughter."

Strong Elk tipped his head, indicating she should continue.

"You have something that belongs to Little Red Fawn," the diminutive woman said with a knowing lift of her white brows. Despite his air of disinterest, Porcupine Quills was fully aware that she had his undivided attention. "Something she prizes very highly and would dearly like to have restored to her."

He turned his head to look over at Rachel where she stood surrounded by the other young women. In the last few days, she had learned enough of their language to ask every available male in the band if he would be willing to guide her back to the Platte. Disappointed at their lack of interest, she'd appeared to lay the cause of their refusal at Strong Elk's feet. Now, instead of merely ignoring his presence, she'd taken to glaring at him whenever he came near.

He had warned the men that the *vehoka* might make such a request, worried that, when she approached them speaking in her broken, garbled Cheyenne, they might misunderstand her innocent entreaty. But he hadn't actually forbidden anyone to accept her offer. No Cheyenne had that much power over another. He'd merely pointed out that any warrior foolish enough to agree to become her guide would miss the entire summer's buffalo hunt.

What would be the chance, he wondered now, of Rachel trying to take off across the plains on her own, once she had her old flintlock rifle back in her possession?

"She will not try to return to her people alone," Porcupine Quills said, as though she'd read his mind. "She told me so, and I believe her." The medicine woman glanced over to see Good Robe Woman leave a group of elderly women, who'd been avidly watching the game. "Ah, I need to go and collect the dress I just won from your grandfather's foolish wife. But come to my lodge for the evening meal, Strong Elk. I have been teaching Little Red Fawn how to cook like a good Cheyenne woman. A fine venison stew might sweeten your disposition."

As the tiny widow moved away, Strong Elk glanced over to find Rachel watching him, a pensive look on her lovely face. He walked up to the cluster of elated winners. At his approach, the other women smiled shyly and retreated, leaving the *vehoka* standing alone.

"Congratulations," he said with formal reserve. He had no intention of being rebuffed in front of the entire camp yet another time. "You played the foot ball game very skillfully."

"Why, I thank you right kindly," she answered. Her marvelous grass-green eyes reflected the pleasure she felt at his compliment.

The Elk tried to deny the glow of happiness that warmed him at the sound of her soft, husky drawl and the brilliance of her engaging smile. It was as though he'd been inside a dark cave and had suddenly stepped into the bright, welcoming sunshine. He cleared his throat, afraid the longing he felt might be betrayed in his hoarse voice. "Porcupine Quills told me that you've given up the idea of trying to return to your people at this time."

"Well, shucks," she answered with a sigh of resignation, "since there ain't nary a single, solitary man in this whole blessed camp a-willin' to guide me, I reckon

I'll jest have to wait till your people are a-headin' south toward Fort Laramie again. Ain't no use beatin' the devil 'round the bush. I know now that I can't possibly cross the plains by myself. I'd most likely run smack dab into the middle of an Injun war party. Reckon I wouldn't have hardly no chance of protectin' myself, if'n I was outnumbered ten to one.''

"I tried to tell you that the first day you arrived," he reminded her gently.

Rachel hooked her thumbs in her trouser pockets and gave him a jaunty smile. "Shoot, when I stumbled into your camp that first mornin', I thought the whole passel of you folks were nothin' but pitiful beggars, hardly able to survive without the white man's charity. Why, the night I lit out of Phil Kearny, I wasn't the least bit afeared of anybody I might chance to meet on the plains, 'cause I figured all the natives were 'bout as peaceable as chicks under their mama hen's wings.''

Strong Elk stared at her in mystification. "I thought all whites newly arrived from the East were terrified of us, certain they were going to be captured and scalped."

"Nope. Leastways, not me," she admitted with an embarrassed chuckle. "Fact is, I'd seen them poor creatures a-crowdin' round the white folks' wagons at Laramie and thought all Injuns were jest the same. But after your warriors fought like wildcats with their tails caught in a trap at Clear Creek, I changed my mind right sudden-like. Reckon when I saw you astride Thunder Cloud on top of that bluff, painted and feathered for war and your big Henry rifle still a-smokin', I realized jest how destructious an enemy you were."

Strong Elk moved closer. "Rachel, what happened at Clear Creek was a defensive action on our part." He lifted his hand impulsively, longing to touch her, but afraid she'd pull away. Keeping himself under strict control, he continued in a low, urgent voice. "I am not your enemy, little girl. I would protect you with my life.''

She looked up at him, her big eyes solemn. "I think you mighta already done jest that. Leastways, I'm not so certain anymore that givin' myself up to Shelby would have prevented anyone's death. Not neither the soldiers' nor the Injuns'. Not after helpin' Porcupine Quills tend your wounded.'' She shook her head in remorse. "Little Moon Shell will be walkin' with a limp from the bullet that struck her ankle for the rest of her natural-born life. And 'twas only by the grace of the Almighty that Beaver Claws's mother survived. The other two who were injured were jest plain lucky as well, I guess.'' She paused and stared down at the toes of her moccasins, then lifted her long russet lashes to meet his gaze with unflinching honesty. "I'm right sorry for the way I've been actin' toward you, Strong Elk. I was lettin' my hankerin' for home get in the way of my good mountain sense. When you told me I needed to grow up, you weren't sayin' nothin' but the point-blank truth.''

Strong Elk stepped even nearer. Her thick curls were damp from the exertions of the game. He pushed back several tendrils that clung to her moist cheek. The feel of her dewy skin sent rivulets of liquid fire through his veins, flooding his heart and constricting his breathing.

He'd dreamed of the trembling fawn and the rutting bull elk again last night and had awakened from the vision, as he always did, with his swollen sex hard and aching. Only this time, he knew exactly whom he was aching for. When he'd stepped out of the lodge into the cool night air, it had taken all his resolve not to turn his bare feet toward the small tipi with the four beckoning stars. He longed to lift Rachel's slim form up in his arms and carry her, still sound asleep, into the sheltering willows. He wanted to bury himself to the hilt in her sweet, delectable flesh and feel her slender limbs wrapped around him, all the while whispering in her ear that no one but she would ever arouse him to such feverish heights. Only the knowledge that Porcupine Quills would have wakened the entire village with her strident admonitions, had he taken so much as a step inside their lodge, prevented him from making a fool of himself.

Now he touched the black-and-yellow feathers in Rachel's glorious hair, feasting his eyes on her vivid coloring. "Little one," he said softly, "I'm certain that Major Bruckenridge would have . . ."

His words were interrupted by the sudden appearance of a party of braves on war ponies. At their approach, Sleeping Bull, the village crier, jumped on his horse and galloped around the camp circle, calling out the tidings that unexpected visitors had arrived. People ran out of their lodges to see what was happening. Several shouted greetings when they recognized members of the group.

Strong Elk watched the eight men ride slowly and deliberately into the campsite, their bull-hide war shields and iron-tipped lances adorned with fresh scalps. The newcomers answered the crowd's excited questions with an aura of immense pride.

"Who are they?" Rachel asked.

"It's my cousin, Wolf Walking Fast, and three of our other young men. They've returned from a hunt," he said evasively. "They have brought some Sioux friends with them." What he didn't tell her was that the braves were known as Bad Faces, warriors who followed the Sioux chief Red Cloud in his war against all whites.

Strong Elk made no move to join the others clustered around the mounted men, and Rachel looked at him questioningly. "Let's mosey on over there and see what the shoutin's about," she suggested. "A body'd think from all the hoorah, they're totin' packs of gold." Reluctantly, the Elk agreed and walked with her toward the center of the camp circle.

As they neared the group on horseback, Wolf Walking Fast stopped in mid-sentence and glared in hatred at Rachel. He was three winters younger than Strong Elk and filled with brash self-confidence. Their fathers, Big Pipe Man and Bellowing Bull, had been brothers. Although slightly shorter in stature than his cousin, Wolf displayed the physical strength and uncommon stamina than ran in their family.

"I didn't know you'd captured a *vehoc, nis'is,"* Wolf called derisively to Strong Elk. "The pony soldiers take no male prisoners over the age of ten. You should have followed their example and slit the boy's throat."

"We do not wage war on children," the Elk replied. "And you are twice mistaken. This is a young woman, not a boy, and she is a guest of our band, not a captive."

Wolf Walking Fast slid from his horse's bare back and strode through the corridor that opened for him. He stopped directly in front of Strong Elk. Silence descended on the bystanders, who were becoming increasingly uneasy at the unpleasant turn of events. Everyone knew of the Wolf's irrational hatred of the white eyes, and they had all grown fond of the *vehoka* in the short time she'd been with them.

"Walk cautiously, my son," Big Pipe Man advised in a quiet voice.

The admonition went unheeded. The battle-hardened warrior stared at Rachel, his long fingers playing idly with the bone handle of the knife at his side. His insolent gaze roved over her tousled red locks, her slender figure, her small feet shod in the Cheyenne moccasins. Slowly, his lips curved into a mocking grin. "Perhaps I should take our guest for a ride over the prairie tonight," he said, his eyes fastened on her delicate features. "She is tiny, but I—"

To Rachel's complete surprise, Strong Elk grabbed the string of wolf claws around the man's neck and jerked him roughly forward, till their noses almost touched. "Do not say another word, my cousin," he warned, "or I will have to punish you for your abominable lack of manners."

Quick as greased lightning, Wolf Walking Fast drew his hunting knife from its sheath and brandished the weapon in front of the Elk's grim visage. "We will see which of us will do the punishing," he taunted arrogantly.

A gasp of shock rose from the spectators who surrounded them. People immediately stepped back to allow the angry pair more room, their dour faces revealing the entire band's disapproval of such wicked behavior in the midst of women and children.

Breathless with fright, Rachel watched as the Elk clamped his hand on the other warrior's wrist and began to force the knife downward between their nearly naked bodies. The two opponents waged a silent battle as each man sought by sheer strength alone to control the movement of the lethal blade. They shifted their stances, seeking better leverage, till their feet were braced wide apart. Their corded thighs tautened visibly under the strain. The muscles in their powerful upper arms bulged, the veins made more prominent by their struggle. Gradually, relentlessly, Strong Elk prevailed. Wolf's hand flew open, and the knife fell to the ground.

In the next instant, Porcupine Quills was at Rachel's side. "Come with me, *nixa*," she insisted shrilly. "I need your help to prepare a poultice for Crane Moving About. He is in terrible pain with a carbuncle on his shoulder blade and needs my good medicine immediately." She grabbed her adopted granddaughter's arm and pulled her away from the throng that encircled the two adversaries.

Baffled by what had just happened, Rachel looked back over her shoulder as the elderly woman hauled her lickety-whoop across the grass toward their lodge. Lord

A'mighty, she longed to see the final upshot of the scrap, but it would have been dang impertinent to refuse Porcupine Quills's request. The widow had been far too kind for Rachel to say her nay.

The two warriors remained surrounded by a company of gravely silent men and women. During the brief wrangle, the braves who'd arrived with Wolf had dismounted and joined the others, but they, too, said nothing. Rachel could hear Flying Hawk speaking in a calm, measured way to his grandsons, but because of her small size, all she could see of the two cousins was the back of the Elk's head, his ornamented and feathered scalp lock clearly visible above the crowd.

''Why was Strong Elk fighting with his cousin?'' she asked the widow. She'd been able to follow only a part of what had been said—and that hadn't made much sense. What started the ruckus in the first place was a riddle she aimed to find the answer to.

But Porcupine Quills just waved her hand, pretending she didn't understand Rachel's muddled Cheyenne. ''I have invited Strong Elk to join us for a small feast this evening,'' she said serenely, the moment they were inside their tipi. ''You had better begin preparing the turnips and onions for the stew.''

Rachel watched in wonder as the medicine woman began setting out the wild vegetables, which had been stored for their journey in stout rawhide parfleches. She hesitated to say anything about her forgetfulness, but it surely did appear that the sweet, old granny had plumb disremembered they were supposed to be making a drawing salve for Crane Moving About's sore shoulder. When she gently reminded her of that fact, the sprightly woman fluttered her fingers in the air as though shooing away dragonflies.

''Do not worry about that cross old man,'' Porcupine

Quills said with a cheerful smile. "You have a courageous and handsome young warrior to feed."

Although the day had been bright and sunny, by early
evening heavy black clouds hung over the high plains
with a promise of rain during the night. Throughout the
campsite, the lodge covers, which had been rolled up to
allow the warm summer breeze to blow through the
dwellings, were now dropped, and most of the village's
women had chosen to cook indoors, lest their evening
fires be quenched prematurely. The small, star-studded
tipi, which had been pitched near a giant bur oak, was
filled with the fragrant aroma of bubbling stew by the
time Strong Elk arrived.

As their guest entered, Rachel looked up from her task
of stirring the cooking pot and gave him a welcoming
smile. She gasped in astonishment when she saw what
he carried. "Jumpin' Jehoshaphat!" she exclaimed.
"You brought my gun!" She left her place near the fire
and moved to stand directly in front of him, her eyes
riveted on the long Kentucky rifle he cradled in the crook
of his arm. The shiny brass inlay on the slender maple
stock winked at her in the firelight like a long-lost friend.

"Before I return it, Rachel," he said with the somber
righteousness of a preacher at a burying, "I want to remind you of your promise."

Rachel felt a blush spread over her cheeks as she recalled the scorching kiss they'd shared on the day she'd
made that promise. Unable to meet his steady gaze, she
stared with mortification at the familiar crescent-shaped
buttplate that fit her shoulder to perfection. "You mean
I'm not to take off for Fort Laramie on my own," she
clarified.

"Not for Fort Laramie, the Platte River, Sugar Hollow,
or parts otherwise known as over yonder."

She looked up to meet his coal-black eyes and felt

unexplainably breathless. As usual, he was clothed only in breechclout and moccasins. The leaping buck elk tattooed on his chest seemed tantalizingly close. Her fingers fairly itched to trace the rack of antlers across his hard, bronzed flesh. The memory of his sun-warmed skin beneath her fingertips stirred an awakening awareness of her own femininity. "I remember my pledge," she said with a catch in her voice.

"Welcome our guest properly," Porcupine Quills chided in Cheyenne from her place on the other side of the fire. "And ask Strong Elk if he is hungry."

"*Epevae tsexehoehneto,*" she said, telling him in her thick accent that it was good of him to come for a visit. "*Ne-haeana-he?*"

"*Hehe,*" he answered politely. His jet eyes were warm with amusement, as a devastating grin slowly spread across his eaglelike features. His bold gaze seemed to touch her everywhere, telling her it wasn't food that he hungered for. She returned his smile shyly, certain he was thinking of how she'd asked if he was hungry that same morning they'd sealed their bargain—and the way he'd teased her about her mountain speech.

He set the rifle down in front of her, butt to the ground. Rachel grasped the barrel just beneath his fingers, the metal cool and reassuring against her palm.

"Sure as I'm a-standin' here," she confessed, "I felt like a newborn calf who'd lost his mama, without my granddaddy's rifle."

The Elk continued to smile, but he still hadn't let go of the gun. "Then you'll be happy to renew your vow not to venture off on your own, should I return it to you."

Rachel gave the barrel a sharp tug, hoping to catch him off-guard. It was like trying to pull a bear through a keyhole. "Well, I hope to spit," she snapped in vexation, "you're one mighty suspicious feller."

The cocksure grin widened. "My mother taught me

never to trust little redheaded white girls with big green eyes.''

''Oh, all right!'' She tossed her head with exaggerated indifference, as if she'd planned on giving in to his demand all along. She put her right hand over her heart. ''I swear on my papa's Bible, I won't go a-traipsin' off to Kentucky alone.''

''Or anywhere else over yonder. Do I have your word?''

''You got it.''

He released his hold, and Rachel lifted the rifle up in front of her. She ran her hand over the gracefully drooping stock, opened and closed the decorative brass patch box on the side of the butt, and thumbed back the hammer, checking to be sure nothing had been damaged. Then she raised the gun and sighted down its slender five-foot barrel.

''You be careful with that, once it's loaded,'' he cautioned. ''I've seen more than one greenhorn Easterner accidentally shoot off his foot.''

At the ridiculous warning, Rachel burst into laughter. She sobered immediately when she saw the glint of displeasure in his eyes. Lordy, she wasn't going to take a chance on him changing his mind.

''Reckon I can handle it,'' she told him, making every effort to simper like she'd seen Lucinda do for her whey-faced beau. ''I'll be right careful where I'm a-pointin' it.''

Apparently satisfied, Strong Elk removed the shot pouch and powder horn he'd slung over his shoulder and placed them on the floor next to a backrest. Rachel returned to the women's side of the lodge, and they both sank down on the fur-covered floor.

For Porcupine Quills's sake, the trio conversed in Cheyenne during the meal. Rachel's sentences were liberally sprinkled with English words, which she used whenever she didn't know the correct ones in their language. But the bright-eyed medicine woman seemed to follow everything that was said. Strangely, neither Strong Elk nor Porcupine Quills mentioned what had happened that afternoon.

Rachel, however, was unable to forget the peculiar welcome Strong Elk had given his cousin. All during the preparation of the meal, she'd tried to figure out just what had gone wrong. It seemed, from Wolf Walking Fast's terrible scowl, that at first he didn't like her. But then he'd smiled and offered to take her riding. At least that was what she'd thought he said. She might have misunderstood, since Strong Elk had reacted with such instantaneous venom.

"Why'd you jump on your poor cousin like a duck on a June bug?" she blurted out in her own language. "All he did was offer to take me for a ride in the moonlight. I thought it was a right mannersome thing for a body to say."

Strong Elk's resolute chin jerked up. At the same instant, Porcupine Quills made a choking sound and started to cough fitfully.

"Are you all right?" Rachel cried. She looked over at Strong Elk, who seemed more annoyed than concerned. "She's choking!" She jumped up and frantically started to pound the tiny woman between the shoulder blades.

Porcupine Quills waved one hand back and forth, indicating she wasn't in any distress. She covered her wrinkled features with both hands, rocking back and forth, alternately coughing and . . . laughing! She lifted her face to meet Rachel's stunned gaze. Tears streamed down her furrowed cheeks. Still seated, she bent forward from the waist and, raising the hem of her soft doeskin dress, dabbed at the corners of her eyes. Then she looked once more at Strong Elk's baleful expression and burst out laughing all over again.

"What did I say?" Rachel asked. She glanced back and forth at the two of them in complete bewilderment.

All of a sudden, Porcupine Quills jumped to her feet. "I promised to take a robe I finished quilling to Standing in Water this evening. I will not be gone long. Strong Elk can stay and keep you company, Little Red Fawn, while you clean and put away the cooking utensils."

Rachel gaped in astonishment at the obvious ploy. "I do not think . . ." she began in Cheyenne, but Porcupine Quills ignored her protest, snatched up the buffalo robe, and left in a rush. Rachel turned to Strong Elk, who smiled his approval of the widow's unseemly exit, his black mood disappearing faster than huckleberries at picking time.

"Tain't hardly fittin'," she finished lamely in English.

Chapter 8

"**S**it down, Rachel," said Strong Elk, "and don't look so worried. Your grandmother will be back before you can possibly succeed in causing any harm to my reputation."

He smiled his reassurance, and Rachel slowly sank back down in her spot on the other side of the small cooking fire. She immediately began to busy herself with the tasks of housekeeping, placing the wooden bowls and horn spoons in a kettle of warm water.

"Your chores can wait," he told her. "There's something I need to talk to you about." She watched him warily as he rose and moved over to where she sat.

"You ain't supposed to be on this here woman's side of the lodge," she informed him. "I've been livin' with your people long enough to know that much. Porcupine Quills has been learnin' me the proper ways to go on."

"If she allows you to continue to sit cross-legged like a man, she's not nearly as fussy as she pretends to be."

Rachel sniffed at his criticism. "If'n you don't approve of my manners, you're free to leave at any time—not like somebody else I know." She picked up a long-handled ladle made from the horn of a mountain sheep and started to wipe it with a piece of damp buck-skin.

Pretending not to notice the petulant jut of her lower lip, Strong Elk dropped down next to her. He took the ladle and cloth from her hands and laid them aside. "I couldn't possibly leave before I told you how lovely you look wearing that necklace," he said.

Her fingers flew to the quilled and beaded band, as though she'd forgotten she wore it. The necklace fit snugly around her throat like a jeweled collar.

"Porcupine Quills gave it to me," she explained with a shy smile. "She won it from Standing in Water, bettin' on my skill at the foot ball game. She said your grand-father's wife makes the prettiest necklaces in the camp."

Strong Elk ran the tip of his forefinger along the band's upper edge, lightly grazing the creamy skin above it. The bright geometric design, fashioned of green and white beads, seemed marvelously exotic against the faded blue flannel of her shirt. Porcupine Quills had chosen wisely. The leaf-green beads were the exact color of Rachel's eyes. Her long, curving lashes fluttered nervously at his touch, casting moving shadows on her pale cheeks. When she raised her eyes and looked into his, Strong Elk felt a jolt of desire so intense, his heart lurched forward and banged against his breastbone.

He slipped his arm around her tiny waist and felt her stiffen with umbrage at his boldness. "I can see why your people call you Rose," he said huskily.

"Rachel Rose," she corrected in a matter-of-fact tone. "But more often than not, it's jest plain Rosie."

He ignored her attempt to scoot away from him. Hold-ing her easily in the crook of his arm, he ran the back of his hand over her smooth cheek. "You're as delicate as the wild rose that blooms on the prairie," he murmured. "Your skin as soft. Your lips as pink. But your sweet perfume reminds me of the lushly petaled blossom that grows in the white man's garden.''

"Oh, that's jest the smell of the wildflowers that Porcupine Quills puts in our mattresses,'' she disclaimed. She peeked at him out of the corner of her eye, clearly apprehensive about the direction their conversation had taken and determined to turn his flatteries aside.

Strong Elk bent his head and brushed his lips across the copper-red curls on her temple. "It's your own personal scent I'm speaking of, little rose.''

At the whispered endearment, Rachel braced one elbow against his rib cage, ready to fend off any further advances. "Lord A'mighty,'' she scoffed, "is that how you track a body down on the prairie? You jest foller her scent like a bawlin'-hound a-trailin' a possum?''

Strong Elk caught her pointed chin in his hand and forced her to look up at him. Just as he suspected, her eyes were sparkling with playful naughtiness. "Miss Robinson,'' he said in a silky, ominous tone, "do you know the meaning of the word *incorrigible*?''

The smile quickly faded. "Does it mean someone who tells fibs?''

"Among other things.''

He knew the source of her sudden uneasiness. She'd asked practically every adult female in the camp exactly what horrible punishment the Cheyenne inflicted on little girls who told lies. At first, they'd stared at her in blank confusion, unable to comprehend her garbled words. When Strong Elk later explained to the baffled women what he'd told the *vehoka* in order to keep her from lying to him, everyone found it a wonderful joke. And no one had ever answered her preposterous question, one way or the other.

"Is that what you were wantin' to tell to me?'' she asked with an anxious frown. "That I'm incorrigible?''

"No.'' He released her and drew back slightly. "I

want to talk to you about what Wolf Walking Fast said this afternoon.''

She jabbed her finger insistently toward the other side of the tipi. "First, you go on over there where you belong. Then we can palaver all you've a mind to."

"I'd rather stay right where I am," Strong Elk countered with a smile of immense satisfaction. "I see your grandmother won a trinket for your hair, as well. She's to be commended on her good taste." He touched the shiny ornament fashioned from a hammered silver disk. Strings of tiny green and white beads dangled from its center. The colored glass swayed enticingly whenever she moved her head, catching the light of the fire and throwing off emerald sparks.

Rachel batted his hand away. "Tarnation! What if Porcupine Quills comes in and finds you a-sittin' beside me?" she scolded. "She'll never invite you to supper again, that's for darn sure. Besides, I can't think proper-like with you a-crowdin' in on me."

What Strong Elk had to say was extremely important. He wanted her full attention. So he rose and moved a slight distance away, sitting down so they faced each other. "How's this?"

"That's better," she said, rewarding him with a bright smile. "Now, what is it you're a-wantin' to tell me?"

He looked into her clear eyes and read the innocence there. He hated to diminish even a tiny bit of that trust, but it was imperative that she know what Wolf's insult had meant. "Rachel Rose," he began and then stopped abruptly.

Her eyes swam with tears, and the corners of her mouth drooped at his words. For the first time, he comprehended fully how very much she missed her home, and his heart was touched by her sadness. As a boy of eight who'd just lost his mother, he'd been taken far away from his own people. He knew how painful home-

sickness could be. When the Elk continued, his voice was
soft with compassion. ''When my cousin said he'd like
to take you for a ride over the prairie tonight, he was
speaking metaphorically.''

She blinked and pursed her lips in reproach. ''Don't
you never talk plain English?''

Strong Elk could tell from the way she looked straight
at him, her eyes wide and filled with artless curiosity,
that she had no notion what he was hinting at. Uncertain
just how much she knew about the mating of a man and
woman, he decided to proceed cautiously. ''Remember
when you told me that your marriage with Bruckenridge
had never been *completed*?''

Rachel sat up perfectly straight and folded her hands
in her lap. A rosy blush crept up her cheeks as she lowered her lids and stared down at her thumbnail. ''Course
I do.''

''Do you understand fully what it was that the major
intended to do that night?''

She lifted one shoulder. ''I've got a pretty fair inklin'.''

''But you don't know exactly.''

''Listen, jest what is it you're a-tryin' to say?'' she
demanded crossly. ''I ain't got all night to sit here jawin'.''

Strong Elk rested his elbows on his knees and shook
his head in exasperation. When had he ever met such an
impudent, willful female? ''Wolf meant that he wanted
to do what Bruckenridge had tried.''

She gaped at him in amazement. ''Holy Moses! You
mean he wanted to rip my clothes and sock me in the
belly?''

''No. That's not what I mean.'' The Elk drew a deep
breath and exhaled it slowly. This was going to be harder
than he'd thought. ''It was Wolf's way of saying that he
wanted to take you by force.''

"Humph." She sniffed, wrinkling her nose in distaste. "If'n he tries to lay a finger on me, I'll learn him some proper manners, real sudden-like."

From the lack of horrified revulsion on her face, Strong Elk realized that Rachel probably had only a muddled idea of what he was talking about. He pulled out the sheathed hunting knife he carried in the beaded leather band at his waist. It was the Bowie he'd taken from her the first day they met. "I want you to carry this with you at all times, Rachel. And I want you to stay close to Porcupine Quills or one of the other women whenever you leave the safety of the camp circle. That means even when you go down to the stream for fresh water in the mornings."

"Shoot, I ain't no helpless, good-for-nothin' city girl," she replied in disgust. She took the weapon, withdrew the long blade with its mother-of-pearl handle from its leather sheath, and balanced it on her open palm. "I don't need no one protectin' me, nohow."

"Fighting off a drunken cavalry officer and defending yourself from a man like Wolf Walking Fast are two very different things," he informed her tersely.

"Don't you go a-worryin' none about me," Rachel said with a confident air. She dropped the knife and sheath on the bearskin rug in front of her and jerked her thumb toward her chest. "I'm a mountain girl, born and raised in the Cumberlands. Why, McDougall menfolk don't never bother with brawlin'. They jest hack, slash, and drag out. Ain't nobody goin' to try and hurt me and get away with it."

Rachel shoved one frayed shirtsleeve up to her elbow. Making a tight fist, she tensed the muscles of her forearm in a brash display of her strength.

Strong Elk stared in consternation. The fragile bones of her hand and wrist were about the size of a large bird's. He couldn't keep the mounting irritation from his voice. She had to realize the seriousness of the threat. "You can't really believe you could ward off an attack by a rapacious Cheyenne warrior," he growled, "just because you were lucky enough to catch Bruckenridge off-guard and break his nose."

Her eyes narrowed wrathfully. She snatched up the Bowie and brandished the blade in front of him. "I'm little, but I'm wiry," she announced. "Why, I'm a wildcat on two feet, oncet I get goin'. So you jest better mind what you're a-sayin, or I'm liable to have to learn you a lesson or two 'bout Cumberland womenfolk. And if'n I do, you ain't never goin' to forget it."

The sight of the little redhead threatening him with her hunting knife tickled the Elk's sense of the absurd. He knew he should try to cajole her by pretending to take her boast seriously. But instead of acting the least bit worried, he grinned. He couldn't help it.

Without a word of warning, Rachel hurled herself at him, spitting epithets like an angry kitten. "Why you high-headed, ripsnitious, biggity-mouthed scalawag!" she cried. She landed squarely on his chest, and Strong Elk obligingly fell over backward, all the while laughing uproariously.

Straddling his large body, the outraged *vehoka* pressed the flat of her blade against his throat. She bent over him, till her face was only inches from his, and spoke through taut lips. "You keep laughin', mister, and I'll put this Arkansas toothpick down your gullet the hard way."

Strong Elk looked up to see the spark of hellfire in her gorgeous eyes. He was only vaguely aware of the cool steel lying across his exposed jugular. The feel of her slim thighs bracketing his flanks, the curve of her soft mound pressed against his abdomen threatened to detonate the charged sexual energy he'd been trying to contain for five long weeks. Completely ignoring the knife, he took her face in his hands and pulled her down, till their lips brushed. Then he cupped the back of her head in his palm and kissed her.

The kiss was wild with an urgency driven by days and nights of carnal frustration. He rocked his lips against hers, moving, adjusting, searching, exploring. Without breaking the kiss, he took the knife from her unresisting fingers and tossed it aside. Then he rolled her onto her back and trapped her legs beneath his thigh, his thickened sex pressing against her softly curved hip.

The sheer pleasure that pulsated through him at that point of glorious contact ignited an explosion of uncontrollable passion like the powder charge of a howitzer cannon. He kissed her eyelids, her nose, her cheeks, her brow, then returned to her mouth once again. Thrusting his tongue inside, he probed and stroked, while his hands sought the buttons of her shirt. He ran his open mouth along the line of her jaw, skimming her lightly with his teeth, then nipped the silken skin beneath her chin. He thrust his tongue into the whorl of her small, shell-like ear, all the while working her buttons free.

The Elk heard Rachel's breath come in short, shallow drafts as she whimpered deep in her throat. Her fingers clutched and tugged on his hair, but he didn't give her time to think or a chance to protest.

He wanted her too badly to stop now.

Hell, he wasn't sure he could even slow down.

Desire, voluptuous and white-hot, pounded and surged through every inch of him. His hands actually shook as he spread open the edges of her shirt.

She wore a thin white chemise as cool and pure as fresh fallen snow, and he groaned with lust as he rubbed his cheeks back and forth over the firm hillocks and valley of her breasts. He took one small, perfect globe in his mouth, flicking the nipple with his tongue through the damp cotton, till he felt her arch upward in sweet, spontaneous response. His hand reached down to cover her mound, pressing and rubbing and fondling in erotic persuasion.

"Nihoatovaz," he rasped. *"Nihoatovaz."*

"Strong Elk," she moaned, "I don't even know what you're sayin'." The sound of his name in her deep breathy voice drove him wild.

"I want you, I want you," he repeated hoarsely as his mouth roved greedily over her breasts. Taking in deep drafts of air, he inhaled the honeyed scent of her female body, and his hardened member leaped up in reflexive reaction. He nudged the edge of the chemise downward with his nose, frustrated that her velvety crests remained hidden from view. With frantic fingers, he jerked the cotton aside, revealing the taut little buds of her rosy nipples.

Strong Elk's breath caught in his throat at the sight of her exquisite beauty. Pushing her breast upward gently, he suckled her, deep and long. The muscles in his tautened loins clenched and spasmed as his engorged manhood searched for its home. He was like the rutting stag in his dreams, heavy and hard and driven by an instinct so deep, so intense, it couldn't be denied.

Cradling her in one arm, he started to slide his fingers under the waistband of her trousers and realized he'd have to loosen her belt. As he began to unfasten the buckle, he heard Porcupine Quills's voice from across the camp circle calling good-night to a friend.

"Dammit," he breathed as he immediately came to his senses. What in the hell was he doing? His heart slamming against his ribs, he sat up at once and began to button her shirt.

Rachel looked up at the magnificent warrior in dazed confusion. The tip of one long side braid, trimmed with otter fur, brushed gently across her cheek. Gradually, she became aware that she was clutching the brass armlet on his bulging upper arm like a drowning victim going under for the third time. She made no attempt to help him fasten her clothing, or even sit up. Her swollen breasts ached from his ardent attentions. She longed for him to continue suckling her. For that, incredibly, was what he'd done. Strong Elk had suckled her like a babe at his mama's breast, and the pleasure had been nearly more than she could bear. He'd fondled her most secret place through her britches, and her whole body had tensed and arched toward him in vibrant, quivering response. She couldn't have been more bewildered by her immediate and overwhelming surrender to his touch than if the stars had just fallen out of heaven.

"Come on, little girl," he urged softly. "Sit up." He slid his arm under her shoulders and lifted her to a sitting position.

As her racing heart slowly returned to its normal beat, Rachel stared into his fathomless ebony eyes, enthralled by the feelings he had conjured up inside her. She cupped his cheek in one hand and placed her outspread fingers over his thudding heart, unable to keep from touching him. He turned his face into her palm and stroked it with his warm, moist tongue. "Strong Elk . . ." she whispered in confusion, uncertain what she wanted to say.

Without another word, he rose and turned toward the lodge's opening, just as Porcupine Quills entered. The little woman cocked her head like a white-crowned sparrow and looked from one to the other, a knowing smile skipping around the corners of her mouth. "Was I gone too long?" she asked in Cheyenne with a feigned air of bafflement. Her gaze lighted upon the dirty dishes that sat beside the fire. "Or not long enough?"

"I was just about to leave," Strong Elk told her sharply, his features harsh and unyielding in the flickering light. Without so much as a backward glance, he charged out of the tipi.

Stunned by his lightning change of mood, Rachel

stared in dismay at the closed flap over the lodge entrance, then turned her head to meet the medicine woman's piercing black eyes.

"Rachel, I think it's . . . time . . . we had a . . . a talk about what goes on between a man and . . . and a woman," Porcupine Quills said in halting, but perfectly understandable English.

Rachel gaped in stupefaction at her adopted grandmother. "You . . . you talk . . ." she sputtered, unable to believe her ears.

"Yes, I speak . . . your . . . your language," the tiny widow said, pausing as she searched for the right words. She sat down beside Rachel, her face crinkled in a merry smile. "It's been so many . . . uh, so many years. I thought I'd forgotten the words. But the more I heard you speak them, the more they started . . . coming back to me."

"But how?" Rachel asked in mystification.

"My first . . . husband . . . was a *veho*—a white man," Porcupine Quills replied, patting Rachel's hand. "That was . . . long before I came to . . . to live with Flying Hawk's band."

"Ain't you Cheyenne?"

The elderly woman's chin came up with pride. "I am Shoshone. The Cheyenne women are . . . known . . . throughout the . . . the Plains tribes for their chastity. The Shoshone maidens are . . . famous . . . for their beauty. And I was Morning Rose, the . . . the loveliest girl in my village. My father was chief of our band. Many young men tried to court me. My father would have none of them for his daughter. Then a white trapper saw me when my father took me with him to a . . . uh, a fur company post to trade pelts. I was only . . . fourteen . . . winters. The *veho* gave my father four ponies and a musket for me. I lived with the white man for nearly fifteen years. During the long, quiet months in our . . . uh, winter lodge, he taught me and our three sons his strange language.''

"What was his name?" queried Rachel in fascination.

"Randall Tackett. He was very good to me. I loved him deeply. I was . . . heartbroken . . . the day he was murdered.''

"What happened?"

The look in Porcupine Quills's eyes grew sad and faraway. "An Arapaho war party . . . attacked . . . our cabin. They killed Randall and my three little boys. They took me captive. One of them tried to make me his woman, but I . . . hated . . . him for what he'd done. I fought him every time he took me. So he traded me to a Southern Cheyenne for a . . . uh, a jug . . . of whisky.''

"You were traded for whisky!" Rachel was flabbergasted. Then another thought struck her. "I didn't know there was more than one kind of Cheyenne.''

The medicine woman nodded. "There are . . . Northern and . . . Southern Cheyenne,'' she explained as she lifted the spoons and bowls out of the kettle's warm water with the long-handled ladle and began to dry them.

"Jest like the North and South where I come from!" Rachel cried. She took the utensils and placed them in their leather pouches. "Did they fight with each other?"

"No," Porcupine Quills answered. "They are of the same tribe, but some of their . . . uh, their . . . customs and words are different. In the old times, the people used to visit one another often. Now they are separated by the white men's road along the Platte.''

"What's Strong Elk?"

Her grandmother smiled at the question. "He is Northern Cheyenne. Almost . . . everyone . . . in Flying Hawk's band is.''

"Did you like the brave who bought you with whisky?"

"Yes, very much." Porcupine Quills's bright eyes danced at the memory. "I was known as Beautiful Sho-

shone Captive. I was Big Bear Killer's . . . favorite . . .
wife. We had a son. Black Moccasin filled the . . . emptiness . . . in my heart carved by the death of my three
little boys.''

Rachel took the dried ladle from her hand and stored
it away. ''How did Big Bear Killer die?''

''He was killed in a battle with the Utes. At thirty-five,
I was a widow once again. But I was still lovely,'' the
medicine woman added with unruffled aplomb. ''Crazy
Mule . . . courted me. I needed a man to provide for my
child, but he was useless. He couldn't hunt well. He
wasn't clever in stealing horses. And beneath the
furs . . .''

She shrugged and waved her gnarled hand in the air.
''For a Cheyenne warrior, he was a sad . . . disappointment. So I threw him away.''

Rachel gasped in delight. ''Can you do that?'' She
grinned at the very idea. ''That's a lollapalozer of a way
to get rid of a husband you don't want!''

''Usually, it is a Cheyenne man who throws his wife
away.'' Porcupine Quills' black eyes twinkled wickedly
as she handed Rachel an earthenware pot to dry. ''But at
a lodge dance one evening, I threw a . . . stick . . . across
the tipi. I shouted that anyone could have my husband,
for I was throwing him away. The women shrieked with
laughter. They dodged the stick, for no one wanted him.
Everyone laughed at the joke. But Crazy Mule was so
. . . ashamed . . . that he never came near me again. After
that, I was not in such a hurry to find another husband.
Many Horses courted me for three years. Finally, he convinced me that he was the one. We were very happy. He
was good to my young son. We had two daughters of
our own and lived together for many years. By the time
Many Horses died, my son, Black Moccasin, had already
been killed in a battle.''

''And your daughters?''

Porcupine Quills's wrinkled features grew suddenly careworn. Rachel had never seen the sprightly widow look so unhappy. "They were both killed by the soldiers at Sand Creek, along with all my . . . my grandchildren. It was then I came to live with Flying Hawk's band. I am called Porcupine Quills for my . . . talent . . . at quilling buffalo robes. No one in camp knows that I am a Shoshone. Or that I can speak the white man's language." She smiled tenderly at Rachel. "When I heard your sweet voice, my grandchild, the day you came into our camp, my heart . . . lit up . . . inside me. I knew that Randall Tackett's spirit had sent you to me, at last, to . . . brighten . . . the cold winter of my lonely old age."

Rachel gulped at her words. "You talk like you were half-expectin' me."

Putting one thin finger to her lips, the medicine woman tilted her snowy head and gazed at Rachel thoughtfully. "I was. When I heard of Strong Elk Heart's . . . vision, I knew that you would come."

"The Elk had a vision about me?" Rachel asked excitedly. "What was it?"

"When he wants you to know, he will tell you." Porcupine Quills drew a cord out of a parfleche nearby. "From now on, *nixa,* you will need some protection. This is called a *nihpihist.* It will guard your virtue from any Cheyenne warrior who might desire you, including the Elk himself."

Rachel looked down at the blue clay pot she held in her hand and spoke in a low, shy voice. "If'n you thought he was a-hankerin' after me, why'd you leave us alone tonight?"

"He knew I would return in a short while. I believed that the Elk would never be . . . satisfied . . . with a hurried mating. He would think of more than his pleasure alone." She tipped her head back and cackled merrily. "From what I saw, I came home just in time."

Rachel squirmed in embarrassment at the memory of what had taken place between her and Strong Elk on the bearskin rug. After outliving four husbands, Porcupine Quills surely had a powerful notion of what had almost happened. "How does that there *nihpihist* work?"

"You wear it next to your skin. I will show you how it fits when you awake in the morning. While you have it on, no man in the camp will violate it. To do so is a great taboo and would bring much shame upon his head."

Rachel took the rope in her hands. "You mean to say that all I've got to do is wear this here little piece of string, and no feller will try to force himself on me?"

Porcupine Quills raised an admonishing finger. "But only a Cheyenne. You will not be safe from a warrior of . . . another tribe . . . or a *veho*. Remember that, *nixa*. As long as you stay near our village, you will be perfectly safe."

"Well, broom me out, if that don't beat all," Rachel said, looking down in admiration at the thin cord coiled in her palm. "What a gollywhopper of an idea!"

When Strong Elk left Porcupine Quills's lodge, the sounds of revelry could be heard carrying across the village. He knew the Bad Faces were celebrating their many coups in Big Pipe Man's large tipi. Many of the band had been invited to the feast, where the warriors, Wolf Walking Fast included, would tell about their brave deeds fighting the pony soldiers. After that, the young men and women would dance. The Sioux warriors would be welcomed by all the pretty girls, for the two tribes often visited each other, and many times a Cheyenne maiden had been courted and won by a handsome Sioux brave. Big Pipe Man had asked his nephew to attend the feast. Strong Elk knew it wouldn't have been a good idea for Rachel to see the warriors parading their trophies, so he'd planned to join the celebration after eating an evening meal with the widow and the *vehoka*.

But when he left the little lodge with its four bright stars, Strong Elk Heart was in no mood for dancing and flirting. He turned, instead, toward the river. The night was black. Storm clouds hid the stars and blanketed the moon. At the river's edge, he stared down at the dark, flowing waters and tried to master his churning emotions. The Elk was furious with himself for what had just happened. Or, more correctly, what had nearly happened. If the widow had not appeared when she had, he would have taken the little white girl. He knew it.

Rachel's sweet, welcoming response to his caresses was no excuse. He was far older than she and far more experienced. Had she called out for him to stop, he wasn't even certain he could have done so. That's what made him the angriest. He had lost control.

He cursed, long and hard, calling himself every foul name he'd ever learned in the white man's language. Remembering the glint of amusement in Porcupine Quills's intelligent eyes, he clenched his fists in remorse and humiliation. Why shouldn't the old woman laugh? He'd behaved like a twelve-year-old *vehoc* groping his first girl in the hayloft of his father's barn. The only thing the Cheyenne people prized as highly as personal courage was self-restraint. He'd been taught that virtue since he was a child.

Strong Elk had endured the agonizing pain of the Medicine Lodge at the age of fifteen, without so much as a flicker of an eyelid. He'd fasted for five days and nights before he'd been sent his first vision. He'd endured blinding sandstorms, freezing blizzards, and a desert crossing than had almost wiped out an entire expedition—without once losing his composure and cool-headedness. He'd killed four men in hand-to-hand combat and untold others with his rifle. He'd mated with more women than he cared to remember, never once taking his own satisfaction without first ensuring theirs. And tonight he'd lost control with a slip of girl because she'd moaned and called his name. *Eaaa!* He was a fool!

There was no sense trying to pretend it hadn't happened. He'd been ready to ram himself into her small body with all the finesse of a charging bull buffalo. She was as delicate and fragile as a butterfly. He was a lumbering oaf.

Strong Elk raised his face to the gloomy sky and felt the first spattering of raindrops on his overheated skin. He knew the cause of his failure. A strain of tainted blood ran in his veins. He'd tried to deny it. He'd refused even to speak of it for the past two years. But it was there, inside him—making him weak. Making him less than a Cheyenne warrior. He had the ugly puckered scar on his back as a constant reminder that he was a breed.

Stripping off his breechclout and moccasins, the Elk plunged into the cold water and swam back and forth across the swift-moving river in the pouring rain, until he was physically exhausted.

By the time he returned to the shore, he'd made his decision. He would keep his hands off Rachel Robinson. He would never forget she was white, and they could never marry. He would see that she returned to Kentucky as pure and undefiled as she was at this moment. If she was to get the annulment she wanted so desperately, she had to return a virgin. And he would show the willpower and strength of character that every Cheyenne male was taught from birth.

The next morning, Rachel decided to take her newly retrieved rifle and go hunting. It had rained during the night, leaving the grasslands smelling fresh and clean. Whenever she was upset back home, she'd take her hound dog and her caplock and wander up and down the nearby hollows, looking for a squirrel or a possum to take back for supper.

She didn't bother mentioning to anyone where she was going. She didn't want to have to argue her way out of camp. She had a pretty good hunch that neither Strong Elk nor Porcupine Quills would approve. So she waited until the Elk had ridden out with a group of men for the daily hunt, and the medicine woman was visiting a friend. Jamming the wide-brimmed cavalry hat on her head, Rachel grabbed the long Kentucky rifle and the Bowie knife Strong Elk had returned to her. She rolled a few things up in the McDougall plaid, tossed it on Spotted Butterfly's back, and rode northward along the eastern bank of Antelope River.

When she came to a spot where she could ford safely, she sat tight on the Butterfly's back, clutching the long black mane as the little mare swam across to the other side. Rachel didn't go far, just far enough to have some privacy and enjoy the sights and sounds of nature in peaceful solitude. She stopped beneath a giant river willow, dismounted, and ground-tied the painted mare where she could graze. Then Rachel sat down in the thick grass and leaned her back against the tree trunk, where she could listen to the cool, frothy water bubbling by.

Back in the Cumberlands, whenever she wanted to have a good think, she found herself a spot beside Sugar Creek and watched it flow on its lazy journey down to the Kentucky River. She'd admire the cowslips blooming on the bank or the unexpected beauty of an opened passionflower nearly hidden in the grass. On the cliffs above her, drifts of azaleas would flutter in the breeze, while the delicate blossoms of the columbine climbed up the limestone bluffs to the pawpaw thickets at the top of the ridge. If she was quiet and still, it wouldn't be long before the little forest creatures would resume their busy lives, ignoring her presence.

Looking out across Antelope River, Rachel rested her forearms on her bent knees and sighed. Lord A'mighty, she was still trying to figure out just what had happened the evening before. While Strong Elk was kissing her, she hadn't much thought about anything else. And when he opened her shirt and put his mouth on her breast, it seemed the world had suddenly shrunk to just the two of them.

Allowing him to go on like that had seemed plumb natural at the time. Now she was purely mortified. She'd whimpered and wriggled and led him on, till it was scarcely a wonder he'd been shocked at her indecent behavior. Porcupine Quills had declared that the Elk wasn't mad at her, he was angry at himself. Rachel found that nigh impossible to believe. When she recollected how he'd touched her between her legs, she was positive she could never look him in the eye again.

She didn't know a whole lot about what all went on in a marriage bed, but she was dead certain, if she continued allowing Strong Elk to fondle her like that, she'd never get an annulment from Shelby Bruckenridge once she returned to Kentucky. Everything depended upon her keeping her virginity—that much nobody had to tell her. And no matter how long it took, no matter how many obstacles were set in her way, come hell or high water, she was going to get back home.

She pictured how surprised Papa would be, the day she came sashaying up that long, tree-shaded lane to Ashwood Hall. He'd be downright bumfuzzled to see her. She prayed Garrett Robinson wouldn't be too aggravated with his oldest daughter because the marriage he'd arranged had turned out so poorly. She'd seen the sorrow in his eyes whenever he looked at her. She was a grievous disappointment, she knew. He'd wanted her to learn to read and write.

When she was twelve, he'd enrolled her in the Wickland Institute for Females in Lexington, but she'd refused to stay there. Miserable and homesick for Gram and Gramps and all her mountain kinfolk, she'd insisted on going back to Sugar Hollow. Then the war came, and everything in Kentucky had been turned topsy-turvy. She'd never had a chance to try her hand at book learning again.

Rachel plucked a blade of grass and chewed on it thoughtfully. She reckoned a divorce was unthinkable. She daren't create a scandal while Papa was running for the Senate. An annulment, however, would be considered fitting and proper, even by Eliza's snooty, fine-haired friends. When Rachel explained what kind of devil's spawn Shelby had turned out to be, and that the groom's bounden duties were never performed on their wedding night, she just knew Papa would forgive her.

Of course, Eliza would never believe that her cousin was a low-bellied snake. In that woman's eyes, no one with the name Bruckenridge could ever be anything short of perfection. Luckily, it wasn't her stepmama Rachel had to convince. That tetchous woman had disliked her for as far back as anyone could remember.

One summer, when Rachel was eight, her father had brought her to Ashwood Hall for a visit. She suspected he'd hoped that she'd stay on. But Eliza had made no secret of the fact that she counted the days until the pathetic, ignorant little mountain girl returned to her grandparents. When Rachel was once again safely back in the cabin beside McDougall's Mill, she'd nearly wept for joy. Later, she'd asked Gram why her stepmama hated her so.

Gram had sat down in her scarred oak rocker and pulled Rachel onto her lap. "Before your daddy ever met your mama, child, Eliza Bruckenridge had set her sights on him. And p'rhaps your daddy returned a little of that affection, I don't know. Then one day, your mama went to Lexington with Gramps to buy some new gears for his waterwheel. Those two younguns met, kinda accidental-like. It was love at first sight for both of 'em.''

"Like when I saw that little puppy at the feed store?"

Gram smiled her wonderful smile and chucked Rachel under the chin. "Yep, I guess you could say it was jest like that, darlin' Rosie. Only more so."

"Then they got married," Rachel said.

"Then they got married. And two happier people I ain't never seen. But back in Lexington, Eliza was as green and sour as a spring persimmon. She threw out flouts against your mama. My little Jenny was awful bad hurt. When she found out she was carryin' you, your mama insisted on comin' back to Sugar Holler. She wanted me to granny her baby. She didn't want nothin' to do with those contrarious flatlanders, nohow.''

Rachel laid her head on her grandma's shoulder. "Eliza should be happy now. She got Papa in the end."

Gram nodded. "That she did. But sometimes, Rosie, child, when we get the thing we think we want most in life, it somehow turns to ashes in our hands. Especially if we get it by hurtin' others. The very day we put your mama in the ground, Eliza came chasin' after your papa. This time, she was bound and determined to get him. And he was hopin' to find someone to take care of his sweet little girl-child. Well, seems like neither one of them got what they really wanted.''

Deep in thought, Rachel stared across Antelope River at the stand of trees that lined the far bank. Tears sprang to her eyes at the memory of Gram. She'd died two years before. Mattie McDougall had been the kindest, lovingest woman in the whole wide world. She'd practiced the healing arts, and she'd never turned away a single soul, ailing in body or spirit, from her cabin door. She had taught her granddaughter that a heap of book learning don't necessarily make a body a better person. Rachel sorely missed her.

Through her blurred vision, Rachel saw a brown-and-white patch move on the opposite shore. She froze and blinked her eyes. A pronghorn was slowly, cautiously making her way to the edge of the creek. The wind was in Rachel's face, and she knew the pronghorn wouldn't catch her scent. She waited to see if a youngster would follow its mama out of the brush, but only the full-grown female bent her head and lapped at the crystal-clear water.

Rachel grinned in satisfaction. She'd brought along a sturdy rope, just as a precaution. She hadn't really thought she'd find any large game so close to the village, but she'd spent too much time roaming around the outdoors to leave camp unprepared. By tossing the braided rawhide over a stout branch, she ought to be able to hoist the small antelope onto Spotted Butterfly's back.

Silently, Rachel reached down and picked up her loaded rifle, hoping her little mare wouldn't catch the newcomer's scent and snort in surprise. She sighted down the long barrel and took aim. Just as Spotted Butterfly whinnied, Rachel let fire. The pronghorn's front legs buckled under her, and she crashed to the ground.

"Well, ol' Betsy," Rachel said to her granddaddy's gun, "seems like we ain't lost our touch after all."

Chapter 9

~~~~~∞∞~~~~~

Late that afternoon, Strong Elk and Young Bear Running, each leading a pack horse laden with game, returned to the village from the day's hunt. They saw Porcupine Quills and Flying Hawk's two wives standing outside the Old Man Chief's lodge. With grave faces, the three elderly women watched the two warriors ride in. The moment the Elk was close enough to see their harrowed expressions, an icy chill snaked down his spine.

The lovely Choke Cherry Blossom, holding her daughter's hand, also waited just in front of the lodge's entrance. On a robe stretched out in the shade of the large tipi, Sweet Feather sat with Thick Braided Hair, whose little son was playing beside her. Everyone's eyes were fastened on Strong Elk and his companion as they rode across the grassy circle.

He brought Thunder Cloud to a halt in front of the lodge. "What is wrong?" he asked, though he was certain he already knew. *He should never have given Rachel her gun.*

"Little Red Fawn has disappeared," Porcupine Quills blurted out before he'd even had a chance to dismount.

Her face was contorted with fear, and she wrung her hands in frenzied agitation. "You must find her, Strong Elk Heart, before it is too late. You must bring her back safely to us."

"*Saaaa!*" Young Bear hissed beneath his breath, as he, too, stopped his horse in front of the lodge.

Strong Elk jumped down from the stallion's back. It took all his willpower to remain cool-headed at the dreadful news. His first impulse was to spring back up on Thunder Cloud and charge out of camp like a madman. The thought of Rachel in the clutches of brutal strangers, Indian or white, twisted a knot in his gut. If any man dared to hurt her, he'd track the bastard down, cut off his hands and feet, and flay him alive.

"When did she leave?" he asked, his words clipped and brusque.

"We do not know for certain," Standing in Water replied in a choked voice. His grandfather's wife covered her cheeks with her gnarled hands and rocked back and forth, moaning in distress. "*Ahahe,*" she lamented. "*Ahahe.*"

At the tortured exclamation of woe, Good Robe Woman put a comforting arm around her older sister's stooped shoulders. "It may have been long before the sun was straight over our heads," Flying Hawk's second wife told Strong Elk. She spoke with more composure than the other two women, but her eyes were clouded with misgiving. "No one knew she was gone until then," she explained. "We all thought Little Red Fawn was with someone else in the village."

The Elk and Young Bear immediately began checking their ammunition. Both men carried Henrys that Strong Elk had acquired during his years scouting for the U.S. cavalry. The light, sleek, repeating rifles could fire over a hundred rounds in five minutes and kill a man at a thousand yards.

"Has anyone gone to search for her?" he questioned as he quickly counted the cartridge boxes in the leather pouch slung over Thunder Cloud's back.

His cousin's plump wife, Thick Braided Hair, rose from the buffalo robe, picked up her son of two winters, and walked over to join them. Her brow was furrowed in apprehension. "Sleeping Bull and your grandfather left the moment we discovered her missing," she said. Prickly Pear patted his mother's cheek, and she absently kissed his chubby fingers before going on. "They rode toward the sacred hunting ground of the Sioux, believing the little Fawn would surely go in the direction of her people."

Strong Elk searched the eastern horizon, hoping for some sign of his grandfather and his cousin, Sleeping Bull. "She is too clever to start out in the direction she intends to go," he told the anxious women. "She will cross the river and ride toward the setting sun, until she thinks she can hide her tracks. Then she will double back."

"Hesc!" Good Robe Woman cried, giving the Cheyenne exclamation for astonishment. She raised her sparse gray brows and met Strong Elk's narrowed eyes. "The *vehoka* would know how to do that?" she queried in disbelief.

"She has done it before. There is no reason to suppose she will not try it again." He lifted the gutted stag from his pack horse's back and laid it on the grass for the women to prepare later. "Young Bear and I will ford the river a short distance upstream and search for her tracks. Tell my grandfather to follow my trail when he and Sleeping Bull return."

"You are angry with her, Strong Elk Heart?" asked Porcupine Quills, her reedy voice high-pitched and quavery. She pressed her shaking hands to her chest as she searched his impassive face for some clue to his intentions once he found the errant runaway.

"No."

Young Bear, who'd already climbed back up on his painted horse and sat waiting for him, tipped his head and silently met the Elk's gaze with incredulous eyes.

But it wasn't a lie. Strong Elk Heart wasn't angry.

He wasn't even furious.

He was stark, blind, raging mad.

She had promised not to take off by herself once he'd given back the rifle. Then the first chance she'd gotten, Rachel Rose Robinson had slipped out of camp unseen and hightailed it for home.

Eaaa! He had meant what he'd said. He would track her down, throw a rope around her neck, and make her walk the whole damn way back, tied to his horse. It was apparently the only method that would impress upon her how dangerous it was for her to leave the village alone.

Livid at the white girl's treachery, he leaped up on Thunder Cloud and wheeled him around. Just as the Elk was about to kick his heels against the rearing stallion's flanks and gallop out of the village, he saw her.

Rachel was sauntering across the camp circle, calmly leading her spirited black-and-white mare, as though she hadn't a care in the world. The carcass of a pronghorn was draped across Spotted Butterfly's back. Her long-barreled rifle was wrapped in a plaid blanket and fastened at the horse's withers with a strip of rawhide. The foolish *vehoka* was heading straight toward them.

Her short curls aflame in the brilliant sunshine, she held her head high, clearly proud of her accomplishment in bagging the cunning, elusive game. Still, she wisely kept her eyes averted from the irate warrior, who sat astride his gray Appaloosa and stared at her with such intimidating ferocity.

His heart thundering, Strong Elk dismounted and strode across the grass to meet her.

"Howdy," she called with an overbright smile, her gaze fastened on the medicine bundle that hung around his neck. She jerked her thumb at the small antelope on the horse behind her. "Look what I brought home for supper."

He didn't answer. Didn't say a word. Just lifted her up, tossed her over his shoulder, and headed for Flying Hawk's tipi.

"Hey, wait a durn minute!" Rachel cried. "You can't do this to me. Put me down!" She grabbed a handful of his hair and yanked as hard as she could. She pounded on his back with her small fists. She scratched and pinched and howled like a she-devil. The Elk bounced her up and down a few times on his hard shoulder, till she had to stop screaming long enough to catch her breath. Then she braced her palms against the straight black hair that hung past his shoulder blades and pushed herself up to look over at the group clustered around the lodge. "Ain't nobody a-goin' to do nothin'?" she screeched in outrage.

No one answered. They watched in silence, knowing that what she'd done had been childishly irresponsible. It was a gift of good fortune from the Great Powers that the rattlebrained white girl was still alive. As he stalked past Young Bear Running, still on his horse, the Elk saw the warrior's wry grin of amusement at the spirited red-head's antics. The women, however, were solemn, their eyes filled with female sympathy. They knew Rachel was about to get exactly what she deserved, but their fondness for her made them wish the Elk would show a little more patience while the headstrong *vehoka* learned their ways.

Strong Elk carried his squirming, wriggling burden inside the empty lodge and dumped her onto the nearest stack of buffalo robes. When she started to scramble to her feet, he thrust one hand out, fingers spread wide in warning. His terse words came short and breathless as rage sent the blood surging through his veins and flooding his heart. "Don't move! Don't say a word, if you value that pretty white skin of yours. I've never been so tempted to take a quirt to a woman's backside in my life."

"What're you rippin' up at me for?" she demanded indignantly. Ignoring his admonition, she shot to her feet and glared back at him in a plucky show of belligerence. Then she lifted her brows and shrugged her shoulders, as though he had no real cause to get so perturbed. "Why, shucks," she dared to complain, "I thought everyone'd be pleased as younguns at a taffy-pullin' with my fancy shootin'."

"You little idiot!" he roared. "Don't you know what would have happened if a group of white trappers had found you? Or their Crow and Shoshone allies? There is a war going on, Rachel! And war breeds every kind of corrupt behavior. How many times do I have to tell you that?"

"I thought you said this here campsite was on Cheyenne huntin' grounds," she countered with a mulish scowl.

He gritted his teeth at her unabashed obstinacy. "That doesn't mean we're completely safe from Shoshone raiding parties bent on stealing horses. Or Crows scouting for the army. Or buffalo hunters drunk on cheap whisky, who haven't seen a white woman since they left St. Louis six years ago."

"Well, hell's bells," she grumbled in her deep little voice, "don't go kickin' afore you've been spurred." She stuck her thumbs in her trouser pockets and rocked back on her heels. Her eyes were fixed, once again, on the medicine bundle around his neck. "I didn't go no further'n a body can shout. Wasn't nobody gonna find me, 'ceptin' maybe somebody from this here camp.''

Strong Elk braced his hands on his hips and strode back and forth across the large lodge, trying to regain control of his anger. The sheer terror for her safety was gradually starting to subside. He took several deep, calming breaths before he turned to look at her. ''Rachel, has any man back home ever really tried to hurt you?''

''Course not,'' she answered with a complacent toss of her head. ''All the menfolk in Sugar Holler are my kin.''

''That's just the point,'' he snapped. ''It's different out here. Our women stay close to the village for their own protection. You can't go wandering off by yourself on the open plains. It's too damn dangerous.''

''For cryin' out loud!'' she protested. ''I can't stay cooped up in this here camp all the time. Why, I'd go plumb crazy!''

''I'm taking back the rifle,'' he told her curtly.

''No, you ain't.''

He reached her in two quick strides. Clasping her arms in a tight grip, he held her anchored in place in front of him. Infuriated by his churlish behavior, she tried to struggle free, which was exactly what he wanted her to do. He wanted her to feel just how helpless she was in a strong man's grasp. ''Do you really think you could fight me off if I wanted to hurt you?'' he taunted. ''Go ahead, Rachel. Hit me. Kick me. I want to see you break my hold and get away.''

With her arms imprisoned, she lifted her pointed chin and glared daggers at him. Their gazes locked for the space of one long, silent minute, as each measured the other's determination. But on this point, he was resolved to assert his dominance. He could feel the fight gradually go out of her as she was forced to admit to herself that it was impossible to match his physical strength. Blinking her lashes rapidly, she turned her head away and looked up in humiliation at the open smoke hole above them. Two large teardrops slid slowly down her cheeks.

At the sight of those silent tears on the proud, heart-shaped face, Strong Elk's wrath melted away. Releasing her arms, he bracketed her waist with his hands and lifted her up, till her head was just above his. She looked down at him in surprise, her misty eyes startled and wary. His hoarse words creaked with raw emotion. "Don't you know, little girl, that you scared me half to death?"

Her lower lip trembled at his gentle reproof. She placed her hands on his bare shoulders, and the feel of her hesitant, shaky fingers sent all his resolutions to remain aloof from the captivating *vehoka* spinning away. "I didn't mean to scare nobody," she said with a catch in her voice. "I jest wanted to do a little huntin'."

His laugh was rusty with relief as he wrapped his arms around her slender hips and pressed his face against her soft, alluring body. He'd thought she had tried to go home, in spite of her promise not to leave without his knowledge. But she was here. She was safe. That was all that mattered. And she was never going to ride out of their campsite alone again. He would see to that. He nuzzled the valley between her small breasts, and the joy that swamped his heart was unlike anything he'd ever felt before.

"My sweet, stubborn little rose," he murmured thickly in Cheyenne. "What am I going to do with you?"

Rachel looked down at the top of Strong Elk's head in muddled confusion. A few minutes ago, he'd looked riled enough to whop the living daylights out of her, just as he'd threatened. Instead, he was holding her close and whispering to her in husky Cheyenne words. The sheen of his blue-black hair made the soft eagle's down that decorated his scalp lock seem incredibly white. The four notched eagle feathers that slanted downward from the short braid on the crown of his head rested against her arm.

Of their own will, her hands slid along the unyielding ridge of his shoulders to come to rest at the base of his neck, where she slipped her thumbs beneath the narrow rawhide band that held the small leather pouch he always wore. She could feel his long, feathered earrings brushing lightly across the back of her hands, and their silken enticement seemed to brush across her heart.

"I'm plumb sorry I stirred up so much aggravation," she apologized. "I'm used to ramblin' around on my own, back in Sugar Holler. I didn't rightly consider how I might be the cause of a powerful lot of frettin' and fussin'."

She bent her head and pressed her lips to the center part in his hair. The fragrance of fresh juniper filled her nostrils. The memory of what he'd told her the evening before—that her scent reminded him of roses—assailed her. "You smell mighty good, too," she whispered so softly he couldn't hear.

But when he lifted his head, his eyes were alight with tender amusement. He lowered her slowly, till their lips were scant inches apart. Rachel's lids drifted shut as she leaned forward. This time, it was she who kissed him. A light, tentative kiss, lips brushing and leaving, only to return. She took his bottom lip between her teeth and nibbled gently, then touched it with the tip of her tongue. She could feel the shudder go through his large frame at her timid explorations and wondered at her power over this magnificent male.

From deep within her, a longing to press her bare skin against his blossomed and spread through her awakening body. What would it be like, she wondered, to lay her cheek on his hard, muscled chest and listen to the solid, steady, comforting rhythm of his heart? Shyly, she traced the seam of his lips with her tongue. When he opened them in coaxing invitation, she slipped inside.

At that exact moment, the three elderly women entered the dim lodge. Rachel's eyes popped open, and she immediately tried to draw away. Strong Elk caught the back of her head in his palm. He met her tongue in a warm, encouraging welcome, then explored her mouth with his own. Rachel could hear the noisy, prattling trio move to the far side of the conical dwelling. Porcupine Quills, Standing in Water, and Good Robe Woman were chattering earnestly to one another as they spread a buffalo robe on the floor for inspection. They never once addressed Rachel or Strong Elk. It was as though the women didn't even see the couple standing there, locked in a torrid embrace.

At last, the Elk ended the sizzling kiss and set her down on her wobbly legs. Breathless, she clutched the brass bands that encircled his upper arms and somehow managed to keep her balance. He threaded his fingers through her tousled hair and stroked her temples with his thumbs. "I have to find Flying Hawk and Sleeping Bull," he said quietly. "They rode out looking for you hours ago."

Her head drooped in shame at his words. "I'm truly, truly sorry, Strong Elk. I guess I feel 'bout as humble as a sheep-killin' dog."

He placed a finger under her chin and nudged it upward. "I know, just plain Rosie," he teased. When she gave him a weak smile, he bussed the freckles on her nose and continued in a conversational tone. "But I'm still taking your gun."

Speechless, Rachel watched him leave. When she turned to the threesome huddled over a partly quilled robe, they ceased their infernal jibber-jabber, looked up at her, and smiled serenely, as though nothing unusual had happened that whole blessed day. Back home in the Cumberlands, no grown man would ever make an open demonstration of his tender feelings toward a woman in front of others, not by so much as a touch of his hand—not even if they'd been married long enough to have a passel of young ones sitting around the supper table. The glow in the three pairs of jet eyes told Rachel these women weren't the least bit scandalized by the Elk's behavior. They apparently thought it was high time the stalwart warrior settled down to some serious courting.

Lord A'mighty, if she lived with them a hundred years, she'd never understand the Cheyenne people.

Chapter 10

⟡

For the next four weeks, Flying Hawk's band was on the move in their unending quest for buffalo. The men would return disheartened and weary each afternoon, only to go out once again in the morning, searching for signs of the huge beasts. As the days went by, the caravan wended its way deeper and deeper into the hunting grounds that had been ceded to the Sioux and Cheyenne by treaty with the U.S. government over fifteen years before.

Rachel knew she was crossing territory that mighty few white men had ever laid eyes on. Porcupine Quills had told her just that morning, while they were packing their belongings and dismantling the tipi one more time, that only a handful of fur trappers had ever crossed these plains on their way to the great Rocky Mountains. A Blackrobe named Father De Smet, whom the Cheyennes had treated as an honored guest, had visited them and stayed in their lodges. Rachel remembered Strong Elk saying that the missionary had helped him improve his knowledge of French, which he'd first learned from the mountain men.

At the thought of Strong Elk, Rachel's heart sank.

He'd avoided her for the entire past month. In spite of the sizzling kiss they'd shared the day she'd returned to camp with the pronghorn, he'd behaved afterward as though she didn't hardly exist. Rachel thought, at first, that he was still angry about her leaving the village without his knowledge, so she'd sought him out and apologized profusely once again. He accepted her apology with grave politeness. After that, he seemed to look right through her. Whenever she smiled and waved to him across the open camp circle, he nodded briefly and went on his way, never once coming over to talk with her. It was all she could do to hide the overwhelming disappointment she felt at his unexplained withdrawal. Rachel went over and over in her mind what she might have said to cause such mean-hearted treatment.

After three weeks of trying to overcome his cold indifference, she finally lost her temper. What right did he have to act like she wasn't no more important than an ant? She took to scowling at him, daring the tall warrior to just try to use his smooth charms on her. He'd see what mountain girls were made of. She didn't give a snap of her fingers if he ever tried to cozy up to her again.

Only that morning, Rachel had caught Strong Elk watching her unawares. The glow in his compelling black eyes made her feel all strange and warm inside, but she steeled herself, refusing to let him see how deeply he'd hurt her or how desperately she longed to be near him. She might be bawling inside, but she sure as heck wasn't going to fall at his feet, no way, nohow.

By late afternoon, excitement was in the air. Even the smallest child seemed to know that something special was going to happen. A group of young boys, led by Strong Elk's nephew Little Man, raced their colts across the grass to meet two warriors who'd appeared at the crest of a hill. The youngsters called out their greetings

in excited voices as they galloped past. What the returning men told the boys sent them tearing back down the
knoll to relay the news to others.

"Look, Little Red Fawn!" Squirming like a frisky
pup, Moon Shell pointed to the top of the rise. "Here
comes Strong Elk and Young Bear Running!" The
seven-year-old sat in front of Rachel on Spotted Butterfly. Wearing a pale yellow buckskin dress trimmed with
long fringes and colorful beading, she lifted her doeskin
doll, garbed in the very same costume, and made it wave
its tiny hand to the tall warriors.

"I see them," said Rachel. "Maybe they've found the
buffalo herd and are coming to tell us." She gave the
lively girl an affectionate squeeze. All the children loved
and admired the two strong, good-looking men. But
Moon Shell's feelings for Young Bear Running bordered
upon adoration.

As Rachel learned more and more of their language,
she also became better acquainted with the people around
her. She realized that quite a few braves were sparking
Moon Shell's beautiful widowed mother. The men would
stand shyly around the lodge of Choke Cherry Blossom's
parents in the early morning, waiting for a chance to
speak with her when she came out of the tipi for fresh
water. Young Bear was one of them. It amazed Rachel
to see the giant of a warrior, who'd behaved with such
ferocious bravery during the ambush by the soldiers at
Clear Creek, grow tongue-tied and awkward whenever
the graceful young woman came in view. At the rate the
Bear was going, he'd be old and gray before he managed
to work up the nerve to pop the question.

The two men rode up to join Rachel and Moon Shell.
"Did you see them?" the little girl asked excitedly. She
grinned, displaying the empty spaces of her missing front
teeth. "Did you find the buffalo?"

"We did, Moon Shell," replied Young Bear with an

affectionate smile. "We saw more buffalo than we could count."

Rachel met Strong Elk's shuttered gaze. "Three days away," he told her in cold, blunt English, as though to point out the fact that she was different from the rest of them. "On the other side of Powder River."

Her cheeks grew warm beneath his icy scrutiny. From his sour expression, a body could never tell they'd ever shared more than a howdy. Rachel found herself suddenly tongue-tied and awkward. Flushing with mortification, she glanced at Young Bear and met his sympathetic brown eyes.

Unaware of the charged emotions swirling around her, Moon Shell looked back over her shoulder at Rachel. "Are you not excited, Little Red Fawn?" she piped, her sweet voice radiating happiness.

"Yes," Rachel replied in her broken Cheyenne. "I have never seen a buffalo."

Young Bear Running looked from Strong Elk to Rachel with a thoughtful frown. No doubt he, too, failed to understand his friend's unbending remoteness toward the young white woman. "Come and ride with me, Moon Shell," the Bear suggested. "We will go find your mother and tell her the good news." He reached over and lifted her onto his horse, careful not to bump her injured ankle. Moon Shell still wore the cast Porcupine Quills had fashioned for her. Young Bear seated the child in front of him, holding her within the curve of his strong arms.

The girl's round face glowed with happiness. She smiled at Rachel and Strong Elk, her dimples peeping out adorably, and even the stern warrior had to return such an entrancing, gap-toothed smile. "Thank you, Little Red Fawn," she called as the Bear's mount cantered away. "Thank you for letting me ride with you!"

Their mounts moving side by side at a walk, Rachel

and Strong Elk followed slowly behind. "Her wound is healing well?" he asked, speaking again in sharp English words.

Rachel's eyes flew to meet his. Tarnation, if he wanted to act like some stuck-up city stranger, she'd dang well follow his lead. She straightened her spine and threw back her shoulders. "It's mendin' as well as a body could expect, I reckon," she said coolly. "Porcupine Quills's skill at healin' is a marvel to behold."

After the ambush at Clear Creek, the medicine woman had shown Rachel how to clean the wound with a poultice of silverweed and yarrow and then sprinkle it with dust from a puffball. Together they'd wrapped Moon Shell from mid-calf to toes in a green deer hide and sewn it tight. As the hide shrank and hardened, the splintered bone was held snugly in place.

Recalling the little girl's courage in the face of agonizing pain, Rachel looked down at Spotted Butterfly's long black mane. "We done our level best," she added, her throat suddenly clogged with sorrow. "But Porcupine Quills allows as how Moon Shell won't never walk without a limp."

Strong Elk saw the dejected slump of Rachel's shoulders and knew what she was thinking. The sprightly, bright-eyed child would never again run and play with the other children because of the callousness of a cavalry officer who'd ordered his troops to shoot down into a milling crowd of women and children. A cavalry officer to whom Rachel had been bound by written vows and whose despicable name she now shared, despite all her attempts to deny it.

It was all he could do to keep from reaching over and lifting her up in front of him on Thunder Cloud's back. Strong Elk yearned to hold her in his arms and kiss that sweet mouth till the sadness that hovered around it changed to a smile of happiness. These past four lonely weeks had been sheer, unadulterated torture. Being so near her and yet so far away. Unable to enjoy the pleasure of her delightful conversation, to watch the glow of emotions in her fascinating grass-green eyes. Unable to feel the smoothness of her skin beneath his touch, beneath his lips.

The need for Rachel had become an unending torment. A torment that battered his senses day and night. Especially night. He'd struggled with every ounce of willpower he possessed to control his lust in a battle that never ceased, while he watched her grow more and more distant and angry and hurt. At least he could soothe her feelings of guilt.

"I've been told that you also have a gift for helping the sick and wounded," he said, hoping to distract her. "People have sung your praises around their lodge fires. They speak especially of your kindness to the frail and elderly."

"My gram taught me that," Rachel answered with sorrowful, unseeing eyes. " 'Twarn't nothin' Gram didn't know 'bout healin'. Folks'd come from as far away as Raccoon Holler for her home remedies. Reckon she set more bones and birthed more younguns than most city doctors."

Strong Elk longed to hold her in his arms and console her. But he'd made that mistake before. After all his resolutions to the contrary, he'd held her in his embrace and kissed her the day she'd returned to camp with the pronghorn. He'd been so relieved that she was unharmed, he had let his control slip once again.

In the dark, sleepless hours of the night that followed, he'd decided that the only answer was to keep an arm's distance between him and the captivating *vehoka* until he regained some measure of his former indomitable self-restraint. A niggling doubt assailed him as he contemplated just how long it might take to reach that elusive goal.

Only moments before, he'd seen the confusion in her expressive green eyes at his coldness and had purposely hardened his heart. Nothing could ever come of their physical attraction to each other. Absolutely nothing.

He was Cheyenne. His people needed his leadership and his intimate knowledge of the pony soldiers, not only in this time of immediate danger, but also in the tumultuous years that lay ahead. The U.S. army was waging a war of total extermination against the Cheyenne because of their well-deserved reputation for being the most courageous warriors on the plains. Only wisdom, caution, and an unwavering determination would save their people from complete annihilation.

He must never forget, not even for a second, that Mrs. Rachel Robinson Bruckenridge was white. She had no part in their future, however tragic or inspiring it might prove to be. She would one day return to her family and her beloved Kentucky, leaving behind any man foolish enough to love her with an aching, empty space where his heart had once been. Even now, the thought of her inevitable departure loomed like an enormous black cloud whose rain-filled shadows threatened to obscure the sun forever. The Elk looked away from the delicate features that haunted his dreams, searching the rolling hills as though somehow he could find an answer to his inner torment in the vast, endless sea of grass and sky that surrounded them.

Just then a young woman who'd been riding alone at the very end of the long column of travelers trotted past the silent pair on her brown-and-white speckled horse.

"Whatever happened to that poor girl?" Rachel asked with compassion. "She stays inside her parents' lodge whenever we're camped. When the women bathe in the afternoons, she keeps to herself, not sayin' nary a word.

In all the time I've been with your people, she ain't never oncet come near me.''

''Mysterious Dancer is deeply ashamed of her scars,'' Strong Elk explained. ''She believes that no warrior will look at her with anything but pity. Nothing could be farther from the truth. Her wounds are a lasting symbol of her tremendous bravery.''

''How in blue blazes did she ever get marked up so bad?''

He was hesitant to tell Rachel the truth. Yet sooner or later, someone would let slip what everyone in the camp had tried to keep from her. It would be better to tell her now, than have her find out through the thoughtless words of a child.

''Mysterious Dancer had the courage to repulse a blue-coat officer who tried to entice her into his tent. He became insistent, and she fought him. In his rage, he cut her so badly with her knife that, when her mother found her bleeding, unconscious body in a nearby ravine, she barely recognized her own daughter. No one thought the once-lovely girl would survive.''

''My God, how awful,'' Rachel breathed. ''What kind of twisted, slimy, no-account varmint would do somethin' like that?'' From the revulsion on her fine-boned features, he knew that Rachel had seen the mass of discolored welts that covered not only Mysterious Dancer's face and neck, but also her chest and arms.

When he didn't answer immediately, Rachel jerked on her reins and brought her graceful mare to a halt. He drew up beside her and waited for the question he knew would come. ''Who was it?'' she croaked, her stricken eyes enormous with suspicion.

''Major Yellow Eyes.''

''Shelby Bruckenridge? He . . . he did that to her? Where? When?''

''A year ago at Fort Laramie,'' the Elk said gently,

knowing the pain his words would bring her. "Her father's band was part of a group of Northern Cheyenne who met, along with some Brulé and Oglala Sioux, in a great council with the white peace commissioner. The soldiers were used to the lax morals of the Indian women who camped near the fort year round and lived off the white commander's handouts. They would go freely into the officers' tents at night. The horse soldiers expected the same of the pretty young newcomers from the north."

Rachel touched a shaking hand to her forehead and squeezed her lids shut, as though trying to ward off the ghastly image of what her husband had done. With a deep, shuddering breath, she forced herself to look into Strong Elk's eyes. "And when Mysterious Dancer refused, Shelby started cuttin' on her like that?"

His heart sank as he met her horrified gaze. It was all he could do not to reach out, catch her trembling fingers in his, and bring them to his lips. "That's why not a single warrior suggested that we give you up to Major Bruckenridge at Clear Creek. They knew what the vicious pony soldier chief might do to you in his brutality."

Her voice was ragged with self-loathing, as though the deeds of her evil spouse had somehow spilled over to stain her own pure soul. "Does Mysterious Dancer hate me for what Shelby done to her?"

"No, Little Fawn," he answered truthfully. "No one blames you."

The corner of her lips curled up in disgust. "Even though they all know I was married to that . . . that skunk?"

His chest ached with commiseration for the kind-hearted *vehoka*. He had to make her understand the sincere compassion they all felt for the young woman who'd been given in marriage to that diabolical fiend. Everyone asked the same question: What kind of parents would allow their daughter to be trapped in such a loathsome match?

"They also know you ran away from him," he told her with an encouraging smile. "There isn't a Cheyenne from Fort Laramie to the Yellowstone that doesn't know Major Yellow Eyes's woman broke his nose, clubbed him unconscious, and left him trussed up like a white man's hog. The story has been told in hundreds of lodges by now, all up and down the Powder River Basin. News like that sweeps across the plains faster than a roaring prairie fire. Our friends the Sioux know of it as well, and laugh out loud at the big-talking, yellow-haired soldier chief."

What Strong Elk didn't tell Rachel was that the gossips also said that the spirited, red-haired *vehoka*, no bigger than a trembling-legged fawn, had ensnared the mighty buck elk. They jested that the heart of the great Cheyenne warrior wasn't so strong anymore. Everyone thought their play on his name was hilarious. It wouldn't be long before the sharp-eared little white girl understood the inane jokes that continued to circulate through Flying Hawk's band. The Elk sometimes wondered if he'd made a mistake in encouraging Rachel to learn his people's language. He would feel far more comfortable if she were kept permanently in the dark on this subject.

Rachel gave him a wan smile that never reached her doleful eyes. "Well, I guess if'n it comes to that, ain't nothin' worse than bein' made a fool of. It'd take the starch plumb out of Shelby's backbone, if'n he knew his enemies were all a-laughin' at him." She paused and stared down at her hands. Her voice was so low, he could barely hear the tortured words. "I can rightly understand your regrettin' ever havin' kissed me, Strong Elk. I don't much like bein' inside my own skin at the moment myself. Reckon the name of Mrs. Shelby Bruckenridge never sounded so downright disgustin'." She kicked her moccasined heels against Spotted Butterfly's flanks and took off at a gallop.

"Rachel!" he called after her. Holding Thunder Cloud on a tight rein, he watched her go. It was just as well she thought he was ashamed of his feelings for her. Now she would keep her distance, until the time when she could safely return to her home. And somehow, in the long, empty years to come, he would learn to live without her.

Chapter 11

66**I** thought you wanted to go hunting, Little Fawn.''

The low rumble of the words, though not their meaning, penetrated the thick fog of sleep that held Rachel in its comforting folds. She snuggled deeper beneath the covers, intent on ignoring the intrusion.

The intruder wasn't about to be ignored. He nudged her insistently. ''Come on, sleepyhead. Wake up.''

Sighing, Rachel rolled over onto her side and curled into a tight ball under the warm buffalo robe. She didn't want to let go of the marvelous sight and touch and smell of home. She'd been dreaming of springtime in Sugar Hollow. Gram was putting a bunch of cherry blossoms into a blue-and-white speckled pitcher on the kitchen table, while Gramps was stoking the fire in preparation for their morning meal of mush and sorghum. Rachel watched from the loft above them where she slept each night, looking down on the homey scene, just as she'd done since she was old enough to remember.

Through her sleepy haze, she gradually became aware of the speaker's presence beside her. He nudged her again with the toe of his moccasin. ''We'll be riding out shortly, Maheszoocess. If you want to chase the buffalo, you'd better wake up and get dressed, or we'll leave you behind.''

Rachel turned onto her back, blinked twice, and stared up at Strong Elk Heart. From her resting place on the willow mattress, he looked ten feet tall. She made no attempt to hide her blank surprise at his presence in Porcupine Quills's lodge. "Huntin'?" she asked, trying to make sense of what he'd just said.

For the last three days, she'd barely caught a glimpse of him. He'd been gone most of the daylight hours, tracking the buffalo herd with a party of hunters. When he came in at dusk each evening, he spent his time with others, never once seeking her out. He'd behaved that way for the past four weeks, but she no longer wondered why.

She knew the cause of his abrupt retreat after he'd kissed her in Flying Hawk's lodge with the three elderly women looking on. Lord above, she didn't blame him. The festering shame of what her so-called husband had done to Mysterious Dancer throbbed like a canker in Rachel's soul. The wonder was that the entire band didn't run her off like some rabid dog who'd wandered into their midst.

The Elk grinned down at her. "I want to see some more of that fancy shooting. I'd like to know if you can hit a moving target twice in a row, or if your success in bagging the pronghorn was merely luck."

Clad in only her chemise and drawers, Rachel clutched the robe to her chest and sat up. "You're takin' me huntin'?" She looked around the tipi in confusion. The first glimmerings of morning light streamed through the open entrance.

Porcupine Quills was already awake and dressed. With a smoother carved from the shoulder blade of a buffalo, she was flattening dyed quills to be used in ornamenting a new robe for a backrest. On the cooking fire, a small kettle of wild chokecherries simmered, their delicious fragrance filling the cozy lodge.

Strong Elk folded his arms and frowned in reproof, but his black eyes glinted with amusement. "How many times do I have to say it?" he rebuked. "Let's go hunting."

The snowy-haired medicine healer looked up from her work. Like them, she spoke in English, for Rachel had let Strong Elk in on their secret. "Ah, the Fawn is always slow to wake in the morning," Porcupine Quills advised the warrior. "The poor girl thrashes around in the middle of the night, whimpering and moaning in her sleep. By the time the sun rises, she's exhausted herself with her unhappy dreams."

Strong Elk immediately sank down on his haunches beside Rachel. He took her hand and ran his thumb gently across her knuckles. "What do you dream of, Rachel Rose, that disturbs your slumber?" he asked in a low voice filled with concern.

"Tell him of the visions you see in your sleep, *nixa*," her grandmother encouraged. "Don't be afraid to talk about the things that frighten you. The Dream Catcher has strong medicine and can explain what you don't understand."

"Jiminy criminy!" Rachel exploded. "We can jaw about that later! A body's dreamin' of Kentucky ain't nearly as important as goin' huntin'. Anyways, I'm plumb rested now." She jabbed a finger toward the entrance and gave Strong Elk a meaningful look. "If'n I'm goin' to get up and get goin', you'd better sashiate right on out of here, so's I can get dressed proper-like."

There was a long, pensive silence as he studied her intently, his thoughts hidden behind half-closed lids. Then he smiled and moved to his feet. "I'll be waiting outside the lodge. Hurry up, Little Fawn. Your spotted pony is all ready to go.''

When Rachel stepped out into the early morning sunshine, she found a party of men in the midst of preparations for the hunt. She'd quickly pulled on a clean shirt and pair of britches and grabbed the wide-brimmed hat she'd taken from Shelby. She hated the constant reminder of the villainous major, but Rachel reckoned if she didn't wear the dark blue cavalry hat, she'd come back with a blistering sunburn. Little by little, her pale skin had taken on a faint golden hue in the past few weeks. She knew from bitter experience, however, that too much exposure to the sun all at once would be disastrous.

Her black-and-white mare waited beside Thunder Cloud, snorting and sidling with nervous anticipation. Strong Elk stood by his stallion's side, checking the leather pouch that held his cartridges. When he heard her approach, he snatched a rifle from the dry grass at his feet and turned to greet her.

''Here,'' he said. ''Let's find out if you're as good with this decrepit old caplock as you claim.'' Holding the weapon by the stock and barrel, he tossed it to her. Rachel caught the gun deftly in both hands.

''You jest hold on to your socks,'' she retorted with a smug grin. ''Anyways, your moccasins. If'n I don't come back with at least one buffaler, I'll eat my hat.''

His gaze moved to survey the offensive headwear, and he arched one ebony brow. ''We'll cook that damn soldier's hat with some liver and tongue and serve it to you tonight as a Cheyenne delicacy.''

''Liver! Yuck!'' She grimaced in disgust. ''I purely hate liver.''

''You haven't tasted the liver of a fat buffalo cow roasted over hot coals.'' His teeth flashed white in a brash grin. "It'll make that tough leather go down all the easier."

A telltale smile flitted about Rachel's pursed lips. "Humph." She sniffed. "I ain't eatin' nothin' cooked with liver."

Strong Elk met her glowing eyes and knew he'd made the right decision. Since the afternoon he'd told her about Mysterious Dancer's scars, Rachel had rarely spoken to anyone except Porcupine Quills. The forlorn *vehoka* had seemed to pull into herself, a sad little figure in white boy's clothes moving silently about the village. As he'd watched her helping her grandmother with their chores from across the camp circle, he'd nearly forgotten his own resolutions. He longed to enfold her in his comforting arms and heal the pain that tortured her with soft, gentle words. Once he'd caught her looking covertly at Mysterious Dancer. The expression of guilt and regret on Rachel's sweet face tore at his insides like red-hot tongs.

Just then, Young Bear rode up on his sturdy hunting pony, interrupting the Elk's sober reflections. The Bear's dark brown eyes twinkled as he met his friend's serious gaze. "The Red Shields will give a feast tonight," he announced. "If the little Fawn brings down a buffalo, she will be expected to come to the celebration and take part in the dancing."

With a confident thrust of her chin, Rachel grasped the barrel in one hand and set the butt of the rifle on the ground. The tip of the gun rose nearly six inches above the top of her curly head. "You point the way," she said in Cheyenne, "and I will bring down a buffalo."

The Elk's heart stirred in captivation at her adorable accent. She drawled the soft syllables of their language with a charming, melodic laziness that made her words take twice as much time as anyone else's. He knew the entire band was fascinated by her speech, especially the children, who giggled in delight whenever she paused to talk with them.

"Boasting about what you are going to do can only lead down the path of humiliation," he chided, scarcely able to conceal the surge of happiness that washed over him at the sound of her deep little voice. *Eaaa,* he had missed her!

She raised her russet eyebrows and looked from one man to the other with an expression of ageless innocence. "That sounds like it must be an ancient Cheyenne proverb," she declared. Her smile was deceptively sweet. "We have a similar one in the Cumberlands."

"Which is?" he prodded.

"The biggest bullet does not always make the most noise."

He gave a sharp bark of laughter. "Is that suppose to mean me?"

She lifted her shoulders noncommittally. "We have another old mountain saying," she added, her eyes sparkling mischievously.

"Yes?"

"If the moccasin fits, wear it."

Strong Elk glanced at Young Bear, who sat on his pony watching Rachel with open admiration and wondering, no doubt, what the little white girl would dare to say next. The Cheyenne people prized an intrepid spirit in anyone, man or woman. "Such insolence in a female should be severely punished," the Elk told his fellow warrior with feigned gruffness.

Young Bear chortled at the reproachful tone. "Little Red Fawn would make a very difficult captive to keep against her will," he agreed. "But perhaps she will make a skillful hunter."

"I doubt that she will," the Elk replied and was rewarded by her gasp of indignation. He bent to cup her small foot, successfully hiding his grin behind the screen

of his long hair. "Come, *vehoka*. We do not want to
delay the others with your foolish chatter."

When Strong Elk tossed her up on the mare, however,
he was unable to keep his hand from drifting down her
trousered leg. That proved to be an enormous mistake.
The brief, casual contact sent a lightning bolt zigzagging
through him. "Damm it," he swore softly in English as
he turned to his own mount, aware that Rachel was staring at him as though he'd suddenly lost his mind.

All around them, the women and children gathered,
chanting the good-hunting songs and giving the warriors
trills of encouragement. Still wearing her deerhide cast,
Moon Shell limped across the trampled grass to reach up
and shyly touch Rachel's foot. "Be careful, Little
Fawn," she said with a worried look.

"There is no need to be concerned," Strong Elk assured the girl. "I will see that the little white woman
returns safely to our camp."

Astride Spotted Butterfly, Rachel spoke with unbounded self-confidence. "I will bring you back the
horns as a trophy, Moon Shell," she pledged.

"Do not make promises you cannot keep," the Elk
warned her with a teasing smile, no longer trying to hide
his mirth.

Holding a cupped hand to her mouth, Rachel leaned
down from her saddle and confided a loud secret to the
seven-year-old. "Pay no attention to the Elk's bellowing,
Moon Shell. He is worried that I will not leave any buffalo for him."

"If the little Fawn brings down more game than I do,
I will wear her ugly hat at the feast tonight," he told the
child. Her big brown eyes dancing with happiness to be
included in the grown-ups' silly game, Moon Shell covered her mouth with both hands and giggled ecstatically.

Strong Elk knew there was no chance of Rachel actually felling a buffalo with that antiquated relic she car-

ried. After each shot, the flintlock had to be filled with powder and the ball rammed down the long muzzle. Riding full gallop beside the herd, she'd never be able to reload and handle her horse at the same time. Rachel would only get off one shot. And he couldn't imagine her aim to be so accurate that she'd bring down a buffalo with her first and only bullet. But her obvious exhilaration made his own spirits soar. He intended to stay right at her side and experience the thrill of the first buffalo chase through her eyes.

The hunting party rode out of camp with Rachel and Strong Elk safely in the rear. He ignored the knowing glances of the other warriors, who refrained from saying anything that would embarrass him in front of the clever *vehoka*. Everyone was well aware of how much of their difficult language she could now understand. Still, he knew they were smiling inside at his obvious tenderness for the lively redhead. He would take plenty of joshing when she was no longer within earshot.

A woman riding alongside the men was not unheard of among the Cheyenne. There had been courageous warrior women in the past who'd taken part in battles. Some had even counted coup on their enemies. However, such valiant women were few in number.

In taking Rachel with him, the Elk was giving up any chance of his own to bring down a buffalo. He would be too busy watching over her and seeing that she did not endanger the success of the hunt. But the herd was large. His grandfather, uncle, and two cousins, Sleeping Bull and Wolf Walking Fast, would get more than enough for their families in this first hunt. And there would be many more opportunities in the coming days for the Elk to provide his share of the winter provisions.

As they moved across the rolling plains, Rachel could see the beginning signs of buffalo in the long coarse grass. Pockets of water dotted the bottom lands ablaze with golden sunflowers. The water in the ponds was fresh and clear. Buffalo skulls lay whitening in the bright morning sunshine.

"Where'd all those little lakes come from?" she wondered aloud.

"They were formed over the past decades by the wallowing of the buffalo," Strong Elk explained. "The bones you see scattered across the ground are from a big hunting party that came through here last year."

Rachel turned her head and stared openly at the large warrior riding beside her. Except for his breechclout and moccasins, he was dang near naked as a jaybird. The downy feathers adorning his scalp lock stirred in the gentle breeze. The medicine bundle hanging around his neck from a rawhide string swung back and forth to the rhythm of his horse's gait. This morning, he wore an intricately beaded headband, along with two narrow side braids tied with sleek otter fur, to keep his long black hair from flying into his eyes at a crucial moment during the hunt. His massive chest and ridged abdomen were bare all the way down to his jutting hipbones, allowing her complete freedom to inspect the pattern of raised welts that crisscrossed his bronzed skin and the exotic elk tattoo.

By now, she was aware that some of the scars had been gained during the Medicine Lodge, when he'd undergone excruciating pain as proof of his courage and as a sacrifice to the Maker of Life. The lovely widow, Choke Cherry Blossom, had explained to Rachel that the Elk had taken part in the Cheyenne people's most sacred ceremony at the early age of fifteen. It was then that he'd also received his first vision.

Rachel swallowed convulsively at the thought of such agonizing torture. The idea of a man letting someone slit the skin of each breast twice, pass a wooden skewer through the cuts, and tie the skewers to a rope by which he would swing from a high pole seemed nigh unbelievable. She couldn't help but compare the fearless warrior beside her to Major Shelby Bruckenridge, whose mustachioed image had tormented her, waking and sleeping, for the last three days.

Strong Elk was supposed to be a heathen savage. Yet even when he'd been madder than a gut-shot painter, so angry he could scarcely talk, he'd done no more than hold her firmly in place in front of him to prove his greater strength. It'd been mighty galling at the time to admit just how puny she was in comparison, but she knew the cause of his wrath had been fear for her safety. The Elk had told her on the day she'd won the foot ball game that he would protect her with his life. Sure as a goose goes barefoot, he'd spoken no more than the point-blank truth.

Shelby Bruckenridge, on the other hand, was a graduate of West Point and supposedly an officer and a gentleman. Rachel's father would never have consented to the marriage if he hadn't believed that. When the major had punched her in the belly on their wedding night because he wanted his own selfish way, she'd figured he was just plain trifling and ornery. She allowed right then and there as how she could never live with the scurvy varmint for the rest of her life. Since then, he'd shown himself to be a merciless butcher who'd kill and maim defenseless women and children without nigh a moment's hesitation.

Every time she looked at Mysterious Dancer, she was reminded of Bruckenridge's low-down, rotten nastiness, and it plumb near broke her spirit to think she carried his name. When she'd learned that he'd purposely mally-hacked a beautiful young woman for doing no more than trying to protect her honor, Rachel had finally realized the full extent of his wickedness. The pretty-faced major was mean enough to bite himself.

Her grandpa had warned her that not everyone in

God's great big world was as peaceable-like as her home-folk in the Cumberlands. Many a contentious fellow from down on the flatlands was bad from the inside out.

If'n a body is born jest naturally destructious, Gramps had said, *you ain't never goin' to change him, Rosie, child. What's bred in the bone can't be beat out of the flesh.*

Rachel reckoned that Shelby Bruckenridge was the most hatefulest creature the Almighty had ever allowed to walk on this earth. And until she got the marriage lines between them erased, she'd never know a single, solitary moment of peace.

With a determined effort, Rachel set her brooding thoughts aside. She was going on her first buffalo hunt, and she wasn't about to let that blackguard's crimes ruin such a glorious day.

The excitement of the warriors was contagious as they talked among themselves of past hunts. Most of the men carried bows and arrows or tall, feathered lances. Some had the Springfields they'd taken from the dead soldiers at Clear Creek. And a few had muzzle-loading caplocks like Rachel's.

She suspected that Wolf Walking Fast had taken his Spencer carbine from the lifeless hands of a cavalry officer killed in the massacre near Fort Phil Kearny the previous winter. Since that first day, when the Elk's cousin had shown such bitter hatred toward Rachel simply because she was white, Wolf Walking Fast had paid her no more nevermind than he would a small child. She knew where his gaze constantly drifted and couldn't hardly blame him. Sweet Feather's quiet grace and feminine ways had ensnared more than one hand-some suitor. But the bonny young woman had eyes for only one man.

Rachel looked over at that man and knew for a fact that Sweet Feather wasn't the only female enthralled by the Elk's overwhelming masculinity. Rachel yearned to feel his arms around her once more, his firm lips pressing against hers. With a sigh, she directed her attention to the men riding ahead of them. "Can the warriors really kill a buffaler with jest their bow and arrows?" she queried in an attempt to school her wayward thoughts.

Strong Elk smiled at the vivacious redhead's foolish question. "The strongest hunters among us can bring down a buffalo with a single arrow, if the point enters at the right spot. The more powerful bowmen can send one straight through the animal to land in the grass on the other side. Such men carry bows that few others can bend."

She squinted at him thoughtfully. "Would you learn me how to shoot with a bow and arrow someday?"

The Elk chuckled, the sound of his amusement rumbling deep in his chest. "First I'd have to make a bow tiny enough for you to use, Little Fawn."

"Well, tarnation," she said huffily, "I ain't all that little! I guess if'n I can handle this here Kentucky rifle, I can sure enough handle a regular-sized bow."

His lips twitched, but he succeeded in keeping his tone steady and even. "Didn't anyone back in Sugar Hollow ever try to teach you how to curb that spitfire temper of yours?"

She glared at him. When she spoke, her husky drawl was steeped in sarcasm as she lingered over every word. "Ain't nobody never learned me nothin' I didn't want to be taught."

"Then let's hope you want to learn how to hunt the buffalo," Strong Elk quipped, "or we may come back with a couple of skinny jackrabbits instead."

He gazed into her expressive eyes, glittering now with vexation, and felt his heart turn upside down at the sight of such animated loveliness. He longed to reach out, haul her up in front of him, and kiss away the impertinence from those delectable pink lips. But the memory of how he'd lost control when he'd touched her before still rankled like a burr caught in his moccasin. He'd made the decision to leave the *vehoka* completely alone. If he didn't have the self-restraint to follow his own resolutions, he wasn't worthy to be called a Cheyenne warrior.

Strong Elk kicked his heels against Thunder Cloud's flanks, and the stallion leaped forward. Rachel's piebald mare followed right behind, just as the Elk knew she would. Moving together as a team, the two horses quickly caught up to the party of warriors.

At last, they saw the faint outline of buffalo far off in the distance. The riders splashed across a shallow ford and moved slowly northward along the east bank of Powder River, careful to stay upwind and well hidden behind any knolls or ridges they could find.

Restless, Rachel glanced over at Strong Elk and wrinkled her nose in exasperation. "Why in blue blazes are we goin' at this snail's pace?" she demanded to know. "It'll take us durn near all day jest to get within rifle range."

"Galloping wildly toward a herd would cause a stampede," he explained. "And that would be extremely dangerous. Once the herd was running, the chase would wear out our horses long before the buffalo tired."

Reluctantly, she nodded her acceptance. "Still, the urge to start tearin' after them is a mighty sore temptation," she admitted.

"Once we do begin the chase," he stated, "I want you to stay right beside me, well on the outskirts of the herd. From a distance, the ground looks flat, but don't be deceived. There are holes and ridges which can easily break a horse's leg. So don't push your mount recklessly. And above all, be careful."

"Don't you go a-worryin' none about me and my little piedy pony," she assured him. She leaned forward and patted the Butterfly's glossy neck. "We'll be jest as fine as frog's hair."

She wasn't bragging. Rachel was confident she could keep up with the others. She might not know anything at all about book learning or the wide world in general. But by the eternal, there were two things she did know how to do—ride and hunt. Gramps had been delighted at her keen aim and cool head in a shooting match. Even Papa, disappointed as he'd been with his oldest daughter's lack of schooling, had been mighty proud of her skill as a horsewoman. Garrett Robinson often said that his little Rosie could soar over Ashwood's highest fence rail and never lose her seat.

About a mile from the buffalo, the men dismounted. Until that time, their attitude had been free and easy. Now members of the Red Shields, the soldier society responsible for leading the hunt that day, took charge. Strong Elk's uncle, Big Pipe Man, was their war chief, and everyone looked to him for direction—even the gray-haired Flying Hawk, who was one of the entire Cheyenne nation's four Old Man Chiefs.

Rachel slid from Spotted Butterfly's back and went to stand beside Strong Elk. "Why's everybody suddenly so serious?" she asked in a near-whisper, aware that her presence kept him at the fringe of the gathering.

"From here on out, the hunters will be guided by strict rules which guarantee that no man will shoot at a buffalo too soon and ruin the chances for the whole band. For a warrior to ignore the orders of the headman in charge of the hunt would bring grave punishment down upon him."

"What would happen?"

"The Red Shields would most likely whip the offender with their quirts," he replied. "Then they'd take away every horse he owned and dismantle and destroy his tipi." The Elk looked up at the top of a knoll where Big

Pipe Man and Wolf Walking Fast were crouched down in the tall grass, peering out over the ridge.

"They wouldn't kill him, would they?"

Strong Elk's head snapped around at her words. He stared intently into her eyes as though searching for a hidden meaning to her question. "No," he answered sharply. "It is forbidden for one Cheyenne to kill another." Gazing once again at the crest of the hillock, he continued in a calmer tone. "The shame of spoiling the hunt would be penalty enough. Back in the village, people would look away when the culprit walked by. Very shortly, he would slip out of our camp and go to live with another band."

At that moment, Big Pipe Man hurried back down the steep slope and gave commands to the waiting men. They were divided into two groups, one of which was to move carefully around the grazing herd to the far side.

"It's time to check your rifle," the Elk told her quietly. All around them, the warriors were tending to their weapons and medicine bundles.

Rachel did as he instructed, inspecting her powder horn and shot pouch, as well as her musket. She patted the nervous Butterfly's nose in reassurance, then looked out at the multitude of huge, shaggy beasts, thicker than sorghum in January, and felt a thrill of heady anticipation.

As their group began to move out, leading the horses behind them, Strong Elk reached over and took hold of the painted mare's reins. "I mean it, Rachel, when I say that I don't want you to take any unnecessary chances. You'll have enough excitement today without bringing down a buffalo."

"Well, I hope to shout," she replied with a confident tilt of her chin. "I didn't come here jest to watch the fun."

"You'll do exactly as I say, or you won't go one step further. And I'll have your word on that."

"You got it," she immediately agreed.

"We're going to walk our horses until we are about three hundred yards from the buffalo," the Elk continued, as though they hadn't just butted heads one more time. "At my uncle's sign, we'll mount and ride directly toward the herd. The men on the far side will do the same. The buffalo will split and gradually begin to move away from us. By the time we're within two hundred feet, they'll break into a gallop. When they do, ride for all you're worth. Pick out a cow or an older calf and head for it. If you don't overtake it in less than six hundred yards, give up the chase." He paused and looked at her sternly. "Is that understood? Don't go breaking down your horse trying to chase the herd for miles. Buffalo have tremendous stamina and can outlast even our strongest hunting ponies, especially in rough terrain."

Before Rachel could answer, Young Bear Running came over to stand beside them. "Remember the danger, Little Red Fawn," he cautioned. "You will not be able to see the ground. If you hit a gopher hole, you could be thrown beneath the hooves of the buffalo."

"I will be careful," she promised in Cheyenne, running her reins back and forth between her restless fingers. Spotted Butterfly stamped and switched her long black tail, as anxious as her mistress to chase after their quarry.

"Stick to me as though your life depended upon it, little girl," Strong Elk told her with a frown. He stared at her through narrowed eyes, and for a moment she thought he was going to change his mind about letting her ride along. "I hope I haven't made a mistake," he added curtly, before he turned and led a prancing Thunder Cloud across the thick grass.

The hunters approached the grazing beasts on foot, taking advantage of the uneven landscape with its maze of deep ravines to hide their presence. Closer and closer they moved, until it seemed as if they were going to walk right into the milling throng.

Rachel could see several huge bulls on the nearer side. Their nostrils expanded, their heads came erect, and their tails cocked in the air as the men drew nearer. Their fiery eyes seemed to flash a warning to come no further. Then Big Pipe Man gave the signal. The party mounted and urged their horses into a gallop, while on the farther side, the rest of the hunters did the same.

In the lead, Wolf Walking Fast and Young Bear Running reached the herd first and fired their rifles. At the crack of their guns, all was confusion, a turmoil of horns and hooves and flying earth. The buffalo were thrown into a panic, trying to run over one another in their attempt to flee. The entire horde started to circle, gathering speed as it followed a lead cow that bolted north toward freedom.

Riding behind the others at Strong Elk's side, Rachel fought the temptation to urge Spotted Butterfly to race even faster. But she was well aware of the large warrior watching her closely, ready to grab her reins and bring her painted pony to a halt if she showed any signs of disobeying him.

Through the clouds of dust, the enormous brutes flew ahead of them. By the time Rachel and Strong Elk reached the herd, it was in full gallop. It split again and again in an effort to avoid its pursuers. Shrill whoops rang out over the deafening sound of a thousand pounding hooves and clattering horns. Rachel kicked the flanks of her mare and flew across the plains, Strong Elk keeping pace at her side.

It seemed impossible to pick out just one animal. Rachel didn't notice any single beast until she saw Strong Elk pointing toward a large cow. She knew he was yelling for her to shoot it. Recalling his instructions, she aimed slightly lower than the center of the shaggy body and just in back of the animal's humped shoulder to strike the vital organs. She was riding without saddle or stirrups, and the recoil of her long Kentucky rifle almost knocked her off the Butterfly's back. She couldn't hear the explosion of her flintlock over the thunder of the hooves on the hard ground, but she saw the buffalo falter and sink to its knees. Elated, Rachel tipped her head back, raised her gun skyward, and gave a wild, ululating Rebel yell. She looked over just in time to see Strong Elk bring down another and then another with his powerful Henry repeater. He dropped six of the massive beasts in less than a minute.

Before she could reload and follow after the disappearing herd, the Elk turned Thunder Cloud, heading Rachel off and bringing her pinto to a halt. "That's enough for one day," he called, grinning at her scowl of disappointment. "Now, don't be selfish, Rachel Rose," he instructed. "Let the others get their share of the game. When you're a little old lady, you can tell your great-grandchildren all about the day you hunted the buffalo. Though no one will ever believe you."

Rachel read the unqualified approval in his eyes, and a tingling glow spread through her. For four long, miserable weeks, he'd hardly spoken to her. He'd remained aloof and withdrawn, scarcely glancing her way. The aching loneliness she'd felt without his presence had been mighty near unbearable. Now she basked in his admiration, her chest swelling with pride.

"I told you I'd bring down a buffaler," she bragged with a cocky toss of her head. "Shucks, I ain't missed nary a shot since I was knee-high to a grasshopper. Why, I bested the whole kit an' caboodle of my McDougall cousins at target shootin' last county court day. Ain't nobody in Sugar Holler can lay claim to outdoin' me when it comes to handlin' a rifle."

At the mention of her kinfolk back in Kentucky, Strong Elk's pleased expression disappeared. "It's time we went back to the camp," he informed her in a clipped voice, his sharp features suddenly forbidding. He turned Thunder Cloud around and urged the big gray Appaloosa into a trot without so much as a backward glance.

Rachel quickly followed behind, wondering what in tarnation made the infernal man so prickly. One moment he was beaming at her with pride. The next he'd returned to his former hidebound self.

The Red Shields, who'd been in charge of the hunt, were going to hold a great feast that evening to celebrate its success. Sleeping Bull, the portly village crier, rode around the encampment, calling out that all were invited. Throughout the circle of lodges, groups of people brought armfuls of wood for the huge fire to be built in the center of camp.

Everyone in the band had worked hard during the day preparing the buffalo. The meat was cut in thin slices and hung on poles to dry in the sun. Later, part of the dried meat would be roasted and used for making pemmican. By early fall, enough food would be prepared and set aside to last through the long, hard winter.

Choke Cherry Blossom and her quiet friend, Sweet Feather, came to the medicine healer's tipi at dusk to encourage the *vehoka* to attend the celebration. "Come to the feast with us," the lovely young widow urged Rachel, once the four women were seated comfortably on the plush bearskins that covered the floor. "Everyone wants to see the little Fawn who brought down a mighty buffalo with her long-barreled gun."

"Yes, please come," Sweet Feather added in her soft, bashful way. Her almond eyes shone with sincere friendliness. "We will show you the steps of the dances. All you will need to do is stay beside us and follow our

movements. For someone who learned the difficult foot
ball game with such ease, it will be simple.''

Rachel knew what a fine, generous character the self-
less offer revealed. For though the Feather tried to hide
her feelings, keeping her gaze cast downward in the
maidenly way admired by the Cheyenne people, she was
plumb smitten with Strong Elk Heart. It was plain as
daylight that the besotted girl thought the tall, handsome
warrior had hung the moon and the stars.

''Thank you for offering to help,'' Rachel told them,
''but Grandmother has already taught me many of the
steps.'' The smile of gratitude she gave her elderly companion quickly faded as she continued. ''I cannot go to
the feast this evening. Not after I learned what the man
I wed did to Mysterious Dancer. People will not want
me there during the merrymaking. I will only remind
them of things they wish to forget.''

''You are wrong to feel that way, Little Fawn,'' said
the Blossom. ''We know that the yellow-haired soldier
chief mistreated you as well. No one blames you for his
evil ways. Each person is responsible for the bad deeds
he carries in his own heart.''

Rachel looked down at the halter she'd been braiding
from rawhide strips. ''Still, I do not think I should attend,'' she replied, fighting to keep the bleakness from
her voice.

Porcupine Quills waved her hand as though sweeping
aside all of her granddaughter's objections. ''We will go
to the feast and stay for the dancing,'' she announced
with an air of finality. ''You are a guest of our band,
Little Red Fawn, and will be welcomed by all. But right
now, I have a gift for you.''

''Another gift? You have given me too much already,
niscem,'' Rachel protested, glancing down at the silver
bracelets on her wrist.

She watched in fascination as Porcupine Quills with-

drew a garment from a large parfleche. When the medicine healer carefully unfolded the tanned skin, the
delicate scent of prairie primroses filled the small lodge.
The Cheyenne purely loved the perfumes of sweet-
smelling grasses, dried flowers, aromatic herbs, pine needles, and prairie sages. No important article of clothing
was ever packed away without being sprinkled with one
of them.

"Hesc!" Choke Cherry Blossom cried in astonishment. "It is truly beautiful." She leaned forward and
stroked her fingertips across the velvety doeskin with admiration.

"Look at the lovely beading," exclaimed Sweet
Feather, who bent forward to examine the design more
closely. "I have never seen finer work."

A lump rose in Rachel's throat as she stared at the
marvelous dress. Bright yellow and white beads, sewn in
an intricate pattern of geometric shapes on a background
of sky-blue beads, covered the shoulders of the creamy
garment. Long, narrow fringes adorned the seams of the
wide sleeves and the bottom of the skirt. "How did you
do it without my seeing you?" she asked in disbelief.

"I did not work on the garment," Porcupine Quills
answered with a sly smile. Her black eyes glittered joyfully at the success of her wonderful surprise. "Good
Robe Woman and Standing in Water made it for you,
my grandchild. We have been saving the dress for a special time. What could be better than the celebration of
the first hunt of the summer? Especially when you were
one of those brave and skillful enough to bring down a
buffalo."

Rachel went over to the tiny woman and knelt beside
her. Putting her arms around the frail shoulders, she
hugged Porcupine Quills close. She looked from her
adopted grandmother to the two serene, graceful women
who watched her with smiles of encouragement. Tears

blurred Rachel's vision. "How can you be so kind to me, when you know who I am married to?"

"What Major Yellow Eyes did has nothing to do with you, Little Fawn," the Blossom insisted. "You helped Porcupine Quills heal my daughter's injured ankle. And you tended all the sick and wounded who came to this lodge seeking relief from their suffering. We judge a woman by her own actions, not by the deeds of her husband. Especially when he is a man not worthy to call you his wife."

Sweet Feather reached over and shyly touched Rachel's hand. "You spread happiness wherever you go with your bright smile and cheerful ways, Maheszoocess. Although your skin is as pale as the cold winter moon, your warm summer heart is Cheyenne. You are one of us now. We love you as a sister."

Rachel fought the tide of emotions that welled up inside her. For how many heartbroken years had she yearned to be loved and accepted as a member of her father's family? A fleeting image of Lucinda's perfect features, screwed up in revulsion as she derided Rachel for her stupidity, brought back all the old feelings of hurt and rejection. The last thing she wanted now was to be known as that sour-faced girl's sister.

"I am so ashamed to have ever been called by the hateful name of Bruckenridge," she said hoarsely. "When I am back among my own people, my father will arrange to wipe out our marriage, so that it will be as if it never happened. But until then, I will have to live with this horrible stain on my life."

The white-haired woman seated beside her waggled a crooked finger under Rachel's nose. "As to that," she said with a cunning smile, "I have an idea."

Listening with growing wonder, the three younger females leaned forward to catch every word of Porcupine Quills's astonishing plan.

Chapter 12

That evening, just before dusk, Rachel went with Porcupine Quills to the feast being held in the center of the camp. They were joined by Sweet Feather and Choke Cherry Blossom, the two loveliest young women in Flying Hawk's band. A huge fire had been built, where the delicacies of buffalo tongue and liver, along with great hump ribs, were being roasted. Most of the people had already put aside their chores and gathered to gossip about the day's events. Children raced around the encampment, pretending to gallop after imaginary buffalo, while puppies barked at their heels. The sound of their carefree laughter rang out in the still, summer air.

"Do not be afraid, Little Red Fawn," the Blossom told Rachel with an encouraging smile as they started across the trampled grass. "We will stay right by your side the whole night long, if you need us."

"Yes," Sweet Feather agreed in her gentle way. She touched Rachel's elbow, her brown eyes filled with sympathy. "When the time comes, we will tell you exactly what to do."

"My granddaughter does not fear a thing," Porcupine Quills declared with absolute certainty. "Why should she? She will be the honored guest of the Red Shield society. I have already spoken to Big Pipe Man, and, as their headman, he has arranged it all.''

Astonished at her grandmother's craftiness, Rachel gave a low, appreciative whistle. "I wish I had half the courage you think I have, *niscem*," she said with a sheepish grin. "But I would rather wrestle a grizzly bear or swing a puma around by its tail than get up and dance in front of the entire village." While her three companions laughed as though she'd told a marvelous joke, Rachel's nervous gaze swept the gathering.

What would *he* think of her highjinks tonight?

Strong Elk looked up from his place on the buffalo robe between Flying Hawk and Young Bear Running to spy the four women walking toward them. At the first glimpse of Rachel, his heart staggered in his chest. He stared in speechless wonder. He'd never seen her attired in anything besides her frayed shirt and worn trousers. Never even imagined her any other way—except, of course, naked in his arms.

The picture of graceful femininity she portrayed caught him totally unprepared. Gone were the oversized boy's clothes. In their place, she wore an alluring Cheyenne dress of pale buff doeskin, the long tassels tied to its skirt swaying provocatively. Tiny bells sewn to the fringed hem tinkled with her every movement. A yellow-and-green headband that matched the sparkling beadwork on her costume was threaded through her coppery curls, while a wide, beaded belt of similar design cinched her slender waist. A quilled collar encircled her throat, and fine silver bracelets jangled on her dainty wrists.

Strong Elk couldn't take his eyes off her. His heart seemed to thump an accompanying beat to the charming, seductive rhythm of those tinkling brass bells.

The stubborn, impudent, brash-talking *vehoka* possessed the fragile loveliness of a wild prairie rose. A shy half-smile played about her pink lips, as though she felt self-conscious and a little awkward in the girl's clothing. It was hard to believe this was the same confident woman-child who, just that morning, had raced after the stampeding buffalo, riding and shooting with the courage and accuracy of a seasoned warrior.

The Cheyenne were tall, strong people. Except for the white-haired medicine woman, Rachel was the smallest adult in the camp. She resembled a big-eyed fawn as she sank down on the women's side of the great fire and looked about her in abashed curiosity.

"Do not be so impatient," Young Bear rebuked the Elk with a chuckle. "The dancing will not begin until after everyone eats their fill of hump ribs."

Dazed, Strong Elk looked down at the top of his friend's ornamented scalp lock. He hadn't even realized that he'd risen to his feet. "I find that I am no longer very hungry," he said distractedly, his eyes fastened, once again, on the little Fawn. But he rejoined his grandfather and the Bear, who sat cross-legged on the outspread robe. And when Standing in Water brought them each a wooden bowl filled with the succulent meat, he accepted it politely and attempted to make conversation with his companions while they ate.

After everyone had finished eating, the soldiers of the Red Shield society entertained their guests. Rachel watched in utter fascination as the grand display unfolded. Most of them wore only scarlet beaded breechclouts. Their upper bodies were painted—some all red, some white, and some striped red-and-white. Each warrior toted a large red shield decorated with a bunch of raven feathers. A buffalo tail dangled from the center of each.

Wearing headpieces made of shaggy buffalo skin with the horns attached, the Red Shield soldiers romped in the firelight. They imitated buffalo bulls, snorting, tossing their heads, pawing the earth, and butting one another, to the great enjoyment of all. Every so often, the dancers turned and charged the crowd. The children screamed with delight, pretending to be afraid. Laughing heartily at the Red Shields' antics, the fathers let their little ones climb into their laps and hug them tight. Rachel watched, purely spellbound, at the warm affection shown by those fierce warriors.

"Can I sit with you, Maheszoocess?" Moon Shell asked with a shy smile. The seven-year-old had been seated on the other side of Choke Cherry Blossom during the meal. While Rachel was watching the splendid jubilee, the girl had left her mother to come over and stand at her side.

"Yes, certainly," she answered, patting the spot beside her. Moon Shell immediately plopped down on the robe, and Rachel put her arm around the child's shoulders. Earlier, she'd presented her with the buffalo horns as she'd promised. "How is your ankle tonight?" Rachel questioned.

"It hurts a little," Moon Shell admitted. She gave a long, exhausted sigh as she tossed her thick brown braids back over her shoulders. "Porcupine Quills says the deer hide can come off soon. Will you stay with me when she cuts it away from my foot?"

"I will be there to help," Rachel promised. She placed a kiss on the worried youngster's forehead and gave her a heartening squeeze. "You were very brave when we put the hide on," she told the child. "I know you will be just as brave when we take it off."

Once the buffalo dance was over, Young Bear Running, who was a member of the Red Shields, stood in front of the fire and spoke of Little Fawn's feat that day, praising her valor and skill. Rachel ducked her head at all the unexpected attention, flushing with embarrassment when he told the listeners how she'd brought down a buffalo with only one bullet. Then the Bear presented her with a red shield scaled down to her size. From its center hung the tail of the huge animal she'd shot that morning.

"Go on, Little Fawn," Porcupine Quills urged when she hesitated to accept it. She poked Rachel in the ribs insistently. "Take the trophy, *nixa*. Show them what a courageous warrior woman my granddaughter is." The medicine healer looked around at the smiling faces, her head held high, her black eyes glittering with pride in the firelight.

Rachel rose to her feet and took the shield. She thanked the soldier society in halting Cheyenne, her voice trembling with emotion as she searched for the right words. When she was seated once more, she snuck a peek at the menfolk seated across the way. Strong Elk was watching her, his razor-edged features softened with the glow of approval and admiration. Her heart lurched at the sudden recollection of what she was going to do that evening. Surely he'd forgive her, then, for having married Shelby Bruckenridge.

Next, the Elk's barrel-chested cousin, Sleeping Bull, entertained the children with tales of talking rabbits and cunning chipmunks, making everyone laugh as he acted out the different parts. After that, the little ones were sent home to bed with their grandparents, while the young men and women got ready to dance.

Seated on the buffalo robe, Strong Elk had been scarcely aware of anyone but Rachel the entire evening. She'd laughed and talked with the other women, seemingly oblivious to his presence. Only once had she looked his way—when she'd been given the shield—and her brow had been creased in a worried frown. Now, as the drums, rattles, and flutes were starting, she looked over and met his gaze again, an expression of tense anticipation on her heart-shaped face.

The young people rose at the sound of the music and

formed two lines, males on one side, females on the other. Rachel stood between Choke Cherry Blossom and Sweet Feather, who were whispering directions to the nervous *vehoka*. From her place among the elderly women, Porcupine Quills sat watching her adopted granddaughter with a look of feverish excitement, and Strong Elk wondered what the cause of their obvious agitation could be.

At that moment, Young Bear Running jumped to his feet. "We had better hurry," he said to Strong Elk, "or they will start dancing without us."

"I am not going to dance tonight," Strong Elk stated, ignoring Young Bear's gape of astonishment. Seated on the Elk's other side, Flying Hawk turned his gray head to stare at his grandson as well. But Strong Elk knew if he joined the young people, he would end up dancing with Rachel. Once he started talking to her, he wouldn't be satisfied until he'd succeeded in enticing her away from the crowd to some secluded place, where he could wrap his robe around her slender form and taste her sweet lips. He wasn't sure he could withstand such an overwhelming temptation.

The Bear raised his brows in surprise at Strong Elk's announcement, then lifted his shoulders as though to dismiss his friend's stubbornness. "You can stay here with the old married men, if you wish," he said cheerfully, "but I am not going to let some other warrior dance with Choke Cherry Blossom."

Strong Elk and his grandfather watched in silence as Young Bear Running muscled his way into the men's line to stand directly in front of the Blossom, edging out two other braves by the simple measure of flexing his upper arms and swelling out his massive chest. Strong Elk's fierce younger cousin, Wolf Walking Fast, hurriedly took his place before the docile Sweet Feather. Thick Braided Hair, her dimples peeping out adorably, smiled a welcome to her husband, Sleeping Bull, who came to stand across from her.

Scowling ferociously, Strong Elk Heart watched in tense silence as a young brave favored Rachel with a bold smile and went to the empty spot in front of her. The Elk glared at the man, nearly choking on his spleen.

A handsome warrior of twenty-two winters, Beaver Claws possessed a head of shiny black hair that fell past his shoulders and had dark, piercing eyes, which he turned on the diminutive white woman with searing intensity.

"I am happy to see that someone is going to dance with Little Red Fawn," Flying Hawk commented gravely. "We would not want our guest to be insulted. It was good of Beaver Claws to think of her feelings."

"Everyone knows the boy is a puffed-up, perfumed dandy," the Elk said, making no attempt to hide his sneer. "He likes nothing better than to dress up in his war paint and finest clothes and ride around the camp circle on his favorite pony, trying to impress all the unmarried women."

"It is true many of them smile at him as he goes by," the Hawk acknowledged judiciously. "But the Beaver is a brave man in battle and has already counted coup. You cannot blame him for wanting to appear well-groomed and attractive to the young girls."

Strong Elk continued to glare at Beaver Claws. The arrogant fop was wearing a finely beaded shirt and fringed leggings, a necklace of beaver claws, and a single notched eagle feather in his scalp lock. At the sight of the lonely feather, the Elk snorted in disdain. "Surely, the only coup that braggart ever made has been greatly exaggerated. He was probably the third and last man to run up and touch a fallen enemy—or maybe it was merely a dead beaver he struck, and he did not know the difference." For the first time, the Elk noticed with disgust the sensuous curve of the fellow's lips. "*Eaaa!* I have never seen any man look so pretty."

This time, the Old Man Chief had the farseeing wisdom not to reply.

Strong Elk made a conscious effort to unclench his fists. He looked around the crowd and realized with shock that Beaver Claws wasn't the only bachelor watching the little Fawn with covetous eyes. Now that he looked closer, there were several married men, as well, gazing at her in speculation, no doubt sizing up the sprightly redhead for a possible second or third wife.

As the musicians and singers began a familiar song, the women started to move slowly forward in a long, swaying line toward the men. Each brave slipped behind the girl in front of him, put his arm through hers, and moved with her to the beat of the music. It was called the sweethearts' dance. Strong Elk watched through a scarlet haze of fury as Beaver Claws bent his head and spoke softly to Little Red Fawn. If the rash fool leaned any closer, his lips would be touching her ear.

The Elk folded his arms and grinned to himself with diabolical humor. Should that happen, he'd have the pleasure of breaking every bone in that strutting prairie cock's body.

The idea that another man might have the rash temerity to flirt with Rachel before his eyes had never occurred to Strong Elk. Everyone in the camp knew she belonged to him. He gritted his teeth as he was forced to admit to himself that she didn't exactly *belong* to him. She wasn't his captive. But in the tradition of his forefathers, she damn well could be. There was an old saying, often repeated with a sly smile by the Cheyenne warriors, that the blood of their enemies ran in their veins.

At that moment, Strong Elk made up his mind.

He was going to keep her.

Like his great-grandfathers before him, who'd raided

the villages of other tribes and made off with their prettiest young women, he was going to keep Rachel for his wife. And like the sobbing, frightened, nubile captives of old, she would eventually forget her lost family and homeland. She would bear his children and live to see their great-grandchildren playing around their lodge. Like the beautiful Shoshone prisoner who eventually became Porcupine Quills, one day, Rachel would be more Cheyenne than she was white.

At the thought of the little Fawn sleeping beside him on a soft, fur-covered mattress, Strong Elk's blood heated to a fever pitch. He forced himself to concentrate on the festivities, only to find that the music had ended and the dance was over.

The men and women returned to their original places, standing in two long lines and waiting expectantly for the next song, which should have been the one for the matchmaking dance. But the tempo of the drums suddenly changed to a much faster beat. To everyone's bewilderment, a small group of Red Shield soldiers gathered near the largest drum and began to sing the words for the throwaway dance. The crowd looked around expectantly, trying to see which man among them was about to rid himself of an unwanted wife.

Since the feast was being hosted by the Red Shields, they assumed that the unhappy husband belonged to that particular society. Yet no hint of gossip had surfaced during the day, which was extremely unusual under the circumstances. In their tight-knit community, serious quarreling between spouses was impossible to keep secret. So an irreparable rift rarely came out of the blue.

But it wasn't a Red Shield warrior who stepped into the center of the grassy dance floor. To the fascinated watchers' astonishment, the little red-haired white girl left the column of women and moved forward alone, her feet flying to the pounding rhythm of the drums. Holding a short stick in one hand, she moved with the grace of a swan in flight down the double row of dancers. Strong Elk watched her performance in awe. Porcupine Quills must have taught her the fast-moving steps, for she never faltered or missed a beat. When she reached the far side of the open area, she danced up to the largest of the drums. The five men who sat around it stopped and waited expectantly. Rachel gave the drum a resounding bang with her stick. The boom echoed throughout the encampment. Then she turned, raised the stick high over her head, and hurled it in the direction of the swaying women.

"I throw my husband, Major Shelby Bruckenridge, away," she cried out in near-perfect Cheyenne as it flew through the air. "Whoever catches this stick may have him!"

The unmarried girls shrieked with laughter as they dodged and scattered in a frenzied effort to avoid being struck by the flying missile. No woman wanted the stick to touch her, knowing she would be teased unmercifully by all the others that she had tried to catch it, and that the yellow-haired white man now belonged to her. Their teasing would be only in fun, but who among them wanted to be the butt of such raillery when the man named was the infamous Major Yellow Eyes?

All the older spectators, who'd sat visiting with one another while they watched the young people enjoying themselves, rose to their feet, roaring with glee. In their lifetime, no one could remember a woman ever having thrown her spouse away to the drum. This was something done only by men. It was a wonderful joke on the pony soldier chief, and they loved it. But it was more than merely a jest. For in their eyes, the little Fawn was absolutely and irrevocably freed from her marriage. She'd just obtained a Cheyenne divorce.

Strong Elk watched, enthralled by her loveliness. In

the light of the flames, Rachel's piquant face glowed with joy and a sense of deliverance. The guilt that she'd carried on her shoulders since Clear Creek had been miraculously lifted away. She hopped up and down in excitement, unable to stand still for a moment. Tears rolled down her cheeks. She was laughing and crying at the same time. Surrounded by the chattering women, who embraced her like sisters, she nearly disappeared from his view.

Unaware of his own movements, he started to cross the open space to the women's side. Before he could reach her, the music and the words changed once again. The dancers returned to their former places with smiles of anticipation. Each girl was given a buffalo robe. At a signal by the leader of the dances, the young women moved slowly forward to the sound of the flutes and the beat of the drums, holding the robes in their outstretched arms. Strong Elk quickly stepped into the line of men to stand at Young Bear's side.

The Bear flashed him a wide grin. "I thought you were not going to join us tonight," he jibed. "Do you really think one of those lovely young girls over there will try to capture a big, lusty elk?"

"Do not worry about me," Strong Elk replied. "Worry, instead, about your own futile attempts to court Choke Cherry Blossom. Maybe that tenderhearted woman will take pity on such a great, lumbering oaf of a bear and choose you for a dance before she leaves the fireside wrapped in her sweetheart's blanket."

Ignoring his friend's honk of laughter, Strong Elk waited impatiently for Rachel to come to him. He knew he'd never be able to stand by calmly and watch her approach any other man, yet it would do him no good to crowd into the space directly in front of her. In this dance, the women chose their partners. Rachel was free to select any warrior that she wished along the entire row of males. Good manners dictated that the brave thus chosen would be a willing partner. They also ensured that the Elk—much as he might want to—couldn't shove the man aside and insist that, for the rest of her life, the enchanting *vehoka* was going to dance only with him.

Rachel smiled at Strong Elk as she drew near, happiness shining in her splendid green eyes. When she was directly in front of him, she stood on tiptoe, stretched her arms as high as she could, and tried to throw the buffalo robe over his shoulders. He was too tall for her to reach above his head. Rather than bend down, he lifted her up, his gaze riveted on her lips. Laughter bubbled up inside her like the sound of a clear, rushing brook as she draped the quilled robe across his shoulders.

"Don't you dare," she warned with a low chuckle, speaking the words in English. "I know what you're thinkin' of doin'."

"What?" he growled softly.

"You put me down," she insisted, refusing to answer his taunting question. "This ain't the way this here dance goes, and I reckon you durn well know it."

Strong Elk set her on her feet. Holding the edges of the buffalo robe in her hands, Rachel danced backward to the women's side, leading the warrior caught in her snare. "Now I have taken you prisoner," she teased, repeating the Cheyenne words of the singers. "And who will set you free?"

All around them, the young men captured in the buffalo robes followed their partners to the other side of the dance area, where a sister or other female member of the warrior's family would present the young huntress with a piece of jewelry or some other trinket, thereby setting the captive free.

"I have no sisters," Strong Elk warned Rachel with a complacent grin. "And my grandfather's wives are too old to skip across the dance floor to free me." He took the robe clutched in her fingers and wrapped it completely around her, enclosing the two of them in a snug cocoon.

The *vehoka* looked up to meet his gaze, her eyes bright with an impudent naughtiness. "Then I'll jest have to keep you for myself, Strong Elk—little as I reckon you're worth—till your kinfolk decide to fetch up a ransom."

At that moment, Thick Braided Hair appeared at their side. With an infectious trill of laughter, Sleeping Bull's wife held out her plump hand. On her open palm rested a pair of silver hoops.

Rachel's mouth opened in astonishment at the sight. "Oh, no!" she cried in Cheyenne. "I cannot take your precious earrings."

"But you must accept them, Little Fawn," insisted the Elk's cousin. Her dark eyes sparkled merrily. "They are not my earrings. They are a gift from Standing in Water and Good Robe Woman." She shook her head in the white man's way. "It would be very bad manners for you to refuse."

Strong Elk brought Rachel even closer, taking advantage of the cozy shelter offered by the large robe. "She's right," the Elk whispered in her ear. "Even though I'd rather not be rescued at all, you must take the gift. Both of my grandmothers would be gravely offended if you refused."

With a laugh of surrender, Rachel turned beneath the quilled covering to face Thick Braided Hair. She reached out and accepted the jewelry. "But I cannot wear them," she reminded the smiling woman. She tipped her head to expose one smooth earlobe. "I don't have any holes in my ears."

"Tomorrow, we will pierce them, Maheszoocess," Thick Braided Hair promised before turning to leave. "You will look beautiful wearing the silver hoops."

Rachel tried to concentrate on the young mother's words. But Strong Elk took advantage of the haven the robe provided, wrapped his arms around her tightly, and pulled her back against his hard form. She could feel his lips brush the top of her head. "That . . . that would be wonderful," she gasped as the air left her lungs in a whoosh.

For over a month, Strong Elk had barely given her a good-morning howdy. But by the eternal, he was certainly making up for lost time tonight! There was only one answer to such a lightning turnabout in his feelings. It was as plain as tail feathers on a turkey. Now that she'd freed herself from Shelby Bruckenridge, the Elk wasn't ashamed to be seen with her.

Rachel's heart essayed a dizzying twirl at the realization of what that meant for the future. She looked back over her shoulder at him. "I reckon we'd better be gettin' back to the frolicatin'," she said. "The next one should be the buffaler-bull dance. Porcupine Quills taught me all the movements. I haven't had a chance to practice tyin' up the hem of my dress, stoopin' down, and pretendin' to be a gallopin' buffaler, but I'll dang sure give it my best."

"They won't begin right away," he said, still holding her snuggled against him. "Everyone will take a rest and get a drink of water first. Let's walk down to the riverbank, where it's cooler."

Rachel hesitated, uncertain what to do. She knew from past experience it'd be nigh impossible to break away, if he hadn't the notion of letting her go. He could hold her pinned to his side as easily as most folks kept a ladybug imprisoned in their closed fists. "Shoot, I don't rightly know," she pondered. "No one told me if'n it's mannersome to leave the doin's with a feller or not. Maybe I should ask my grandmother first."

"Oh, it's perfectly good manners," Strong Elk assured

her. His voice sounded unusually deep and husky. "You don't have to say anything to anyone. We won't stay away long. No one will even realize we're gone."

Rachel raised her eyebrows at *that* bodacious mouthful of bunkum. Seemed like everybody in the village minded everyone else's business, as far as she could see. She reckoned no one had ever told them they ought to kill their own snakes first.

"Well, I don't allow as how it could hurt . . ." she said uneasily.

"Come on," he coaxed. He took the robe from their shoulders and folded it over his arm. Then he moved to her side, slipped his other arm around her waist, and hauled her up against him. "I promise, I'll bring you back the minute you want to return."

Short of hollering for help, Rachel really didn't have much choice. Strong Elk had the strength of two grizzlies once he made up his mind. Fact was, he was moving her away from the milling dancers with each word he spoke. He was right about one thing, though. It'd be a whole lot cooler down by the water.

As they left the camp circle, Rachel glanced back with a worried frown. Porcupine Quills stood in the glow of the firelight, watching them with a little catlike smile. When the medicine healer didn't call out for the pair to stop, Rachel guessed it was all fitting and proper-like.

"Let's hurry," she said to the determined warrior beside her. "I surely wouldn't want to miss the last sashay round the fire this evenin'."

Chapter 13

Rather than going directly to the riverbank, where several other couples stood wrapped in their blankets and talking in the moonlight, Strong Elk headed in the direction of a dense stand of willows. "Let's go to a spot that's not so crowded," he suggested in an offhand manner. "I want to talk to you where we won't be interrupted."

Rachel nodded in unquestioning acceptance. "I guess you were mighty surprised at my fancy caperin' tonight," she said with a happy little skip beside him.

"Very," he agreed, his mind racing ahead to the privacy offered by the trees. "I had no idea you were such a good dancer. Your grandmother did a fine job. You didn't miss a step."

Rachel giggled irrepressibly. "You ain't never goin' to call me Mrs. Bruckenridge again, I reckon."

"Never," he promised.

She allowed him to guide her with complete faith, not for a moment suspecting his intent. Why should she? For four torturous weeks, he'd held himself on a relentlessly tight rein, never once giving a hint of the sexual tension coiled inside him. For all the lighthearted redhead knew, he hadn't spared her a moment's thought since the day she'd returned to their camp with the pronghorn. The same day they'd kissed in Flying Hawk's tipi.

A twinge of guilt raked his conscience at her heedless innocence.

But his goal was fixed.

He planned to seduce her as quickly as possible, fully aware that, according to the white man's laws, once he'd taken her virginity, she'd no longer be able to get a dissolution of her marriage with Shelby Bruckenridge. In Strong Elk's mind—and the mind of every other Cheyenne—Rachel was free to wed whomever she wished. But according to the beliefs of her people, the vows she'd made so foolishly last spring still held her bound to that merciless bastard. Once an annulment was out of the question, her hopes of ever returning to Kentucky and being legally freed from Shelby were doomed.

And the sooner Rachel gave up all thought of going back to Sugar Hollow, the sooner she'd accept the fact that she was going to remain at Strong Elk's side for the rest of their lives. Hadn't the Powers revealed her destiny to him long before they'd ever met? Even her own grandmother had envisioned her out on the plains, running away from an unknown enemy—an enemy who could only be the yellow-haired major. The Elk knew, beyond a doubt, that Rachel Rose Robinson was the white-tailed fawn of his dreams. She belonged to him. Maheo had sent her to be his wife and the mother of his children.

When they reached the grove of river willows and wild plums, Strong Elk dropped the buffalo robe on the brown summer grass. The circle of drooping branches and shrubbery that surrounded them created a rustling screen in the balmy night breeze. Only the steady chirp of katydids and the occasional splash of a sandhill crane, as it waded through the cattails by the water's edge, disturbed the silence.

Leaning against the trunk of a large willow tree, the Elk widened his stance and drew Rachel between his thighs. The soft doeskin of her skirt grazed his bare legs, and his groin muscles tightened rapaciously. The ache he'd endured all evening long, as he'd watched her laugh and talk with the other women, pulsated through him now like an escalating war chant. Without saying a word, he bent his head and brushed her lips with his.

"Whoa, now!" she cried softly. She braced her forearms on his chest and leaned back against his supporting arm. "I thought you were a-wantin' to talk."

"We will," he said with quiet gravity. "Later."

In the shadows, he could barely make out her pale features, but his other senses were heightened by the darkness that enveloped them. He inhaled the scent of prairie primroses in her hair and listened with a lover's delight to the tinkling bells on her dress. He lifted her slowly upward, dragging her luscious female form along the length of his tautened male body. The feel of her unbelievable softness pressing against his hardened manhood sent the blood roaring through his veins. His voice was thick with desire as he murmured cajolingly, "First, Rachel Rose, I want to show you how proud I am of you."

He covered her dewy lips with his. When she immediately opened her mouth like a trusting baby bird, he thrust his tongue inside. She returned the kiss freely, making a faint sigh of contentment as she slid her arms around his neck. He realized with an inner smile that this time she wasn't yanking on his hair or screaming at the top of her lungs. This time she was snuggling closer, her high, firm breasts smashed against his naked chest.

Holding the back of her head in his palm, he plundered her incredible sweetness, prolonging the kiss with a fierce, dominating insistence, until her breathing grew ragged and her tongue tangled wildly with his. He could feel her heart pounding in an increasingly frantic rhythm.

Her unguarded response to the invitation of his lips was as spontaneous and natural as all her other actions. Unlike the pucker-faced white women who followed the horse soldiers, the little Fawn was open, candid, and impulsive. She welcomed his overtures with such carefree joy that he knew instinctively that she would be a generous and passionate lover. At the thought of their mating, the thrill of the hunter on first sighting his prey reverberated inside him.

Rachel broke the kiss to drag air into her suffocated lungs, then rubbed her cheek against Strong Elk's hard jaw. "Lord A'mighty," she panted as she struggled to catch her breath. "I ain't never felt like this afore! It's like to drive me insane."

For the past month, she'd pined for just a smile from his lips. She'd hoarded every glimpse of him like play-pretties in a child's treasure box. Her fingertips grazed the medicine bundle he always wore as she smoothed her palms across his scarred chest, over his shoulders and bulging upper arms. She was nigh starved for the feel of him.

His muscles flexed beneath her touch, and Rachel felt her own limbs tremble for no reason at all. An unfamiliar, urgent warmth spread through her body. She leaned against his unyielding frame, glorying in the feel of his sinewy arms around her. Just being alone with him tonight was like riding to heaven on a cloud.

He spanned her waist with his hands and lifted her higher. Taking his own sweet time, he nuzzled her breasts and gently nipped their pliant tips through the velvety doeskin. The pleasure he gave was so keen that Rachel couldn't help but whimper a mite when he set her on the ground once more.

"Mm," she purred encouragingly. "I reckon our jawin' can wait a spell, if'n you'd like. I ain't partial to cavortin' round like a buffaler, anyways.'' Without conscious thought of what she was doing, she brushed her lips across his chest and touched the leaping stag with the tip of her tongue.

''There's no need to hurry back,'' he concurred.

Strong Elk dropped to his knees on the grass before her and pressed his mouth to her alluring form. She was as slim and supple as the reeds that grew along the riverbank. *''Nihoatovaz,''* he whispered, keeping the words so low she couldn't hear him. ''Rosie, love, I want you.''

With one hand cupping her round little rump, he held her fast in front of him. He ran his palm down the enticing curve of her hip and thigh to her shapely ankle. Gradually, deliberately, he pushed the fringed hem of her long skirt upward. The jingle of the tiny brass bells filled their shadowed hideaway, and his heart sang to their bewitching music.

Strong Elk moved with exquisite care. He didn't want to startle her by giving away his intentions too soon, or she'd turn and dash for safety like the little red fawn of his dreams. For he intended to lay Rachel down on the thick buffalo robe beneath the concealing thicket of plums. To spread her legs and taste her intoxicating female body, till he heard her convulsive sobs of pleasure and felt her shudders of release as she cried out in ecstasy. When her pink folds were slick and moist from the warmth of his caresses, he was going to ease his thickened sex slowly and carefully inside her tight virgin's passage, penetrating her tender flesh deeper and deeper, until he'd made Rachel his—totally, completely, and forever.

Inching his hand up her bare calf, Strong Elk felt himself swell like the rutting bull elk. His fingers touched the unmistakable coolness of cotton—and he stopped dead.

''Maheszoocess,'' he admonished with a throaty

chuckle. "Cheyenne girls don't wear drawers under their dresses."

"I ain't Cheyenne."

"You will be."

Strong Elk didn't wait for her inevitable response to that brazen remark. His heart was a war club, hammering out the sure knowledge that tonight he would take her for the first time. No longer would he have to beat back the inescapable lust that had tormented him, waking and sleeping, since that wondrous afternoon she'd strolled into their camp.

He wasn't the least concerned about the unexpected garment. More than once, he'd peeled off a provocative tart's lingerie, a single layer at a time. He should have realized earlier, while he was watching the little Fawn dance in the fire's glow, that seventeen years of wearing undies couldn't be changed in one night.

"What a sight you would have made," he teased, "trying to imitate a galloping buffalo with your frilly white drawers showing beneath your skirt."

"I don't reckon that'd be nearly so indecent as allowin' you to put your hand under my dress," she retorted huffily. "Back home in Kentucky, you'd be a-gettin' your face slapped good and hard, jest about now. But like I said, I ain't Cheyenne, so's I don't rightly know what's considered fittin' and proper out here in the jillikens."

Despite her chiding tone, she caught his long side braids, wrapped them around her hands, and tugged gently. She bent and kissed his forehead, then lightly bit the bridge of his nose with her sharp little teeth as though to warn him that he'd best behave, if he knew what was good for him.

Strong Elk ignored the warning. His searching fingers grazed the lacy ruffle that encircled her knee. Heated blood crackled through his veins like a prairie fire, threatening to sweep away every last vestige of his self-restraint. He was burning with need.

"I'll show you what's fitting and proper," the Elk rasped. He found the narrow bands at her waist that held the two nearly separate pieces of the undergarment together and slipped his fingers inside the opening. The smoothness of her cool skin beneath his hot flesh nearly robbed him of his breath. He slid his palm across her flat stomach . . .

. . . and froze in shock as he touched the women's protective string.

"If you're not Cheyenne," he demanded with a low, rumbling growl of frustration, "what the hell are you doing wearing the *nihpihist*?"

"Porcupine Quills gave it to me the day your cousin threatened to ride me over the prairie," Rachel answered blithely. "*Niscem* said there wasn't nary a man in camp who'd dare to molest me, long as I was a-wearin' it."

"That was very good advice on her part," he admitted grudgingly. "And a far better idea than my returning your knife and gun." As he willed his racing pulse to slow its frenzied pace, he lightly traced her navel with his fingertips in an ever-widening circle. "But your grandmother wasn't thinking of me when she gave it to you," he informed the naive *vehoka*.

"Yeah, she was."

"What makes you so certain?"

"She mentioned your name point-blank."

The Elk gave a short, dry bark of laughter. "I'm going to wring that interfering old woman's neck," he muttered. He withdrew his hand from the garment and kneaded Rachel's adorable bottom through the cotton material. He couldn't go any further without her willing cooperation.

"You need to take the *nihpihist* off, Little Fawn," he

coaxed, his hoarse words raw with passion. "Nothing more can happen unless you do."

"That's exactly what *niscem* told me," she answered breathlessly.

The Elk sat back on his haunches and braced his hands on his thighs, trying to read her expression in the shadows. There was a long pause as each waited for the other to speak.

Rachel stood in front of the stunned, silent warrior with her head bowed and her hands clasped tight in front of her like a sinner about to witness at a prayer meeting. The smothering pain in her chest was nearly more than she could bear. If Strong Elk retreated behind his cold mask of indifference once more, her poor heart would surely break in two. A rising tide of despair threatened to engulf her. She needed his teasing smile, the warmth of his glance, the touch of his hand, or she'd dry up and shrivel away like a thrown-out old apple peel.

But she couldn't give Strong Elk what he asked for. Not if she ever wanted to go home again. She tried to pierce the darkness, to see his coal-black eyes and glean some clue to what he was thinking, knowing all along it was plumb useless to hope that he'd ever understand.

His words were strangely cool and unemotional when he spoke at last. "You have no intention of ever taking off the protective string, do you, Rachel?"

"No."

"Not until you're safely on your way back home. Is that right?"

"That's right."

Strong Elk remained perfectly still, comprehension exploding in his brain. Through the blaze of raging carnal need that consumed him, he could hear the blood pound in his ears. Damn! His plans had been thwarted by a crafty old crone, who'd probably watched them leave the camp circle knowing full well what he intended to do.

At that very moment, the tiny widow must be laughing herself silly at the mighty stag's foredoomed attempt at seduction.

Eaaa! He couldn't blame Porcupine Quills. She'd done exactly what any loving Cheyenne grandmother would do—she'd protected her virtuous granddaughter from being deflowered.

"It . . . it ain't that I'm a-wantin' to contrary you," Rachel said in a mournful tone. "And it purely ain't 'cause what I'm a-feelin' inside isn't finer than the flag on the Fourth of July. It's jest that when I get back to Lexington, I have to be . . . I've *got* to be . . ." Her words melted away in anguished mortification.

Strong Elk rose to his feet and placed his forefinger against her lips. "I know," he said with aching tenderness. He took a deep breath and exhaled it slowly. "You don't have to explain, Rachel Rose. I already know what you're trying to say."

Her deep little voice creaked with relief. "You do?"

He slid his hands behind her neck and pressed his lips to her worried brow, trying to ignore the fact that beneath his breechclout he was stiff with lust. No wonder that great, bugling bull elk in his dream lowered his antlers and charged every other male in sight. At that moment, Strong Elk Heart felt like ripping up the nearest tree by its roots and hurling it into the river. He smiled in spite of his agonizing frustration. "Every girl should have a grandmother like yours," he told her quietly.

"Yep, she's a pistol," Rachel agreed.

He lifted the robe from the ground and draped it over the *vehoka*'s slender shoulders. "The buffalo-bull dance will be starting any minute now. You'd better hurry, if you want to join them."

"Ain't you a-goin', too?"

He could hear her unspoken plea for understanding and wondered if she had any idea of the strength of will he was exercising at that moment. He doubted it—or she would have bolted for freedom long ago. "I think I'll stay here for a while," he said.

Rachel turned to leave. She pushed the curtain of fluttering willow branches aside, then stopped and looked back. "You ain't mad at me 'cause of this here *nihpihist*, are you?" Her voice quavered dolefully. "What I mean is . . . I hope we can still be friends . . . and all."

"No, Little Fawn, I'm not angry," he soothed. "Now go on and join the dancers. I'll talk to you tomorrow."

Strong Elk followed her a short way, watching until she was safely inside the circle of firelight. He returned to the river's edge and stared for a moment at the rippling, black current. As he looked up to the pale, summer moon in the star-studded sky, he swore long and fluently in both of the white men's tongues he knew so well. Then, with a groan of resignation, he dove into the water. Breechclout, moccasins, feathers, and all.

The next afternoon, Strong Elk heard two voices singing in English as he neared the river. One was a throaty contralto. The other, a child's clear soprano.

"Down in the valley, valley so low," the pair warbled together. *"Hang your head over, hear the wind blow."*

He smiled to himself at Rachel's accomplishment. During the past weeks, the injured Moon Shell, unable to keep up with the other boys and girls, had frequently sought out the cheerful *vehoka*'s company. He should have realized that Rachel would teach the eager seven-year-old some of her language. Exactly what kind of English the child was learning wasn't hard to guess. To any *veho*, the little Cheyenne girl would sound as if she'd been born and raised in the Cumberlands.

When he'd returned from the day's hunt, Choke Cherry Blossom had told Strong Elk he would find her daughter with the redheaded Fawn, picking wild plums.

Moving through the willow trees that grew along the bank, he discovered them resting on a plaid blanket spread on the grass. The two fruit gatherers were accompanied by Porcupine Quills, who sat listening to their song as she worked diligently on a new lodge cover. A basket piled high with ripe plums sat nearby.

"Look, Strong Elk Heart!" the child cried the moment he stepped from the cover of the trees. "My ankle is all better now!"

Rachel refused to look up. Seated cross-legged in front of Moon Shell, she cradled the girl's bare heel in her hands. The beautiful doeskin dress of the previous evening had been put away, and the stubborn *vehoka* wore her white boy's clothing once again. She blushed enchantingly as he laid the parfleche he carried on the ground and crouched down beside them.

"We took the cast off this morning," Rachel said in her lazy, drawling Cheyenne, keeping her attention focused on the child. "The wound has healed well."

Captivated, Strong Elk watched the sun's late afternoon rays dancing in Little Fawn's coppery curls. Her hair was longer now than when he'd first mistaken her for a boy, but it was still far shorter than anyone else's in the village. She wore the beaded collar Porcupine Quills had given her. Sometime that morning, while he was away, the young women had pierced her ears, just as Thick Braided Hair had promised. His grandmothers' silver hoops dangled enticingly from the *vehoka*'s small pink lobes.

"If the injury is completely healed, what are you doing now?" he asked, his gaze locked on Rachel's delicate profile. Her russet lashes fluttered at the sound of his voice, telling him she was well aware of his scrutiny.

"Little Red Fawn is putting her special potion on my foot," Moon Shell piped joyfully. "She says that before the first frost comes, I will be able to run and play games with the other children.''

Strong Elk couldn't conceal his surprise. ''Is this so?'' he asked the young white woman.

She nodded, not yet sparing him a glance, as she vigorously massaged the child's calf, ankle, and foot. It was clear from the Fawn's unusual reticence that her thoughts were on his bold ploy of the night before. Seeing her rosy cheeks, he had to fight to keep from grinning. She didn't know the half of what he'd had planned.

''The bone has knitted perfectly,'' Rachel said, ''thanks to *niscem*'s skill. But the muscles are stiff and sore from the deer hide cast. For the next few weeks, I will rub Moon Shell's ankle every day with a liniment made from wormwood sage. Porcupine Quills showed me how to prepare it.''

The Elk glanced across the pink-and-lavender blanket and met the snowy-haired widow's shrewd gaze. For a moment, they stared into each other's eyes. A smile of victory flitted across the elderly woman's features, only to be replaced by a reproving scowl. She'd obviously surmised what had happened in the sheltering thicket, though he was certain Rachel hadn't revealed a word of it.

Unrepentant, Strong Elk grinned in reply to Porcupine Quills's unspoken reproach. He knew, however, that he'd have to go far slower than he'd planned, courting the innocent *vehoka* in the age-old Cheyenne way. Although Rachel's grandmother may have won the first skirmish, he was far from vanquished. He would simply have to make certain that the little Fawn was safely wedded and bedded before Flying Hawk's band came into contact with any white man who might be willing to guide her home. And the sooner he and the strong-willed redhead were married, the better for everyone concerned.

He shifted his gaze back to the pair beside him. ''Por-

cupine Quills's medicine is very strong," he acknowledged gruffly.

"You ain't jest whistlin' Dixie on that one," Rachel
asserted beneath her breath in English, as she continued
her nursing.

"I liked your song," the Elk said, addressing the
brown-eyed child once more. "Will you sing it for me
sometime?"

"Yes," Moon Shell agreed happily. "Maheszoocess
taught me all the *veho* words. Her other grandmother
used to sing it to her when she was my age."

The child cocked her head like an inquisitive chicka-
dee as Strong Elk pulled the dreamcatcher out of his parfleche. When he placed a finger in front of his lips to
indicate that it was a surprise for the little Fawn, Moon
Shell's eyes sparkled with excitement. She was delighted
to be a part of the warrior's secret.

Rachel looked up and, seeing her patient's wide, gap-
toothed smile, turned her head to meet his eyes at last.
"I thought teaching her a song would make the time go
faster while her ankle was healing. I wanted to keep her
mind off the boredom of being an invalid." Her gaze
dropped to his hand. "What is that?" she asked curiously.

"A gift for you."

"For me? What is it?"

"It is a dreamcatcher!" Moon Shell announced with
a gurgle of laughter. "Strong Elk saw one in a vision."

"Take it, Little Red Fawn," he urged quietly. "I made
this especially for you."

"You made it for me?" Astonished, Rachel took the
strange object from Strong Elk's hand and lifted it up,
examining it in fascination.

Inside a hoop crafted from a willow branch and
wrapped with cream-colored buckskin was a webbing of
sinew nearly as fine as spiders' silk, with only a small

hole left in the very center. Caught here and there in the fragile net was a sprinkling of tiny shells. A cluster of bright yellow-and-black oriole feathers decorated one side of the hoop, while long buckskin tassels fell from the other. It was a fantastical, fairylike creation.

Rachel turned the dreamcatcher over in her hand, inspecting it from every side. "You made this for me?" she repeated in awe. She gave the Cheyenne woman's exclamation for surprise. "*Nakoe!* It is beautiful!"

"Long ago," Strong Elk explained, "before our ancestors moved out onto the plains to follow the buffalo, the Cheyenne lived along the shores of great lakes. They fished and gathered food to survive. Although our way of life changed with the coming of the horse and the bow and arrow, many of our stories go back to that time when we were a woodland people. One ancient legend tells of the Dream Catcher, a mystic warrior who could ensnare a person's bad dreams in his net and hold them, until they were destroyed by the first rays of the sun. Only good dreams could find their way through the maze of his net to become a part of the dreamer's life."

"Hang the dreamcatcher above the backrest of your mattress, *nixa*," Porcupine Quills directed. "You will no longer thrash around and cry out in your sleep, for you will have unhappy dreams no more."

Rachel stroked the silken feathers with her fingertips. "Thank you, Strong Elk," she said with a catch in her voice. "Now all my dreams of home will be happy ones."

Moon Shell leaned forward and patted Rachel's knee in a consoling gesture. "Strong Elk is called the Dream Catcher, too," she told her friend artlessly. "My mother says his power to understand visions is stronger than anyone's."

Rachel placed the dreamcatcher in Moon Shell's lap for the child to look at more closely. She was touched by the fierce warrior's thoughtfulness—especially after what had happened between them the night before. The idea that he would fashion something so fine and dainty just for her, something to remedy the constant ache of homesickness that fairly plagued her, brought tears to her eyes.

Strong Elk returned her trembling smile. "I brought you something else," he said. "Something I hope you will like just as much."

"Another gift?" Rachel was floored by this sudden display of generosity. Jumping Jehoshaphat! He'd avoided her for the entire past month. Now he was showering her with presents. What in tarnation was he going to do next?

"What else did you bring her?" Moon Shell demanded with girlish impatience. "May we see it, too, please?"

Rachel stared in horror as Strong Elk pulled his next surprise out of the parfleche. Speechless, she dragged her incredulous gaze from the book in his hand to his thick-lashed eyes. At the tenderness in their ebony depths, her heart seemed to tilt on its side and bang up and down her rib bones, *whackety-whack.*

"For me?" she croaked, hurriedly trying to cover her dismay with a smile of delight.

"Yes. I thought it would bring you some comfort to read the familiar words."

When Rachel didn't reach out to take the present, he placed it on the plaid before her. She wiped her hands on the knees of her britches and stared in holy terror at the red leather cover with its large gold lettering in words she couldn't decipher, nohow. Nary a blasted, blue-blazing, god-awful one of them. She raised her lids to find him watching her with the clear expectation that she'd read the name of the book out loud and make some grateful noises. Her heart, which had been rolling around in her chest like a pumpkin in a near-empty wheelbarrow, squeezed itself into a tight lead ball.

"I . . . I did not know you . . . you could read, Strong Elk," she stammered in awkward Cheyenne. "I . . . I knew you spoke many languages, but I never thought . . . about your reading them. Can you . . . can you read in French as well?"

He shrugged, clearly disappointed in her middling response to his precious offering. "Some."

Painfully, Rachel swallowed the lead ball that was lodged high in her throat. She purely hated admitting to anyone outside of Sugar Hollow that she couldn't read a lick. She'd endured enough flouts at the Wickland Institute for Females to last the rest of her natural-born days. The thought of telling the bravest, smartest, most handsomest man she'd ever met that she was plain ignorant when it come to book learning was downright unbearable. She turned her head, searching in panic for some means of escape, and met her grandmother's laughing eyes.

In a flash of inspiration, Rachel clutched at the nearest straw. The onliest straw. Porcupine Quills had once said that her white husband had taught her and their three little boys to speak English. Maybe, just maybe, that sainted Randall Tackett had also learned them how to read before he'd gone to his grave.

Rachel sprang up, hurried to where the widow sat on the far side of the McDougall plaid, and crouched down beside her. "Look, *niscem!*" she cried, thrusting the volume under her grandmother's nose. "A book! Is that not wonderful?"

Porcupine Quills laid down her awl and bone needle and took the leather tome in her aged hands. She nodded and smiled indulgently. Pointing to a row of gold letters stamped on the cover, she read out loud in English, "D-I-C-K-E-N-S." Her wrinkled face glowed with pride as she looked up and met Strong Elk's astonished eyes.

Relief flooding through her, Rachel leaned over the medicine woman's frail shoulder and placed her own fingertip on each shiny, golden mark. "D-I-C-K-E-N-S," she repeated, letter by letter. She glanced up to meet the Elk's gaze. "That sounds like a wonderful story! I know that I will enjoy it. *Niscem* and I can read it together when our chores are done this evening."

She grinned at him in exultation, all but bursting with happiness that she wouldn't have to admit her lack of schooling to a man who not only could declaim in several languages, but could read in at least two of them, as well. What a dunce he would have thought her!

As Strong Elk watched her take the book from Porcupine Quills's grasp and lay it carefully aside, Rachel held her breath, hoping against hope that he wouldn't ask her to read any more than the name of the story. Leastways, not right then and there. She immediately returned to her spot in front of Moon Shell and busied herself with the task of rubbing the child's stiffened ankle.

She would have her grandmother read part of the tale to her each evening by the firelight. When she saw Strong Elk the next day, she'd tell him how very much she was enjoying his gift. Which wouldn't exactly be a lie.

"Can I see it, too?" the little girl asked.

"Yes," Rachel replied, "but not now. First, we have to be sure to get all of this medicine worked into your sore muscles." She peeked at the warrior from the corner of her eye. Seated cross-legged on the tartan, he was studying her thoughtfully.

Please, Lord, don't let him ask, she prayed. *Don't let him ask me to read any more of that dang book than its name.*

He didn't.

He rose instead and turned to Porcupine Quills. "I have a haunch of venison for your lodge, Grandmother," he said with the stilted politeness of a county judge addressing the preacher's wife. "When you return from gathering plums, I will bring it to you."

The old woman beamed as though he'd just offered to fetch her a bag full of gold. "Thank you, my grandson, for your kindness. Please join us this evening and share our meal."

"I would not want to impose upon your goodness," he replied in a tone that said he'd purely love to come.

"Do not be foolish!" she admonished with a saucy wag of her gnarled finger. "You are always welcome in my tipi."

What in God's creation was going on? Rachel wondered. First a dreamcatcher as delicate as a spider's web, then a fancy book covered in red leather and stamped with gold. And now the two of them—who'd bickered and snapped at each other like two bad-tempered hounds trapped under the same porch in a rainstorm since the day she'd arrived—were behaving as though they'd just discovered they were kissing cousins on the spindle side. It was enough to give a body a bad case of the golly-wobbles.

If she lived to be a hundred and one, she'd never understand the Cheyenne people. Not never, nohow. And that was a fact.

Strong Elk watched the play of emotions on Rachel's lovely face. He realized that she'd listened to their formal exchange in complete bafflement, unaware of what had just taken place when she'd accepted his gifts and her grandmother had not insisted she return them immediately. He met the elderly widow's black eyes, shining now with merriment. The two of them were well aware of the sudden change in circumstances.

The courtship had begun.

Chapter 14

Fort Laramie
Wyoming Territory
September 1867

"**I** know it can work, General Sheridan. If we strike those bloody savages while they're holed up in their winter lairs, we'll catch them unprepared. We'll take the offensive and hit them right where it hurts."

Philip Henry Sheridan pushed his chair back from his desk and rose to his feet. He scowled as he strode past Lieutenant Colonel Shelby Bruckenridge and went to stand by the window. Rubbing his bearded chin thoughtfully, he looked across the parade ground, with its flag snapping high in the autumn breeze, to officers' row and the bustling sutler's store.

"You may be right, Colonel," he said. "You may be right. God knows, I'm sick to death of these wily redskins scalping and pillaging during the summer, then signing our treaties in the fall when it's to their advantage to be cooped up on agency land eating agency beef all winter. But those damn mealymouthed humanitarians in

239

the East have been mighty noisy lately. Some of them are still whining about Sand Creek, and that was three years ago.''

''With all due respect, General,'' said Shelby, ''may I suggest that the Indian commissioners sent out here from Washington, and all the other do-gooders making inflammatory speeches, know nothing of the true nature of these vicious, unpredictable creatures. The only way to treat the red man is the same way he treats us. Show him no mercy.''

Sheridan pulled a fat cigar out of his pocket, bit off the tip, and spat it through the open window. After striking a match on the sole of his boot, he lit the other end. He leaned one hand against the window sash and puffed in silence.

As commander of the Department of the West, Phil Sheridan had grown bored with his desk job and had decided to make a tour of inspection around the frontier posts. He turned to stare for a moment at Shelby in pensive contemplation, and his harsh features seemed to soften.

''Your father-in-law has demanded that every attempt be made to rescue his daughter,'' he said, not unkindly. ''As a candidate for the Senate in the coming elections, Judge Garrett Robinson has some very influential friends in Washington who have the ear of the president. I understand the judge's determination, and your own, Colonel, to track down and punish the band of hostile Cheyennes who took Rachel Bruckenridge captive. Your bravery in trailing the rascals deep into their hunting grounds was commendable. It was unfortunate that you were beaten back by overwhelming odds before you could free her. Still, I have grave doubts about your present proposal.''

Shelby stood taut and straight, determined not to give away the consuming rage that left him nearly speechless at the very mention of that redheaded little bitch. He clamped his lips together as he regained control of his virulent anger, then forced himself to speak in a tone of heartfelt grief. "I have every reason to believe that my wife is still with the cowardly butchers who kidnapped her, General."

The short, stout officer narrowed his eyes and peered at Shelby through a wreath of smoke. "You can't possibly think you're going to rescue her at the risk of an entire regiment of troopers," he said gruffly.

"My only motivation for a winter campaign would be to bring an end to the murdering of innocent whites, sir. Using the element of surprise, we can thrash these Cheyennes so severely they'll never take a white woman captive again. As for my wife, I have little hope of ever recovering Rachel alive."

Sheridan returned to his desk, where he braced his hands on the cluttered surface and stared down at an outspread map, the burning cigar clamped between his index and middle fingers. "I can't deny that your proposition has merit. But as it is, the army's spread far too thin. We have ninety-three forts to maintain on the frontier, all of them pitifully undermanned." The general moved his hand over the map in a sweeping gesture. "There are approximately three hundred thousand Indians scattered across the plains, at least half of them hostile at any given moment. Apache, Comanche, Sioux, and Cheyenne. In the past, the cavalry's policy of chasing small hit-and-run raiding parties over miles of open country has proven goddamn useless. Our grain-fed horses can't keep up with their tough little ponies. And our supply lines slow us down to a maddening crawl. Hell, our soldiers spend most of their time just trying to stay alive out here."

"That's exactly why my plan will work, sir," Shelby argued. He moved closer and pointed to the Powder River territory on the chart before them. "During the coldest months, the warring bands are forced to find shelter for their women and children. The terrible weather on the northern plains makes game and forage for their herds scarce, forcing them to conserve fuel and food supplies. If we take advantage of their temporary immobility and mount surprise attacks on their villages, we'll catch them off-guard. We can destroy their provisions and their lodges, wipe out the entire structure on which their primitive way of life depends." Shelby clenched his fist exultantly in front of him. "Victory is ours for the taking."

"And what about prisoners?" Sheridan questioned mildly. He straightened and flicked his ashes on the planked oak floor. "How could you possibly transport the captured women and children to an Indian agency in the middle of a blizzard?"

Shelby met the general's austere, uncompromising gaze with heightened resolve. He knew the man standing before him had systematically devastated the entire Shenandoah Valley, burning homes and barns, killing or driving off livestock. Sheridan had stripped one of the most fruitful regions of the South so bare that he could report to Washington, in truth, that even a crow flying over the place would have to take his supplies with him.

"When the Indians see the size of our cannon, General," Shelby stated tersely, "they won't expect to be allowed to surrender. Nor will we let them. There will be no prisoners."

"How long will it take you to train your men?"

"We'll be ready to move with the first snowfall. By that time, the wild tribes will have settled into their winter quarters, never suspecting the change in our tactics."

"And how do you propose to find their winter quarters?"

"I have three Crow scouts who know the Powder River Basin like the backs of their hands. They can track a mountain goat over sheer rock. For the sake of blood vengeance, they're willing to guide me all the way to the Yellowstone, if need be. We'll find the Cheyenne, General. And when we do, we'll teach those filthy murderers a lesson they'll never forget.''

"I'm going to let you try your plan, Colonel Bruckenridge,'' Sheridan said as he lowered himself into his chair once more. "I'll write the necessary orders in the morning, putting you in command of the Second Cavalry. You can draw whatever supplies you need from the quartermaster here at Laramie. We'll send you equipped for an entire winter's campaign. One that had better be successful.'' Sheridan waved his cigar in a careless gesture. "My belated congratulations on your promotion, Colonel. You're dismissed.''

"Thank you, sir. You won't be disappointed,'' Shelby promised. Grinning in triumph, he snapped a salute and turned to leave.

"Oh, one more thing, Colonel,'' the general called. "I want you to take Major Feehan with you on this campaign. He served under my command at Five Forks and won considerable distinction when we routed Lee from Richmond. The major shows great potential for leadership, but he needs more experience in Indian fighting.'' The bearded man's sudden smile dispelled his usual severity. "Terence's father and I were childhood friends back in Perry County, Ohio. I'm rather fond of the lad and have taken an interest in his career.''

"With all due respect, sir,'' Shelby blurted out, "Major Feehan and I were stationed together at Fort Phil Kearny. We don't exactly see eye to eye when it comes to dealing with savages.''

But Sheridan had already resumed his study of the map and didn't even bother to look up. "Nevertheless, he'll go as your second-in-command. That will be all, Colonel.''

* * *

Strong Elk was waiting for her again that morning. Rachel peeked up at the tall warrior from beneath her lowered lids, wondering if this time she could simply pretend not to see him.

Criminently, it'd been the same for the last six mornings in a row. Ever since he'd given her that confounded book. Each day at dawn, she went down to the river's edge to fetch fresh water—and found Strong Elk waiting for her on the way back, a blanket wrapped around his broad shoulders. This time he was leaning against a large cottonwood tree. He straightened the moment he saw her approach.

"Hello, Little Red Fawn," he said quietly. His shuttered gaze swept over her, taking in every detail of her tattered shirt and patched britches. He'd never mentioned the beautiful beaded dress since she'd packed it away in one of the parfleches Porcupine Quills had given her. But Rachel knew from that smoldering look in his sinful black eyes that he longed to see her wearing it again.

She tried to scoot past him with no more than a curt nod. "Hello yourself."

The Elk stepped squarely into her path, blocking her way. The timbre of his deep, masculine voice set her heart a-twanging like the strings on Cousin Lemuel's store-bought banjo. "Did you have a pleasant night's sleep?"

"Now that you mention it, I did," she told him with perfect candor. "That there dreamcatcher seems to be a-workin' jest fine, thank you kindly."

Her cagey attempt to edge around him failed. He merely moved closer, till her hip brushed against his, and the now-familiar shiver of excitement ricocheted through her innards. She knew what was coming next, and she ought to say something. She ought to tell him she was far too busy to dally here by the riverbank with the likes of him every morning.

But she didn't. She just watched in mute fascination as he opened his scarlet blanket with its wide white stripe. He drew her within the soft folds, raising it up till their heads were covered and they were standing freckled nose to bare chest. She knew that if she refused to stretch up on her toes and tip her head back to meet his gaze, he'd simply lift her up to eye level.

"Don't you never wear no clothes?" she snapped. She clutched the buffalo bladder filled with water to her breast, keeping it carefully wedged between their bodies.

"Certainly, I wear clothes," he replied, clearly unimpressed by her fractious temper. "If you'd look at me, instead of staring down at the waterskin in your hands, you'd know that I'm wearing a breechclout and moccasins. In the winter, when it's cold, I'll put on a shirt and leggings, too." The brilliance of his smile was enough to stop a body's heart from beating. "Why? Does my lack of garments bother you?"

"Humph." She sniffed. "It don't make no nevermind to me, if'n you want to run around half-naked all the time. It's jest that I don't allow as how we should be a-cuddlin' up like this every mornin'. I mean . . . bein' this close and all, I can't help but touch your bare skin."

The sun's early rays streamed through the blanket, casting a rosy glow over their heads and shoulders. Inside their cozy haven, the delicate perfume of wildflowers blended with the sharp, fresh tang of juniper. Bending over her, Strong Elk brushed his lips against Rachel's temple and stroked the inner curve of her ear with his tongue. "What's wrong with that?" he countered softly. "I enjoy having you touch my bare skin." He nudged the silver hoop that dangled from her earlobe out of his way and nibbled lightly on her silken neck. Then lowered his voice to a suggestive murmur. "I'd enjoy touching yours even more."

"Stop that!" she commanded. She jerked her head

away. "Whatever are people a-goin' to think when they see us a-standin' here under this blanket?"

"No one seems to think a thing about it," he pointed out with a complacent chuckle. "Not even your strict grandmother."

Rachel had to agree with that astonishing pronouncement. What's more, it happened all the time—and not just with the two of them.

"It purely amazes me," she muttered crossly, "how a grown man and woman can stand smack dab in the middle of the village, wrapped in a blanket and talkin', and no one pays them the least nevermind."

Strong Elk grinned at her belated display of righteousness. She'd seen couples doing it since the day she'd arrived and had never lodged a complaint until now. "A warrior can't take his sweetheart for a walk out on the prairie," he explained with infinite patience, knowing full well that Porcupine Quills had already told her about their customs. "It wouldn't be safe. If an enemy raiding party found them, he wouldn't be able to protect her and defend himself at the same time. So my people allow us the privacy of our courting blankets. That way young men and women can get to know each other. How else can a girl decide which brave she wants to wed?"

In spite of her previous intentions, Rachel stood on her tiptoes and, for the briefest of seconds, touched her lips to his left breast. Square on the nose of the great bull elk leaping over his heart. She sent the tall warrior a jaunty smile. "If'n that's the way it works," she jibed, "shouldn't I be a-cuddlin' with a few more menfolk?" At her teasing words, he gripped her so tightly, she had to gasp for breath.

"No."

He didn't bother to explain. He didn't need to. The first morning Strong Elk had stood waiting for her, Beaver Claws had tried to approach her as well. The Elk had

glared at the poor young brave with such fury, he'd
turned and left the scene without saying a word. Not
exactly fair play by Cheyenne standards, but from what
Rachel had gathered, her persistent suitor wasn't too worried about breaking the rules when it came to wooing
her.

"Well, you may have all day to lollygag around," she
stated with her nose in the air, "but I jest happen to be
busier than a bee in a tar barrel this mornin'. Porcupine
Quills is a-goin' to show me how to put a lodge linin'
together. So I'd best be a-gettin' on home."

Rachel held the water container tight against her
breastbone, for all the world like it was a cork bobbing
up and down in the middle of the ocean and she was a
drowning man. She was plumb terrified that if she set the
histai wittsts down, she'd throw her arms around Strong
Elk and start kissing him, just like she'd done the morning before.

Beneath the blanket's protective covering, he never
tried to touch her intimately—at least not in the scandalous way he had before he knew she was wearing the
nihpihist. But the Elk happily accepted all the caresses
she cared to hand out—whether such boldness on her
part was proper manners according to his people's courting customs or not. Considering how demure and shy
Sweet Feather was, Rachel had a hunch her own ramptious conduct was pretty brazen.

Still, the large warrior gladly let Rachel press herself
against him, till it was purely shameful the way she wriggled and squirmed, as though she couldn't get enough of
a good thing. Fact was, she'd come to realize that she
could trust Strong Elk completely—leastways, as long as
she wore the magical string that Porcupine Quills had
given her. But Rachel's own behavior was enough to
send the devil running for home. Old Mr. Satan must

have been stoking his hearth yesterday morning with a grin of gleeful anticipation.

Last night, just before falling asleep, Rachel had decided she'd been stirring up hellfire with a long spoon, and it'd be her own wicked fault if she got scorched, good and proper-like. She gulped as she recovered her faltering determination. "I need to be a-moseyin' on."

"Don't go just yet," Strong Elk urged. "Your grandmother was young once, too. She won't mind if you're a little late. Put the waterskin down and stay for a while."

"Nope, I ain't a-goin' to." Rachel shook her head adamantly. "Not anymore, Strong Elk. I can't be a-huggin' and a-kissin' you every mornin' like this. For one thing, it ain't fair to be a-leadin' you on, when I know for a fact that sooner or later I'll be a-leavin' for Kentucky. It'd be jest tormentin' us both for no good reason." She started to push away, but he wouldn't allow it.

"Stay," he whispered, his cool breath brushing against her temple and tickling her ear. His lips twitched suspiciously. "Don't worry about being unfair to me, little girl. I'm a big, brave, Cheyenne warrior. I can endure all the hugging and kissing you can torture me with, right up until the day you say good-bye."

She laughed at his outrageous remark. "Oh, I'm mighty sure you ain't a-goin' to cry uncle 'fore I do!"

Strong Elk bent and kissed her, a gentle, reassuring kiss. "You can trust me," he told the innocent womanchild, reading the sudden wariness in her enormous green eyes. He smoothed his chin along her delicate cheekbone and brushed her sweet-smelling skin with his open mouth. "I would never violate the *nihpihist*. You have my word on that, love."

"It ain't your behavin' I'm a-worryin' about," she confessed. "My addled brain tells me that I ought to take off a-runnin' for high ground the moment I spy you a-comin'. But when you put your arms round me like this, my feelin's get all mixed up, so's I don't rightly know if'n I'm startin' or stoppin'.''

He pressed his lips against the pulse in her throat. ''Listen to your heart beating, Rachel Rose. Put your fingers here and feel it pounding out a message anyone can understand. Even a stubborn, willful *vehoka* like you.''

Hesitantly, Rachel allowed him to pry one of her hands from the bulging water container and place it against the base of her neck. Beneath her fingertips, she could feel the throbbing beat of her heart. She shook her head in confusion, scarcely able to speak.

''No . . . I don't understand, Strong Elk,'' she said, her throat choked with sobs. ''The onliest thing I know for a fact is that I want to be able to go home to my kinfolk when the time comes. Now, please, I'm a-beggin' you kindly to let me go.''

Strong Elk released her and stepped back, the blanket slipping down past his shoulders. Tears blurred Rachel's vision, but she refused to change her mind. Refused even to meet his solemn gaze. Though it felt like her pitiful heart was being torn right in two, she turned with unwavering resolve and started to walk away.

''I can teach you to read,'' he uttered so softly that, for a moment or two, she didn't even realize what he'd said.

Rachel stopped in her tracks. *He knew.* That was why he'd never once asked how she liked the book. He'd known, from the afternoon he'd first given it to her, that she couldn't read a word of it.

For the past six evenings, Strong Elk had joined her and Porcupine Quills for their meal. Rachel had waited in agony for him to inquire if she was enjoying the story. She'd learned, to her crushing disheartenment, that Porcupine Quills couldn't read neither. Nary a line on the page. Randall Tackett had taught his family the names of the letters. That was all. Shucks, even Rachel knew most of their names.

During her two short weeks at the girls' school in Lexington, she'd managed to master the alphabet. But that hadn't helped one teensy bit. Once, in her papa's library, she'd pulled down a book, opened it to the first page, and named the letters softly to herself. L-A-W. She'd named them fast. She'd named them slow. 'Twarn't any use. None of it had made a tad of sense.

Rachel whirled and stared at Strong Elk, not daring to hope he had spoken the truth. His hatchet-sharp features were wiped clean of all emotion. He'd folded his striped blanket over his arm and was watching her with infuriating calm. She stepped closer, trying to detect a hint of laughter sparkling in his eyes.

"Do you jest reckon you can learn me," she demanded testily, "or do you know it for certain?"

"I can teach you to read," he replied. "I'm sure of it." Without further explanation, he turned and strode away, heading toward the river.

Rachel followed at his heels. "Prove it," she said to his broad back, not daring to believe he really could, but afraid he just might—by some happenstance misbobble—be able to do what he claimed. Sure as Old Coaley had a tail and it was forked, she wasn't about to lose her very last chance through her own muleheaded stubbornness.

She watched in bafflement as he laid the blanket aside, hunkered down on the sloping bank, and picked up a twig. In spite of her doubt, she stepped closer and stretched her neck to peer over his shoulder.

Papa had offered to teach her how to read several times after Gramps had died and she'd gone to live at Ashwood Hall. But she'd refused to even try, terrified that she would prove to be just as thickheaded as Eliza and Lucinda had foretold. She'd dared not risk failure and lose what little of Papa's approval she'd already earned.

Strong Elk drew the letter R in the soft dirt. "This says *rrr*," he told her matter-of-factly. "It sounds like a puma growling, '*Rrr, rrr, rrr.*' "

Rachel looked from the feathered scalp lock on Strong Elk's head to the moist ground in front of him, suspecting that he was trying to gammon her. Jiminy, criminy, she was in no mood for fritter-minded games.

"This says *A*."

"I already know that!" she snapped in wretched disappointment. She straightened, prepared to leave. "And it ain't never done me no good a-knowin' it afore."

He didn't seem to pay her any attention. Next, he wrote C-H. "These two together say '*chuh*,' like the great iron horse when it's puffing along the tracks." He glanced back at her and repeated, "*Chuh-chuh-chuh.*"

Rachel changed her mind about leaving. She might as well give him a tinker's chance. Hell's bells, he already knew she couldn't read. 'Twasn't no sense in trying to deny it. "I suppose that says '*eee, eee, eee,*' like the fifth little piggy a-squealin' all the way home," she said sulkily, as she pointed over his shoulder to the next letter.

"No, love," he answered, completely unmoved by her sarcasm. "In this particular word, that letter makes no sound at all."

She lifted her brows skeptically, but kept her tongue in her mouth on that one. No sense in getting him riled, till she found out if he could really learn her something useful.

He drew an L. "This one sounds like the steady hum of a steamboat engine pulling into a dock, *ulll.*"

Rachel crouched down next to him, wondering what in blue blazes he was going to say next. Strong Elk immediately put his arm around her and drew her closer. "Now watch," he said. "All you have to do is put the sounds together.'' He pointed to each letter as he spoke. *''Rrr-A-chuh-ulll.''*

Rachel lifted her hands in amazement as a bolt of wonder went through her. ''It says *Rachel*!'' she cried. ''That there word says my name!'' She pointed to each letter and made the sound he'd taught her. *''Rrr-A-chuh-ulll.* RACHEL!'' She tipped her head back and crowed with delight. ''I can read my name!'' She met his amused gaze, jubilation filling her. What would Papa think when she came back home and read to him right out loud? In front of Eliza and everybody! ''Is that all there is to it?'' she asked, incredulous.

Strong Elk lifted the excited *vehoka* to her feet. ''That's all,'' he said with an encouraging grin. ''You just learn the sound of each letter, or combination of letters, and put the sounds together like beads on a string.''

''Only sometimes they're silent?''

''Sometimes they're silent.''

''How many letters are there?'' she asked breathlessly, staring down at her name written in the riverbank's soft earth.

Slipping his arm about her slender waist, Strong Elk bent his head and nuzzled the side of her throat, just below the swaying earring. ''Twenty-six.''

''And the combinations?''

''I've never actually counted them,'' he admitted. At her sudden tensing, he quickly added, ''Not all that many.''

''How long do you think it will take?''

Her lithe form quivered with exhilaration, and he had to bite his inner lip to keep from laughing out loud at the overwhelming success of his stratagem. He caught her chin in his hand and turned her adorable face to his. ''That's exactly what I keep asking myself,'' he murmured against her lips.

Rachel drew back slightly and frowned in concern. Her

luminous eyes were shining with hope and doubt. She
clutched the brass bands that encircled his upper arms,
as though afraid he'd disappear from sight. "Will you
teach me to read, Strong Elk? Please, oh, please, say
you'll teach me to read!"

"Yes," he whispered, just before he kissed her with
all the passion and love he felt in his heart.

Flying Hawk's band of nomads moved steadily northward, following the wandering buffalo herd. Rachel had
no idea where they were. Only that Sugar Hollow was
miles and miles away. The days were starting to grow
shorter, the mornings and evenings crisp, although the
afternoon sun still warmed them as they traveled, dragging all their belongings behind them on the loaded travois.

Across the open grassland, blue and white asters, sil-
very lupine, and bright yellow-and-brown sunflowers
competed for the eye, along with goldenrod blooming in
great, billowing drifts. Enormous flocks of migrating
meadowlarks, snowy plovers and killdeers, curlews, and
pipits flew overhead, darkening the sky.

Early one morning, the air suddenly resounded with
the clarion cries of trumpeter swans winging their way
southward. Rachel watched from astride Spotted Butterfly and felt her heart leap with joy at the mere thought
of going along with them. The image of Papa and Ben
galloping across Ashwood's meadow on two sleek Kentucky Thoroughbreds brought tears to her eyes, and she
furtively wiped them away.

The next day, they spotted eight giant geese and five
smaller ones, flying in arrowhead formation across the
blue sky. Canadian geese, Strong Elk told her, coming
down from their summer in the Arctic, where they'd
raised their goslings, to spend the winter along the warm
shores of the Gulf of Mexico. He must have read in her

uplifted gaze the homesickness she'd been trying to hide, for he reached over and touched her hand in silent understanding.

Rachel met his magnificent almond-shaped eyes, filled at that moment with tender compassion, and a searing pain shot through her. For though the memories of home and kinfolk still beckoned, she could no longer imagine life without him.

What in God's name was she going to do?

"Choke Cherry Blossom told me that you visited Mysterious Dancer in her lodge yesterday," the Elk said quietly. A smile of sincere approval curved his lips. "That was very kind of you."

Rachel shrugged with embarrassment. " 'Twarn't no such thing," she denied. "I wanted to tell her, personal-like, jest how sorry I am about what Shelby done to her. I asked her to forgive me for havin' once borne the disgustin' title of Mrs. Bruckenridge."

"And you gave her the shield that the soldier society awarded you?"

"Yep," Rachel admitted bashfully. "I figured she had more right to it than me. It don't take no real bravery to shoot a buffaler. What takes gumption, and lots of it, is to keep on livin' when you'd rather be dead. And from the pain I'd seen in those big, sad eyes of hers, I figured that was exactly what Mysterious Dancer was thinkin'."

Strong Elk smoothed his knuckles across Rachel's cheek in a gesture so loving it brought tears to her eyes. "How did such a little thing like you grow up to be so wise?" he teased softly.

She heaved a sigh, shook her head, and peeped up at him from under her lashes. "Reckon it was that Cumberland Mountain upbringin'," she declared with an impudent grin.

* * *

That evening, they stood beneath the spreading branches of a large box elder, watching a pair of red-tailed hawks swoop over the grass in search of their prey. It was nearly dusk and growing colder as the shadows deepened. Very shortly, they would have to return to the safety and warmth of the circle of lodges nearby.

A Tale of Two Cities had been set aside. The two of them were enveloped in the sheltering folds of the Mc-Dougall plaid, both aware that the changing weather would soon make it impossible for them to continue their blanket courtship.

"We can't keep doin' this," she whispered hoarsely.

Strong Elk smiled and kissed her brow. "Yes, we can," he said. His dark eyes glinted with amusement. "It would be foolish for you to quit now. You're making excellent progress in learning to read."

"I wasn't talkin' about my readin'," she croaked, "and you dang well know it. I'm at my wits' end tryin' to figure out jest what to do."

"I told you before," he replied. "Listen to your heart, Rosie, love. We can stay wrapped in each other's arms like this for the rest of our lives."

But Rachel knew better.

Like a greedy little bear cub who squeezes his paw into a crack in the tree trunk to steal the honey and then finds he can't pull free without letting go of the treat, Rachel discovered herself caught in a trap of her own making. But instead of having to bat away a swarm of angry bees with one hand while stubbornly holding on to the sweet, sticky honeycomb with the other, she was busy fending off a determined warrior's single-minded seduction as she tried to study how to read. It was an impossible situation, and one that, little by little, she realized she wasn't going to win. What was worse, she was no longer sure she even wanted to.

For two whole weeks, her will had stood firm against

his. Strong Elk never once denied her continued requests for another lesson, and yet another. But somehow, the book learning always took place while they were snuggled together beneath his striped blanket or the lavender-and-pink tartan.

The Lord above knew, she didn't have to touch him. She didn't have to crowd closer and closer, till she ended up sitting in his lap with her arms around his neck, her open mouth pressed to his throat or her lips skimming across the hard flesh and bone of his shoulders. She didn't have to bury her fingers in Strong Elk's long black hair or wrap his narrow side braids around her wrists like satin fetters or run her hand down his heavily muscled thigh. She didn't have to do any of those things.

But she did.

Her intentions of being a scholar forgotten, Rachel had stroked him and hugged him and pressed her body against his much larger frame, till she was one pulsating mass of unrequited sexual longing.

Frowning down at the toes of her beaded moccasins, she shook her head in denial of all that she felt inside. "We can't be together for the rest of our lives," she grumbled, "and you dang well know it."

"Give me one good reason," he insisted.

Rachel looked up to meet his heavy-lidded gaze and forgot all her fine-sounding excuses. "Well, for one thing," she announced, grasping at a straw in the wind, "you're a way too tall. I get a crick in my neck jest talkin' to you."

He grinned like the devil himself. "That is a serious problem," he agreed with a muffled laugh. Before she knew what was happening, he'd lifted her up to stand on a nearby log. He arched one black eyebrow in inquiry. "How's this? Better?"

She leaned forward and traced the sensual line of his lips with the tip of one finger. "'Tain't half bad," she murmured, before tilting her head and adjusting her mouth to fit his.

The kiss turned wild as their tongues moved together in an ancient ritual of mating. Beneath the plaid's sheltering folds, Rachel threw her arms around him and smashed her aching breasts against his chest. The uncontrollable desire to feel his bare skin against hers swept through her, shattering all her resolutions. With trembling fingers, she unbuttoned her flannel shirt and slipped her arms out of the loose sleeves. She pushed the thin straps of her camisole over her shoulders, till the delicate garment fell to her waist.

"Ah, my sweet little rose," Strong Elk whispered. His gaze openly caressed her pale flesh, scorching her with its naked hunger. A low, agonized groan tore from his throat as he lifted her off the fallen log.

Rachel wrapped her trousered legs around his waist. He bent his head to suckle her, and the sleek otter fur that fastened his side braids brushed across her puckered nipples. A thrill of pure, unalloyed pleasure vibrated through her entire body.

"I'm burnin' with need," she said hoarsely. She pressed even closer, squeezing her legs tight around his body, rubbing herself against him shamelessly. "Oh, God, Strong Elk, I jest can't get enough of you. Wakin' and sleepin', it's plumb drivin' me crazy."

His voice was coaxing and deep. "Only your stubbornness is standing in our way, *zehemehotaz.*"

Impulsively, Rachel started to unbuckle her belt. "Swing me down," she said with a choked sob. "It's these britches that are standin' in the way right now."

But he didn't let her slide to her feet. Instead, he held her locked to his hard frame. "Marry me, Rachel Rose," he urged.

"Let's jest make love," she replied in agonized frustration. "We don't need to swap no promises 'bout forever."

He kissed her forehead, her eyelids, her chin. "Yes, we do," he contradicted.

Rachel braced her palms on his shoulders and leaned back to meet his eyes. The unswerving resolution she found there stunned her. "I thought you wanted me to take off this here *nihpihist*," she said, making no attempt to hide her disappointment.

Strong Elk smiled tenderly at the confusion and unhappiness mirrored in her grass-green eyes. Her cheeks were flushed with mortification at what she perceived as his rejection. "When you do take the protective string off, Little Fawn," he told her gently, "you'll be my wife."

The Elk wanted nothing more than to lay Rachel down on the plaid blanket and assuage the fever raging inside him. The last few weeks had been torture of the most exquisite kind. He ached with need for her. The longing to move his hands over the silken curves of her breasts and hips, to taste the honey of her intoxicating femininity, to probe her softly blossoming petals and feel her delicate tissues flutter in ever-deepening spasms around his swollen sex had seeped into the very marrow of his bones. He yearned to watch the enraptured expression on her face as he planted his seed deep inside her, binding them together in a living promise that could never be denied.

But he was determined to win not just her body, but her mind and her heart. He would no longer be satisfied merely to trap her into marriage by stealing her virginity, forcing her to wed him because of the white man's foolish laws. He wanted the enchanting *vehoka* to come to him freely, in the Cheyenne way.

Wordlessly, Rachel slumped against him. She cradled her face in the hollow at the base of his neck. "You know I can't make that promise," she said mournfully. "I can't give up the hope of someday goin' home.''

He rubbed his chin across her coppery curls, his voice rusty with passion. "One day you'll realize, Maheszo-ocess, that this is your home.''

She pushed her upper body away from his, tipped her head back, and searched the canopy of autumn leaves above them. "Where?'' she taunted, irony and frustration sharpening her words. "Here beneath this tree?''

He loosened his hold as though to drop her, and she clutched him in startled surprise. "Here,'' he said with a low growl. "Right here in my arms.''

Chapter 15

⟨~⟩◦◦⟨~⟩

For two days, Rachel never caught sight of Strong Elk. She was told by his kindly grandmothers that he was riding far ahead of the caravan. Elk and his cousin, Wolf Walking Fast, were scouting for a place where Flying Hawk's band could stay safely through the winter.

Rachel tried hard not to give in to the mullygrubs that had plagued her since their tryst under the McDougall plaid. They had returned to the village without nary a word between them. Only as they'd neared her grandmother's tipi had the Elk said, real quiet-like, that he wouldn't be seeing her the next day. He'd offered no further explanation. Stricken with fear and scarce able to breathe, Rachel watched him walk across the camp circle. A paralyzing dread that he wouldn't even bother to turn around, should she beg him to stay for a few minutes more, squeezed her throat, making it nigh impossible to call out.

For the first time since she'd hung the pretty dreamcatcher above her willow mattress, Rachel lay awake into the still, wee hours of the night, unable to get a smidgen of sleep. She went over and over in her mind everything they'd said beneath the falling leaves of the box elder tree.

Zehemehotaz, he had called her. *Thou, my beloved.*

She tried to picture him, once again, as he'd looked on that high bluff at Clear Creek, wearing the primitive eagle feathers and heathen paint, carrying his war shield decorated with grizzly bear claws, and holding the powerful repeating rifle he used with such deadly accuracy over his head in the sign of conquest. Never had she dreamed that the ferocious warrior she'd seen astride the rearing gray stallion would murmur the tenderest, wonderfulest, most sweetest endearment she'd ever heard in all her natural-born days.

Thou, my beloved. She hadn't even responded to his soft-spoken words. She'd been too afraid to admit her own feelings, lest he insist on her making a promise she knew dang well she couldn't keep. All that night, tears of pure misery had trickled down her cheeks at the thought of the love she had so stubbornly refused to accept. Lord A'mighty, it seemed like she'd been crying ever since.

Guided by the two scouts, the travelers arrived in a peaceful valley bordered on the west by the Rosebud Mountains. To the east, empty plains stretched for as far as the eye could see.

They reached Tongue River just in time. Gray, snow-filled clouds came scudding off the nearby mountaintops while the women hurriedly put the buffalo-skin coverings over their raised lodge poles. The temperature dropped steadily all day long, leaving Rachel shivering in her thin flannel shirt. By dusk, she'd wrapped the warm woolen tartan around her and hovered close to the cooking fire.

Strong Elk failed to come to Porcupine Quills's tipi for the second evening in a row. During the meal, Rachel tried to follow her grandmother's lively conversation, but her melancholy thoughts kept drifting away. She was wracked with a heap of self-doubt. She'd always considered honesty one of her strongest virtues. Sometimes her onliest virtue. Back home, she'd prided herself on saying what she meant and meaning what she said, in spite of her techeous stepmother's advice to the contrary. But for longer than she dared to admit, Rachel had been lying to Strong Elk. And, what was even worse, she'd been lying to herself.

The plain truth was, she loved him. Yep, she loved that great big aggravating hunk of humanity with all her heart and soul. It had taken these last two miserable days without him for the enormity of it to sink into her addle-pated brain. And as soon as supper dishes were done, she was going to take the lavender-and-pink tartan, sashay on over to Flying Hawk's tipi, and do a little blanket courting herself. She was going to wrap her arms around Strong Elk and tell him that she purely loved him. Just come right out and say it. She prayed to God that the wild, untamed Cheyenne warrior would lift her up to eye level, flash that devastating, heartbreaking grin of his, and tell her, for a fact, that he loved her, too.

As Rachel helped her grandmother clean the wooden bowls and horn spoons and store them in their parfleches, the faraway strains of a love flute wafted clearly through the dry, frigid air She tipped her head in beguilement at the first haunting notes, wondering what smitten young brave was going to play for his sweetheart that night. Coming ever closer, the sound rose and fell in plaintive seduction.

Holy Moses!

Rachel's mouth dropped open in blank surprise the instant she realized exactly what lovely, sentimental tune was being played on the Cheyenne flute. Why, a child could have knocked her over with a feather!

Rachel jumped to her feet and raced outside into the frosty night, the plaid blanket forgotten on the lodge floor. Spinning in a circle, she tried to detect which direction the music was coming from, then looked toward the cottonwoods that grew along the riverbank and smiled. Only moments ago, she'd been wallowing in the doldrums. Now her misery turned to laughter. Her heart sang like a jaybird a-trilling on a fence rail, soaring skyward right along with the wailing of the flute.

The lilting melody that floated across the meadow seemed to wrap itself around Rachel, warming her very soul. She pressed her palms to her cheeks and listened in wonder to the achingly familiar song. How had he ever managed to carve a flute that would play a mountain ditty? Porcupine Quills had told her that everything the Elk made was filled with magic. Dreamcatchers, peace pipes, and love flutes. Law, she hadn't believed nary a word of it, until now.

Suddenly, Rachel realized she wasn't the only one in the village who'd recognized the charming ballad. Moon Shell, clearly visible in the moonlight, slipped out of her mother's lodge and ran to the center of the camp. She cocked her head, first to one side and then the other, listening intently, then clapped her hands in childish glee. With the unrestrained enthusiasm of youth, she lifted her sweet, clear soprano to the piping strains of the flute.

"*If you don't love me,*" the seven-year-old sang in English, "*love whom you please. Throw your arms 'round me, give my heart ease.*"

Rachel's heart overflowed with joy. Tears streaming down her cheeks, she joined in, adding her foggy voice, choked with emotion, to the little girl's high, pure tones. Their words floated up into the brisk night air, carrying clearly to the warrior, who stood somewhere out there by the river's edge. "*Give my heart ease, love, give my heart ease. Throw your arms 'round me, give my heart ease.*"

The moment Strong Elk stepped from the shadows of the tall trees, Rachel raced toward him. She was vaguely aware that he was dressed in a fringed shirt and leggings, with the flute now tucked safely into the beaded band of his breechclout. He caught her by the waist, lifted her high above his head, and twirled her around and around.

"Yes!" she said hoarsely, her throat choked with sobs. She clutched his side braids and tugged insistently, till he lowered her down to eye level. She was laughing and crying at the same time. "Yes, oh, yes, my sweet darlin'. I'll gladly jump the broom with you, if'n you still want me."

Strong Elk kissed her in reply, letting his heart tell her how very deeply he loved her. Telling her without words that, no matter what happened in the months and years to come, he would never let her go.

"Are you going to marry the *vehoka*, Strong Elk Heart?" a high-pitched voice asked. They broke the kiss and looked down to find Moon Shell standing right beside them. She stared up at the couple, wide-eyed and entranced.

"Yes!" Rachel exclaimed in Cheyenne before he could say a word. "Strong Elk and I are going to be married."

"When?" the child demanded.

"Right away," declared the shivering *vehoka* as she laid her head on Strong Elk's chest and sighed blissfully. She cuddled against him, slipping her hand beneath his deerskin shirt for warmth and smoothing her palm across his bare flesh. His groin muscles tightened in instantaneous response. The little Fawn had no idea the effect her slightest touch had upon him.

The Elk placed his hand on top of hers and gently pressed her fingers flat against his suddenly overheated body. In spite of his previous boast, he'd taken all the torture he could endure at the moment. "We will marry as soon as we have her grandmother's permission," he told Moon Shell.

Rachel's spontaneous laughter bubbled up inside her. She lifted her head, happiness bringing an added glow to her vivid coloring. Her cheeks were rosy from the cold, her green eyes brilliant beneath the long russet lashes glistening with teardrops.

"We have to get *niscem*'s permission?" she asked in surprise. "That should not be too hard to do. Porcupine Quills has invited you into her lodge every evening since you gave me the dreamcatcher."

Strong Elk looked around the village. In front of every painted tipi, people stood watching in frank curiosity. Everyone was gesturing and talking at the same time. Flying Hawk with his two wives. Young Bear Running beside Big Pipe Man. The Elk's cousin, Sleeping Bull, and his plump wife, Thick Braided Hair, with Prickly Pear in her arms and six-year-old Little Man between them. Sweet Feather stood close to Wolf Walking Fast, a courting blanket draped about their shoulders. And Choke Cherry Blossom was hurrying across the trampled brown grass to take her daughter's hand. All of their family and friends smiled their delighted approval.

But when the Elk's gaze drifted to Porcupine Quills's lodge, he wasn't surprised to find Rachel's snowy-haired grandmother nowhere in sight. There would be no more invitations to visit the small tipi with its four bright stars until the marriage proposal was transacted to the widow's complete satisfaction.

Strong Elk wasn't worried. He placed a kiss on the top of the *vehoka*'s coppery curls and smiled with limitless confidence. He would offer such a staggering number of ponies that even the proud, unpredictable Shoshone medicine woman would be suitably impressed.

It snowed that night. Not unusual, even in early October, for winter often came hard and fast on the northern plains. Outside Porcupine Quills's lodge the next morn-

ing, forty ponies stamped and snorted, their breath white
puffs in the frosty air. The animals had been chosen with
special care, for every one of them was trained to the
halter and gentle enough for an elderly woman to ride.
Young Bear Running appeared at the tipi's entrance and
waited politely for the call inviting him in.

With her hands clasped tight in her lap, Rachel sat on
a fur rug and watched in tense silence as the Bear entered,
placed a white buffalo robe in front of the seated Porcupine Quills, and sank down on the men's side. The
outspoken white girl had been warned by her grandmother that proper manners required a shy, chaste maiden
to listen quietly while her elders did all the palavering.
Rachel was supposed to sit there and pretend she didn't
even know what was going on. Jeeminently!

In honor of the occasion, Young Bear Running was
dressed in his finest regalia. His shirt and leggings were
lavishly beaded, quilled, and fringed. He wore a magnificent breastplate and a necklace of bear claws. "I bring
Strong Elk Heart's proposal of marriage," the large man
said, once the formalities had been completed. "These
horses and the robe are offered as a sign of my friend's
deepest respect and admiration."

The tiny widow waved her hand in a dismissive gesture. "If Strong Elk is proposing marriage to me," she
told Young Bear, "then these few ponies are adequate.
But if his intentions are directed toward my beautiful
granddaughter, I find them a paltry gift, indeed."

"Niscem!" Rachel cried, purely horrified. She was so
rattled, she had to search for the right words in Cheyenne.
"It . . . it is not as though Strong Elk is trying to . . . to
buy me. I have already . . . told him I wanted to be . . .
his wife."

Porcupine Quills ignored the unseemly outburst and
continued speaking directly to the stunned, silent man.
"Little Red Fawn is skilled in all the ways of a good

Cheyenne wife. She has helped sew a lodge cover and lining for her first home. She has quilled a robe and a pair of moccasins and knows how to prepare strong medicine for the sick and injured. Yet the great Elk offers only forty mares for a warrior woman who has brought down a buffalo with only one bullet. Mm.'' She lifted her slight shoulders. ''I am not impressed.''

Young Bear never once glanced Rachel's way. ''I know I speak for my friend,'' he replied, ''when I say that Strong Elk considers your granddaughter priceless. Nothing he could offer would exceed her worth. Any gift you name, he will give gladly.''

Rachel pressed her hands to the front of her worn blue shirt and held her breath, wondering what on earth her irascible grandmother would say next.

Porcupine Quills smiled serenely, but her shrewd black eyes were alight with mischief. ''Randall Tackett gave my father a stack of prime beaver pelts as tall as his new bride, three mares, and a stallion, along with a shiny new musket. Surely, Strong Elk places as much worth upon my granddaughter as my first husband placed upon me.''

Young Bear's eyes narrowed at the staggering bride-price the old woman had slyly inferred. He opened his mouth to speak and then closed it without making a sound. Clearly, he wasn't about to make such a monumental decision for his friend.

''What good are mares without a stallion?'' Porcupine Quills muttered, as though in afterthought. She pushed the rare white buffalo robe back toward her guest.

Rachel jumped up and waved her hands excitedly. ''Tell Strong Elk that his forty ponies are accepted,'' she informed the Bear. ''I would marry him if . . . there was no gift at all.''

Neither of them paid her the least bit of attention.

The tall, muscular brave rose gracefully to his feet and addressed Porcupine Quills. ''I will tell my friend all that

you have said.'' Without so much as a word to the stu-
pefied *vehoka,* he picked up the robe and left the tipi.

An appalled hush settled over the entire village as
Young Bear Running, with the help of Sleeping Bull and
the Wolf, moved the forty ponies back to the large herd
on the hillside.

No one could believe what had just happened.

Strong Elk's proposal had been rejected.

The next morning, seventy ponies, fifteen of them
trained for the buffalo hunt and fifteen trained for war,
neighed and tossed their heads spiritedly outside Porcupine Quills's tipi. The sacred war shield that had once
belonged to Strong Elk's father, Bellowing Bull, now
stood on a tripod in the snow. Beside it was a tall lance,
with its cluster of owl feathers dancing in the breeze. At
the very front, ground-tied by the entrance, stood Thunder Cloud, painted and perfumed, his bridle lavishly decorated with eagle feathers and strips of braided rawhide.
On the pad of antelope hair thrown across the great stallion's back was a parfleche filled with cartridges and the
precious Henry rifle.

Not a person in the camp could have mistaken the
meaning of such an unbelievably generous gift. The Elk
would willingly impoverish himself to win Little Red
Fawn for his wife.

This time, the ponies remained all morning long. When
Young Bear Running returned to the small lodge, he carried three quilled buffalo robes, a One-Thousand dress
covered with elk teeth, a finely ornamented saddlecloth
of antelope hide, and four pairs of intricately beaded
moccasins.

The sun was straight overhead when Porcupine Quills
stepped out into the snow and took the reins of the splendid Appaloosa stallion. Beaming with pride, she announced to the inveterate gossips nearby, many of whom

had loitered around the camp circle for hours, "My granddaughter has accepted the mighty Strong Elk Heart—a brave warrior who has won many coups in battle and has proven his courage to all—as her first husband."

"Niscem!" they heard the white girl cry out in mortification from inside the lodge. "Strong Elk will be my first and *last* husband!"

But when he was told of the old crone's outrageous words, Strong Elk just grinned the carefree, besotted grin of a prospective bridegroom.

The Elk's feelings of unbridled elation didn't last long. After the ritual giving of gifts by Standing in Water and Good Robe Woman to their future granddaughter, and the words of solemn advice for his grandson from Flying Hawk, who harked all the way back to the advice given him by *his* grandfather, the wedding was only a day away. There would be a great feast the next morning that would last most of the day. Toward evening, Rachel would be carried into their new lodge on a blanket and presented to her captivated bridegroom.

Rachel was filled with impatience.

Strong Elk was terrified.

Every time he looked at her, she seemed to have grown a little smaller, a little more delicate, a little more fine-boned than the last. He'd spent weeks of agonizing frustration attempting to seduce the innocent redhead. Now, as their wedding night approached, he was tormented by unimaginable fears.

It wasn't that he was without knowledge of carnal relations between a man and a woman. None of the other tribes of the western plains placed such a high value on the chastity of their women. In the course of his travels as interpreter for the army, he'd slept with many willing and lovely females. There had been eager young girls, lonely widows, a few flirtatious wives grown restless in their marriage, and even some daring white harlots, seeking a thrill from sharing their feather mattress with a copper-skinned savage. But he had never bedded a virgin.

Added to that, he'd seen enough victims of rape in his duties as a scout to know that any female, even a large, big-boned one, could be lacerated horribly by a brutal assault. One pathetic white girl he'd found at the scene of an Apache raid had hemorrhaged and died in his arms, her life's blood soaking her tattered skirt and white petticoat and pooling on the dirt floor of her family's cabin.

Strong Elk tried to picture just how tiny Rachel might be and broke into a cold sweat. He'd learned one thing for certain from the plain-spoken whores. His male member was unusually large.

"Lordy, Lordy," one trollop had declared with a loud, appreciative whistle, "if you ain't as big as a hoss, I ain't ever laid eyes on a man's bare ass before!"

He decided to go to Black Rabbit, the wise old medicine healer, who could put an injured warrior into a deep sleep with the shake of his rattle and the drone of his chant, then work his medicine while the patient slept. Strong Elk walked slowly toward the venerable man's lodge, debating how to put his apprehension into words. He changed his mind when he neared the entrance of the Rabbit's tipi. Knowing how to sew up knife gashes, tend arrow wounds, set broken bones, and dig out bullets didn't necessarily mean the wizened elder would know any more about females than Strong Elk did. Black Rabbit had taken only two wives in his entire life. That didn't offer much likelihood that he had the farseeing wisdom required to advise the Elk about lying beside a diminutive, untouched bride.

Strong Elk continued to walk, gradually turning his steps toward the small lodge by the grove of cottonwoods. There was only one person in the village as tiny as Rachel: a widow who'd outlived four husbands. If anyone would have sound advice for the worried groom, it would be the canny old medicine woman. He stood outside the tipi, torn by indecision. He was about to turn and leave when Porcupine Quills called out for her visitor to enter.

Strong Elk went in and sat down.

"Little Red Fawn is not here," the widow announced cheerfully. "She is with Choke Cherry Blossom and Sweet Feather. They have gifts for the day of her wedding."

He tried to return the welcoming smile. It felt as though his face would crack under the strain. "Yes, Grandmother," he answered in a tone far more serious than he'd intended. "I saw Little Fawn going into the Blossom's tipi."

Porcupine Quills gave no hint of surprise at his words. She was pounding dried berries for the making of pemmican. Beside her, in wooden bowls, were piles of wild turnips, onions, sage, peas, rose hips, and prickly pear cactus for stew. The busy widow wasn't the only one engaged in the preparation of food that day. Every woman in Strong Elk's family would cook something for the huge feast to celebrate the nuptials. Along with buffalo, there would be rabbit, venison, and quail flavored with dried plums, nuts, and sweet thistle. The entire village would be invited to share in their joy.

Rachel's grandmother continued her work as she waited in silence for him to explain why he'd come.

"The Fawn is very small," he said at last.

She looked up from her mortar and pestle and gazed at him with an expression of utter serenity. "That is why they call her Little Fawn."

There was a long, awkward pause.

"Her hands and feet are nearly as small as a child's,"

he added gruffly. "When I first saw her, I thought she was a child."

The medicine woman smiled in agreement and bent over her work once again.

Strong Elk stared at the center part in her white hair, then glanced up at the smoke hole in mounting irritation. It was no wonder Rachel and her headstrong grandmother got along so well. As any white man would say, they were two of a kind. "Yesterday, when I was holding her hand," he continued, "I noticed, especially, how very small her fingers are in comparison to mine. The nails on her littlest fingers are surprisingly tiny."

"Little Red Fawn is tiny all over," agreed Porcupine Quills.

Strong Elk waited through another uncomfortable pause, the steady bang of the stone maul the only sound in the lodge. He cleared his throat noisily. "I am a very large man," he admitted in a strangled voice. "Everything about me is large."

Without a word, the medicine woman rose to her feet and moved to a parfleche stashed behind a headrest. She withdrew a small clay pot with a lid, which had been tightly wrapped in deerskin, and turned to him, her intelligent eyes flashing with humor.

"That thought occurred to me as well, Strong Elk," she remarked, "on the very day you gave my granddaughter the dreamcatcher. Randall Tackett was nearly as large a man as you." Coming to stand beside him, she stooped and placed the pot in his hands. "I made a salve from the crushed new leaves of the yellow columbine and the roots of the white water lily. Use it to ease your entry the first few times you take your new bride in your arms. After that, it will no longer be necessary."

Strong Elk looked up at her in shock, then back down to the clay bowl. He was rigid with embarrassment, but he had to be certain that Rachel would be absolutely safe. "You are sure?"

She smiled with boundless confidence. "Nature works a magic all its own," she told him, "even for a big rutting stag like you."

The Elk rose to his feet to tower over her. He didn't know whether to grind his teeth in exasperation or laugh out loud. He did neither. "Thank you, Grandmother," he said sincerely. Holding the pot as if it were made of gold, he started to leave.

"Strong Elk," the widow called softly. He turned and waited, wondering what surprising revelation she would make next.

"I mixed a small amount of crushed wintergreen leaves into the ointment." The shadow of a smile flitted across her wrinkled features. She winked at him broadly as she added, "To enhance the pleasure."

He stared at her, dumbfounded.

Porcupine Quills lifted her thin brows and raised both hands, palms outward, in the sign of peace. "I was young once, too, you know."

Strong Elk's hearty laugh boomed out.

At that moment, Rachel entered the tipi. She looked from one to the other, obviously pleased that they were getting along so well. "What are you two talking about?" she questioned happily in Cheyenne as she moved to stand beside Strong Elk. The moment he put his arm around her, she snuggled against him with complete trust.

"I was telling Strong Elk how much I am looking forward to having great-grandchildren," Porcupine Quills said with a sly glance at the soon-to-be bridegroom. "Lots of them and as quickly as possible."

Rachel looked from one to the other, and her wide smile vanished instantly. It was plain that the sprightly, impulsive *vehoka* had not, until that moment, given a thought to bearing his children.

Chapter 16

⟨≈≈≈≈⟩

"Rachel, what are you doing?"

His new bride peeked around her staggering burden, a quizzical look on her face. "I'm gettin' our bed ready. What in tarnation do you reckon I'm doin'?" she asked as she shifted her balance to straighten the load. The stack of furs in her arms reached higher than the top of her curly head. Going to the willow mattress, she spilled the entire batch on top of the sleek bearskin that had already been spread out for the wedding couple by one of their grandmothers.

Strong Elk folded his arms across his chest and smiled at the comical sight. He'd been so distracted by thoughts of the coming evening, he hadn't realized, until now, that Rachel had busily gathered almost every pelt she could find in their new lodge and piled it on top of their marriage bed. "Why so many of them?" he questioned with a chuckle.

"I don't know about you," she replied, clearly amazed that he'd have to ask, "but I've been freezin' to death at night. It's colder than an icehouse in January out there."

"You won't need more than one buffalo robe," he told her.

She raised her russet brows dubiously. "I haven't been warm since it started a-snowin' three days ago," she complained. "I swear, I'm chilled right down to the bone."

He shook his head at the strange workings of the female mind. For the same number of days, all he could think about was how small she was in comparison to him. Apparently, she'd been troubled over nothing more consequential than having enough covers to keep her warm at night. She should have told him. He could have allayed her fears on that score quite easily. His worries, however, were a little more serious.

He walked over and placed his hands lightly on her shoulders. Rubbing his thumbs across her collarbone in a soothing motion, he pressed a gentle kiss to her forehead. "Trust me, *nazheem*. You won't be cold tonight. I can promise you that."

Rachel looked up to meet his reassuring gaze and smiled. "I like hearin' you call me your wife."

"I like it, too," he said.

"You looked mighty fine at the feast this morning." She smoothed the fringes on the front of his buckskin shirt with quick, nervous pats. "I don't reckon I've ever seen you with so many clothes on afore, and all of them so fancy, too."

"A man likes to dress up for his wedding," Strong Elk reminded her wryly. He cupped her heart-shaped face in his hands and bussed the freckles on her pert little nose. "You looked so beautiful when they carried you into our lodge on the white buffalo robe this evening, I thought my heart was going to stop beating and never start up again."

Rachel stared down at the floor, flushing with happiness at his praise. She was wearing a white doeskin dress trimmed in rabbit fur, with matching moccasins and leggings. Above each ear, downy feathers clustered in her bright curls like pure white clouds.

"Shucks, I reckon you ain't never seen me in such a fancy get-up, neither," she demurred. "You can thank Choke Cherry Blossom for that. She and Sweet Feather prettied me all up in this here weddin' rig. Cherry Blossom's mama made the dress for her when she got married. 'Twas mighty kind of the Blossom to lend it to me."

"I'll be sure to thank them tomorrow," he said huskily. "Right now I think it's time for us to go to bed."

"You . . . you go on," she said. "I'll join you in a minute."

He smiled indulgently. "I thought you were freezing to death."

"Oh, I ain't cold right now!" she disclaimed. "I'm jest thinkin' about when the fire dies down later tonight, and that old wind comes a-whistlin' round the tipi."

He watched with tender amusement as she scurried to the woman's side of the lodge and started rifling through the contents of a parfleche. Turning his back to allow her some privacy, he pulled off his shirt and draped it across a backrest. He removed his moccasins, then untied his leggings and slipped them off. He shoved all but the black bearskin at the bottom of the stack of furs out of the way. Wearing only his breechclout, he sat down cross-legged on the soft pallet to wait for her.

"I made something for you," she called shyly from across the lodge.

Strong Elk looked over to find that she'd removed her moccasins and leggings. Her bare feet were nearly buried in the thick wolf pelt she stood on. She was watching him now with enormous eyes, a folded garment in her hands.

Rachel stared at her bridegroom in pure captivation. For a fact, he was the most perfectest human being God ever created. The flickering light of the lodge fire played across his bronze skin, drawing her gaze to his broad chest and upper arms. Aside from the beaded breechclout, he wore only his leather medicine bundle around his neck and golden hoops in his ears. His flat abdomen and massive thighs were corded with muscles. His blueblack hair fell straight down his back in a sleek, silken cascade. The short, braided scalp lock was decorated with eagle feathers and a hammered brass disk.

She tried to smile, but found her lips trembling dangerously. At the moment, he looked mighty dang serious himself.

Rachel had a pretty fair idea of what was going to happen when she joined him on that there bearskin. Any mountain girl with eyes in her head could learn a lot just walking through a meadow in springtime. Added to that, she'd helped care for the newborn babes her gram had brought into the world. Rachel had swaddled many a squalling manchild in his first quilted comforter, so the differences between the sexes weren't exactly unknown to her. It was the particulars that left her wondering.

He was waiting for her to come to him, clearly giving her all the time she needed. With her gaze never once leaving his, she moved across the fur-covered floor. She sank down on the sleek bearskin, facing him, and held out the shirt she'd worked so hard on.

"Thank you, Little Fawn," he said, his black eyes soft with tenderness. He unfolded the golden-brown deerskin, which she'd beaded and quilled in precise geometric designs under her exacting grandmother's direction. He looked up to meet her gaze, and she could tell he was sincerely touched. "It's wonderful," he told her.

"Well, shoot," she said, all of a sudden drowning in self-consciousness, "I don't know 'bout that. I jest hope it's big enough." She took the garment out of his hands and held it up against his chest. "Yep, looks like it's a-goin' to be a perfect fit. But you may want to try it on, jest in case.''

''I'll try it on later,'' Strong Elk promised as he took the shirt and carefully laid it over his leggings on the backrest nearby. He lifted Rachel onto his lap. Bringing her closer, he brushed his lips across her trembling mouth and gently nuzzled her ear. He could feel the quivering tension in her slender body. ''Right now, I want to show you how pleased I am.''

''With my sewin'?'' she asked on a soft exhalation of breath.

''With my bride,'' he murmured.

The pressure of her firm little rump wedged between his thighs sent the blood rushing to his already swollen sex. Every time he'd looked at her today, he'd felt himself harden in anticipation.

At the feast held in Flying Hawk's large tipi, people had come and gone all day long, bringing gifts for the newlyweds and food for the marriage celebration. Now, at last, he had her alone.

He kissed her deeply, exploring the sweetness of her mouth, while his hands moved hungrily over her delicate curves. He hadn't allowed himself to touch her intimately since the evening of the throwaway dance, when he'd discovered the chastity rope beneath her white cotton drawers.

Strong Elk had no idea if Rachel still wore the *nihpih-ist*. He was certain, however, that her grandmother had explained that bashful young brides often kept the rope on for several nights, sometimes as long as a week. A Cheyenne husband did not hurry his bride, but allowed her time to become accustomed to sleeping beside him. A newly married couple would often lie in each other's arms and talk for hours into the night, becoming better acquainted, getting to know each other's secret dreams and hidden longings.

He had always thought the Medicine Lodge—when a young man hung from a pole by skewers lanced through his flesh without revealing a trace of the pain he endured—was a true measure of a warrior's indomitable strength of will. Now he knew better.

Rachel caught the Elk's long, silky hair in her hands as she delved her tongue into his warm, welcoming mouth. "Mm," she sighed against his lips, "kissin' you is jest like sippin' pure honey from a comb. I keep listenin' for those bees to come a-swarmin' round my head." She could feel his smile of male satisfaction at her words. "I reckon you knew all along you had me caught in your trap, jest like a hungry little bear too stubborn to let go of the sweetnin'."

"You are the one who's sweet, little love," he averred, his voice coaxing and deep. "I've been longing to taste your exquisite honey since the day we met."

Rachel sighed with pleasure as he cupped her aching breasts through the lovely white dress. She could feel his arousal thrust boldly against her bottom and shifted in his lap, suddenly wary.

Strong Elk broke the kiss to trace the shell of her ear with his tongue. "Sweet Little Fawn," he whispered huskily, "let's take off your dress so I can see you."

He felt her stiffen at the suggestion and held himself sternly in check, prepared to discover that she still wore the protective string. Yet he needed to know before he went any farther. There were limits to a man's willpower, and he was fast approaching his.

Rachel pulled back from the embrace, her lids lowered bashfully. Without a word, she slipped out of his lap to kneel before him on the thick fur. She raised her long, curving lashes to meet his gaze. The trust shining in her brilliant eyes sent a shudder of insatiable need through the Elk. He was determined to let her set the pace, even while knowing that it would take every ounce of his vaunted self-restraint.

Strong Elk moved to his knees in front of her. He threaded his fingers through her curls and kissed her smooth cheek in a gentle, reassuring gesture. Hesitantly, Rachel leaned forward and placed a light kiss on his naked chest in return. When she traced the outline of the leaping elk with the tip of her tongue, he gasped for breath. A jolt of white-hot desire speared through his groin like a fiery war lance. Graphic thoughts of what he intended to do to his beautiful bride rose in his mind.

"You always set me a-thinkin' of Christmas," she whispered in sweet innocence against his bare skin.

Bewildered, he looked down at the feathers entangled in her curls and sucked in a deep draft of air. His brain reeled with the conflicting images of her guileless remark and his erotic intentions.

"Christmas?" he asked in a choked voice

"Yeah," she sighed. She stroked her fingertips across the ridge of his collarbone. Offering no further explanation, she continued to place soft, lingering kisses on the thick scars that marked his initiation into manhood.

Strong Elk removed the wide quilled belt from around her slender waist as he tried to follow her convoluted reasoning. He was familiar with the white man's religious celebration, with its tradition of gift-giving, and could see no likely similarity to himself. "Why?" he queried. "Because I gave you presents?"

She looked up to meet his gaze and ran her finger, which he immediately kissed, playfully across his lips. The corners of her mouth turned up in a winsome smile. "Nope, because you always smell like a wreath of fresh evergreens."

Grinning, he reached down to take the fringed hem of her dress in his hands. "It's the juniper branches my grandmothers put in all their lodge pillows," he explained. "The scent must stay in my hair."

She smoothed her cheeks across his flat nipples and inhaled with a dramatic sigh. "What a purely marvelous idea."

Strong Elk slowly lifted the white deerskin skirt that pooled about her knees. His heart smashed against his ribs like a war club as his fingers grazed her bare thighs. "I was half-expecting to find you wearing white girl's underwear beneath this Cheyenne wedding dress," he teased, trying vainly to keep the relief from his hoarse voice.

"I told you before, Choke Cherry Blossom and Sweet Feather helped me get ready," she said. Her eyes sparkled mischievously. "When I tried to pull my drawers on under the skirt, they both nearly died of an apoplectic fit."

"I'll have to thank them for that as well."

"Don't you dare!" she warned. "Leastways, not when I'm around."

Strong Elk eased her bridal dress up over her head. Laying it aside, he sank back on his haunches to look at her. The sight of her loveliness took his breath away. She was perfection. Her creamy skin was flawless. Her small breasts were round and firm, the nipples a deep, velvety rose in the glow of the flames. Heated blood raged through his veins as his eyes followed the delicate curve of her waist and hips to the puff of curls at the juncture of her pale thighs.

His heart thudded out the glorious message to his fevered brain.

She was not wearing the protective string.

Strong Elk bracketed her hips with his hands. The perfume of wild roses assailed his senses. He leaned forward and suckled her deeply, feeling her tense and arch her spine in undeniable pleasure. He kneaded her smooth buttocks, then slipped his hand between her legs to cup her soft mound. Threading his fingers gently through the coppery cloud, he stroked her delicate petals. His heart stalled for the space of a second. She felt so tiny and dainty beneath his large hand. Beads of perspiration suddenly formed on his upper lip. But she was already moist, and the proof that she wanted him was indisputable.

Rachel gasped at the intimacy of his caresses. She jerked reflexively and clutched his hair. ''Strong Elk, I . . .'' she cried softly, the surprise in her voice unmistakable.

''What, little love?'' he whispered as he held her close. ''Does my touch bring you pleasure?''

''Yes, oh, yes.'' She sighed. ''It pleasures me beyond all knowin'.''

He covered her lips with his open mouth, probing rhythmically with his tongue as his fingers stroked her fragile tissues. Then he lowered his head to lave the pliant crests of her uptilted breasts into tight little rosebuds.

Rachel would have slumped to the bearskin in a heap, if Strong Elk hadn't been holding her up. Her entire body seemed to pulsate beneath his gentle fondling.

He eased her down on the sleek bearskin and bent over her. His hands were everywhere. His lips were everywhere.

''Zehemehotaz,'' he murmured, the hunger in his deep voice a raw, throbbing ache. ''Nihoatovaz.''

His long hair brushed across Rachel's naked body like a curtain of black silk, the narrow side braids with their otter fur trim awakening every slumbering nerve. She could feel the golden hoops he wore bump lightly against her legs. As he kissed the sensitive skin inside her thighs, he repeated the words hoarsely in English. ''My beloved, I want you.''

The realization of what he'd meant about tasting her exquisite honey—and that he intended to do it right now—slowly penetrated Rachel's pleasure-fogged brain.

She tried to deny it, at first. He couldn't be thinking of that! She grabbed a handful of his hair and tugged, comprehending, too late, that this must be one of those particulars that no one had bothered to tell her about.

Strong Elk scooped his hands beneath her bum and lifted her hips toward him. Rachel could feel his cool breath float over her as he parted her sensitive folds. When he licked her with his moist tongue as though she really were made of honey and he was a ravenous bear, she cried out in a pleasure so keen it was nearly pain.

He wouldn't let her pull away. He even growled deep in his chest to warn her not to try. He held her, writhing and sobbing, as he built the most wondrous, most excitingest, most unbelievable feeling inside her, till her heart was banging madly and her breath came in short gasps.

She couldn't think of nothing but what he was doing to her. She'd purely die of embarrassment if he didn't stop. And she'd surely die of heart failure if he did. She called his name in a long, drawn-out sigh as a glow of purest bliss spread through her.

Gradually, Rachel became aware that Strong Elk was on his knees between her spread legs. When she saw that he had removed his breechclout, she tried to sit up, then sank back down on her elbows in shock.

Jumpin' Jehoshaphat.

His erect, swollen manroot was enormous.

Seeing a little boy-child back in Sugar Hollow had never prepared her for this. She met his gaze and clamped her lips tight to keep from blurting out just how huge he looked to her inexperienced eyes. But her strangled sob betrayed her.

"Don't be afraid, little rose," he crooned softly.

"I ain't afraid," she lied.

Rachel squeezed her lids shut and tensed her body, expecting Strong Elk to try to wedge that thick male part of him inside her.

He'd never fit.

She didn't know much about procreation, and nothing at all about the particulars, but, jiminy, criminy, even she could see that.

Her eyes flew open as she felt his finger sliding gently inside her. He teased her sensitive flesh with his thumb, and a cool, tingling sensation spread all through her private parts. The scent of wintergreen filled her nostrils as he cupped her breast with his other hand and lightly tugged on her nipple.

Rachel gazed up at him in bafflement. "What are you doin'?" she asked with a moan of pure pleasure. She arched her back and shamelessly opened herself wider to him. It was as though she couldn't get enough of his magical touch.

The moment Strong Elk felt her relax, he slid two fingers inside her small passage, stretching her gently, caressing her softly. "You're so tiny," he said in a soothing voice. "This will help make it easier for both of us the first time. Give yourself to me, little bride. Trust me completely. Let me bring you all the pleasure a man can bring the woman he loves."

"I trust you," she said, and this time, he knew she was telling the truth.

Strong Elk entered her as carefully and gently as he could. His heart was about to explode from the surging blood that flooded through it. He'd never before experienced such mind-numbing pleasure. She was so incredibly tight. He inched slowly inside her, the cooling balm easing his way, till he reached the barrier he sought. Resting his weight on his hands, he bent over her slender white body. She was looking up at him with a mixture of awe and doubt, her luminous eyes enormous in her pale face. The torturous weeks of waiting had taken their toll, and he knew that he couldn't postpone his release much longer.

He kissed her deeply, passionately. "Rachel Rose," he said in a ragged whisper, "sweet, little Rosie, I love you." With one powerful surge of his hips, he thrust deep inside her. He heard her cry out in surprise as he broke through the maidenhead and touched her womb.

He stopped for a moment, letting their bodies get used to the marvelous feeling of being joined so tightly together. He kissed her closed lids, tasting the salty tears at the corners of her eyes. But when his mouth sought hers in an unspoken quest for forgiveness, she moved her tongue across his lips and into his mouth in a wildly erotic dance of female enticement.

Rachel wrapped her legs around Strong Elk as the throbbing pleasure built up within her once again. The feeling of overwhelming fullness seemed to ignite a fire inside. Fire and ice, for the cool, tingling sensations that had awakened every inch of her female core still tantalized and excited. The pressure of his muscled flanks between her thighs, the heavy maleness of him deep within her, the steadily increasing rhythm of his movements as he thrust and withdrew brought the glow of rapture to an ever higher level. She cried out, calling his name over and over as wave after wave of pure, sweet ecstasy washed through her.

Rachel felt Strong Elk tense as he held himself braced above her. His powerful body jerked in spasms, and she knew instinctively that he shared the same unimaginable pleasure he'd given her. With a low groan, he rolled to his side, bringing her with him, her head resting on his shoulder. When she started to move away, he clamped his large hand on her thigh, holding her tight against him.

"Stay right here," he whispered. "Don't go away. Not yet."

Rachel felt his member moving reflexively inside her, and she realized, numbly, that they were still joined together, and he was still hard and erect. His lids were closed, the thick black lashes shading his tawny cheeks. She studied his ax-sharp features, awed at the overwhelming love she felt for him. A love she was afraid to put into words, knowing once she told him, he would never let her go. Never.

Strong Elk opened his eyes and found her staring at him with an expression of utter solemnity. He smoothed her flushed cheek with the back of his hand. "So fragile . . . so delicate," he murmured. "I wonder that I dared to touch you."

She smiled as she traced a pair of horizontal lines across his cheekbones with the tips of two fingers, then drew one vertical line from the top of his forehead down to his chin. "So savage . . . so fierce," she replied in a hushed whisper. "I wonder that I dared to let you."

He knew she was thinking of the ambush at Clear Creek. "Did I frighten you with my war paint?" he asked softly.

"I hope to shout you did," she replied with an impish grin. "You scared the holy bejeezus plumb out of me. Why do you reckon I kept tryin' to get my grandpappy's gun back?"

"Liar," he said with a low growl. "You were never afraid of me. Not from the moment you came strolling into our camp and told me that ridiculous story about visiting with friends and heading back over yonder."

Her green eyes sparkled with playfulness. "Well, to tell the truth of it," she said, "we've got a whole lot more in common than you most likely think. Gramps told me oncet how his forebears used to paint themselves blue and ride into battle in the raw. And that ain't the half of it. The rest of the time, the menfolk sashayed 'round with blankets wrapped about their hips and nothin' on underneath. That there lavender-and-pink plaid of mine is one of them very blankets, brought over from the Scottish Highlands by Gramps's own pappy."

He touched the tip of her freckled nose with his finger, delighted at her fanciful tale. "Why blue?" he asked with a grin.

She giggled. "Shoot, I never thought to question the color. The fact they painted themselves up like a bunch of wild Injuns was bewitchin' enough for me. When I was a little girl-child, I used to draw lines on my face with red ocher from the clay banks down by the river and whoop blood-curdlin' yells, till Gram complained that old Bossie's milk was startin' to curdle, and the poor wee calf was a-bawlin' her lungs out."

"I wish had known you as a child," he said.

"Well, everyone in Sugar Holler used to say I was somethin' else again. Course there ain't a soul in the holler who's not my kin." She looked at him speculatively. "Now that we're a-swappin' secrets, there's one thing I've wanted to know ever since I came wanderin' into your camp."

"What's that?"

"I've asked every durn female in the village, from the youngest to the oldest, and not one of 'em has even bothered to answer my question."

"Which is?"

"What *do* the Cheyenne people do to little girls who tell lies?"

Strong Elk's roar of laughter filled the lodge. "Little Red Fawn," he said between guffaws, "if you haven't figured that out by now, you don't deserve to be told the answer."

She scowled as she pushed her hands against his chest in a futile effort to move away. "I don't reckon I see what's so all-fired funny," she muttered.

His large hand cupped her bottom, holding her tight against him with disgusting ease. Rachel could feel his manhood move tantalizingly inside her, and she stared at him in surprise. He thrust upward as he guided her legs around him once again. Only this time, she was on top and he was on the bottom. He fondled her breasts, his thumbs flicking lightly across their swollen cherry-red buttons.

"We shouldn't be doing this again so soon, *nameo*," he told her almost gruffly "If you feel too tender, I'll stop right now. After all those weeks of wanting you, I could stay hard all night."

Rachel bent down and kissed him. "What does that there word mean?" she asked, as she nibbled on his lower lip. "I ain't heard nary a soul use it afore."

"My lover," he answered thickly. Despite his gallant offer to quit, his hands continued to move over her body, as though he could never stop touching her.

"*Nameo*," she whispered shyly in his ear. "*Nihoato-vaz.*"

Chapter 17

*I*t was Maxhekonene, the moon of the strong cold and hard frost. Snow lay in great drifts across the landscape. Antelope, deer, and elk moved steadily downward from the higher elevations, seeking sustenance on the frost-cured grass below. A herd of twenty-eight elk hurried across a lower valley, pushed along by a blizzard that had been roaring above them on the mountaintop for the past two days.

The lead bull elk was an imperial stag with a magnificent rack of antlers. There were three younger bulls in the herd to help protect the cows and yearlings and the seven calves that had been born the previous spring, plus a wily old cow to guide them.

In the midst of the elk herd was a young white-tailed doe who had somehow been separated from her own kind. Her shiny red coat gleamed like a flame against the snow. As the herd traveled, she stayed close to the mighty bull elk, always at his side.

They browsed through the day, but when the tail end of the storm swept down into their small valley, the elk herd took shelter in a stand of aspens and spruce, huddling together for protection. The hard driven snow piled up in drifts nine feet tall, and the elk were soon penned in a yard bordered on all sides by high snow banks. By evening, the howling of wolves could be heard in the distance, and the elk formed a circle, the calves and yearlings in the middle.

The wolf pack continued to move closer during the night, till suddenly they appeared, their dark shapes silhouetted against the snow in the moonlight. They watched the elk from the top of the banks, growing steadily bolder as the hours wore on. Finally, tired of the waiting, one huge gray wolf leaped down into the yard's trampled snow and snapped at the flank of an older cow. Two of his snarling cronies took advantage of the diversion to strike at a frightened yearling.

The great bull elk lowered his head and lunged. He caught the two wolves, sweeping them up on his branching antlers and tossing them high into the air, his sharp tines goring them fatally. He immediately turned and plunged toward the crafty old loner. The wolf abandoned his try for the cow and scrambled to the top of the bank, where he turned and watched with cold, yellow eyes.

The stag shook his antlers and bugled a challenge to the waiting predators. But the pack had had enough for the moment. They moved off, as the calls of others on the trail of easier prey carried faintly through the night.

Toward morning, a warming Chinook wind circled through the elk yard, melting the top layers of snow. Instinctively, the bull elk knew the herd must leave then, if they were ever to reach the safety of the flatlands below. He trampled his way through the high drifts, the slender, white-tailed doe on his flank.

But as the herd hurried across the snow-covered meadow, with the old lead cow in the vanguard, the wolves appeared again at the edge of the timber. They stalked the elk warily, following behind them in groups *of twos and threes, waiting for the weak or lame to stumble and fall in the icy drifts.*

All that day the rank smell of wolf was carried on the wind. First a calf went down, exhausted from lack of rest and food. Then an older cow. The wolves fell on them, snapping at one another in their frenzy to gorge themselves on their kill.

The herd slowed and came to a halt. Moving closer together, the cows nudged the weakened calves into the center. The younger bulls ranged around the outside of the circle, pawing the ground restlessly, ready to charge. The powerful lead bull elk snorted his defiance at the pack and shook his antlers. In the deep snow, two wolves crept forward, hoping to spring up and hamstring him. The bull charged and caught them in mid-leap on his great rack. Two wolves lay dead, their blood staining the snow around them in bright red pools.

Once again the herd bolted for freedom. But this time the little white-tailed doe couldn't keep up with the much stronger elks. She gradually dropped behind, and because she was a deer and not an elk, she panicked. Driven off the path of trampled snow laid down by the others, the terrified doe was forced onto a frozen river by the howling wolves. Skidding and sliding across the ice, she was scarcely able to keep from falling. The wily pack knew that if the doe fell, she could never get up again.

The great bull elk turned and bounded for the river as the wolves formed a circle around the helpless doe and slowly began to close in . . .

Strong Elk came awake, fully alert in less than a second. His heart beat wildly in the aftermath of the terrible dream. He looked down at the curly head resting against his chest and knew it had been no dream, but a vision sent by the Great Powers to warn him. He lay still beneath the buffalo robe, waiting for his pulse to return to normal.

His bride of two weeks lay cuddled against him, sound asleep. As usual, she'd flung an arm and a leg across her husband during the night, seeking the warmth of his body.

The Elk kissed the top of her head. He'd promised she wouldn't be cold at night, and he'd kept that promise. Even though they slept naked on the soft bearskin with only a single buffalo robe for a cover, Rachel had soon learned that her bridegroom had more than enough body heat for the two of them.

Strong Elk eased away from his little wife and moved out from under the robe. She grumbled something unintelligible in Cheyenne, clearly unhappy about his leaving, even though she was still half-asleep. He put on his breechclout and winter moccasins, then grabbed a thick robe from a stack of furs. He picked up the Henry rifle that his grandmother-in-law had presented to him on his wedding day. Porcupine Quills had returned the thirty ponies trained for battle and hunting, along with the gray stallion and the parfleche of cartridges. But she'd kept the forty gentle mares. She wasn't the least bit hesitant about announcing that she was now the wealthiest woman in the village.

The gray light of early morning bathed the sleeping encampment in its faint rays as Strong Elk stepped out of the lodge with the robe wrapped around his shoulders and the rifle cradled in the crook of his arm. He searched the foothills across the river for the least hint of a suspicious movement. Only the herds of shaggy ponies, huddled together for warmth, gave any sign of life. Strong Elk turned and stared, long and hard, across the open, snow-covered plains to the eastern horizon. Not even a bird in the sky disturbed the peaceful scene.

But the Long Knives were out there somewhere. And

like a pack of wolves, they were coming in stealth. There was no doubt in the Elk's mind what his vision had meant. The white man with the yellow eyes hadn't given up the chase. Shelby Bruckenridge was bringing an army through the snow in an attempt to reclaim the woman he still considered his wife.

Certain that the camp was safe for the time being, Strong Elk returned to his lodge. He laid the quilled robe and the rifle aside, removed his breechclout and moccasins, and returned to bed.

"Ooh, you're cold!" his wife complained, a scowl creasing her forehead. Her lower lip jutted forward in an enchanting pout. With her eyes squeezed shut, she rolled to her other side and turned her back on him.

Strong Elk ran his hand along the curve of her waist and hip, smiling to himself at his bride's naiveté. She assumed, no doubt, that she'd just administered a stinging rebuke not to stand outside in the frosty air and then return to their warm bed, chilled to the bone. He pressed his much larger body against her enticing backside, enjoying the feel of her little butt cuddled up against the hardening muscles of his groin. Slipping his arms around her, he pulled her closer and boldly searched for the soft pink rosebuds that now belonged to him. And only him.

Not yet fully awake, she purred lazily and wiggled her bottom. His thickened sex leaped up in wild excitement. He played with her silken folds in light, sensuous strokes, till he felt the delicate pink petals grow moist and turgid beneath his fingertips. He smiled in satisfaction as her slumberous body began to move involuntarily against his hand.

Rachel's eyelids fluttered open. She tried to turn around and discovered that she was held fast in her husband's arms. Confused and still groggy, she jabbed him with her elbow. He imprisoned her arm firmly beneath his powerful forearm.

"What are you doin'?" she mumbled. "I was goin' to tell you good mornin'."

"Good morning, *nazheem,*" Strong Elk rasped in her ear. He lifted his wife's slender thigh to allow him better access and buried his aching manhood deep within her warm, delectable body.

Rachel groaned with the unexpected pleasure and tipped her head back to rest on his muscled shoulder. Moving from a state of dreamy languor to breathless urgency, she could do nothing but accept the dazzling erotic sensations his insistent male body was awakening in her unresisting female flesh.

"Am I still cold?" he asked tauntingly.

She shook her head, too overwhelmed by the vibrant, radiating currents of pleasure to lie. "I reckon we're both on fire now."

His rich, husky voice shimmered with the heat of sexual conquest as he continued to batter her senses, thrusting into her again and again as though driven by some ancient, primal instinct. "I thought this would be a good way to warm us both up," he grated through clenched teeth. "What do you think, *nameo*? Did it work?"

Rachel yielded to her husband's sudden, primitive need to exert his male dominance. "You ain't jest whistlin' Dixie on that one," she gasped. As the deep, reverberating thrill of release consumed her, she clutched his forearm and gave him what he sought so intensely: her long, low cry of complete surrender.

Strong Elk climaxed at the same moment, pouring his seed deep inside her, where he hoped it would take hold and flower in her womb. The red-haired *vehoka* was not aware of it, but he prayed to Maheo each morning that the little Fawn would soon grow big with child.

No matter what the cost, he was never going to lose her.

Never.

When their breathing had calmed, he turned her to face him. "From now on, Rachel," he said in a tone that brooked absolutely no disobedience, "you are not to step foot outside this camp without me."

She looked up at him with disbelieving eyes. "Whoa!" she cried, scowling mutinously. "We ain't a-goin' through that again!"

Chapter 18

〜✦✧✦〜

"**H**old on tight, Rosie, girl," Strong Elk instructed. "I don't want to lose you halfway down the hill."

Rachel snuggled closer, her arms wrapped around her husband's solid torso. In spite of the frigid weather, she was cozy in the buffalo coat and beaver hat her grandmother had fashioned from the hides he'd provided, along with high winter moccasins and mittens lined with rabbit fur. It was a riddle to her how he could stay warm in just his deerskin shirt and leggings. She suspected it had something to do with the fact that he'd sashiated round all summer long with only a breechclout covering his crotch.

She was seated behind him on the sled, her cheek pressed flat against his muscled back. Her legs, bent at the knees, were propped against the top of the runners on either side of his flanks. "You ain't a-goin' to lose me," she said, giggling in excitement. "I'm a-hangin' on to you like a mama hen with a big fat worm."

They were at the crest of a high, snow-covered hill which ended on a frozen creek bed at the bottom far below. The sled, fashioned of boards for the seat and smooth buffalo ribs for runners, was poised at the brow of the steep slope.

"You're sure you want to do this?" he asked for the third time. "You'd be a lot safer on a woman's toboggan."

"Goin' down on a slab of birch ain't exactly what I call thrillin'," she replied. "So quit your jawin' an' let this Injun contraption go!"

"All right, *vehoka,* you asked for it!"

The sled flew over the crusted snow, faster and faster down the hill. Rachel screamed in delight. Strong Elk had warned her that they would fly over the ground swifter than a horse could run. He'd been right on that score.

They soared over the snow, Rachel's piercing Rebel yell echoing all the way down the hill. They hit the frozen ice of the creek with a flying bump and continued, the buffalo-rib runners adding their shrieking whine to the excitement of the wild ride. Eventually, the sled came to a rest in a snow bank, where they tumbled off together.

"Let's do it again!" Rachel cried. "Come on! Get up! Let's do it again!" She tried to struggle to her feet, no easy task in her winter clothes, but her husband held her down beside him in the snow.

Strong Elk wrapped his arms around the small bundle of fur that was his wife, his laughter ringing out in the cold, dry air. He kissed her lips and playfully bit the tip of her red nose.

"You're insatiable, *nazheem,*" he said with a chuckle. " 'Play with me,' all day, 'Play with me,' all night. I can't keep this up!"

Rachel threw her arms around her husband's neck and kissed him right back. "You're the one who claims we're supposed to sleep under that there buffalo robe without nary a stitch of clothin' on," she protested. "I'm jest goin' along with your ramptious Cheyenne ways. I purely can't help what happens after that. So don't go a-blamin' me, if'n you can't keep up.''

Strong Elk rolled his wife over on her back, pinning her in the snow with one muscled thigh. ''I'll keep up with you,'' he promised with mock gruffness. He kissed her again, his tongue searching for hers in mounting passion. ''Let's go back to the lodge,'' he said huskily, ''and I'll prove it.''

''First, let's coast down the hill a few more times,'' Rachel begged, barely able to suppress her laughter. ''Everyone in the village is talkin' 'bout the way we keep disappearin' inside our tipi in the middle of the day and not comin' out till the next mornin'. They're goin' to start callin' you Big Stallion instead of Strong Elk.''

He grinned, his black eyes glinting with devilment. ''I'm only making up for lost time.''

''What lost time?'' she demanded.

''All those weeks you kept batting my hands away underneath our courting blanket, and I couldn't do a thing about it because you were wearing the *nihpihist*.'' Strong Elk rose to his feet and swung her up beside him. ''Two more slides down the hill, little girl, and then I'll take you back home. You can scream in my ear while we play with each other in bed.''

She planted her mittened hands on either side of her woolly coat and wrinkled her nose at him with saucy impudence. ''I don't scream in bed,'' she denied on a gurgle of laughter. ''I'm a-hollerin' for help, but nobody never comes to save me!'' She took off through the snowdrift, her husband right behind her with the sled.

They were stopped at the foot of the hill by Young Bear Running, who came riding toward them on a shaggy pony.

''Strong Elk!'' he called the moment he was near enough to be heard. ''We have found signs of a grizzly bear not two days' walk from the camp.''

"A grizzly!" Rachel exclaimed in Cheyenne. "But a bear should be sound asleep in its cave this time of year."

"It must have been disturbed," Strong Elk said grimly. "And it will be hungry after all these weeks." He looked up to meet Young Bear's concerned gaze. "I will take Little Red Fawn back to camp and join you as soon as possible."

"Let me go with you," Rachel pleaded the moment their friend rode away.

Strong Elk shook his head. "No, little girl. Tracking an angry grizzly that's been disturbed from its winter sleep is not like chasing after a buffalo herd or hunting pronghorns. It's far too dangerous. Having you along would be a distraction I couldn't risk, and an added concern to the other hunters. I want you to stay with Porcupine Quills while I'm away. We could be gone for several days."

"Shoot, I ain't afraid to sleep by myself in my own tipi," she protested. She scowled at him in irritation as they trudged through the snow.

For the past four weeks, her husband hadn't allowed her to be alone once. Sometimes, when he went hunting, he took her with him. The few times he'd left the village without her during the day, he'd insisted that she stay close to either Porcupine Quills or his two grandmothers. Rachel knew he'd spoken with Flying Hawk about looking after her whenever he was gone, though neither man had admitted it when she brought the subject up.

"Nevertheless, you're going to do as I tell you," her husband declared in his most highhanded manner. "You can stay with Porcupine Quills or sleep in Flying Hawk's lodge. That's your choice."

"When you decide to have your own way, you're as contrarious as an old billy goat," she grumbled. "I keep lookin' to see if'n you're a-growin' a skinny white beard at the end of that cantankerous chin of yours.''

"That's why the All-Knowing One made me so much larger than you," Strong Elk explained with a grin, making no attempt to hide his amusement. "With a strong-willed redheaded *vehoka* for a wife, I must have some means of enforcing my decisions. And when it comes to this decision, I am going to have my way, Rachel Rose.''

He watched her from the corner of his eye as she marched along beside him. In their six weeks of marriage, she had stubbornly refrained from telling him that she loved him. She readily admitted that she wanted him. But not once had she said the words he longed to hear.

So he'd held back as well knowing he couldn't force the issue. After their wedding night, he expressed his physical need for her, but not his love. Not in words. He'd told her frequently how much he desired her. It was enough for now. If she ever realized just how much he adored her, she would try even harder to get her own way.

And on this issue, there would be no compromising. He had shared his dream of the wolves stalking the elk herd with Flying Hawk and the council chiefs. None of the elders had questioned his explanation of the vision's meaning.

Only Wolf Walking Fast and a few other warriors had refused to see the need for heightened caution. They were impatient young men, who scoffed at the very idea of being attacked by the horse soldiers and were quick to boast about their own prowess in battle. But the wise elders, not the hot-tempered braves, made the decisions for the entire band. The headmen were not about to risk the lives of the women and children unnecessarily. The entire village had been put on alert for a possible attack by the Long Knives.

For the space of one moon's time, pickets were posted and scouts were sent out, day and night. But no one could really imagine the pony soldiers mounting a campaign deep into the heart of the Cheyenne-Sioux hunting grounds during the harshness of winter on the northern plains. It had never been done before. So, gradually, the need for scouts seemed less important as the possibility of a sneak attack appeared less and less likely. After several deep snows, not even pickets were considered necessary. Still, the dream continued to haunt Strong Elk, and he refused to allow his wife to be left alone.

The couple reached their tipi to find about twenty men impatiently waiting for him, all of them eager to track the grizzly. Thunder Cloud had been brought in from the herd and readied by Little Man. The six-year-old sat astride his cousin's gray Appaloosa with a proud smile.

The group was made up of the bravest warriors in the band, including Wolf Walking Fast and Beaver Claws, as well as Young Bear Running. Every man carried a repeating rifle, and most were known for their marksmanship. Each one hoped to be the fortunate brave to count first coup on the great bear.

Strong Elk turned to his recalcitrant wife. "You will remember your pledge, Little Fawn," he said quietly, making it a statement of fact and not a question. "You will not leave the camp without my permission. I don't want you even to go to the river for water in the morning, unless my grandfather or my cousin, Sleeping Bull, is at your side."

She looked at him through narrowed eyes, a willful expression on her lovely face, then turned her head to stare off into the distance. "Shucks, I guess I'll remember, right enough. But I ain't no puny, good-for-nothin' city girl, and the sooner you realize that, the whole lot happier I'll be."

"Kiss me good-bye," he said.

She pretended not to hear him.

The moment Strong Elk started to walk away, Rachel

flung herself on her tall husband, her mouth seeking his in a passionate kiss. It would be their first night apart since their wedding. "Strong Elk," she began in a breathless whisper, "I . . ."

"Tell me, little wife," he murmured. "Say what your heart wants you to say."

"I'll miss you."

"I'll miss you, too, *nazheem.*"

Rachel watched her husband ride out of camp with the large party of hunters. She stood there in the snow until they'd forded the icy Tongue River and disappeared from sight in the pine-covered foothills that led up into the Rosebud Mountains.

Criminently! She'd nearly blurted out just how dang much she loved him. She continued to tell herself that if she never admitted it, he'd be willing to let her leave when the time came. But the scoffing voice inside her head told Rachel she was plain crazy even to think that way. First off, her husband knew she loved him. Lord A'mighty, she couldn't hardly keep her hands off him, day or night. And secondly, even if she never told him she loved him, Strong Elk had absolutely no intention of ever letting her go back home to Sugar Hollow. Not never, nohow.

A fusillade of rifle fire erupted at dawn. Rachel sat up, clutching the buffalo robe that covered her. Her first thought was that her husband was gone and something was terribly wrong. Filled with dread, she looked across the lodge to find that her grandmother had already sprung to her feet and was reaching for her clothes.

"Pony soldiers!" Porcupine Quills cried. "The village is being attacked!"

Rachel scrambled out of bed, threw on her dress and moccasins, and picked up her shot pouch and powder horn. "We have to get out of here fast!" she called to the frightened medicine woman. She grabbed her rifle leaning beside the lodge entrance and took Porcupine Quills's elbow. "Quickly, *niscem*. Quickly!"

The two of them dashed from the tipi.

Warning shouts rang through the encampment. The village—peacefully sleeping only moments ago—was in chaos.

Dazed, Rachel looked around in confusion. People were running everywhere. Women carried babies and toddlers in their arms. Bewildered boys and girls clung to their mothers' skirts.

A withering barrage of gunfire raked the Cheyenne as they raced through the snow. On the hills across the river, the large pony herds stampeded, galloping madly away— their thundering hooves nearly drowning out the *rat-tat-tat* of the rifles.

Blood spattered across the ground in front of Rachel . . . rich scarlet patches in the pure white snow. Fear and horror sent her heart smashing against her ribs. People were falling in crumpled heaps . . . innocent toddlers . . . defenseless old ones . . .

The startled cries of the wounded pierced the steady boom of gunfire. Screams of terrified women and children rent the air.

"Stay beside me, *niscem!*" Rachel shouted. Her grandmother clutched her arm and motioned for Rachel to keep going.

But where?

Warriors with rifles and cartridge belts hurried past them to form a line of defense, most of them barefoot and wearing only clouts. Entire families fled toward the protection of the thickly wooded riverbank.

Bullets churned up the snow at Rachel's feet. She looked past the circle of lodges, and her heart lurched at the sight before her.

Merciful God . . .

A formation of soldiers in their dark buffalo coats nearly encircled the camp. They must have come in stealth during the night! The dismounted cavalrymen formed a skirmish line from the southern end of the village all the way across the eastern side. They'd waited in silence for the first light of day to catch the Indians asleep in their lodges.

Rachel glanced over her shoulder and groaned in despair. More soldiers were in position on the hillsides across the river.

The Cheyenne were trapped in a crossfire.

"No!" she screamed at the advancing line. "No! Don't shoot! These people are peaceful! You're makin' a mistake!" Her voice floated like a wisp of smoke into the deafening roar of the guns.

Someone touched her arm, and Rachel jerked in surprise.

"Quick, Little Fawn," Flying Hawk shouted. "Take cover in the trees. Get your grandmother to safety. Hurry!"

His words brought Rachel to her senses. She grabbed Porcupine Quills's hand. "Yes," she told the Hawk. "Don't worry about us! Do what you must to save the others."

Together they joined the helpless ones fleeing for their lives into the stands of cottonwoods and willows along the riverbank. Their only hope was to work their way northward through the underbrush, to slip past the tightening cordon of soldiers. Bullets sang all around them, kicking up the snow as they ran.

Rachel's breath came in terrified gulps. She looked over at her grandmother and immediately slowed down. Porcupine Quills was panting for air, her chest heaving in great shudders.

"Go, Little Fawn," the medicine woman croaked. "Leave me."

"No!" Rachel shouted over the roar of the battle. "I'm not leavin' you!" She put her arm around the thin, aged body, offering the strength of her support. They started running again, their moccasins dragging through the snow.

Dog Men from the northern end of the village came tearing past them, making their way toward the oncoming soldiers. Zigzagging behind tipis ... kneeling to shoot ... rising to run again ... they hurried to create a living wall between the withering rifle fire and their vulnerable loved ones.

Rachel chanced a quick glance behind her. On the east, a company of mounted cavalry plowed their way through the deep snow toward the far end of the encampment, swinging wide in an attempt to outflank the fleeing Cheyenne.

Some of the warriors in that part of the campsite raced to the edge of the timber. They took up positions behind the trees and boulders to cover the escape of their families. Caught suddenly in their deadly rifle fire, the on-rushing troopers dismounted, stumbling and awkward in their buffalo coats. Holding their horses' reins, they knelt in the snow and returned fire. Each time a cavalryman tried to rise and move forward, a hail of bullets from the trees stopped him in his tracks.

At last, Rachel and Porcupine Quills reached the trees by the river and sank down in the snow, exhausted ... safe for the moment.

Horrified, Rachel watched from her hiding place behind a large cottonwood. All was turmoil and confusion. Bullets spattered everywhere. The shouted orders of the officers could be heard faintly amid the terrifying din, along with the whooping cries of the charging warriors. To the south of the camp, armed troopers were running into the village.

Rachel covered her trembling lips with one shaking

hand. Tears poured down her cold cheeks. Her throat choked with sobs.

God help them!

The soldiers were shooting everyone in sight . . . the old . . . the young . . . children . . . babies . . . anyone who moved.

Some of them were trying to burn the lodges with people still trapped inside. The tough buffalo hides were covered with frost and wouldn't easily catch fire, so the men started slashing at the tipis with their long sabers in a blood-chilling frenzy of hatred.

The soldiers still on the eastern skirmish line were firing volley after volley into the camp, the bullets ripping through the tipis. The dense blue smoke from their guns drifted in billowing clouds on the cold winter air. Several frightened cavalry mounts had broken away. The horses galloped wildly through the people, churning up great chunks of snow, adding to the chaos.

A thrill of pride coursed through Rachel as she spotted Big Pipe Man leading a group of half-naked Red Shields toward the soldiers. Their shrill whoops pierced the din.

"Follow me, warriors!" the courageous war chief bellowed. "Fight for your women and children. It is a good day to die!"

Rachel looked over her shoulder at those nearby. Good Robe Woman and Standing in Water huddled behind several large boulders, their gray heads close together, their arms around each other's shoulders. Not far away, Choke Cherry Blossom crouched at the base of a large tree. She held Moon Shell tightly in her arms, trying to shield her little daughter with her own body.

Rachel turned to her grandmother, who lay beside her, flat in the snow on her stomach. "Are you all right, *niscem?*" she cried. Paralyzing fear slammed through her. Had the medicine woman been shot?

Porcupine Quills lifted her head. "Yes, do not worry

about me," she called, undaunted. "Use your rifle, *nixa*. Shoot them!"

Rachel stared down at the musket in her hand. Her heart leaped to her throat. Killing another human being had not—until that moment—occurred to her. Dear Lord above! She wasn't sure she could, even now.

"I am going to see if I can get closer," she said in Cheyenne to the women nearby. "Wait here."

Crouching, Rachel raced toward a ravine that led from the river. She wiped away the tears that blurred her vision and peeked cautiously over the snowy embankment.

Men were fighting at close range now. The warriors used bows and arrows, rifles, war clubs, lances, knives . . . desperately holding their ground before the advancing well-armed troops. All of the soldiers carried Spencer repeaters, with Colt revolvers holstered at their sides.

She looked in the opposite direction. On a pine-studded knoll across the river, a group of staff officers astride their horses was watching the progress of the battle. With a cry of horror, Rachel recognized her papa's magnificent chestnut stallion.

McDougall's Pride!

She could see the rider's yellow locks. A moan of anguish from deep inside wracked her. She'd know that ugly handlebar mustache anywhere.

It was him.

Lord, she should have known . . . who else but Shelby Bruckenridge would lead these men in such a cowardly sneak attack on a peaceful, unsuspecting village?

Suddenly, Rachel realized that someone on the hillside was shooting over her head toward a patch of higher ground at the edge of the camp. Stretching her neck to look over the bank, she spotted a child in the snow.

Prickly Pear!

The two-year-old was wandering in circles around the fallen body of his mother, wailing in desolation. Bullets kicked up puffs of snow near his tiny bare feet.

Talons of fear clutched at Rachel's heart when she realized what was happening. One of the men on the knoll above her was using the crying toddler for rifle practice.

"Prickly Pear, get down!" Rachel hollered at the top of her lungs.

Dropping her long Kentucky rifle, she scrambled up over the slope and raced toward the child and his mother. The moment she reached them, Rachel knew the sweet young woman with the dimpled smile was already dead. The soft brown eyes, always so filled with laughter, stared vacantly into the gray sky above her.

As Rachel scooped Prickly Pear into her arms, another bullet zinged into the snow at her feet.

She straightened to see Shelby.

He'd ridden forward several yards from the tight cluster of soldiers and was looking at her down the slender barrel of his powerful Spencer carbine.

He knew who she was.

Her short, curly hair stood out like a bright red flag against the snow.

Bruckenridge took careful aim and shot again, missing her by mere inches. The putrid varmint was taunting her. He wanted Rachel to get down on her knees and beg for mercy before he killed her.

He had her dead in his sights.

She knew she'd never be able to make it back to the ravine alive. But if she fell with the child beneath her, she could possibly save Prickly Pear's life.

"*Shelby!*" she screamed up at him. "You miserable spawn of the devil! May your rotten carcass burn in hell!"

Her hysterical words were carried upward on the cold winter wind. The Kentucky Thoroughbred reared and

pawed the air at the sound of her voice. The next shot
went high over her head.

Behind Rachel, unshod hooves thudded in the snow.
She turned to find Strong Elk, stripped for war and
painted frighteningly, galloping toward her on Thunder
Cloud. He didn't even slow the Appaloosa down . . . just
reached out, caught Rachel around the waist, and scooped
her and the child up in front of him. They were within
the safety of the ravine before Shelby could calm his
excited mount and fire again.

Strong Elk slid off his horse and lifted his wife to the
ground. "Are you hurt?"

His heart thundered in terror at how close she'd come
to being killed right before his eyes. As he checked her
swiftly for any sign of blood, she ignored his question
and examined Prickly Pear instead.

"No," she said at last, her breath coming in gasping
pants. "We're both fine. But his mama's dead. And I
ain't seen Little Man nowhere." She looked up to meet
his gaze, her lips trembling. Her eyes were enormous in
her stricken face. Two plump tears made their way
slowly down her wind-reddened cheeks.

"Little Man is with his father," Strong Elk told her.
"I saw them while I was searching for you. They're both
alive."

"You go on, then," she insisted, her voice catching
on a sob. "I'll take care of the child. We'll be safe."

"First, I'll get you back into the cover of the trees
with the rest of the women," he said. "Some of our
hunters are on the ridge above the officers' command
post. We have them pinned down. It will be over
shortly."

Rachel retrieved her rifle from the snow. She turned
and peered over the top of the embankment to search the
foothills above them. But by then, Bruckenridge had disappeared from sight.

"Let's go, Maheszoocess," Strong Elk said gently.

Together, they hurried to the protection of the cotton-woods and river willows, where Porcupine Quills huddled close to several other elderly women. Young Bear Running stood beside the Blossom and Moon Shell, his carbine clutched in his hand and a look of deadly intent on his angry face. Flying Hawk waited beside his two wives, ready to lead the group of women to safety through the thick stand of trees.

Good Robe Woman came over and took Prickly Pear from Rachel, crooning a Cheyenne lullaby to her grandson.

"Stay with my grandfather," Strong Elk told his wife. He started to leave, turned abruptly, and wrapped his arms around her. "You have the heart of a warrior," he said, his words filled with pride and love.

"I ain't brave," she cried, "I ain't brave!" She clung to him, sobbing and nearly incoherent. "I could have k-killed that low-down skunk. I could have killed him! But when I ran to p-pick up the youngun, I threw down my gun like a prankin' fool. It would have b-been as easy as barkin' a squirrel in a tree, but I d-didn't have the guts to use my rifle."

Porcupine Quills moved quickly to her side. "Come, *nixa*," she soothed. She patted the little Fawn's shoulder consolingly. "We must let Strong Elk join the other warriors. And you must help me take care of the wounded."

Lieutenant Colonel Shelby Bruckenridge found himself lucky to have escaped the merciless accuracy of the Cheyenne sharpshooters, who'd appeared out of nowhere on the hill above him. Two of his aides-de-camp had been killed as they'd all scrambled down the snow-covered slopes. Shelby and the rest of his staff swam their mounts across the icy-cold river and galloped, hell-for-leather, to join the troopers at the southern end of the encampment.

In the village, the tide had turned with the sudden arrival of close to twenty young bucks. The outnumbered warriors, fighting recklessly for the lives of their women and children, had beaten back the troopers in savage hand-to-hand combat. Scattered companies of soldiers, their officers dead or mortally wounded, were hastening in retreat, with little or no semblance of order.

Realizing that the savages could mount a counteroffensive once their families were safely away and their stampeded horses recovered, Shelby ordered an immediate abandonment of their position and a full-scale withdrawal to an elevated benchland on the plains to the east. There they would regroup while they waited for the wagons and howitzers to be brought up from the supply base five miles away, where he'd left them.

Shelby had known they'd never get the cannon near enough for a surprise assault. But the need for secrecy was long past. When he had his big guns in place, he'd blow that frigging Indian camp right off the map.

Four days ago, Shelby had sent Major Terence Feehan and half of the Second Cavalry on a reconnaissance mission into the Rosebud Mountains. The Ohioan had argued fiercely against splitting up their men, but Shelby had insisted that his orders be followed, no matter what the major thought. He had divided his force of twelve hundred soldiers because he wanted his lackluster second-in-command far away from all the action—and the glory. Now he waited impatiently for Feehan to rejoin them so they could finish the job they had come to do. Hell, as the ranking officer on the battlefield, Shelby would still get all the credit.

Chapter 19

❧ ∽⟩⟩◯◯

In the aftermath of the brutal attack, the mourning families quickly buried their dead. Rachel and her grandmother walked through the camp circle together, searching for anyone who might be wounded. All around them, women slashed their arms and legs, keening in the high-pitched Cheyenne way of funeralizing.

They found the mutilated body of Mysterious Dancer. She'd been trapped in her tipi when the soldiers first swarmed into the unsuspecting village. The knife she'd used in a vain attempt to defend herself was still clutched in her icy hand. Close by lay the shield with the long buffalo tail that Rachel had given the young woman to show her sorrow for what Shelby had done—and to beg forgiveness. At last, in death, Mysterious Dancer would have the peace that had eluded her in life.

Together, Rachel and her grandmother wrapped the scarred, broken body in a quilled robe and buried it beneath a pile of stones on a hillside across the river. As they finished their sad task, they looked up to see Wolf Walking Fast carrying Sweet Feather in his arms. His face twisted with grief, the warrior brought his beloved burden to lie near Thick Braided Hair and Mysterious Dancer.

Rachel had never known such terrible anguish. The three young women had been ruthlessly cut down by white men who hadn't known them, hadn't nary a reason to hate them, not even the paltry, puling excuse of taking revenge for some past misdeeds. A laughing mother of two pert little ones; a brave, lonely woman horribly scarred by a lust-crazed officer; and a shy, sweet maiden, who wouldn't have harmed nary a living soul in this whole, wide world—all murdered by men who killed for pay. It was a practice beyond understanding to their grief-stricken Cheyenne families.

In all, thirty-two people had been slaughtered by the soldiers and the Crow scouts who'd led them there. Most of the dead were women and children caught in the first few moments of the carnage.

Rachel saw Strong Elk only once after the surprise assault had been repulsed, when he came to speak to her briefly before the men met in council. She knew he had many duties at Flying Hawk's side, for it was his grand-father's wish that the Elk would someday take his place as one of the Old Man Chiefs of the entire Cheyenne nation.

"Our hunting party discovered the presence of a large troop of soldiers in the mountains," her husband told her. "That was why we hurried back to the village so quickly."

Now that the fighting was over, he wore his shirt and leggings again, but he still had dark slashes of war paint on his face. His gaze searched her features, as though reassuring himself that she hadn't nary a scratch on her. "We must thank the Great Powers that we arrived in time," he added quietly.

"Gram told me oncet that a body had to live through things to rightly have a knowin' of their meanin'," Rachel said, pressing a hand against her chest. Her heart ached so bad she could scarcely talk. "But if'n I live to be a hundred, I reckon I'll never know the meanin' of what I witnessed here this mornin'. What kind of folks would do a thing like this?"

Strong Elk cupped her wet cheeks in his hands and wiped away her tears with the pads of his thumbs. His words were filled with a calm resolve. "The two cavalry forces are only hours apart from one another. Their combined strength will far outnumber our warriors. Perhaps as much as ten to one."

Rachel placed her hands on top of his, wishing she could draw some of his enormous strength into her trembling body. But her frightened voice cracked pathetically when she spoke. "What, in God's name, are we goin' to do?"

He put his arms around her comfortingly and held her tight for several moments, then stepped back. "Be prepared to move quickly, *nazheem*. And stay close to your grandmother or mine at all times. Remember, Flying Hawk will be nearby."

A party of young men and boys retrieved most of the stampeded ponies, while the elders and seasoned warriors met in the war council. Rachel was helping Porcupine Quills bind up the wounded when they were told of the council's decision. The band would move out immediately and travel far into the night, making their way northward toward the Yellowstone as quickly as possible.

Dazed and numbed by the horror she'd seen, Rachel worked in silence beside Porcupine Quills. They helped each other take down the stiffened buffalo-hide coverings from the lodge poles. Beneath their feet, frozen pools of blood still stained the snow, where bodies had lain in every direction. Rachel wiped the sleeve of her shaggy coat across her eyes again and again, trying to sop up the tears that wouldn't stop falling.

The entire band had departed the campsite by midday, the injured carried on travois behind the loaded horses. Her heart wracked with unbelievable pain, Rachel rode Spotted Butterfly alongside a pony that pulled the lodge poles for her tipi and all her household possessions. She assumed that Strong Elk was far ahead, somewhere with Young Bear, scouting the route. At the rear, a party of Dog Soldiers waited till everyone was safely away.

She looked about her at the people who rode in near silence. A solemn, unsmiling Moon Shell was seated in front of her mother on their brown-and-white pony. What did the little girl think of the funny *vehoka* now? Rachel wondered sadly. Even Little Man rode straight and tall beside his father, though the six-year-old knew he was leaving his mother buried in the rocky hillside behind them. The courage of the somber children tore at Rachel's heart. She asked herself over and over, what kind of men would do such a thing?

As they traveled across the snowy plains, she tried to keep from sobbing out loud. Everything that had happened that morning was her fault. If it weren't for her, Shelby Bruckenridge would never have tracked them down. Surely, every member of Flying Hawk's band, from the oldest to the youngest, must realize that fact and despise her for it.

There was just one thing Rachel could do to set it all right. She could return to the white man who hated her so badly that he'd followed her across miles of unmapped Indian territory in the dead of winter. If her surrender would keep him from butchering an entire band of people—people who'd treated her as kindly as if she was kin—she'd submit to being his wife, till he ended up killing her in a fit of glassy-eyed rage.

She would go back and plead with Shelby.

Her life for theirs.

And if he refused to leave these good folks in peace,

there wasn't but one thing left to do. She'd kill the skunk. Sure as dogwood bloomed in the springtime, she was the onliest person who could get close enough to the no-good varmint to do it.

She'd slip back to the soldiers, while her docile pack pony kept moving forward with the other horses. It'd be easier than hunting possum with Cousin Lemuel's brag dog. All she had to do was backtrack along the wide trail left by their travois in the snow, then follow the footsteps of the retreating troopers. In the confusion of decamping, Porcupine Quills had ridden on ahead with Good Robe Woman and little Prickly Pear. Nary a body would notice that she was gone till they'd reached the next campsite. With Strong Elk scouting far in the lead, it would be hours before he learned of her disappearance. By then, it'd be too late.

"Colonel Bruckenridge, you've got a visitor."

Shelby looked up with a scowl from the tin plate in front of him. At the sight of her, he laid down his knife and fork and rose slowly to his feet, the look on his face betraying his complete surprise. All around the table, his supper companions jumped up and stood politely in front of their camp chairs at the unexpected appearance of a female.

"Rachel!" cried Terence Feehan in shock. He threw down his napkin, shoved his chair out of the way, and took a step toward her. He halted, as though suddenly realizing that she was married to the man standing beside him.

Her gaze flew to meet the stocky Ohioan's astonished eyes. "Howdy, Major," she said with a heartsick smile. "Congratulations on your new rank. The sergeant here told me about it."

She looked around the group of officers, who were staring at her in discombobulation. Some of these no-

good buzzards were to blame for the massacre she'd witnessed that morning. The sight of them in their warm
winter uniforms sickened her nigh to death. But she'd
come here for a reason, and it wasn't to tell them just
how low-down rotten they were.

Rachel put her hand to her brow with a dejected sigh
and turned to the one man she loathed most of all. "After
that whoppin' you gave 'em, Shelby, them Injuns jest
run me right on out of their camp. I ain't got nowheres
else to go. So . . . so I allowed as how you might take
me on back home with you."

They were standing in the officers' mess tent, where
Sergeant Croft had immediately brought her after she'd
called out to the bewildered sentry in the dark. Rachel
hadn't had a lick of trouble finding the location of the
entire Second Cavalry. The two forces Strong Elk had
told her about had clearly joined up. The light of their
fires could be seen for nearly a mile away in the cloudless
night sky.

When Shelby failed to answer, Rachel shrugged out of
her buffalo coat and folded it over her arm. After pulling
off her beaver hat, she held it in one hand and her rabbit-
fur mittens in the other. She wore a fringed deerskin dress
and leggings, along with winter moccasins, a quilled collar, silver hoop earrings, and a wide, beaded belt. Shucks,
they might as well take a real good gander at her and get
it done with. She reckoned they found her quite a sight,
because they just stood and stared at her for a mighty
long time before anyone could think of a fitting thing to
say.

It was Major Feehan who finally broke the silence.
"Are you hungry?" he asked kindly. "We were just fin-
ishing supper." He looked around for an orderly.

"Naw, not really," she said. The sight of the food
scraps on their plates made her stomach queasy. She'd
just as soon get the whole thing over with as fast as

possible. She looked at Bruckenridge. "I'd like to talk to you personal-like, Colonel, if'n that's all right with you."

In the light of the lanterns hanging from the tent poles, Shelby's amber eyes glittered with a kind of wild excitement. He picked up his wide-brimmed hat from the table and fiddled with the gold cord around the crown, then jerked his chin in the affirmative, as though he'd just made up his mind about something. What to do with her, she suspected.

"Of course," he said, his pale features contorted by a twisted, weasely smile. "We'll go to my quarters, where we can speak privately." His silky smooth voice made her skin crawl.

"I don't think that's a good idea," Major Feehan stated without a moment's hesitation. He was staring straight at Rachel—real meaningful-like. The stern cast to his boyish features betrayed his low opinion of Shelby Bruckenridge's character. The barrel-chested major didn't back down none, neither. Not even at his commanding officer's snarl of contempt. Terence continued in the smooth, mannerable way of a gentleman. "May I suggest that I go along with you, Rachel, as an old friend?"

The rest of the men, still standing at their places in front of their forgotten tin dishes, looked back and forth at one another, flabbergasted at what was going on. Several murmured comments about the irregularity of it all. Rachel reckoned they had no idea who the red-haired white woman standing before them was.

"You forget yourself, Major," Shelby snapped. "Mrs. Bruckenridge and I have some things to discuss, and we're going to do it in private." He stepped forward and motioned for the sergeant standing next to her to move aside.

"Rachel," Terence said earnestly, "I beg you to reconsider. Have me or another officer accompany you. Please.''

"Shucks, I reckon I ought to talk with my husband alone," Rachel told him. "After all this time, it's the least I can do. But I thank you right kindly for your concern, Major Feehan."

She turned and moved toward the entrance. It didn't surprise her none to hear Shelby's steps just behind her.

Once out of the large mess tent, Rachel clamped her lips tight to hide their telltale quivering. She hadn't bothered to bring her rifle along. She knew Shelby would take it from her before he ever agreed to see her alone. But her Bowie knife was hidden inside her high winter moccasin. She'd give the chicken-livered polecat every chance to be reasonable before pulling it on him. If worse came to worse, she'd use her Arkansas toothpick to carve a new hole in his miserable gullet.

As they walked across the packed snow to Shelby's quarters, Rachel realized that Terence Feehan was following them. Her knees started to shake at this unforeseen problem. The well-meaning major was liable to ruin everything.

But Terence stopped several yards short of his superior officer's canvas tent. "I'll be right outside," he called to Rachel. "If you need me, all you have to do is holler."

Too anxious about her plans to answer him, she merely nodded her understanding and kept on walking.

Shelby spoke quietly to the guard positioned several feet in front of the entrance. "I'm going to be visiting with my wife, Private. See to it that we're not disturbed for any reason."

"Yes, sir," the soldier answered.

Rachel squared her shoulders and stepped inside, her husband right on her heels. The tent flap fell in place behind them. Afraid her eyes would give her away, she spoke without turning around. "Shelby, I—"

Her words were cut off. He'd looped a cord around her neck in a lightning movement, and Rachel fought the terrifying effects of strangulation. She reached up, frantically trying to loosen the noose that pressed against her windpipe just below the quilled collar. She pulled and tugged in silent frenzy. He wasn't letting her make a sound that could be heard outside the tent.

Rachel choked and gurgled deep in her throat. Everything started to grow dim. She reached out blindly, trying to find something to strike him with, and clawed at empty space. No matter how she bucked and kicked, Shelby just kept pulling the string tighter and tighter. She struggled for air, staggered, and collapsed.

When she regained consciousness, Rachel was lying on the cold oilcloth that covered the floor, bound and gagged and completely naked. Dazed, she searched the tent till she found him. He was seated on a camp chair, watching her with those strangely excited, yellow eyes. The moment he realized she was awake, he stood up and smiled.

"Well, well, Mrs. Bruckenridge," he said softly, "we meet again. And how many dirty, thieving bucks have you slept with in the meantime, I wonder." He slowly removed his sword belt and slid the sheathed saber off its sling. Then he wound the strip of tooled leather around one hand, leaving its ornate gold buckle dangling evilly.

Her heart racing in terror, Rachel tried to sit up and failed. Her hands were firmly lashed behind her back. Her ankles were tied as well. She screamed. The sound was so muffled by the cloth, she knew she'd never attract anyone's attention.

"It's time you received the disciplining you deserve, Rachel," he drawled. "And I've been waiting patiently to give it to you." He stepped closer and bent over her. His high cavalry boots, with their fancy brass spurs, were so bright and shiny she could see the blurred reflection of her pale body in the polished black leather.

"It's too bad I won't be able to hear your pleas for mercy," he whispered in the sugar-coated tones of a Louisville beau. "Much as I'd love to hear you beg, I don't dare take that gag off." He straightened and smoothed his mustache with a finicky motion. "You understand, don't you? Your nosy friend out there would want to put a stop to all my fun."

Rachel tipped her head back and stared at him. From the insane glow that lit his pasty-white face, she reckoned she'd never survive the beating. As he brought his arm back to strike the first blow, she closed her eyes and prayed she'd pass out quickly. She cringed, waiting for the lash to fall.

She heard, instead, the sound of a vicious thud. Her lids flew open just in time to see Shelby pitch to the oilcloth in front of her. Then Rachel did something she'd never done before in her life.

She fainted.

Strong Elk stood over Shelby's crumpled body, wishing he could do more than smash the bastard's skull with the butt of his Henry rifle. But he dared not risk another sound. And there wasn't a second to lose.

Rachel lay unconscious at his feet. He was so angry with the little wretch for what she'd done, he wanted to shake her awake, so he could roar at her, until she bawled like a baby. *Eaaa!* She'd never do anything like this again. Not if he had to keep her trussed up for the rest of her life.

Grabbing the buffalo robe he'd brought with him, Strong Elk rolled up his wife and her clothes in its folds and threw her over his shoulder. He left as quickly and silently as he'd entered—through the slit he'd made with his knife at the back of the tent. He tossed his precious bundle across Thunder Cloud's back and jumped up behind her. At his signal, the gray stallion leaped forward, with Spotted Butterfly following in their snowy wake.

The guard standing at the front of the tent heard the noise and hurried to see what was happening. Major Feehan, who'd been pacing back and forth a short distance away, darted after him. They were just in time to spot an Indian riding away with a suspiciously large bundle up in front of him and a black-and-white pony galloping alongside.

The guard raised his carbine and aimed.

Terence quickly pushed the barrel aside. "Hold your fire, soldier," he ordered. "That buffalo robe just may have a woman inside. You can't take a chance on hitting her."

"A woman?" the guard asked incredulously. He turned from the officer to stare out into the darkness where the Indian had just disappeared. "Who, sir?"

"Why, Mrs. Bruckenridge, man. Who else?"

"Shouldn't we go after them?"

"I don't think that's necessary," Terence replied with a deliberative shake of his head. "I think the lady is probably better off right where she is."

Rachel regained her senses to find herself lying on her belly across the back of a galloping horse. She was still tied, hand and foot, with a silk bandana over her mouth. Only now she was rolled up in a buffalo robe. If it weren't for the hide's thick padding, her innards would have been jarred to a pulp.

She had no idea whose horse she was on. Well, shoot, that wasn't exactly the truth of it. She had a pretty good hunch who the horse belonged to, seeing as how the rider didn't say a word when she started squirming and wriggling to show him she was awake and wanted to sit up.

When he didn't respond, she thumped her head against

his leg and made muffled noises through the gag. When that didn't get nary a squeak out of him, she tried to shove her shoulder into his crotch. That got a response. Finally.

The rider reined his horse to a halt and dismounted. Rachel felt herself being lifted from the snorting animal and laid, belly down, on the snow. She flopped around like a catfish in a net, trying to get out of the robe, until she felt him put his foot on her backside and give her an irritated, little shove. She lay still after that, and the shaggy hide was slowly peeled away from her face.

The bright moonlight reflected off the snow, lighting her husband's blade-sharp features as he met her worried gaze.

Ooo-whee, he was mad!

Strong Elk just stared at her, his eyes as hard and black as two cinders from hell. His jaw was clenched so tight a muscle twitched at the side of his cheek.

When he drew his knife from its sheath, she blinked in surprise at the sudden movement. He shoved the robe back out of his way and cut the cord that tied her hands and feet, then started massaging them to help get the blood flowing again. She couldn't help whimpering a mite from the pain, but he never paused for a second, letting her know she was getting exactly what she deserved.

The freezing night air swirled around Rachel's naked body, and she started to shiver uncontrollably. She tried to untie the scarf with her shaking hands while he worked on her feet. It wouldn't come loose. Without saying a word, he pushed her fingers away and cut the knot.

"Strong Elk," she gasped, "thank—"

He clapped his large hand completely over her mouth and pressed her nostrils together between his thumb and forefinger, the way a Cheyenne mama did when she taught her baby not to cry in time of danger.

"Rachel," he bit out savagely, "don't say a word. Understand?"

She nodded vigorously.

He released her and stood up. "Now get dressed."

The sound of his cold, clipped voice sent a shudder of foreboding through her. She recollected what he'd told her once. That if she ever tried to leave without telling him first, he'd put a rope around her neck and make her walk all the way back tied to his horse. She put her fingertips to her throat and winced in pain. There was a raw, searing burn around her neck, where Shelby had nearly strangled her to death. She peeked up at her husband from the corner of her eye to find him watching her every move, his face a mask of complete indifference. Well, shucks, so much for getting a lick of sympathy from him.

Beneath the sheltering warmth of the robe, Rachel quickly slipped into her dress, leggings, and moccasins. She pulled on her coat and hat and rose awkwardly to her feet. Tarnation, it felt like a million needles were sticking into her toes. To her joyful surprise, she turned to find Spotted Butterfly not far away. She hadn't realized her pony had been with them all along. It'd been too hard to hear anything, wrapped up like a little pork sausage in the buffalo hide.

She waited to find out what would happen next. From the long, nerve-wracking silence, she suspected she was going to do a whole lot of walking before the night was over. To her relief, Strong Elk picked up the robe and wrapped it snugly around her. Then he lifted her up and set her sidesaddle on Thunder Cloud. She heaved a sigh of eternal thanksgiving.

"You deserve to walk all the way back," he stated without a trace of emotion as he mounted behind her. "But I can't spare the time it'd take." He put his arms around her and gathered up the reins without any explanation at all about why she wasn't riding her own pony.

Within the protection of her husband's strong arms, Rachel felt like she'd purely died and gone to heaven. She tilted her chin and looked up at him, tears of joy blurring her sight. "Strong Elk, I—"

"We'll talk about this when we get back to our lodge," he said, sounding just like Old Coaley himself, promising a visit to hell.

"But I want—"

"Rachel, shut up."

She decided to take his advice.

They rode in silence at a steady trot, her piedy little pony keeping pace right beside them. Eventually, Rachel's heartbeat returned to normal. She tried not to think about what had happened in Shelby's tent. Or what would have happened if Strong Elk hadn't followed her. She laid her head on his solid chest and let the tears flow silently. Lord A'mighty, she was so thankful. She didn't care what heinous Cheyenne punishment her husband had in mind for his vexatious wife. She'd gladly walk all the way to the Yellowstone River, dragging the lodgepoles behind her. She was just so plumb grateful to be back in his arms again.

When they arrived at the camp, nearly everyone was sleeping. Strong Elk had signaled the pickets with the low, hooting sound of a snow owl. Rachel saw Porcupine Quills standing at the entrance of her own small lodge when they rode in. The moment her grandmother spied them coming, she waved a silent greeting and then disappeared inside her tipi.

Strong Elk lifted Rachel down in front of their lodge, which some of the other women must have put up for them. She staggered inside to find they had even lit a fire. Exhausted and grateful, she fell on top of the bearskin that covered their willow mattress, still wearing her coat and hat.

When her husband came in after unbridling the horses, Rachel waited for him to speak first. Everything about him screamed of anger, though he didn't make nary a sound. She'd never listened to such a fearful quiet in her life as he stripped off his clothes and laid them aside.

Stark naked, he came over and crouched down beside her. Without a word, he undressed her, just like she was a little doll. Off came the coat and hat. Next the moccasins, leggings, and quilled collar. When he went to pull her dress over her head, she squirmed in sudden embarrassment, and he met her bewildered gaze. That's all he had to do—look at her. She read the silent message in his eyes and gave him her complete cooperation.

Rachel waited as he went to get something from a parfleche and returned to their bed, carrying a small, lidded bowl. She was lying on her back, the glow of the fire flickering over her bare body.

Without saying a word, he examined her.

Everywhere.

He was as gentle as a mama counting the fingers and toes on her newborn babe, but she knew Shelby Bruckenridge's fate—if he was still alive—hung in the balance. Whether the varmint would die a quick death or suffer days of prolonged, agonizing torture depended on what Strong Elk found. There mustn't have been a mark on her, except for the rope burns, for when he sat back on his haunches and braced his hands on his thighs, some of the tension was gone from his face.

Then her husband tenderly rubbed the salve from the little clay pot over the burns on her wrists, ankles, and throat. His touch was so incredibly soft, Rachel's heart ached with love for him. The cooling scent of wintergreen filled the lodge, bringing back honey-sweet memories of their wedding night.

Two fat tears rolled down her cheeks. When Strong Elk looked at her questioningly, she shrugged her shoulders. "I lost my grandpappy's knife," she offered lamely.

His expression turned thunderous. The single, clipped word rang out like a gunshot in the still tipi. "Why?"

Rachel covered her face with her hands and mumbled into her palms. "I couldn't help it. Shelby came up behind me afore I ever got a chance to pull it on him."

"Rachel," he barked in exasperation, "why did you go there in the first place?"

She realized she'd misunderstood his question. She peeked through her fingers, amazed that he'd even have to ask. "I was a-goin' to tell Shelby that if'n he'd leave you folks in peace, I'd go back with him and be his wife. And if'n he wouldn't promise me that, I was a-goin' to kill him."

Bracing his weight on his elbows, Strong Elk covered his wife's small body with his much larger one. He buried his fingers in her coppery curls and smoothed his bare skin across her satiny flesh in a declaration of absolute ownership. His thickened male member stabbed at the softness of her inner thigh, and he rubbed it against her in a deliberate, purposeful manner.

"Little Fawn," he grated in her ear. "Can you feel that?"

"Yeah," she answered with a stifled sob.

"That means I'm the warrior in this family. I get to do all the killing." He braced up on his hands and reached between them to gently stroke her delicate tissues as he looked into her wide, wondering, tear-filled eyes. "Do you feel this?"

She swallowed noisily. "Yep."

"This means you're the wife. You get to do just what I tell you. And you are never going to leave our camp without my permission again. Do you understand?"

"Yep."

"Good. Now kiss me."

Their mouths and tongues met in a kiss of uncontrollable passion. Rachel threw her arms around him, straining to be closer. As he came inside her, she broke the kiss to meet his smoldering gaze. The controlled anger she'd seen earlier was still there, but most of it had turned to desire. A burning, carnal desire that seemed to pour over her like liquid fire, scalding her right to the bone. She clutched his straight black hair and arched her back, thrilling to the familiar touch of his braids as they brushed lightly across her sensitive breasts.

He drove into her, pounding and thrusting, and she sobbed with happiness and thanksgiving. He'd never before taken her so quick and hard and savage. She knew, instinctively, it was because he'd come so close to losing her.

Strong Elk bent his head and kissed her again. "This time I want the words, little rose," he said harshly. He thrust his hips upward, his sex buried deep inside her.

Currents of shimmering sensations pulsated through Rachel. She caressed his tight buttocks, straining and taut with sexual tension. Her hands moved hungrily over his hard-muscled flesh, over his flanks and the beautiful curve of his back, up the bumps of his spine to his massive shoulders, as every inch of her female body responded to his overwhelming maleness. She purred way down in her throat, the vibrant feelings so exquisite, she felt close to swooning.

"I want the words, Rosie," he insisted. "I want to hear you say them tonight."

He kissed her deeply as he moved inside her. Rachel matched his rhythm, lifting her hips, keening her pleasure. Her nails clawed at the bulging muscles of his upper arms, while the urgency grew inside her to a frantic, insatiable need.

His powerful body suddenly stilled above her, and her lungs spasmed for air. She knew he was bending her to his will. He was determined to keep her, to never let her go. And equally determined to hear her confess her true feelings.

"Don't stop now," she pleaded. "Oh, darlin', don't stop."

Her husband resumed his steady, pumping strokes, increasing the tempo till he brought her once again to heaven's door. She was vaguely aware that she was crying, long, drawn-out, plaintive cries of female submission. And in the onrushing throes of ecstasy, Rachel admitted to herself what he was resolved to hear her say.

She would never leave him.

Never.

He spoke in her ear, his voice low and compelling. "Tell me now, *zehemehotaz*. Tell your husband now."

"*Nahyam,* I love you!" she sobbed as she soared on her way to paradise.

Strong Elk tensed above her, every muscle in his body quivering with the strain of his iron control. Then he drove deep inside her, again and again. "*Namehota, nazheem,*" he groaned, as convulsions of pleasure rocked his whole frame and his seed spurted within her soft, welcoming warmth. "I love you, too, little wife."

Rachel's eyes were closed, but she knew her husband was smiling. Spent and languorous in the afterglow, she made no attempt to move away. She knew him too well, by now, even to try. She would have several more tastes of pure, genuine rapture before she fell asleep in his arms.

Just as she expected, he rolled over on his back, taking her with him, still deep inside her. She sprawled on top of his magnificent body, her bent legs pressed against his jutting hipbones. She kissed the broad, muscled chest and inhaled the wonderful mixture of juniper and heady male scent. She smoothed her hand across his brown nipple and lightly traced the outline of the elk above his pounding heart. His manhood jerked reflexively at her touch, and she smiled with absolute contentment.

"If you'd been born a Thoroughbred stallion, 'stead of a Cheyenne warrior," she said huskily, "you'd have been the prize stud of the Kentucky Bluegrass." Without raising her head from his chest, she reached up and felt his mouth. "Yep, I knew you'd be grinning at that one." She chuckled. "I like you a whole sight better, *nahyam,* when you're not mad at me."

He drew her fingers inside his mouth and ran his tongue across the pads of her fingertips, then bit them.

"Ouch!" she protested, as she jerked her hand away. She nestled her head at the base of his throat and sighed happily. "Leastways, I surely am glad you followed me."

"I didn't follow you, Maheszoocess," he answered, rubbing his chin across the top of her curls. "I was at the soldiers' camp when you arrived. You can imagine how I felt when I heard you call out to the sentry and then saw you ride Spotted Butterfly right into the middle of my enemies' tents."

She braced her arms on his chest and lifted her head to look into his eyes, scarce able to believe him. "You were already there?"

Strong Elk smoothed the tangled locks away from his wife's lovely face and touched the silver hoops in her ears to set them swinging gently. "I'm the only one in our band who speaks English well enough to understand what the officers were saying."

She raised her russet eyebrows at that, and he amended quickly, "Other than you. And believe me, Rachel Rose, the thought of sending you to spy on the Second Cavalry never once occurred to me."

He put his hands on her waist and eased her to a sitting position above him. Cupping her silken breasts, he stroked their pink crests with his thumbs and continued. "My years with the army made it easy to pass myself off as one of their scouts. One Plains Indian looks pretty much like another to raw recruits from the East. I had to get as close as possible and hear their plans."

"Did you hear them?"

"Yes." He kneaded the firm globes gently, his gaze fastened on the twin rosebuds that puckered beneath his touch. He could feel her delicate muscles flutter and tighten around his throbbing hardness. His mouth curved upward in a satisfied smile. She had admitted she loved him.

"What's goin' to happen to us?" she asked, her green eyes wide with apprehension.

"I will wake my grandfather and the other council chiefs shortly. Once they've heard what I learned, and our decision is made, the rest of our people will be awakened. The old and the young need all the sleep they can get tonight. We'll be leaving well before dawn and moving as fast as we can."

"Where are we goin'?"

"Canada."

Strong Elk sat up. Keeping her still on top of him, he shifted so he could lean against the backrest at the head of the mattress. He cupped her smooth bottom in his hands, brought her even closer, and nuzzled her breasts. She gasped in response, whether to his answer or his greedy lips, he wasn't sure.

"Canada!" she exclaimed. She arched her back and lifted the milky-white mounds higher, giving him better access to their rosy tips. "If'n we're leavin' before dawn, hadn't you better get some sleep?"

"I'm not through disciplining my wife yet. And I've been waiting patiently to do it."

She started to pull back in surprise. He held her right where she belonged. "You heard what that skunk said?"

"I had to move both horses to the back of Bruckenridge's quarters from behind the mess tent," he murmured. "I got there just in time to hear him." He took one smooth globe in his mouth and flicked the tight bud with his tongue.

Her engorged breasts rose and fell, as her breathing grew deeper. "That's when you decided I was in trouble?" she asked on a ragged sigh. "When he said he was goin' to discipline me?"

"I knew you were in trouble when you didn't answer him, love." He moved to her other breast, laving the sweet rosebud, as he breathed in the intoxicating scent of wildflowers and wintergreen.

She bracketed his cheeks with her hands and tugged his face upward, so she could look into his eyes. She was frowning in concentration, her deep voice confused and doubtful. "I don't reckon I rightly understand."

"Nazheem," he said with a grin as he thrust up inside her, "when have I ever heard you willingly stop talking? I knew you had to be either gagged or unconscious."

"But I—"

"Rachel, shut up and kiss me."

She decided to take his advice again. Twice in one evening. Lord A'mighty, that ought to take some kind of prize.

Chapter 20

Flying Hawk's band slipped away from their encampment on Tongue River before the coming dawn had bathed the tipis in its wintry light. Nearly half the lodges remained standing, their fires still lit. The smaller homes, with tattered buffalo hides covering old lodge poles, were left scattered over the campsite. The larger ones had been dismantled and packed for the long journey ahead.

From a distance, it looked as though most of the village still slept. The oldest and weakest horses of the large herds roamed the hillsides across the river. Members of the Dog Soldier society and the Red Shields remained in the camp, some of them dressed as women. They moved about the circle of lodges as though doing the normal morning tasks. A few of these courageous men had taken the suicide vow, promising to remain and fight until they were killed by the soldiers. In this way, the fleeing elders and children would have the longest time possible before the discovery of the ruse. Wolf Walking Fast was one of them. Big Pipe Man embraced his son, knowing they would not meet again until he joined the Wolf in the spirit world.

Strong Elk had learned while he was in the soldiers' camp that Shelby Bruckenridge planned to wait until his cannon were brought forward through the snow from five miles away. The Second Cavalry's commanding officer seemed captivated by the idea of training the howitzers on the Indian village, even though several of his advisers, including the outspoken Major Feehan, suggested that the badly outnumbered savages should be given a chance to surrender before being blown to pieces. The yellow-haired colonel's fascination with his heavy artillery would prove to be his undoing.

On the first afternoon of their escape, Strong Elk insisted that his wife ride with him for several hours. Rachel protested, embarrassed to be treated like a child. She was so exhausted, however, that she fell asleep in his arms the moment she quit muttering her complaints about having a ripsnitious, biggity-mouthed mule for a husband. As he rode with her cradled against him, he prayed to Maheo once again that Little Red Fawn would soon grow big with child. He smiled in anticipation. The signs were already favorable.

Most of the men who'd stayed behind caught up with the band the next day, leaving only the young warriors who had vowed to fight to the death at the deserted campsite. The returning braves reported that the wagons carrying the cannon were buried in the snow a night's sleep from the soldiers' campsite. The entire Second Cavalry appeared to be waiting for their commander to decide whether the big guns were to be abandoned.

The Great Powers intervened on the third day, sending the Chinook, a warming wind coming through the mountains to the west, to melt away the top layer of snow and completely wipe out the tracks of the fleeing band.

In the weeks that followed, the Cheyenne moved quickly northward along Tongue River to the Yellowstone. From there they struck out across the snowy plains to the Missouri. They avoided contact with all whites as they crossed the two frozen rivers. For mile after mile, they saw no other party, and they knew the Great Powers were guarding them.

The smaller children were wrapped in heavy buffalo robes and frequently rode within the shelter of their fathers' arms. The babies rested snugly against their mothers' warm bodies. The pace was hurried, but not harsh. Each day they left the horse soldiers—hampered by the transport of cannon—farther behind. Several families slept together in the large lodges each night, shielded from the sweeping winds. Strong Elk and Little Red Fawn curled up near Porcupine Quills in his grandfather's tipi. They were crowded, but cozy and safe.

During the journey, the Elk began to worry about his usually vivacious wife. He knew that Rachel continued to blame herself for the massacre. The death of Sweet Feather especially seemed to haunt her, and the little Fawn would frequently break into tears without any warning. By the end of the second week, she refused to speak a word of English, even when he teased her unmercifully in an attempt to get her so riled she'd forget her guilt-ridden grief. He yearned to see her sunny smile and hear her colorful speech. But the crowded lodge made it difficult for him to discuss with her the shame she felt at being white.

Finally, by the third week, he again insisted that she ride in front of him on Thunder Cloud. This time she made no protest. She snuggled up against him with a weary sigh, burying her sad little face in the buffalo robe he wore around his shoulders.

"Did you ever wonder, Rosie, girl," he queried, "how I came to speak French?"

She cocked her head, instantly alert and curious. "You learned it from the mountain men and from the white missionary, Father De Smet," she replied in Cheyenne.

"They helped me improve my knowledge of the language," he explained, still speaking the *veho* tongue. "But I first learned it as a small child from my trapper grandfather, Antoine Tréfouret. He and my mother, Evening Star, who was half-white, taught me to speak French practically from the day I was born."

Rachel sat up straight and stared into his eyes. "You are part white?" she gasped in Cheyenne.

Strong Elk smiled at her unqualified astonishment. "Yes, love. I have white blood in me."

His wife narrowed her eyes and scowled at him in disbelief. "You're jest a-sayin' that to be kindly," she accused. "Reckon I've been in the mullygrubs a mite lately."

"No, I'm not just being kind," he denied, grinning with satisfaction. It was so good to hear her quaint mountain dialect again. "I don't tell whoppers like some little white girls do."

"Why didn't you never tell me this here yarn before?"

Strong Elk grew serious. "Like you, Little Fawn," he said, "I was ashamed of my white heritage."

"But you were a guide for the army," she pointed out incredulously. "You worked for the whites, and so did your papa."

"And I deeply regret those years," he confessed. "When I was a young, unfledged warrior, I thought the white man's road was the only answer for the Indian. I attempted to live the *veho* way of life. As a scout and interpreter, I was extremely proud of my ability to speak their languages and to get white captives released by hostile tribes."

"Well, I hope to spit," she declared. "You should have been proud." She patted his chest with her mittened hand in wifely approval. "What you did was mighty fine."

"Not everything," he answered wryly. "When I was

eighteen, I nearly killed another Cheyenne scout. We were both drunk on whiskey and got into a knife fight over an Arapaho woman.'' He met her wondering gaze and added truthfully, ''I don't even remember what she looked like, let alone her name.''

''Darlin', I'm so sorry,'' she whispered, her eyes soft with commiseration. His wife knew the Cheyenne people had a strict taboo against killing a fellow tribesman. If the other man had died, the Elk would have been shunned by Flying Hawk's band, perhaps for the rest of his life. At the very least, he would never have been able to smoke the pipe at a council fire again.

''I never touched a drop of alcohol after that,'' he said. ''I was deeply ashamed. The scar left from falling into a fire during the brawl was a permanent reminder of my foolishness.'' He looked at her questioningly. ''You must have noticed it on my back.''

She clucked her tongue with an air of amused resignation. ''You've got so many scars on your big body, *nahyam,* I don't rightly reckon I even know which one you're a-talkin' 'bout.''

''The puckered one across my shoulder blades.''

''Oh, that!'' she exclaimed. ''I thought that was jest somethin' left over from the Medicine Lodge. But didn't you stay with the army after your fight with that other Cheyenne?''

''Yes. For many years, I thought I could help my people by riding with the Long Knives. Only after the horrible butchery of a band of Southern Cheyenne at Sand Creek over three years ago did I turn from the white man's way completely. I wanted to forget there was a drop of *veho* blood in my veins.''

Rachel clasped his forearm compassionately. ''Do all the folks in your grandfather's band know about your bein' part white?''

''Of course, *nazheem.*'' He kissed her forehead,

touched by her tenderhearted sympathy. "They knew my mother and her parents well. My grandmother was Choke Cherry Blossom's great-aunt."

"Tarnation," she gulped in awe. "Why, they treat you jest like you was pure Cheyenne."

"In their eyes, I am," he assured her.

They rode in silence for a while. Rachel rested her head against his chest, apparently thinking of what he'd just told her. He could tell from the quiet tension in her small frame that she still harbored doubts about her own worth. His heart ached with love for her.

"Little Fawn," said Strong Elk tenderly, "do you know you are carrying our child?"

She jerked up straight and braced her hands on his shoulders, gazing at him in amazement. "No! Are you sure?" she demanded, her deep little voice filled with delight.

He nodded.

"How do you know?"

He smiled as he tucked a stray curl under her bearskin hat. "Do you realize how many weeks it's been since you last—"

She clapped her rabbit-fur mitten over his mouth, her green eyes big with embarrassment and wonder. "It purely amazes me the things you'll say right out loud," she scolded. She chewed her lip, mentally counting back the weeks. "Now that I recollect..." A glow of happiness lit her fine-boned features. She threw her arms around his neck and sprinkled kisses all over his face. "A baby! We're goin' to have a baby!"

"Our child will have both white and Cheyenne blood," he reminded her soberly.

"Yeah." She shrugged at the obviousness of his statement.

"Are you going to be ashamed of our child because he's part white?"

His wife glowered at him. "Course not!" she exploded. "Why, 'twon't be the little babe's fault what some low-down, chicken-livered white men done back there at Tongue River."

"And it's not your fault either, Rachel Rose."

Taken aback, she stared at him. "It isn't, is it?" she said thoughtfully.

"Were your grandparents capable of such cruelty?"

"No! Gram and Gramps were the bestest, most wonderfulest folks in the world. They could never have done such a terrible thing."

"Neither could mine," he said. "The blood that was spilled at the Tongue is not on your hands, *vehoka*. There was nothing you could have done to prevent it. Had you stayed with Bruckenridge, he would have killed you. You know that, don't you?"

"Yep, he'd have killed me for sure," she readily agreed.

"Then don't keep blaming yourself. We're going to teach our children to be proud of who they are. That means we have to first be proud of ourselves."

She grinned at him in admiration. "How'd you get so smart?"

"It must be the Cheyenne blood in me," he answered.

Rachel turned and hollered to Young Bear Running, who was riding not far away. "We're going to have a baby!"

The Bear smiled, but showed no surprise. "I know," he shouted back. "Your husband already told me."

She looked around, spied Porcupine Quills on a gentle mare, and cupped her mouth with her hands. "We're going to have a baby!" she cried in excitement.

"Yes, Little Fawn," her grandmother called, her wrinkled face beaming with pride. "In Meanesehe, the summer moon."

"July!" Rachel said softly. Her eyes aglow, she slid

her arms around her husband's neck and smiled shyly. "Which night did I . . . did we . . . ?"

Strong Elk's hearty laugh rang out. *"Nazheem,"* he said, "some things even your Cheyenne husband doesn't know."

By the middle of December, the Cheyenne crossed the Medicine Line into Canada. Not even Lieutenant Colonel Shelby Bruckenridge would dare to lead his command across the border that separated the two friendly nations. Such an act would be considered a violation of the British queen's sovereignty.

The band settled in a beautiful valley surrounded by hills covered with pine for new lodge poles and a small river running through it. In the distance, the snowy peaks of the Rocky Mountains rose up against the western horizon.

Strong Elk knew that a group of Santee Sioux had fled to Canada after an uprising in Minnesota seven years earlier, and the queen's government had allowed them to remain. He hoped Flying Hawk's band would be treated in the same tolerant manner.

Three weeks after they arrived, two members of the North West Mounted Police, accompanied by a half-breed guide and interpreter, rode out to their encampment from Fort Walsh.

On the banks of Tongue River in Montana, the Americans had amassed a force of over a thousand soldiers to launch a surprise attack on Flying Hawk's band. Here in Canada, two policemen rode boldly into the Cheyenne camp. Either these Mounties were very wise or very foolish. Strong Elk suspected it was the former.

Constable McLean and Inspector Legaré introduced themselves. Both men, somewhere in their mid-thirties, had great, bushy mustaches with long curling ends. They wore buffalo coats, black bearskin hats, woolen scarves around their necks, and warm moccasins made of hide. Strong Elk was impressed with their hardy appearance. They were clearly able to survive in the outdoors, despite the bitter elements and the many dangers of traveling through a wilderness.

Once the Mounted Police realized how much better at translating the difficult Cheyenne language Strong Elk was than the part-Blackfoot scout they'd brought for that purpose, they agreed to use the Elk as interpreter for both sides. They met with the council of elders and chiefs in Flying Hawk's lodge.

"Why have you come?" McLean asked, once the peace pipe had been passed around.

"My people have been driven into the land of the Great White Mother by an overwhelming force of American pony soldiers," Flying Hawk replied in his dignified way. "The Long Knives attacked our sleeping village. They killed thirty-two of our band, most of them women and children. The soldiers made no attempt to take any prisoners or to offer the helpless ones a chance to surrender."

The Mounties exchanged knowing glances. It seemed they'd already heard of the United States army's brutal policy toward the Indians.

"Your people will not be bothered as long as they keep the queen's laws," Constable McLean said, looking directly at Flying Hawk when he spoke. His piercing blue eyes revealed an honest, forthright manner. "Our government plans to make a treaty with the tribes in the North West Territories this spring. Your band will be invited to the great council. It will be decided then if you'll be allowed to stay permanently. In the meantime, I'll send word to my commissioner of your presence in this valley. He will contact our prime minister, Sir John Macdonald."

"We will harm no one," the Old Man Chief promised.

"I will see that my young warriors obey all of the White Mother's laws."

"This also means you must cause no trouble with the other tribes," cautioned Inspector Legaré, his brown eyes somber. Like his partner, he exuded an air of calm authority tempered by humane compassion.

"We will send messengers to the head chiefs of the Blackfoot and Cree nations, telling them we come in peace," Flying Hawk assured him. "We will smoke the pipe with our former enemies and fight no more."

The policemen rose and shook hands with all the chiefs and elders, and the council was ended.

Afterward, Rachel visited with both Mounties, who assumed, for one startled moment, that she was a captive. They bristled with indignation until she explained that she'd married Strong Elk Heart of her own free will and lived with the Cheyenne by choice. With warm smiles, the men accepted her invitation to share the evening meal and the shelter of their lodge for the night. They confided that she was the first white woman they'd seen in nearly three years.

Inspector Legaré and her husband jawed away in what she assumed was French, while she visited with the constable in English. McLean happened to notice the lavender-and-pink plaid folded over a backrest in their tipi. When she learned that his father had been born in Scotland, Rachel told him about her McDougall kinfolk and her life in Sugar Hollow.

Rachel was touched by the honest and open friendliness which these tall, strong men showed to everyone in the village. She sensed instinctively that they considered the life of an Indian as sacred as that of a white and believed that all men were truly equal in the eyes of the law. Under the protection of the North West Mounted Police, Flying Hawk's band would be safe at last.

After the policemen had left the next morning, she

asked her husband what the words *Maintiens le Droit* on their badges meant.

Strong Elk's mouth curved upward, as he put his arm around her and drew her close. The timbre of his deep, quiet voice was filled with hope for his people. "Uphold the right."

As the harshness of January set in, their valley was cut off from the outside world by snowstorms. Deer, elk, and other game abounded in the wooded hills, and the hunters continued to bring in fresh meat. Because of Strong Elk's fearless leadership and his know-how of the fighting ways of the U.S. cavalry, the band had managed to tote most of their winter provisions and household goods with them across the snowy plains.

Rachel had never been happier. The occasional bouts of queasiness in the mornings and sleepiness in the afternoons didn't once lower her spirits. Long winter nights beneath the buffalo robe, wrapped in her husband's brawny arms, left her as content as a bullfrog floating facedown in a barrel of moonshine. No amount of urging on her part, however, could convince Strong Elk that he didn't have to treat her like she was made of glass. Even when she scratched and bit him in her wild excitement, he continued to make love to her with a gentleness that would have put a big-eyed heifer with her first calf to shame.

During the day, she played games in the snow with her husband—or anyone else available, when he was too busy. She chatted with the other women while quilling or sewing or preparing food. Sometimes, Strong Elk took her hunting. Other times, Porcupine Quills and Moon Shell came to visit Rachel in her small, cozy tipi. And she often helped Good Robe Woman and Standing in Water care for their motherless great-grandchildren. To

Rachel's unbounded joy, Prickly Pear had started to laugh again.

Each evening, Rachel smoothed her palms over her bare stomach, trying to tell if she showed any sign of carrying a child. "I need a mirror," she complained to her husband one night. "I purely can't tell nothin' this way."

She stood on the wolf pelt beside their mattress, naked as the day she was born. Strong Elk sat cross-legged on the black bearskin, watching her go through her nightly ritual.

"You'll be able to tell soon enough without using a mirror," he assured her with a complacent smile. "Now come here, little rose, and get in bed with your husband, where you belong."

He was right.

By February, she was definitely pooching out.

By March, she was carrying a firm, round ball inside her. Now every evening, Strong Elk would smooth his cupped hand over her belly and kiss her swollen body. It was a riddle to her how he could take such a grand delight in watching his wife turn into a gigantic white watermelon. When she told him so, he tipped his head back and roared with laughter.

Gram had scored a bull's-eye when she'd assured her worried nine-year-old granddaughter that it didn't matter none if a body did have red hair. Love was blind.

The only thing to mar Rachel's bliss was a recurring dream, which first came in April, when the spring thaws started to break up the ice on the river that ran through their valley. She dreamed that Papa was calling to her over and over. She awoke in the middle of the night, trembling and certain Garrett Robinson was standing just outside their tipi. Strong Elk held her in his arms and soothed her with gentle words till she fell asleep again.

The third time it happened, her husband offered an

explanation of her disturbing dream. "Now that the snows are melting and the rivers are navigable once again, your father will come out to the plains to search for you, Little Fawn."

Rachel could hear the unspoken dread in Strong Elk's hushed words. "Don't you fret none, *nahyam*," she whispered as she snuggled against his warm body. "I won't never leave you, not even if'n Papa should find me. If'n you recollect, darlin', I happen to love you."

He kissed her, his hands caressing her tenderly, making her forget her worries, turning her misgiving into ecstasy.

The Mounted Police returned the third week of April, grim-faced and solemn. This time there were eight of them, as well as their hired scout. The policemen wore scarlet tunics with shiny brass buttons, dark blue pants with yellow stripes, and high black boots. Their white gauntlets and pith helmets sparkled in the spring sunshine. From the four pack horses they'd brought along, it was clear they were prepared for a journey.

Constable McLean immediately requested a meeting with the chiefs and tribal councilors. This time, however, Strong Elk wasn't invited to do the interpreting. Three of the policemen waited outside, while the other Mounties went into Flying Hawk's large tipi to parley with the Indian leaders.

The men were barely gathered inside the council lodge before Rachel heard her husband and Inspector Legaré hollering at each other in French. When the two stormed out like angry bulls, still bellowing at the tops of their lungs, she hurried over.

"What in tarnation is goin' on?" she demanded.

"Nothing," Strong Elk gritted in Cheyenne, not even glancing her way. He glowered at the inspector as he continued to speak to Rachel through clenched teeth.

"Go into our lodge, *nazheem,* and stay there, until I tell you to come out."

Dumbfounded, she turned to Legaré. "Will you tell me what in blue blazes is wrong, sir?"

"Rachel!" her husband shouted before the man could open his mouth. "Do as I say!"

She didn't budge.

The war chiefs of the Kit Fox Soldiers, the Dog Men, the Bowstrings, and the Crazy Dogs, along with the seven other Mounties, gathered around the three of them, all listening somberly.

Rachel looked over at her husband's uncle, Big Pipe Man, war chief of the Red Shields, and then at Flying Hawk, the Old Man Chief of the entire band. Both men were watching her with sincere compassion, tinged with the calm resignation of the very wise.

"Is this about me, Grandfather?" she questioned in Cheyenne. Her heart started to work its way up into her throat, making her deep voice drop even lower. "I have a right to know if this argument is about me."

"Rachel," Constable McLean said gloomily, "we received orders from our government in Ottawa two days ago. You are to be returned to your father, Senator Garrett Robinson, and your husband, Lieutenant Colonel Bruckenridge, who are both waiting for you at Fort Benton. We're to escort you to the border, where we will be met by two companies of the U.S. Second Cavalry. They will take you safely into Montana Territory."

"She's not going," Strong Elk growled. With the Henry rifle clenched in one hand, he stepped closer to his wife.

"So Papa won the election!" Rachel exclaimed happily. "Lordy, that's nice!" She met Constable McLean's anxious gaze and smiled. "Strong Elk's right," she announced breezily. "I ain't a-goin' to leave my husband, nohow. Maybe Papa can come up here for a visit, though. I'll jest write him a letter and ask him.''

McLean's face fell at her proposal. "I'm afraid not."

Undismayed by his dour expression, she rested her arms on her bulging tummy. "Oh, I can read and write now," she assured him blithely. "Won't my papa be proud of me?"

"I'm afraid that a letter won't be enough, ma'am," the Mountie clarified. "We're under orders from our commissioner to escort you to the frontier. Your father has written directly to Prime Minister Macdonald requesting his help in the matter. I'm sorry, but we have no choice."

"My wife is staying right here with me," Strong Elk bit out furiously. "You can see she's expecting a child."

"Mrs. Bruckenridge must be returned to her father and husband," Inspector Legaré interjected. His grim features were resolute. "If she isn't, the prime minister won't allow your band to remain in Canada. Your people will not be included in the great council to take place in a few weeks. Instead, everyone here will be forced to leave this valley, and the American army will be notified of the time and place of your return across the border."

"Lord A'mighty, sir, they can't go back!" Rachel cried. She clasped the constable's red sleeve in terror. "These folks will all be killed by the soldiers, if'n they cross the Medicine Line."

McLean covered her hand with his and patted it sympathetically. "This is one set of orders I am loath to enforce, ma'am, but I am prepared to do so, whatever the cost." He met Strong Elk's enraged gaze without flinching. "We have no choice."

"Then I reckon I'll have to go with you," Rachel said. She looked about forlornly at the people she'd come to love so dearly. "If'n my return to my father will mean the difference between life and death for these good folks here, I ain't hardly got no choice.''

Strong Elk's deep, steady voice was implacable. ''If my wife goes back, I go with her.'' He met Rachel's sorrowful gaze, his black eyes scorching. ''Little Fawn, take your hand off that man's arm and come stand beside me.''

''No, *nahyam,* you ain't a-goin' back with me,'' she answered mournfully. She fought back the sobs that threatened to choke her. Instead of joining her husband, she moved to stand partly behind Constable McLean. ''You can't go, Strong Elk, and you dang well know it. If'n you show up at that border with me, you'll land smack in the middle of the Second Cavalry. If'n they don't shoot you right off, they'll save you for a hangin'.''

''Rachel,'' Strong Elk grated, ''I am not letting you go back alone. Bruckenridge will be there waiting for you.''

''Don't go a-worryin' none about that no-account varmint,'' she assured her husband. ''Papa won't let him hurt me, nohow. Besides, I still got my Kentucky rifle.'' Wiping her wet cheeks with her fingertips, she looked at the constable and managed a trembling smile. ''How soon do we leave, sir?'

''Right now, ma'am.'' McLean squeezed her fingers compassionately. ''I'm terribly sorry. You only have time to pack your things and say your good-byes. We brought a tent along for your privacy. We'll reach the frontier in three days, four at the most.'' Still covering her hand with his, he glanced over at her husband. ''We'll set a slow, careful pace, Strong Elk. She'll come to no harm with us. You have my word on that.''

''You're not taking my wife without me!'' Strong Elk roared. He shoved McLean away from Rachel. As the constable staggered and caught his balance, the other Mounties drew their pistols and pointed them straight at the Elk's heart. All the warriors immediately aimed their rifles and arrows at the policemen.

Her heart pounding in fear, Rachel turned to Flying Hawk and the other chiefs and pleaded in Cheyenne. "If Strong Elk goes back with me, the American soldiers will kill him. You must not let that happen. You must see that my husband stays here."

At the Old Man Chief's signal, the braves slowly lowered their weapons.

Constable McLean gave a quick nod. While the other policemen held Strong Elk at gun point, two of them shackled his wrists behind his back. It was obvious the Mounties had been prepared for the powerful warrior to put up a fight, for they'd even brought leg irons with them.

No Cheyenne interfered. They knew that Rachel had told the truth. Flying Hawk spoke to his grandson quietly, trying to calm him. Strong Elk jerked his head, acknowledging his grandfather's words, then turned to meet his wife's stricken gaze.

"Your promises are worth very little, *vehoka,*" he sneered. "For someone who vowed never to leave without my permission, you certainly are leaping at the first chance you get."

"I'm dreadful sorry," she said, her lips quivering pathetically. "But there's nothin' else I can do."

"You'd best get ready, ma'am," McLean urged.

There was very little for Rachel to pack. She left all of her household goods for her husband. Porcupine Quills helped her gather the few things she'd need on the trip to Fort Benton and put them in a parfleche.

The widow's black eyes glistened with tears as she framed Rachel's face in her time-worn hands. "I shall miss you, Little Red Fawn," she said sorrowfully. Tears rolled down her wrinkled cheeks. "You have brought the sun's bright rays into my lonely old age."

Rachel put her arms around her tiny grandmother and started to bawl. "*Niscem,* I'm a-goin' to miss you, too. Thank you for everything you've done for me."

Next, Rachel said a tearful farewell to Choke Cherry Blossom and her sad-eyed daughter. Getting down on her knees, she hugged Moon Shell tight.

"I do not want you to go away, Maheszoocess," the girl said unhappily. "Stay with us and teach me more *veho* songs."

Rachel took off her silver earrings and placed them in Moon Shell's small hands. "I have to go, little friend," she whispered. "Keep these to remember me by."

Weeping openly, Rachel embraced Good Robe Woman and Standing in Water, Little Man and Prickly Pear, and so many others.

At last, she approached her husband, who stood gun-barrel straight and as foreboding as a peek into hell, despite the heavy shackles. His strong jaw was taut with silent rage.

Rachel was crying so hard, she could scarcely talk. "Please t-tell me g-good-bye, Strong Elk," she pleaded.

His bronzed features were wiped clean of any emotion except total and complete indifference. He stared off toward the mountains in the distance, refusing to look at her. Inspector Legaré stood beside the Elk with a warning hand on his broad shoulder.

Rachel threw her arms about her husband's muscular torso, sobbing uncontrollably. Unless he bent down, she wasn't even tall enough to kiss him on the mouth. She kissed his chest instead. Right above his heart.

"I l-love you, *nahyam,*" she whispered, her throat aching with despair. "Please, s-say you love me, too." She clung to him, certain her poor heart was going to break. "Please, oh please, darlin', don't do this. If'n you d-don't love me no more, at least tell me good-bye.''

The Mounties held back, none of them wanting to be the one to pry her away from the disdainful warrior, who stood as though carved in granite.

Finally, Porcupine Quills went up to Rachel and gently took her arm. "Come, *nixa*," she admonished softly. "Be brave for the little one's sake. You must take care of yourself for the baby who is to come."

The gentle reminder of the unborn child she carried gave Rachel the strength she so desperately needed. She stepped back and searched her husband's icy features. "I'm a-beggin' you to forgive me for breakin' my promise, Strong Elk," she croaked. "I wouldn't be a-goin' if'n I didn't have to. But there jest ain't no other way."

Little Man had brought her pony down from the large herd grazing in the hills above the village. Rachel allowed Constable McLean to help her up on Spotted Butterfly's back, and then the policemen mounted their horses. Only Inspector Legaré stayed behind to guard her silent, aloof husband.

Not daring to look back, she rode off with her escort of North West Mounted Police. She could hear the women singing a strong-heart song, asking the Great Powers to give Little Red Fawn the courage to act like the Cheyenne warrior woman she was.

With his hands shackled behind his back, Strong Elk watched his pregnant wife go without a word. Only his indomitable willpower kept him from calling after her, begging her to come back so he could tell her how much he adored her. But the Elk had learned during his years with the horse soldiers how to keep a tight rein on his emotions. If he was to convince Legaré to release him from the irons, he had to remain absolutely impassive.

It was imperative that he be freed as quickly as possible, so he could follow Rachel. For Strong Elk knew there was only one way that she would ever be completely safe. He had to kill Shelby Bruckenridge.

"Nom de Dieu," Inspector Legaré said in disgust. "You could have at least pretended to care, until the poor little one had disappeared from sight."

Strong Elk glanced at the French Canadian and smiled sardonically. "Beneath the buffalo robe," he replied with cool dispassion, "one woman is as good as another. And that jealous redhead would never have allowed a second wife into our tipi." He shrugged placidly. "I'm better off without her."

Chapter 21

Situated at the head of navigation on the Missouri River, Fort Benton was a former stronghold of the American Fur Company. Constable McLean had told Rachel, as they rode over the rolling green hills to the border, that the Montana settlement was little more than a sagebrush Sodom. The Mounted Police went there occasionally for supplies and in search of fugitive whisky traders who crossed into Canada and sold their vile, homemade brews illegally to the Blackfoot and Cree.

The tumbledown buildings along the boardwalks were crowded with what looked to Rachel like the most by-guess-and-by-God assortment of humanity that could be gathered in a single spot. Rubbing shoulders with one another were cowboys, soldiers, buffalo hunters, trappers, harlots, Indians from many different tribes, and even a genuine preacher man.

''The people here call this place the Chicago of the Plains,'' Major Feehan told her as their horses trotted down a muddy street littered with refuse. A column of mounted troopers from companies D and F followed directly behind them.

''Phew!'' she exclaimed with a quick toss of her head.

"Must be 'cause it stinks jest like a stockyard."

Terence laughed. "There's thousands of pack animals and beef on the hoof right outside town. As soon as the ice breaks on the river, the sternwheelers come up from St. Louis bringing livestock and goods of every description. The levee here is the center of the freighting business for the entire northwestern plains. And a jumping-off place for frontiersmen heading into the wilderness. Adventurers, prospectors, outlaws on the run—you name it, this place's got it."

Rachel wrinkled her nose in disgust. "Reckon I've been away from civilization a mite too long. What's that all over the roadway there?" she asked.

"Playing cards," Terence replied. "They were dropped on the floor of the gambling saloons last night and swept out this morning. A fresh pack has to be opened at the start of each new game to make certain nobody's marking the cards."

"Nice sorta folks that live in these parts," Rachel commented wryly. "Whyever do you suppose my papa wanted me to meet him in this miserable shantytown?"

"Fort Benton is the farthest he could come up the Missouri by steamboat and the closest he could get to where you were finally located in Canada. His choice makes sense, in spite of the wild-and-woolly atmosphere."

Rachel smiled gratefully. "Thank you kindly for comin' to meet me at the Medicine Line, Major."

"I requested that I be allowed to personally lead your escort from the border," said Terence. "Colonel Bruckenridge only agreed to it after your father insisted." Expelling a long, uneasy breath, he paused and met her gaze.

"I was mighty glad it was you who came."

The plainspoken officer's features puckered with worried regard. "Rachel, I'm more than willing to speak to Senator Robinson about Shelby's character—or lack of it, I should say. I can't stand to think of you being in the clutches of that depraved son-of-a-bitch again. When we found him unconscious on the floor of his tent, we had a pretty good hunch what he'd been planning to do. His sword belt was still wrapped around his hand.''

Touched by his offer, she reached out and grasped her friend's arm. ''Don't you go sayin' a word,'' she warned him. ''Don't go stickin' your neck out and end up ruinin' your army career. My papa will believe me when I tell him what kind of ornery polecat Shelby Bruckenridge turned out to be. Papa won't make me stay with that skunk. You'll see.''

''I'm not leaving until I know for certain what's going to happen,'' Terence stated. He motioned toward a hitching post and announced with forced cheerfulness, ''Here we are. Just remember, I'm right behind you.''

They entered the Buffalo Horn Hotel, a sky-goggling building of wood and shingle, its crooked frame pitifully askew. It looked more like a den of iniquity than a place where a body could safely lay his head on a pillow without having to keep one eye peeled most of the night. A barkeeper from the saloon just off the bare lobby led Rachel and the major to a private sitting room, while the cavalrymen tromped into the bar to wet their whistles.

Rachel stepped through the doorway to find her father and her brother, Ben, seated on a worn velvet settee. Close by, her stepmother, Eliza, and Shelby Bruckenridge perched stiffly on a pair of faded upholstered chairs. Major Feehan followed Rachel in and closed the door behind him.

Her family rose to their feet and gaped at her in speechless shock. Rachel suddenly realized how different she must look in her quilled and fringed doeskin dress. Her hair came down to her shoulders now, with the yellow-and-black feathers of an oriole clustered over one ear. A powder horn and shot pouch were slung across her shoulder. She carried her grandpappy's long-barreled rifle in one hand and a parfleche in the other. Their disbelieving gazes roved over her small frame, from the top of her tangled curls to the toes of her beaded moccasins, and then locked on the obvious bulge protruding where her flat stomach used to be.

Rachel chewed her bottom lip as she met her father's anxious eyes. He'd grown thinner since she'd seen him last. His hair had turned almost completely gray. A wave of guilt washed over her at the thought that she was the cause of so much suffering.

When her father smiled and opened his arms to her, she thrust her musket at Major Feehan, dropped the parfleche on the floor, and ran to him. "Papa!" she cried. "Oh, Papa!"

He embraced her, kissing her cheek and brow and resting his chin on the top of her head. "Rosie, Rosie," he said, his low voice breaking with emotion. "My sweet little Rosie, child."

"Oh, Papa, it's so dang good to see you!" She hugged him tight, laughing and crying at the same time. "And Ben!" She pulled her little brother into her arms. "Lord A'mighty, you've grown a foot since I last saw you."

His hazel eyes sparkling with excitement, Ben grinned at her. "Hi, Rosie," he said with brotherly affection. "I missed you."

"I missed you, too," Rachel answered. She glanced quickly around the room. "Reckon Lucinda didn't come."

"Nope," said Ben. "She's visiting Grandmother Adelaide in Louisville. Lucy couldn't leave all those sweet-talking beaux swarming around her. Besides, she's scared to death of being scalped by the Indians."

Shelby moved to stand beside them. When he put his hand on Rachel's shoulder, she jerked away as though she'd just been bitten by a rattler. "Hello, Rachel," he drawled with infuriating calm.

"I don't want him a-touchin' me, Papa," she said wrathfully. She pointed an accusing finger at the tall colonel. "He ain't nothin' but a yellow-bellied coward, who mallyhacks innocent womenfolk and murders younguns in their sleep."

"Shut up!" her stepmother hissed as she hurried to her cousin's side. "You're talking about your husband, you stupid little twit."

"Eliza," ordered Garrett Robinson sternly, "go sit down on that chair and keep your mouth closed."

"Law, I got a husband, all right," Rachel told the sour-faced woman, who looked like she'd been chewing on a mouthful of briars. "But it surely ain't ol' Snake-in-the-Grass Bruckenridge here. My true husband's name is Strong Elk Heart. And I'm a-goin' back to him—if'n he'll ever forgive me for breakin' my promise—jest as soon as me and Papa and Ben have a visit. By the by, Eliza, howdy to you, too."

The shapely blond sank down on the tattered seat and gasped for air. As usual, she'd laced her corset too tight and couldn't hardly breathe. Eliza pulled a hanky out of her reticule and waved it in front of her face. "Why, I've never been treated like this in all my life," she whined tragically. "I'm certain I'm going to swoon. Come over here and sit beside your mother, Ben."

The others, including her son, chose to ignore her.

"Don't talk nonsense, Rachel," reproached Shelby with the practiced deceit of a prize hypocrite. "Of course we're married. That could be my child you're carrying, for all we know."

Rachel put her hand on her swollen belly protectively as she jabbed her finger into his chest with each scathing word. "This ain't your baby, you hog swill, and you dang well know it."

Her father grasped her by the shoulders and gently turned her to face him. "Is this Strong Elk Heart you spoke of the same Indian who kidnapped you twice?''

''Strong Elk never kidnapped me once,'' Rachel scoffed. She glared at Shelby from the corner of her eyes.

Her father cupped her chin in his hand, and she met his puzzled gaze. His learned features were soft with a loving forbearance. ''Major Bruckenridge claims the red man stole you for the second time after the battle with the Indians at Tongue River. Shelby said when you came to the soldiers' camp to plead for his help, the Indian crept into his tent, knocked him out, and took you away.''

''The child could have been conceived that very night,'' Shelby lied smoothly. ''The officers who were in the mess tent when you arrived can testify to the fact that you went willingly with me to my quarters.'' He looked over at Terence, who'd waited politely at the door. ''Isn't that right, Major Feehan?''

''Rachel was in your tent for a very short while,'' Terence answered truthfully. He gazed at his superior officer with open contempt. ''Probably less than a quarter hour.''

Shelby smirked. ''Long enough to father a child, I believe.''

Rachel took her father's hands. ''Papa, the onliest time this lyin' skunk laid a hand on me was to sock me in the belly and rip my clothes off on what was supposed to have been our weddin' night. And when I was in his tent after the massacre on the Tongue, he stripped me bare naked while I was unconscious, after nearly stranglin' me to death with the cord from his hat. The last I seen of Shelby, he was a-plannin' on whippin' me with his sword belt. He would have killed me, too, if'n Strong Elk hadn't come to save me.''

''What poppycock!'' Eliza exclaimed from her place on the chair. ''My cousin would never dream of raising a hand to a defenseless female.''

''Your weasel-faced cousin cut up a Cheyenne woman so bad she was scarred for life,'' Rachel told her stepmother. "He's meaner than a meat-ax and twice as dangerous. And if'n you're a-tryin' to claim different, you're a-barkin' up the wrong holler." She narrowed her eyes and stared at the woman, real meaningful-like. "But I got an inklin' you already knew that when you sent me out to Fort Laramie."

Shelby stiffened and took a step closer, elbowing Ben rudely aside. His yellow eyes glittered feverishly. "Garrett, I think I should be allowed a chance to speak with my wife in private."

"I don't believe that would be a very good idea, Senator Robinson," stated Major Feehan from his place in front of the closed door.

Rachel's father looked from one cavalry officer to the other with a thoughtful frown. "My daughter and I are going to discuss this matter alone," he stated in a tone of absolute authority. "Now, if both of you gentlemen will be so kind as to leave us?" Papa glanced over at his wife and continued smoothly. "Eliza, please allow Shelby to escort you to your room. I'll join you later." He smiled fondly at his son. "Go with your mother, Ben."

The peevish female jumped to her feet and twitched her satin skirts contemptuously. "I'll be delighted to leave you with that ignorant slut. What decent white man would want her now, anyway?"

The moment they'd left, Papa drew Rachel to the settee and they sat down together. He put his arm around her shoulders and drew her close. "Now, Rachel Rose Robinson, suppose you start from the beginning and tell me everything, just as it happened."

Rachel grinned triumphantly. "Papa, you ain't a-goin' to believe this, but I can read!"

He beamed at her with fatherly pride and touched the tip of her nose with one finger. "I knew you could learn how. All you had to do was try. Who taught you, sweetheart? Major Feehan?"

"I'll tell you the whole story, jest like it happened," she promised.

Little Red Fawn chuckled softly to herself. There were a few things she'd best leave out. She didn't want to embarrass her father—or give him any more gray hairs than he already had.

At daybreak the next morning, Rachel slipped out of the ramshackle hotel and walked down to a bend in the river, almost out of sight of the levee. She wanted to be alone in the peace of early dawn, before the rest of the town stirred to life. Trying to sleep in a lumpy bed in the cramped, stuffy room had made her long for her sweet-smelling lodge in their lovely, wooded valley.

She stared out across the river to the other side, thinking how terribly much she missed her husband. She recalled the fury in Strong Elk's eyes as he'd reminded Rachel of her promise never to leave. Would he ever forgive her? She swallowed back the lump in her throat and blinked repeatedly. He had to forgive her—or she didn't know what she'd do.

Wandering through a stand of willows that grew close to the river's edge, she thought of her papa's kindness. When he'd heard the entire story, her father had assured her that she would never have to go near Shelby Bruckenridge again. Papa promised to get her a divorce, once they returned to Lexington. Then his eldest daughter could decide whether to live with him in Washington, to stay at Ashwood Hall, or to return to the cabin in Sugar Hollow.

Her father hadn't doubted a single word that Rachel told him. He'd believed her, right from the get-go. But when it came to her returning to live with Strong Elk, Papa wasn't quite so understanding. Only after she threatened to run away did he agree to journey with her into Canada.

"If I can be convinced that this red man really cares for you, Rosie," he declared with a severe frown, "and that he can provide for you and the child, I will consider allowing you to remain with him.''

Rachel smiled to herself as she recollected her father's foolish assumption that he was still the bull goose. One thing was plumb certain. If Strong Elk wanted her back, he wouldn't pay the least nevermind to Papa's decision—unless it just happened to agree with his. But she'd let the two strong-willed men figure that out, once they met each other.

She plucked a prairie violet from the grass at her feet and sniffed its delicate perfume. Leaning against a tree trunk, she watched the sun's rays dance on the water and counted the hours till she'd be on her way back home to her husband. She hoped Ben would be allowed to come with her and meet her adopted people.

Rachel's happy daydreams were suddenly shattered by a chilling sound.

''So, Mrs. Bruckenridge,'' came the familiar Louisville drawl from just behind her, ''I see you like to take early morning walks, too.''

Rachel whirled to find Shelby less than a yard away. ''You mean you followed me here, don't you?''

She could have kicked herself. Like a greenhorn, she'd left her squirrel rifle back in her room. She hadn't thought Shelby would dare to harm her with her father so near. Not after all that Papa knew about him. From the crazed look in the colonel's golden cat eyes, she'd been dead wrong on that score.

She tried to make a run for the water's edge. There was a chance she'd be seen from the levee. But with her added bulk, she was far too awkward. She dare not risk falling. Shelby caught her by the arm and jerked her to a painful halt, just as she broke through the trees.

''You're not going anywhere, you redheaded bitch,'' he snarled, ''because I'm going to rip that frigging little bastard right out of your belly.'' He chortled with the wild-eyed wickedness of Satan himself. "Everyone will think it was a suicide," he said. "What white woman could face returning to her home breeding a dirty red-skin's whelp?"

Rachel's heart stalled at the sight of Gramps's Bowie clutched in Shelby's hand.

Not the baby! Oh, dear God above, not the baby!

"Shelby, please," she begged. She spread her hands in surrender. "Don't—"

"Save your breath," he sniggered.

"Put the knife down, white man," Strong Elk commanded tersely, "and move away from my wife."

In one swift movement, Shelby pivoted and yanked Rachel in front of him. He threw his arm around her chest and gripped her shoulder, pulling her backward to imprison her against him. With his other hand, he held the blade's razor edge to Rachel's throat. She could hear his harsh breath rasping in her ear.

Rachel searched frantically for her husband. Strong Elk stood with his shoulders propped against a nearby tree. He was stripped to his breechclout and moccasins and painted for war. The notched feathers in his scalp lock pointed skyward. The black and red slashes on his face and chest gave him such a terrifying appearance, for a moment she was purely taken aback. How the fierce warrior had managed to get so close without being seen or heard was nigh unbelievable.

Rachel's husband lounged against the willow trunk, holding his Henry in one hand by its long, slender barrel. His hunting knife remained in its sheath.

"Shoot him!" she cried. "Shoot him!"

"I'll slit her throat before I die," Shelby howled like a maniac. "I swear to God, I'll take her with me."

Strong Elk moved away from the tree and took a step nearer, but he didn't even raise the rifle. "Let her go now," he ordered.

"Not until you throw down your weapons," Shelby bargained, his voice rising shrilly. Rachel could feel his frenzied heartbeat smashing against his chest.

"There's no need to hurt her," Strong Elk said calmly as he inched closer with every word. "She's just a woman. There's no honor in that. It's me you want to kill."

"Hell, I'm not going to kill her, unless I have to," Bruckenridge snickered. "Least, not right away. Rachel needs to be taught how to be a proper, submissive wife. It'll probably take me years to train her right, but I'm no shirk. I'll do whatever has to be done. And your half-breed brat will be sent to a reservation in Oklahoma, unless you agree to leave right now—without your weapons—and return to Canada, alone."

"Shoot him," Rachel pleaded. "Don't pay no never-mind to what this putrid varmint says. He's goin' to kill me anyway. Oh, darlin', do as I tell you and shoot him."

Strong Elk had closed most of the distance between them. His eyes fastened on Bruckenridge's face, he hurled his rifle and knife into the thick underbrush.

As Shelby watched the weapons disappear, Rachel reached up and grasped his wrist. She pulled the hand holding the knife down, pinning it to her chest. At the same moment, she shifted her balance and swung her hips to one side. She smashed the edge of her fist as hard as she could against Shelby's suddenly exposed crotch. He groaned with pain and hunched down in agonized reflex.

Strong Elk was there instantly. He grabbed a hank of wavy blond hair. With a vicious jerk, he yanked the *veho* sideways past his hip, peeling the brute away from Rachel. Shelby's knife arm flew outward with the unexpected motion, leaving her completely unscathed.

Bruckenridge fell on his back, rolled, and regained his feet, still holding the knife. From a crouch, he slashed out at Strong Elk's bare legs, seeking tendons and bone. The Elk jumped back, just barely avoiding the eight-inch blade. Before Shelby could recover his fighting stance, Strong Elk kicked him square in the chest. The impact of the blow knocked the white man backward into the icy river.

Rachel hurried to find the Henry, lost somewhere in a tangle of branches. Panting, she crawled on her hands and knees through wild berry bushes, searching desperately. She had to find the rifle in time.

Shelby struggled to his feet and dashed the water from his eyes with his sodden sleeve. His chest heaved as his breath came in retching gasps. Standing knee-deep and weighed down by his high, spurred boots, he gripped the lethal knife with whitened knuckles and snarled his hatred.

Strong Elk waded into the river after him.

The *veho* lunged for the Elk with a maddened roar, trying to stab him in the side of his neck with the Bowie's sharp, curved point.

In a lightning, upward motion, Strong Elk blocked his opponent's right forearm with his left. He pinned Shelby's arm beneath his own and forced it downward. Grabbing the officer's throat with his other hand, he pushed against the windpipe, his thumb crushing the vulnerable larynx and cutting off the air supply.

Strong Elk held his adversary's extended elbow locked in the crook of his own. He brought Shelby's arm inexorably upward, till he heard the satisfying pop of cartilage severing from bone as it snapped at the elbow. Then he wrenched the white man's body backward across his braced leg.

Shelby grunted in terror as he realized the implacable strength of his Cheyenne foe. He struggled vainly to regain his balance on the slippery river bottom.

With his enemy's throat in his unremitting grasp, Strong Elk forced him relentlessly back over his bent knee, till the blond head and blue-coated shoulders were plunged beneath the sloshing surface of the river. Bruckenridge thrashed wildly in desperation, the broken arm pinned to Strong Elk's side, the other flailing about uselessly as his lungs began to fill with freezing water. The death-throes gradually subsided, and Shelby hung limp.

Strong Elk released the lifeless body, shoving it out into the strong current. He watched the corpse being carried down the Missouri, then turned to find his wife holding the Henry pointed straight at his chest. Her face was drained of color, her eyes bewildered and frightened.

She set the gun butt on the grassy bank and glared at him. "Holy Moses!" she shouted. "Why didn't you jest shoot him?"

The Elk splashed out of the cold water, took the rifle from her grasp, and laid it on the ground. "Because I wanted to kill him with my bare hands," he said.

"Why?" she demanded angrily. She pounded on his chest with her fists. "Why take the chance on gettin' yourself killed?"

"There was never any danger of my being killed, *nazheem*," he chided her. "This way, when the body is discovered, it will look more like an accident than an execution. A drowning victim's arm could easily be broken against the rocks on the way down the river. No one will question it. No one will want to." The Elk smiled as he met her outraged gaze. He drew her close, and she stopped beating on him. "And for another thing," he added quietly, "I simply wanted the pleasure of doing it."

Rachel threw her arms around her husband's neck. "Jumpin' Jehoshaphat," she warned him, "this time, you'd better not refuse to kiss me, if'n you know what's good for you."

Strong Elk lifted her up, carefully adjusting her firm, round stomach to his flat abdomen, so she wouldn't be squashed. He gave her a scorching kiss, filled with blatant, masculine possessiveness. "You should be punished, Little Fawn, for breaking your promise," he murmured against her lips.

"Yeah, well, you've got all the time it takes to get me back home to think of a real good one."

He set her down and framed her adorable face with his hands. Deep inside, Strong Elk felt as though his spirit was slowly dying. It took every bit of his iron resolve not to beg her to stay with him.

"Now that Bruckenridge is dead," he told her, "you're free to go home with your father. I know that all these months you've never stopped dreaming of the day you'd return to Kentucky. I won't try to keep you against your will."

Rachel wrapped his long side braids around her hands and tugged gently. "It's true, *nahyam*," she answered in a hushed voice, "that I've longed to see my kinfolk. I've yearned for the forests and streams and the peaceful old water mill in Sugar Holler. But if'n I never see them again, they'll always be a part of my childhood. I'm a woman grown now. I love you, Strong Elk, and I won't never leave you. My home is right here in your arms."

Her grass-green eyes shining with love, she stretched up on her toes. He bent toward her obligingly, and their lips brushed in sweet devotion.

"I will always love you, Little Red Fawn," he said, his hoarse voice aching with tenderness. "You will be my mate for the rest of my life."

It was just as Strong Elk's vision had foretold.

The mighty bull elk and the little white-tailed fawn together.

Forever.

Epilogue

~~~~~~~~

North West Territories, Canada
Meanesehe, the summer moon
July 1868

Strong Elk watched in terror as Porcupine Quills calmly prepared the beautiful quilled and beaded cradleboard. She pointed to a spot beside her on the buffalo robe that had been spread in the shade beside his lodge.

"I should have taken the little Fawn to Fort Walsh," he stated, ignoring her gesture and continuing to stand. "There is a *veho* doctor there."

The widow sniffed disdainfully. "A drunkard, I've been told, with filthy hands and bleary eyes. My granddaughter wants me and your grandmothers to help with the birth of her child, not some clumsy, whisky-soaked white man."

Driven by a mounting sense of alarm, Strong Elk went back inside the lodge. His diminutive wife sat propped against a backrest. Her coppery locks were soaked with sweat. Her distended abdomen was enormous. He knelt on one knee beside her, his throat clogged with fear, and gazed into her tortured eyes.

367

"You ain't suppose to be in here," she groaned as the pain took hold of her again. "This is woman's work."

"I'm not leaving your side, *nazheem*," he protested. He took her hand, and she squeezed his fingers in a vain attempt to soothe him. Even in her misery, she could see he was starting to panic.

The next minute, Good Robe Woman and Standing in Water returned to the tipi, carrying bladders of water, bowls of warm buffalo cow fat, swaths of clean doeskin, and soft, absorbent mosses. They smiled encouragingly at Rachel and scowled at Strong Elk Heart.

"Out! Out!" the gray-haired women scolded as they set the items down and fluttered their hands toward the entrance.

Strong Elk stepped back outside and took a deep, steadying breath. It'd been like this for the past eight hours, beginning well before dawn. In and out. In and out. Talking to his grandmothers. Talking to Porcupine Quills. Looking helplessly at Rachel.

Those three cheerful, old crones were without a shred of sympathy for the father-to-be. *Eaaa!* He deserved none. Why had he ever laid a finger on his delicate, fine-boned wife?

"She is too small to have such a large baby," he said to Porcupine Quills. "I have never seen any woman grow so big with child. These last few weeks, the little Fawn could hardly get up and down from our mattress. I have lain awake night after night, since the beginning of the summer moon, worrying about this day."

"You will have a fine, strong, warrior son," the elderly woman assured him as she continued to place prairie puffballs in the bottom of the decorated cradleboard. "Did you think any child you fathered would be tiny?"

The Elk met her astute black eyes. "I did not think," he admitted hoarsely. He rubbed the back of his neck with his hand and paced back and forth in front of the lodge.

"Ah, it is ever so," she replied with exasperating serenity. "Try to sit still, Strong Elk, and stay out of our way. Do I or your grandmothers go with you on a hunt and try to tell you how to bring down a mighty buffalo?" The medicine woman glanced up and smiled. "Look, here is Young Bear Running, come to sit with you while you wait."

The two warriors sank down on the robe together as Porcupine Quills went inside the lodge. Young Bear was wise enough not to attempt a conversation. He just sat there, offering the support of his presence to the terrified man beside him.

In a few moments, Flying Hawk came to join them in the shade of the tipi.

"You should have warned me never to get married," the Elk told his grandfather in an accusing tone.

The hint of a smile played around the Hawk's mouth. But with the far-seeing wisdom of an Old Man Chief, he didn't say a word.

At the first faint, quivery wail, Strong Elk leaped to his feet. "At last," he said with a groan of relief, "my son is born." He raised his eyes to the sky above and offered a prayer of thanksgiving to the Maker of Life.

The wails grew stronger and closer together, till it seemed as though even a lusty young warrior couldn't make all that noise. Then Porcupine Quills stepped out of the lodge, her wrinkled face glowing with happiness.

"Little Red Fawn?" questioned the Elk in a choked voice.

"The new mother is fine," she replied. Her black eyes fairly danced in delight.

"And my son?"

She chuckled mysteriously. "Strong Elk, you do not have a son, as we had all expected."

He gaped at the medicine woman in blank astonishment. This had to be the biggest girl ever born. "My daughter is well, then?" he managed to ask.

"Yes," Porcupine Quills answered. "Both of them." She hurried back inside the lodge.

Strong Elk glanced at Young Bear, meeting the brave's open-mouthed stare in dazed confusion, and then followed on her heels.

Good Robe Woman and Standing in Water were hovering over Rachel, who now lay flat on the mattress, her head propped up on several soft deerskin pillows. Snuggled in the crook of each arm rested a slumbering infant.

Strong Elk walked slowly to the bed and crouched down beside his wife and daughters. Filled with awe, he smoothed Rachel's brow with a shaking hand. She smiled up at him weakly, too exhausted to talk. When he looked at the babies, his heart stumbled painfully.

They were the tiniest human beings he'd ever seen.

The Elk looked up at the three older women standing near the bed, searching their compassionate eyes for some sign of hope. Surely these fragile newborns could never survive. He blinked back the tears of sorrow that sprang to his eyes. What a terrible, terrible heartbreak for his sweet, young wife.

"They are so tiny," he whispered to Porcupine Quills.

She nodded her snowy head. "Everything about them is tiny," she agreed with a confident smile. "But everything is perfect."

Rachel gently kissed each little forehead. "Shucks, my gram told me I wasn't much bigger than a large man's fist when I was born. And jest look how wiry and tough I grew up to be. You wait, Dream Catcher, 'cause you're in for double trouble, now. They're a-goin' to be wildcats on two feet, if'n you get them riled."

Strong Elk grinned blissfully as tears of joy ran down his cheeks. "I guess I'd better get busy making another cradleboard," he said, his voice aching with tenderness. He bent and gently kissed his wife's soft, pink lips. The love in his heart was beyond anything he'd ever dreamed of.

Good Robe Woman and Standing in Water left to prepare the evening meal for the new mother and father, while Porcupine Quills stayed to help with the babies.

Bursting with pride, Strong Elk sank back on his haunches and gazed at his family. "What shall we call them, *nazheem*?"

Little Fawn smiled down at her twins. "Morning Rose and Evening Star," she told him softly.

Porcupine Quills leaned over the bed and patted Rachel's cheek. "Thank you, Little Fawn," she said with delight. "I am so proud to have one of your daughters bear the name I was first given by my people."

"And my mother's name for our other daughter is a wonderful choice," Strong Elk added huskily.

His wife looked up at him, a slight scowl creasing her forehead. When she spoke, her tone was serious. "There's jest one thing I want you to promise me."

He took her hand and kissed it. "Anything."

Rachel glanced down at her tiny baby girls and then back to her husband. She met his loving gaze and sighed. "Well, *nahyam,* seein's how they're part white, it's purely possible that once in a while they might tell a teeny-weeny, itty-bitty fib. Now, I don't rightly know jest what it is that the Cheyenne do to little girls who tell whoppers, but if'n our daughters spin a tall tale or two, I want you to promise me that I'll do all the punishin'."

Strong Elk stared at her, his handsome features suddenly blank. "You have my word, *nazheem*," he said, his low voice strangely hoarse. He moved to his feet and left the tipi without nary a smidgen of explanation.

Porcupine Quills followed him outside.

To Rachel's befuddlement, she could hear the sound of her husband's deep laughter boom out like a cannon, accompanied by her grandmother's shrill cackle. Then Young Bear and Flying Hawk joined in, till all of them were roaring with hilarity.

Little Red Fawn looked down at her twin girls, sleeping peacefully through all that racket, and shook her head in pure discombobulation.

"If'n I live to be a hundred and five," she told them in strictest confidence, "I ain't never goin' to understand the Cheyenne people."

Author's Note

Readers familiar with the history of the Royal Canadian Mounted Police will know that they were established in May 1873 under Prime Minister Sir John Macdonald. Originally called the North West Mounted Police, they were a force of three hundred peace officers sent by the government in Ottawa to maintain law and order in an area of 2,250,000 square miles. The plains were sparsely inhabited, with a population of nomadic bands belonging mainly to the Blackfoot, Cree, and Assiniboine tribes, plus a handful of fur traders and Hudson's Bay Company employees.

The Mounties brought with them to that great expanse of wilderness the Canadian government's policy of firm benevolence. Under the Mounted Police, laws were administered with unwavering justice, and these brave men became living symbols of integrity to the native peoples. Their assumption that all human life is sacred was in glaring contrast to the policy of the United States government toward its native population, which was enforced with such appalling results by the U.S. army.

Forgive me for exercising the privilege of an author of

historical fiction by altering the calendar to suit my needs. For it is imperative that our two little girls be raised under the jurisdiction of the North West Mounted Police, safely out of harm's way.